KYRA
OF THE NORTH

DAVID DECKER

MOUNTAIN SIDE MEDIA, LLC

Book Cover Design by David Decker
Cover Illustration by Leslie Casilli
Map Illustration by David Decker

Published by Mountain Side Media, LLC
www.mountainsidemediallc.com

ISBN: 979-8-9915342-0-8 (Paperback)

ISBN: 979-8-9915342-1-5 (eBook)

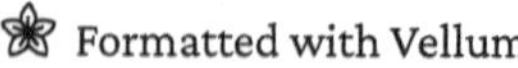 Formatted with Vellum

DEDICATION

If it wasn't for my family and friends, who kept encouraging me to continue down this creative journey and challenging process, I might not have finished. I want to say thank you for all the questions, working sessions, and messages I exchanged with them throughout all of this.

There is one special person that I want to thank the most: my wife. Not only did she support me through all of this, but she went above and beyond by spending countless hours working with me, reading out loud each page, and forcing me to challenge myself to make this story the best it could be. I can not express how grateful I am for her commitment to me while I went through this creative effort.
Hun'ala, my love.

MOUNTAIN SIDE
VALLEY OF THE NORTH
LAKE SHORE
TRADING POST INN
THE GREAT PASSAGE
MIDLANDS
RIVER SONG

PROLOGUE

Sitting in my bedroom window, I feel a cool breeze blow against me. It feels refreshing after being in the sun all day, clearing our field. I hear Mother downstairs preparing our evening meal. The aromas of roasting chicken with herbs and butter fill my home, which smells delicious.

Looking out, I only see a few clouds in the night sky. They are illuminated by the twin moons of Adian and Adelynn as their light fills the valley below them. Lantern flies are flickering their green and orange lights in the fields just past our rock wall. In the distance, I see the dots of warm lights from the homes throughout the valley that lead to the city. As always, I'm fascinated by the dots of light coming from High Rock and how they travel up the cliff face. I wonder if anyone in High Rock is doing the same thing I am: imagining what their future holds.

Lately, I've been feeling restless and want to experience more. Every day seems to blend into the next: working our field and tending to our animals. The only fun thing I have is an evening swim at the pond near our home to cool off and bathe. I want to see what other opportunities are available and meet people. Even though

Mother and I are very close, sometimes I wish I had friends my age to talk to.

I wish we had plans to go to the city soon to get supplies for Mother's soaps and ointments. I like seeing all the people and feeling the energy throughout the city. Mother is the total opposite of me. She wants to be in and out of the city as fast as possible. She's always worried we might get caught up in a disturbance due to Lowlanders trying to fight for more equality. For as long as anyone can remember, Lowlanders have been disadvantaged because the residents of High Rock use their wealth to influence city officials, furthering their agendas. There has been more tension than usual, making Mother more cautious than ever.

This tension will likely calm down when the harvest season starts. It's the one time of year when everyone seems to get along for a while. Without working together, there would not be enough food to survive the long and cold winter season.

I need a change, or I will go crazy. Being seventeen, it's time for me to start standing on my own and making choices for myself. There has to be more to life than this.

"Kyra, our meal is ready. Come down and eat." Mother calls to me.

"Coming."

PART ONE

FINDING ONESELF

CHAPTER 1
THE HARVEST

Why am I holding this girl's hand? Why is she pulling me through a crowd of people?

"Come on, we are almost there," she says.

It looks like she's guiding me to the city center. I notice the sun catching her brown hair, which sways with every step. When the sun shines on it, the color reminds me of wheat. She's wearing a blue dress that flares out at the bottom with accents of white lace. Who is she? We finally stop, and she starts to turn to me.

Opening my eyes, I see the ceiling above me ... no time to think about that dream. I reach over to turn up the brightness of my light crystal lamp. Swinging my legs over the edge of the bed, I sit there for a minute, collecting my thoughts. Today is the first day of the harvest, and I hope to find work as a field hand. It took me weeks to convince Mother to allow me to try to find work this season. She finally caved when I told her how I was feeling as of late.

Heading over to my clothes hanging on the wall, I try not to hit my head on the large oak beams that span across my room. I can still feel the last time I whacked my head on one. This wasn't an issue a few months ago, but since my last growth spurt, they have become a constant reminder for me to duck while in my room. Mother keeps referring to me as a vine, as I grew almost a foot in the past few seasons. I'm not her little girl anymore, as she keeps saying. I pick my heavier-weight top and field pants. The work I may get could be in the fields or the orchards, and these clothes will work no matter what. After dressing, I look at myself in the mirror and run my fingers through my short black bedhead hair to make it more presentable. As usual, a bit settles over my light blue eye, making my hazel eye stand out. I turn down the lamp and slide down the ladder from my room. Looking over, I see Mother sleeping. Her long black hair partially covers her face.

"I'm heading out. I want to make sure I get there early," whispering to her.

Mother softly answers, "I hope you get work, but don't be upset if you don't. They can't hire everyone. I left some food wrapped in cloth on the table for you to take. Be cautious and try not to show them too much, if at all."

"I will."

Walking out, I grab my satchel hanging by the door and place the food in it for safekeeping. Making my way down the path, I turn down the Western Road that will take me to the city. As I'm walking, the sun is starting to rise between the mountain peaks in the distance, filling the valley with light. The light hits the snow-capped mountains and the lush green valley below them, and a new day starts.

The smell of morning dew and freshly hayed fields is heavy in the air. Looking at the field next to me, I see a group of Blue Tails playing with each other as they sweep and chase one another over the growing fields of my neighbors. Their long sapphire-feathered tails reflect the morning sun as they fly high above me. When I'm about halfway to the city, High Rock is starting to peek out from the clouds that surrounded it overnight. The buildings have a golden and warm look as the sun casts its light on them, as do the waterfalls from the aqueducts filling the holding pools hundreds of feet below them. I can even see the trams moving up and down from High Rock. I've always wondered what it would be like to visit High Rock, but the only reason a Lowlander like myself would be up there is to work or make deliveries.

When I get to the Western Gate, I realize I am not the only one to arrive early. A large crowd is standing around waiting to be picked for work. I sit under a tree near the city wall to observe and get my bearings. A few feet away, my ears overhear a conversation between two men.

"Let's get on John's team again. He works for the largest land owner, which means more pay," one tells the other.

Hearing this, I walk over, along with a few others who I believe overheard their conversation. I guess the attraction of more pay appeals to all. I want to talk to them and ask them a few questions to make sure I know who this John person is. As I'm about to ask them, everyone notices three individuals walking onto a stage near us. One of them, a rather heavy-set dwarf wearing a red shirt that can barely hold his belly, starts ringing a bell to get everyone's attention.

"Jacob, stop ringing that! A few times would have been more than enough," the man in a blue shirt shouts.

"Welcome to the harvest. Thanks to the gods, it's been an excellent growing season again. We have fields and orchards that need to be harvested. I know you would like work, but we can't hire you all. If you are not picked, you can try at the Eastern and Southern Gates. They need just as many workers, if not more.

Along with myself, these other foremen will be selecting workers for the orchards and the fields. To make things easier, we want everyone to get into groups to help us make our selections based on skill and experience. If you have ever worked the orchards, stand over there. If you worked the vegetable fields, stand in front of me. Finally, if you worked the wheat fields, please stand there. If you haven't worked the harvest before, pick a group you want to work with," the man announces.

Everyone reorganizes into new groups, trying to stay in front for easy selection. I move to the group with the two men I overheard talking about working for John.

We watch the foremen leave the stage and head to one of the three groups of workers. The man in the blue shirt walks over to my group. This must be John. He's a tall, stocky man with a groomed brown beard. You can tell he spends time in the sun because his face has a tanned leather look, making his blue eyes stand out.

"If you don't know me, I'm John Ridgewater. I'm in charge of the western vegetable fields. If selected, you'll earn fifty silver coins this season. I need twenty pickers and five transporters," he announces.

Looking over the group I'm with, he definitely has options. I wonder what he is looking for in a worker. He scans the group and stops at the two men beside me.

"Edward and Phil, back again? Get behind me and help get everyone organized by the carts. You know what to do," he tells them.

Both men slap hands and walk to the carts behind John. I notice them take a large sack out of a cart and place it on the ground. John looks over at the hopeful workers and continues his pick. I notice he picks the girl in the green outfit, the halfling next to her, and a big man in the back. Every time John picks someone, they tell him their name as they walk by him, and he writes it down on a board he's holding. John continues picking one person after another. I think to myself, How many is that? It must be close to eighteen, if not more. After several more picks, he looks up and announces, "That does it. My team is full. Thank you all for coming."

Everyone that wasn't picked grumbles, including myself. That's it. I spent weeks convincing Mother to allow me to work, and I didn't even get picked. I'm so frustrated. The others start to disperse, and I watch John check over his clipboard when Phil walks over.

"John, we are all set except for one transporter. The last guy you picked could barely lift the test sack, so I let him go."

"Do you know anyone else we can get?" John asks.

"Not today, but maybe tomorrow," Phil replies.

Watching John lower his head at this news, I see my opportunity and approach him quickly.

"I can be a transporter. I move bales of hay back home all the time. I'm stronger than you think I am," I announce.

John lifts his head, sizing me up.

"Lifting these sacks all day takes a toll on anyone. I have seen the strongest people break down after a few hours," John replies.

I need to show them I can lift the test stack. I walk straight to the sack. "If I can pick this up, I can be a transporter," I state.

They look at each other and then back at me, smiling. John nods to give me the go-ahead.

I grab one corner of the sack to give it a test tug. It's heavier than I expected, but it's still not an issue. A few people around me start to chuckle as they think I won't be able to lift it. Mother said not to show too much, but I can't let this opportunity pass me by.

I look up at everyone and lift the sack with one arm holding it in front of me.

Looking back at John. "I can be a transporter?"

John smiles and shakes his head slightly, gesturing for me to join the others in the cart.

"What's your name? I hope you don't burn yourself out on the first day. One sack is different than sack after sack. You'll see," he yells over to me.

"Kyra Everwind," I yell over.

I jump into the cart excited and hear Phil say, "I wasn't expecting that, were you? She lifted it with one arm! It takes me both arms to lift that."

"I wasn't, but sometimes surprises are good. Let's keep an eye on her," John answers.

As everyone settles into the carts, John and Phil jump onto the driver's bench of the cart I am in. Edward is ready to drive the other cart. They give the horses the go-ahead, and we are off. I lean back with a smile on my face. I did it; I got hired. Looking around at the people I am sitting with, I see the girl in the green outfit talking to the halfling who was standing next to her before. She sees me looking at her and smiles, so I smile back.

Arriving at the fields, everyone jumps out of the cart.

John gathers everyone up. "We have a long effort ahead of us. Pickers, take a bushel of sacks with a knife to trim off the tops. This field behind us has carrots, turnips, and parsnips. Fill each sack up with one crop type. Leave a few inches at the top free so the transporters can tie it off before carrying it to the carts," John says, pointing to them.

Looking over, I see three oversized wooden carts at the edge of the field road.

"Transporters take one of these balls of twine, and when a sack is ready, tie it off and carry it to one of those carts. Remember, don't mix the crop types in the carts; they must be stored separately in the storehouses. I don't want us to unpack a cart at the end of the day because someone combined crops. It happened last season, and it caused quite an issue. We hung a sample on each cart so this doesn't happen again. We must fill all three carts each day, or we won't make our timeline. During our midday break, we can get out of the sun and drink water under the large tent provided by the landowner. Be thankful as not all landowners are so gracious to us workers," John tells us.

Phil interjects, "My suggestion of ale instead of water wasn't approved?"

John looks at Phil briefly, then turns his attention back to us. "Let's get going."

Everyone disperses, including me.

As I pass John, he pulls me aside. "I'm taking a chance on you. I saw that you're strong, but don't overdo it. Remember, one sack is very different than your tenth or twentieth. Use both arms. Do you have any questions?"

Shaking my head, he gives the go-ahead to start working.

Over the next few hours, I get into a rhythm of tying off sacks and carrying them to the carts. While heavy, they aren't too bad to lift and carry. I even start carrying two sacks at a time, one on each shoulder, to save trips. Every once in a while, I look over and see John watching me. I think he's still unsure of me, but I catch him shaking his head occasionally with a smile.

Around midday, we all hear a bell ring, and John yells, "Everyone, take an hour for your break. Remember to drink water and eat if you have something. I don't want anyone passing out on me."

I'm not hungry, so I rest in the corner of the tent and watch everyone as I drink water. The girl in the green outfit and halfling are still together, eating and talking. They must be friends as they have been together all day. Watching them converse, I notice her look at me, and she smiles and waves. I raise my hand to acknowledge her wave. I bet it's nice having a friend here to talk to and share things with. It's been just Mother and I my whole life. The break goes by fast. Standing, I notice my legs don't move as easily as I was used to.

As the day progressed, I understood what John meant about the difference between one sack and many. My arms and legs are wearing out, and my back is starting to hurt from all the lifting. Even with my strength, the repetition is getting to me. I don't know how many sacks I transported today, but I'm exhausted and covered in dirt and sweat.

As I head back to the field to grab another sack, I hear John calling out to us, "That's day one. Good work, everyone. Go home and get some rest. Be back at the Western Gate at sunrise. We only cleared a portion of the first field today and have five more fields to go."

After finishing my first day, I realize working the harvest might not be as fun as I thought. It's exhausting work, and I don't think I have ever been this dirty. Even the fieldwork at home doesn't make me this dirty. I also learned I have muscles I didn't know of because I could feel every muscle in my body; even my fingers hurt. Making my way into the cart, I hear John talk to me.

"You made it through your first day. I'm impressed. What's your name again?" he asks.

"Kyra," I answer tiredly.

"Well, Kyra, see you early tomorrow, and keep it up." Slapping my back softly.

I try not to make a sound, as I know he meant the light slap as a gesture of kindness, but the slap causes my back to tighten up and cramp. Sitting down, I try to work the cramp out by rubbing it. The ride back to the city seems much longer than this morning. Most likely due to my exhaustion. Everyone else might feel the same, as there is very little talking. I pull my food from my satchel to eat something, as I haven't eaten anything all day. Maybe that's why I am so tired. Across from me is the girl in the green outfit again. She's just as dirty and looks as exhausted as I am. Looking at her this time, I couldn't help but notice her emerald green eyes and how they stood out. She sees me looking at her. I tear off a piece of my food and hand it to her.

"Thank you," she says, taking it from me.

Her friend is leaning his head onto her arm with his eyes closed.

"Is he alright?" I ask.

"Yes, he is just tired. I think we all are," she explains.

I make an agreeing gesture and continue eating, looking out at the valley and the setting sun.

Arriving back at the city, we all disperse in different directions. I notice the girl and her friend are heading into the city. Walking home, every muscle in my body hurts. All I want is to clean up and go to bed. Approaching home, I see Mother, and she waves at me.

"I guess you found work, congratulations," she tells me.

"Congratulations to me. I'm exhausted, and I can barely move. Not to mention, I'm covered in dirt."

"I thought you would need a bath, and I see I was correct. I filled the watering trough in the barn with hot water for you. There's soap and a sponge next to it as well. I will serve you some stew while you bathe," she tells me.

Hearing I have a bath ready, I head straight towards the barn as fast as possible, stripping off my clothes and flipping them in the air, creating a dust cloud behind me.

"I can almost cry, but I am too tired," I tell Mother.

When I get to my bath, I flop into the water and start to wash, quickly turning the water brown and murky.

"Thank you, Mother. You don't know how much I need this." Scrubbing the last portion of my arm. I look over, and Mother is picking up my clothes from the ground.

Mother says, "I feel more laundry is coming in my future."

Smoky, our horse, looks at me from his stall. I close my eyes and let the hot water work on my muscles.

I'm no longer in the barn. I'm in front of the castle again, and as before, I enter and make my way to the dark ballroom filled with people dressed in gowns and formal attire. They are holding drinks, talking, and laughing. When I look at them, their faces are blurry and distorted. I also can't understand what they are saying, as that's distorted and muffled. Even though the room is dark, I can see wall tapestries and other adornments. In the back of the room, I see him again sitting in an oversized chair. On the wall above him is a crest comprised of the moons with a wolf's head in front of them.

"Don't be afraid, come. You are on the verge of your awakening," he tells me.

"What do you mean, my awakening? Who are you? What do you want?" I ask.

I feel a force start pulling me towards him. I try to stop myself from moving by planting my feet forcefully into the floor while leaning backward, but the force becomes stronger and continues to pull me toward him. I try to resist even more, but it's no use. He extends his hand to me when I am only a few feet from him.

"We need to talk so you can understand," he tells me.

I wake up, splashing the water and breathing heavily. I hate every variation of that dream. I don't understand why I have them or what they mean. Lately, they seem to be becoming more intense with each one I have.

Looking out the barn doors, the sun has set, but there's still a tiny bit of warm glow at the horizon. The twin moons are rising in the sky, with stars starting to appear. Standing from my bath, I feel the cool air on my body as the warm water mists off of me. Looking next to the tub, I see fresh clothes. Mother must have placed them there for me while I was asleep. I dress and go inside to get some food with Mother. Entering the house, I see a bowl of stew on the table and a large slice of bread covered with seasoned fat. Looking over, Mother is already asleep in her bed. I guess she had a busy day as well. I'll have to tell her about my day another time. I sit down and eat my meal. After finishing, I wash the bowl and head to my room to pass out.

Making my way up to my room is a struggle. Every step on the ladder is an effort, as my legs have no strength left in them. With each step, I laugh as this has never happened to me before. I hope my body adapts to this work quickly because this is ridiculous. Stepping onto the landing of my room feels like an accomplishment. I fall across my bed, planting my face into my pillow, and close my eyes. I think to myself. Is this what it will be like while working the harvest?

CHAPTER 2
FRIENDSHIP

Over the past few days, I've fallen into a routine of waking up early to ensure I arrive at the Western Gate to catch my ride to the fields. During the midday break, I have something to eat and drink like everyone else. I learned eating something during the break allows me to keep my energy up, so I'm not so exhausted at the end of the day. Sometimes, I sit with the workers, trying to get to know them, but I mainly listen to their conversations and don't say much. Today is no different, except for the green-eyed girl and her friend walking up to me.

"Can we join you?" she asks confidently, sitting beside me.

I move over to give them more room.

"I am Jenniver, but please call me Jenny. This is Rox. What is your name?" she asks, crunching on an apple.

"Kyra," I reply, chewing.

I notice her sparkling green eyes again. Today, her hair is tied up in a ponytail, and she is wearing a head scarf to keep the dirt out, but her face is still covered in dirt. Rox is a halfling. His small round nose and roundish cheeks framed by his short brown hair give him an almost adolescent look.

"Are you from the city or valley?" she continues with questions.

"The valley by the Western Pass," I answer, folding up the cloth that held my food. "I think I saw you both walk back into the city on our first day. Do you live in the city?"

"Yes," she answers, taking another bite of her apple.

Rox finally jumps in. "I have been wondering since you did it."

"What?" I ask.

"The test sack. How did you lift it with one arm? Everyone uses two."

"It wasn't that heavy. Back home, I work in our field, carrying bundles of hay to our barn. They're twice as heavy, and I can carry one on each shoulder at the same time if I have to," I answer.

"How is it being a transporter?" Jenny interjects, taking the last bite of her apple before tossing it to the ground.

"The lifting and hauling isn't too bad. However, I never get this dirty working our field back home," I explain, wiping dirt off me.

"I know I could not do your job," Jenny tells me, pushing up one of her sleeves to show me one of her slender arms. She leans in and looks at me. "Your eyes are two different colors. How did I not notice that right away?"

I am surprised she didn't notice them. Most people see them right away and ask about them. Over the years, I learned not to let this bother me, and I tell everyone who notices them for the first time the same thing.

"My mother says my blue eye matches my father's, and my hazel one matches hers."

"That's interesting, let me see," Rox says.

John enters the tent and announces, "Breaks over, back to work. We have a long way to go."

Everyone heads back out for another exciting second half of the day working the fields. As I walk out, Jenny and Rox walk out with me.

"Ride back with us tonight?" Jenny asks.

"Sure. I will look for you at the end of the day."

When Jenny asked me to ride back with them, I was surprised. Maybe she wants to get to know me better. I am curious to learn more about her and her friend.

~

Since that day, the three of us started spending more and more time together. Even at home, I couldn't stop talking about them to Mother. They are usually my last thought before falling asleep, especially Jenny. Over the past few weeks, I noticed small things about her. How she talks and carries herself is different than most of us. Plus, I have been looking at her and thinking about her in ways I don't fully understand. I think I'm developing a crush on her, and I'm not sure how to handle it, as I haven't ever had feelings like this toward anyone before. I wonder if she might feel the same about me. I noticed she keeps doing small things like giving me hugs playfully or holding my arm when we walk together. These are things that people do when they like each other; at least, that's what I think people do. Sometimes, I want to talk to Mother about my feelings for Jenny, but I'm nervous about what she might say or think. Allowing me to work the harvest was a big thing; it took weeks for her to agree to it. This might be a bigger deal. With the harvest ending shortly, I hope we will continue to see each other. I would really miss my new friends, especially Jenny, if we don't.

~

It's the final stretch, and we only have one field left to clear—unfortunately, it's the potato field, the dirtiest of the crops. Jenny, Rox, and I are resting under the tent at the midday break.

John starts rallying everyone, "After today, we only have one day left to clear the last field. Afterward, we can enjoy celebrating the harvest with our families and friends. Now let's get back to work."

We dust off our backsides as we stand and head back to the fields; John pulls me aside. "Have a second?"

Jenny turns and walks backward. "See you at the cart later."

"See you later," I answer.

"You're a workhorse. The other transporters can't come close to you," he says, placing his hand on my shoulder. "Allowing you to be a transporter has paid off. Remind me to hire you next season," John says while patting my back, producing a dust cloud.

I smile at John and head back to the fields.

A few hours have passed since the midday break. I hear screaming from the carts and look over to see one of them toppled over. Workers are frantically pulling sacks of potatoes out.

"It's too heavy; we'll never get it off, John!" I hear one of them yell.

Hearing John is trapped under the cart, I run as fast as possible to see if I can help. Several workers are pulling sacks out of the cart while others try to lift it with little result. John is trying to push the cart off himself but can't. He's coughing and struggling to breathe. I can see blood coming from the corners of his mouth due to the crushing weight on him. Without thinking, I squat next to the cart, grabbing the bottom of it while pressing my back against it in the hopes of lifting it. At first, nothing, but I kept trying. I start to feel it shift as my feet push into the ground from the weight of the cart. Calling all of my strength, I scream, and my legs straighten.

I yell to everyone, "Get him out; I don't know how long I can hold this!"

I watch Phil and Edward pull John out from under it to safety, and they give me the go-ahead to drop the cart. When I let go, it crashes to the ground. Feeling lightheaded, my shaking legs give out, causing me to fall to the ground. I hear people talking, but I can't understand what they are saying due to the strain I just placed on myself.

A moment later, I hear someone from a cart yelling, "Go as fast as you can to the nearest healer. We don't have much time!"

I feel someone place their hand on my shoulder and ask, "Are you hurt?"

Shaking my head, I look up to see Jenny standing above me.

"Are you sure?" she asks.

"I think so," I answer, standing but shaky. Leaning on the side of the cart to help keep myself vertical.

After a moment, I get my legs back under me and start looking around. Everyone's whispering and looking at me. I begin to step back, feeling nervous. This is what Mother was concerned about: people finding out about my unnatural strength. When I'm away from everyone, I run as fast as my legs allow me back home.

As I run away, Jenny yells, "Wait! Please stay!"

When I make it home, I try to act like nothing is wrong—just another day in the fields.

"You're home early," Mother states.

"We will finish up tomorrow. These potatoes are the worst. They are the dirtiest, as you can see," I tell her. "I am going to wash up and go to bed. I'm exhausted."

"I know you wanted to work the harvest, but maybe next season, you can find other work that isn't so physical and requires you to be gone all day. You're always exhausted at night; honestly, I could use your help around here a bit more," explains Mother. "Anyway, your bath is ready, and I will get you some clean clothes and your meal ready."

"We only have a day left, and then I can help out here more. You might be right about working next harvest."

Walking over to the bath, I feel guilty not telling her what happened, but I think it's for the best. I undress and step into the warm bath. While in the tub, I notice my hands are shaking. I don't know if it's my emotions or the physical strain I placed on myself. As

I bathe, I scrub harder and harder, trying to wash the day off of me, but I can't. Eventually, I start splashing the water by striking with my arms. As I do this, I begin crying, as I can't hold my emotions back anymore. Mother comes running over to me.

"What's the matter, child? Why are you crying?" she asks.

"John ... John ...," I muddle between cries and breaths.

"Who's John?" Mother asks, holding me.

"He's the foreman who has been overseeing our work. There was an accident today. He got badly hurt, and I don't know if he's going to live," I explain.

"That's terrible. What happened?" Mother asks, sitting on the side of the tub.

"A cart toppled over on him somehow. He was being crushed by it, and I reacted. Somehow, I was able to lift it enough so they could pull him from under it. Afterward, everyone was staring at me and talking. I'm sorry, Mother. I didn't mean to," I sob.

Mother hugs me, trying to comfort me, but it's not helping.

"Try not to worry. You did what you did to help. I am sure everyone will see that. We knew this might happen someday, and now all we can do is wait and hope for the best," she tells me.

Mother places a set of clean clothes next to the tub that she must have been holding when she came running. She stands and tells me, "Nothing will happen to you. I will make sure of it, my precious girl. I love you." Before leaving, she wipes the tears from my cheeks.

"I love you too."

Looking at the sponge floating in the water, I grab it and finish trying to wash this day off of me, as I want to forget it.

Entering the house, I see Mother is in her room. She's combing her hair and humming a song she sang to me when I was little to help me fall asleep. On the table is a bowl of hot steaming stew and bread. It smells delicious, but I don't have an appetite tonight. I sit down and pick at it for a while. My nerves are still getting the best of me. I keep thinking of John and everyone looking at me and talking about me. Maybe I shouldn't go tomorrow; it might be better that way. However, I want to see Rox and Jenny. I remember that Jenny was concerned about me, and I ran away. I don't want her to worry. I guess I have to go back. If things go bad, I can just run back home.

Mother comes out of her room and sits next to me. "Not hungry?" she asks.

"No, I think I'll just go to bed," I tell her. I place the bowl by the wash bucket and head to my room, wondering what tomorrow will bring.

Arriving at the Western Gate, I'm nervous and tired. I barely slept because I kept going over yesterday's events all night. Jumping into the cart, a few workers smile at me. I don't see Jenny or Rox anywhere, which adds to my nervousness. Just before the cart leaves, they jump in and sit next to me.

"Sorry, we were running a little behind today," Jenny tells me.

Having them beside me makes me feel better, and my nerves calm down as Jenny holds my hand. I eventually lean my head onto Jenny, who holds onto me with her free arm.

Rox quietly asks, "You ran off suddenly, and we were worried. Why did you run away?"

"I got nervous and scared," I tell him.

"Why?" Rox asks.

"Everyone was looking at me funny and talking about me," I explain.

"Everyone was amazed at what you did. That's all," Rox tries to reassure me.

As we continue to the fields, my attention is drawn to a conversation between two others in our cart.

"Any update on John?" One asks the other.

"No, I haven't heard anything. Phil's not here either. Must be bad," another worker states.

Jenny squeezes my shoulders to comfort me. "They got him to a healer. He will be fine."

When we arrive at the field, the dwarf who rang the bell on the first day of the harvest is already there.

"I'm Jacob Leadrock. I'm your replacement for John. I don't have any updates on him. So don't ask. Let's get to work. We need to complete the harvest today," he states coldly.

Hearing this, I immediately feel worse. Everyone heads out to the field quietly, knowing we should complete the work as John would want us to.

While working, a few workers look at me occasionally and smile. I keep wondering what they are thinking when they smile at me. Are they uneasy around me or just being nice? Whenever I get a chance, I grab a sack of potatoes from Rox or Jenny just to be close to them. They always greet me with a big smile and check on me.

We finish clearing the last of the field as the sun gets low in the sky. Placing my last sack in the cart, I notice a silhouette of a man walking out of the tent, holding his side as he yells, "We're done here! Gather your things and come get your wages."

Knowing that voice, a smile appears on my face from ear to ear. We all run to the tent to find John sitting at a table. He doesn't look great, but he's alive. There is a large lockbox on the table in front of John.

"First, I want to thank everyone for yesterday. Because of you, I am here. I still need more time to heal and a few more visits to a healer, but I will be alright. I wasn't going to miss the last day of the harvest. Now then, who wants to get paid?" he asks, sitting behind the table.

Everyone cheers, and John starts to call the workers' names, inviting them to receive their wages. As each worker goes up to get their purse of coins, they make their mark next to their name on John's sheet of paper. Seeing Rox go up to get his wages was fun. Rox does a small roll into a stand as he reaches the table, which causes everyone to chuckle, even John.

"Don't make me laugh. It hurts," John tells Rox.

After reading through a few more names, John pauses for a second, and then I hear my name.

"Kyra ... Kyra Everwind. Come get your wages," John announces, with a softer tone.

I make my way through the workers, and I feel Jenny touch my shoulder as I walk past her. I see a purse of coins on the table in front of me. I take the pen and write *received* next to my name.

Taking my pay, John places his hand on mine. "Wait ... I was told what you did. I don't know how you did it, but thank you. My family thanks you as well," John tells me. He leans down and places another purse of coins on the table. "This is a portion of my wages. I talked to my family about this, and we want to help your family. It is because of you that my family is still whole."

I tell John, "No, I didn't do what I did for money."

"No, please take it and use it as you wish. I wouldn't be here if it weren't for you," John insists.

I stand in front of John for what seems like an hour, but it's most likely a few seconds. I finally nod and take the extra pay before moving to the back of the crowd.

After a bit of time, everyone gets their wages, and John gives his final orders. "The harvest is when we work together so the city has enough food during the winter season. It's hard and long hours, but the reward is here. Most of you will spend your pay on ale and whatnot, but try to keep some for another day. Now go and celebrate and enjoy yourselves."

Everyone raises their arms cheerfully at his final words, and we head to the carts. Walking to the cart, I feel an arm wrap around mine.

"Ready for some fun? Rox has a plan," Jenny informs me.

"A plan? I plan to go home and clean up," I explain as we walk.

"Home? You must come to the city to celebrate with us," Rox begs.

"I'm dirty," I reply.

"Come on, just a drink or two. You earned it, and we're all dirty," Jenny insists. "We just want to celebrate together. What do you say?"

"I don't know. Mother is expecting me home tonight, and I must tell her how the day went. It's important to her," I answer.

Jenny asks me again, "Come on, one drink. It will be fun! Then you can go home and tell your mom about everything."

She holds my hands and looks at me with her big green eyes, which has an effect on me that I wasn't expecting. I can't say no to her, plus I have been curious about how the city celebrates the harvest for a long time. Mother and I would have a few ciders after we finish our harvest, but that's about it.

"Let's go for one drink, maybe two drinks, but that's it," I answer.

"Great, let's get going," Rox says.

We jump into the cart for our last ride back to the city.

"How much extra did you earn?" Rox asks me.

"I don't know," I answer, opening the extra coin purse.

My eyes go wide looking at gold coins. I quickly close the purse and put it away.

"How much?" Jenny asks quietly.

I whisper to them, "It's full of gold coins."

"John gave you—," Rox tries to say aloud as I cover his mouth with my hand and nod.

I lower my hand from his mouth and place my finger over my lips.

Rox whispers to me, "First round is definitely on you."

Jenny laughs at the two of us, and we laugh with her.

CHAPTER 3
A SURPRISE

The three of us jump out of the cart one final time, making our way through the Western Gate, where the sounds of the Harvest Celebration have already started. Children are running around, laughing with streamers in their hands. A baker is passing out treats to people passing by him. I look towards a fountain and see a street performer casting illusion magic for children for coins. All the shops and cafes are full of patrons celebrating. Some are toasting each other, while others have arms over each other's shoulders, laughing and singing together. Rox guides us down the Western Boulevard, and then we take an alleyway and another. Walking through the dimly lit alleys, I pull Jenny closer as we pass different storefronts and people.

"Where are we going?" I ask.

"We're going to the Dragon Tail. It's my favorite place to get an ale and some food," Rox informs me.

"Do you know what this place is like?" I ask Jenny.

"Not really, but I heard Rox talk about it a few times," she answers.

After walking for a bit longer, Rox stops and turns to us.

"We're here," he proclaims.

I see a metal dragon sculpture protruding from the stone exterior above a window to the left of the tavern's door. It's drinking a mug of ale, and wisps of smoke exit its nose. From within the tavern, we hear laughter and music. I look through the window and see a crowded tavern full of people drinking and celebrating together.

"Come on, let's get inside before all the tables are taken. It sounds like the local violinist is playing tonight. I can also smell the roasting meats from out here," Rox announces.

Rox runs up to the door and reaches for the doorknob. When he opens the door, laughter and music from within spill out into the alleyway.

I look at Jenny and tell her, "After you."

Entering, I see a small, spritely elf woman with blond hair dressed in a multi-colored outfit. She's tantalizing the patrons with her movements through the crowd as she plays her violin. A man is playing a long wooden drum on a stage, creating a beat to accompany her playing. The tavern is packed with field workers who seem to have come straight from the fields or orchards. I guess I didn't have to worry so much about being dirty. My stomach growls as the smell of ale and roasting meats hits my nose, as I haven't eaten anything since yesterday.

"There's a spot over there. Let's grab it quickly before anyone else does," Rox announces.

He runs through the crowded tavern quickly due to his size and grabs the table in the nook.

As Jenny and I push through the crowded tavern, a tavern maid yells to us, "Ales for you bunch?"

Jenny shows the tavern maiden three fingers as we sit at the table.

I grab the chair next to the wall so I won't worry about people behind me. As I settle in, I ask Jenny the question I have been wondering about for a while now. "We've gotten to know each other over the past few weeks. I've wanted to ask you something but have been a little nervous. I hope you don't mind. You're not from the Lowlands, are you?"

Rox looks at Jenny, smirking.

It takes Jenny a few seconds to answer, "No, I am not. I am from High Rock. How did you figure it out?"

"Subtle things such as how you talk and move. You never use Lowlander words or pronounce things like Rox or I. You must tell me what living up in High Rock is like." I say.

"There's not much to say. I live about halfway up. My father plays the politician, but he's not. He sells and trades different commodities, such as spices and ores. More recently, he started trading wines. He says wine will become more popular than ale. My mother is a traditional lady of High Rock. She was born there and will always be in High Rock. She doesn't like to come down from it unless she has to. She spends her days entertaining guests by hosting dinners, midday teas, or doing the most boring things possible," Jenny explains, cradling her chin on her hands.

"What about you, Rox? Do you live up in High Rock? I notice you speak like I do."

"Yes, but it's different," he answers. "My mom has worked for Jenny's family since I was young. We live in a room attached to the back of the kitchen."

"So that's how the two of you got to know each other," I reply.

"Due to my parent's busy social schedule, I was often left alone, so Rox and I started to play together and quickly became best friends. I'm also very close with his mother. She was always there to help mend a hurt knee or just someone to talk to about things. As we got older, my parents tried to limit our time together, as it wouldn't be proper for a Morant to be seen with the cook's child. We didn't want to cause trouble for Rox's mother, so we kept our friendship quiet," Jenny adds.

At this moment, the tavern maiden drops three large ales and a plate of mixed meats on the table, holding her hand out for payment. "One silver for the ales and four copper for the plate of food."

"We didn't order any food, but that looks delicious," I reply.

Rox smiles at me. I reach into my coin purse and pay for our drinks and food.

Both Rox and Jenny raise their mugs to me and start to drink.

"You're getting the next round," I inform them.

Enough about us. I knew you were strong, but how could you lift the cart," Rox asks, taking a piece of meat. "I can barely carry a satchel of potatoes."

"I don't know," I muddle with my mug in front of my face.

"How much do you think you can lift?" Jenny asks.

"I don't try to lift things as a practice. Lifting the cart pushed me to my limit," I answer.

Staring at the plate of meats, my growing stomach forces me to grab a piece to try.

"That's good. I like how they season it, heavy on the salt and herbs," I tell my table mates, chewing on what I believe is elk.

Jenny grabs my arm and squeezes it. "Your arms are like stone," she tells me.

As she says this, I'm taking another large swig of ale, and a tremendous belch unexpectedly explodes out of my mouth. This silences everyone at the table and around us for a second. A second later, Jenny and Rox bust out laughing.

"Now that's power," Rox proclaims.

"I'm happy you worked the harvest as I got to meet you, but don't take this the wrong way. It sounds like you didn't have to, Jenny. Rox, what about you?" I inquire.

"Unlike Jenny, who does this type of thing for fun, I do it for the money," Rox replies to me. He then turns to Jenny to say, "This was not fun: hot, tiring, dirty, yes, but not fun. Next time, we should be more thoughtful about what we consider doing together as a fun activity.

Whenever I can earn a few extra coins, I do. Whether it's being a messenger or working an angle. I have pretty good street smarts."

Jenny raises her hands and waves to Rox to be quiet.

"It's my turn now. Tell us about your family. Do you have any brothers or sisters?" Jenny asks.

"It's just Mother and me. I don't have any brothers or sisters. I don't remember my father either. He left when I was a baby. My mother told me he had to leave to protect us, but she never explained why. By the way, I finished my ale; I believe one of you owes me one," I answer.

"That's fair. Let me get you another, as I can use one myself. Jenny, you want another?" Rox asks.

"Yes, I will take one," she answers.

Rox heads to the bar to get our drinks. Both Jenny and I pick at the plate of food. As I eat, I feel something touch my leg. I lean down and see Jenny is touching my leg with hers.

"Is that alright?" she asks.

"I like it when you touch me," I answer. Did I just say that? I am such a bonehead.

"Good." She smiles at me.

As the celebration progresses, we play several games of darts and drink one ale after another. At times, the effects of the ale start to show as we begin to laugh more, along with a stumble here and there. Finishing up our last game of darts, we walk over to a large table in the tavern's center with a few open spots. Looking around the tavern, it's even fuller than before. The elf girl sits on the stage by herself, playing a slower song while her band member hangs out with a few people across the tavern, enjoying a drink with them.

"So much for one or two drinks," I tell Rox.

"So much," he says, shrugging his shoulders at me.

"One last ale, and then I have to get home. I am sure Mother is wondering where I am and is likely worried about me. Do you two need one?" I ask.

They indicate they are still drinking their last one.

Making my way toward the bar, I pass a few of the field workers I worked with, and they smile and raise their mugs to me. I guess things will be alright, I think to myself. Passing the elf girl, I drop a few coins in her tips chest to thank her for the music. I feel a slight tap on my butt, which causes me to turn and look back. I see the elf girl smiling at me. I smile back before continuing to the bar.

The barkeep is taking empty mugs off the bar to be washed. He turns to me, smiles, and asks, "Another ale?"

"One last one before I head out," I answer, sliding a silver coin on the bar.

The barkeep pushes the coin back to me and tells me, "I can't take that. I heard what you did for John. I have to buy you a drink. It's the least I can do. I've known John my whole life. Just give me a few minutes, and I will get your ale."

Today has turned out to be such a good day. Waiting for my mug of ale, I look back to our table and see Jenny and Rox talking to each other. It seems like Rox is teasing Jenny, and she's smiling and turning red. Suddenly, I feel someone squeeze my butt.

"She's a pretty one. Tall and firm as well. I'm not sure if this is the girl people are talking about," someone says drunkenly behind me.

I turn around quickly and see a table with three men in red jackets staring at me. The one that grabbed me was average size, with medium-length brown hair to his shoulders. He has a scar across his cheek and is overall ugly. The other two are much larger and command a presence. One in particular is huge with tree trunk arms. It looks like he cut the sleeves off his jacket, most likely due to the size of his arms. Even sitting, he towers over the other two. His hair is tied back, and you can see a tattoo that covers a portion of his face on one side that goes from his forehead to his cheek.

"I don't know; what girl are you looking for?" I ask in a snide tone.

"We keep hearing about a girl who worked the harvest this season and how strong she is. I want to meet her. I like strong women and want to see how strong she might be, maybe more if you know what I mean," answers the big one, laughing into his mug.

I turn back to the bar, hoping my mug has been filled so I can return to my friends.

Without looking at them, I say, "I'm sure I am not the girl you're looking for. If you find her, maybe she might teach you a few manners."

"She does feel nice," the small one tells his friends, grabbing my butt once again.

I quickly turn, leaning down, putting my face in his, and I tell him, "If you want to keep it, remove it!"

The man laughs, squeezing my butt, and tells me, "Ah, come on, pretty one. We want to have some fun. It's been a while since we've had the comfort of a woman."

I grab his hand off my backside and firmly place it on the table in front of him. Based on his expression, I didn't think he expected me to do that. How am I going to get out of this situation? These assholes are asking for it. I straighten up and grab a chair near me, swinging it around so I can sit at the table with them.

"You three want to have some fun? Let's see what fun we can have. I know. Do you like to gamble?" I ask.

"I do. What's the gamble?" asks the huge one.

"Up for an arm wrestle?"

"With you?" he asks jokingly.

"If I win, you buy me a drink and let me go back to my friends. If I lose, I hang out with you three, and we see how the night goes. Deal?" I ask. "Who's first?"

The three stare at me and laugh out loud, slapping the table.

"Let's see if you can take me," the big one says, followed by a smile.

He leans forward, placing his elbow on the table and opening his hand.

I put my elbow on the table and place my hand in his. As we close hands, his completely covers mine, with only my finger tips poking out. I look around, and I can see the tavern is starting to notice us. People are watching and talking to each other. Some of the field workers I know begin to smile, knowing this asshole is going to have a surprise in a few moments.

"Ready?" I ask.

The man nods and says, "You want to do this; let's go."

I feel him start to apply pressure and allow him to move my arm down towards the table. I'm sure he thinks he is being nice by only using a small portion of his strength. I push back slightly against him and feel him apply more pressure. I see a slight change in his expression as I look at him. It went from fun and smiles to a bit more serious, as he couldn't move my arm down anymore. I look at his companions, who are laughing and teasing him now.

"You can't move her arm down. You are going to let this girl beat you," they state.

In the background, I hear, "Looks like you found her. I would be careful."

As we continue our match, I see the man's face turning red, and he's squinching it.

He utters, "I don't get it. I keep pushing, but I can't move it. What's going on?"

This game has gone on long enough. I tighten my grip, constricting my muscles, and move his arm until I have the advantage of pushing downward. When his arm is just an inch away from the table, I tell him, "I win," and slam his arm to the table.

I stand and say, "Don't worry about the drink. I have to get back to my friends."

The tavern cheers and a few people slap my shoulders and back in victory.

"That was great," one says.

Standing from the table, I turn to the bar and see my mug filled. I grab it and head back to Jenny and Rox. I only get a foot or two from the bar when I hear Jenny yell from across the tavern, "Watch out!"

I turn and see the big man coming at me, holding his arm.

"No one does that to me. What are you?" he yells.

"You lost. It was a fair match. I want to get back to celebrating with friends," I tell him as I start to back up from him.

He reaches for me, but I step back quickly so he can't grab me.

The tavern suddenly goes silent as everyone is watching us. I am starting to get nervous, as I don't want to fight.

"Leave the girl alone. It was in good fun," barks the barkeep.

His companions jump in to support him and look ready to fight.

The next thing I know, I'm on the floor with broken glass all around me. He must have pushed me or something.

The big man yells at the bartender, "You stay out of this!"

Feeling like a horse just kicked me in the chest, I look down and see drops of blood hitting the floor. I touch my face, and it's wet. I look at my hand to see blood on my fingers. I laugh at the sight of my blood. I place my fingertips to my mouth for some reason. As soon as I taste my blood, I feel my heart pulse. A second later, it pulses again but more intensely. I turn my head and look at my attacker, but something is different. Everything is amplified. From the sounds around me to how everything looks. It's almost too much for me to take in. It's disorienting in a way. What's going on?

"What are you going to do now, pretty?" the man states.

Hearing this, I snap and lunge at him angrily, lifting him off the ground.

"You couldn't just leave it," I yell at him. I toss him into the tavern wall with all that I have. When he hits the wall, he's knocked out instantly. I turn to the larger of his remaining companions and move in to attack him. He swings at me, but I dodge his attack. I deal an uppercut to his chin, which launches him in the air and onto a table. Lastly, I turn toward the last one and walk towards him, which causes him to back up out of fear. I don't think he expected me to go through his companions so quickly.

"Now you don't want anything to do with me," I yell at him.

I grab him before he can get away, looking at him face-to-face.

"Help, help me. She's crazy. Her eyes," he screams!

Before he can say anything else, I headbutt him in the center of his face, breaking his nose. I let go of him, and he drops to the ground. I stand there, adrenaline pumping through me. Gathering myself, I see myself in a mirror. My face is half covered in blood, and my eyes look different. I grab a rag off the bar to wipe the blood from my face. As I am wiping, I see everyone looking at me and the carnage around me.

"Did you see that?" one person says.

"She took those Red Jackets out quickly," I hear another say.

I have to get out of here before things get worse. Making my way through the tavern, I see Jenny and Rox at the table, and they look shocked at what just happened. I reach the door and start to run down the alleyway. As I run, my vision flashes white every few seconds, which prevents me from seeing a crate in front of me, which causes me to trip and fall to the ground. In a panic, I push myself to the edge of the alleyway and lean against a building. My vision keeps flashing white and back to normal until it stops. As I look around, everything looks as bright as day, but there's no color. I can see everything, even in the unlit portions of the alley. I rub my eyes, and I look again to make sure I am seeing this. When I look again, my vision is normal again. I lean against the building wall, holding myself, wishing I was home. I should have never come here. This was a mistake. All I want is to be home.

The feeling of a soft, wet thing repeatedly touching my face wakes me. Opening my eyes, I see a small, scruffy-looking black puppy with a white tuff on his chest licking my face.

"Stop, stop," I tell it.

Pulling it away from my face, I hold it in front of me. I look around, and I'm still in the alley. I must have fallen asleep here last night. I can't believe I slept in the alley. This is not my finest moment. Looking down at a puddle next to me, I see my reflection and the dried blood on my face, which causes me to remember what happened last night. I get up slowly, thinking I am going to be hurt, but I'm not. I have to get home. I am sure Mother is really worried about me. Making my way down the alley, I realize I'm still holding the puppy.

"Sorry. Find your owner or your mama," as I place it on the ground.

It stays there looking at me, twisting its head right and left. It finally barks at me.

"Go ahead. Go home. I have to get home too. Mother is going to be very upset with me," I tell it.

Continuing on my way, I look down, and the puppy is right next to me.

"No, no, you can't follow me," I tell it.

The puppy tilts its head and barks at me a few times. I stand there looking at it.

"Keep up if you can, but I am not going to wait for you," I tell it.

To my surprise, the puppy keeps up with me with his little legs as we go through the city and down the Western Road. I wonder what Mother is going to say when she sees my face. How am I going to explain it? I get about ten minutes from my home when I see two figures in the distance. Based on what I see, I think it's Jenny and Rox. They must be checking up on me. They see me and run over.

"Where have you been?" Jenny asks. "We ran after you, but we couldn't find you. Please do not leave us behind again." Jenny breathes deeply in surprise and exclaims, "Look at your face! Does it still hurt?!"

I shrug and tell her, "A little, but overall, I'm not hurt even though I should be. You know where I live?"

"Well, not really, but we knew you lived by the Western Pass. We thought we would head this way and ask around," she says.

"Who's dog is this?" Rox asks.

"It followed me from the city for some reason," I answer, rubbing my cheek.

"Take this and wipe your face," Jenny tells me, handing me her handkerchief.

I wipe my face to remove the last of the dried blood.

"How's the cut above my eye?" I ask them.

"It is not too bad. It is just above your eyebrow. Most people would not even notice it," Jenny, let me know.

"I have to figure out how to tell my Mother how I got it," I explain.

"Last night was crazy. We saw you sitting down with those Red Jackets, and you were arm-wrestling one of them. The next thing we saw was the Red Jacket kicking you into the table, and everything went crazy. Jenny and I were about to run over, but you took them out like rag dolls," Rox injects excitedly.

"I know. I lost control. I wasn't myself. Something came over me. I'm sure I'm in trouble with the tavern owner and even the city guard. Tell me, how badly did I hurt them?" I ask.

"They'll be fine. You broke one of their noses and another one's jaw. Nothing a healer can't fix. The one you threw against the wall had his pride hurt more than anything. As for being in trouble, don't worry about it. Didn't I tell you why I like the Dragon Tail so much? What happens there stays there. Fights happen all the time, and they're never reported to the city guard," Rox explains.

"So I'm not in trouble?" I ask, scratching the top of my head.

"You're good, trust me. You have to tell us what happened and where you went," Rox asks.

"Can we walk so I can let Mother know I am safe?" I ask.

"Sure, sure," he says.

Walking home, I explain what happened after I ran out of the tavern. When we reach my home, I see Mother feeding the chickens. She looks up, runs over to us, and hugs me tightly.

"Where have you been? I was so worried as you never made it home last night. I was up all night pacing."

"Sorry about that. Everything seems to be fine regarding what we were worried about. I joined Jenny and Rox for a celebratory drink within the city, and things got carried away. This is Jenny and Rox. This little guy followed me home. I can't seem to get rid of him," I explain.

The puppy walks over to Mother, placing his front paws on her while wiggling his tail.

"Hello, little one," Mother says.

"Nice to meet you, Miss Everwind," Jenny says, extending her hand.

Mother shakes her hand and then extends her hand out to Rox, and he returns the greeting.

"So you are the two that have captured my daughter's attention. There's some fresh bread on the table if you all like some. You need food in your bellies instead of all the ale or spirits you might have had. Kyra, we will be discussing the cut above your eye and your punishment later," Mother informs me.

"Yes, ma'am."

We all stand there for a second, and I am sure Rox and Jenny feel just as uncomfortable as I do. When Mother becomes this way, she can be pretty intimidating.

Rox finally breaks the awkwardness. "You don't have to tell me twice. I like bread, and I didn't have breakfast," Rox says, walking to the house.

I nervously smile at Mother as Jenny and I walk to the house for some food.

Before we get to the house, Rox is already back in the doorway, holding a piece of bread and chewing.

"It's good, Jenny. It reminds me of my mom's bread," he yells, spitting food as he talks.

"Glad you like it," I answer.

Entering the house, Jenny starts looking around my home.

I say to her, "I'm sure your home is very different than this."

Jenny looks at me and says, "It's nice. I might live in a bigger home, but I can tell this home is big in different ways. Even though your mom might be upset with you, it's because she loves you. I would take that over what I have at home."

We make our way to the table, and Rox is already starting on his second piece of bread. I grab the homemade jam that Mother makes and pass it to Rox. I cut a piece of bread for myself and pass the knife to Jenny so she can also cut a piece. We don't say much to each other while we eat. I wonder what the two of them are thinking. I feel uneasiness as I am unsure what to say or do, but the silence is killing me, so I break it.

"What are you two doing today?" I ask.

They look at me, and Jenny says, " You mean the three of us, right?"

"You still want to hang out with me? I wasn't sure after last night," I ask.

"Why wouldn't we?" Rox answers with a full mouth.

I shrug my shoulders and look at them both.

"We're friends, and friends stick by each other," Rox states.

I look up at both of them. "Thanks; that means a lot. So what is the plan for today?"

"There are so many things to do. There's the archery competition, the dances, and the fireworks at night. However, before we do anything, you have to clean yourself up. Your clothes are soiled, and you smell of the alleyway you slept in," Jenny informs with a smile.

I pull my shirt up to my nose, sniff, and stand embarrassed. I smell like piss and other things I don't want to think of.

"Why didn't you tell me I smelled like this? I need to bathe and get fresh clothes. Jenny, can you go up to my room and get me a clean outfit? I am sure you can put something together for me. I don't have that many clothes. I am going to head to the barn to bathe."

"The barn," Rox asks.

"That's where we keep the watering trough for the animals. We turn it into a bathtub when we want to bathe," I explain.

Running out of the house toward the barn, I fill my tub with water from the well, wishing I had hot water from the fireplace to warm it, but I will have to make do with a cold bath. I strip down, grab the bar of soap, and quickly sit down, feeling a shocking sensation travel up my spine from the freezing water.

"That's cold!"

I start to wash quickly as there's no time for a soak. As long as I remove the dirt and the smell of the alley, that will be good enough. I grab my soiled clothes and scrub them with soap. Once clean, I ring them out and toss them on two hooks on the wall to drip dry.

As I am getting close to finishing up, I hear Jenny from the barn door, "It's me. I have your outfit."

"Can you put it on the stool over there?" I ask.

She walks over and places my clothes on a stool beside the tub.

"Do you need anything else?" she asks.

"No, I'm good. Just finishing up here, and then we can get going," I say.

I feel her hand on my shoulder, which sends a tingle through my body, but not the way the cold water did a bit ago.

"I will wait outside with Rox," she tells me, walking to the door.

"Wait," I say. "Can I ask you something?"

"Sure," she replies.

"I haven't had many friends in my life. To be honest, you two are my first. I don't have much experience with this and need to know. Does my strength make you or Rox nervous?" I ask.

I watch Jenny walk back over to me and kneel next to the tub. She's twirling her finger in the water and then looks at me. "I am pretty sure Rox finds your strength fascinating," she answers.

"What about you?" I ask again.

"No, you do not make me nervous, far from it," she says. She raises her hand and touches my cheek with the back of her finger. She then leans in and gently kisses me. "I hope you did not mind that."

I shake my head a tiny bit in disbelief at what just happened.

Jenny smiles and says, while standing, "We need to get going. Rox has a short attention span and will come in here asking us to hurry up. We should talk later, but let us get ready and head back to the city for some fun."

I step out of the tub to get dressed. As I'm dressing, I look over to Jenny, who is looking at me oddly.

I ask her, "What? Haven't you seen a naked girl before?"

"Not like you. Your body is different," she says.

"What do you mean?" I ask.

"Your body is not like most girls. Most girls are soft and do not have muscles as you do. Have you always been that way?" she asks.

"Kind of. As a kid, I was kind of twiggy, but as I grew, my body changed. All the chores and field work most likely had a hand in it as well," I answer.

I finish dressing quickly in the outfit Jenny picked out for me. She chose my light blue top, brown leather pants I hadn't worn in a while, and brown boots. I grab the money purses and attach them to my belt.

I turn to her and say, "Ready!"

She walks over and sniffs me. "You no longer smell like the alley. I approve."

I stand there befuddled at her statement as she walks out. I notice Smoky, who has been watching us the whole time, shake his head playfully at me.

"I don't want your opinion," I say to him.

As I exit the barn, I see Jenny and Rox playing with the puppy by the house. Mother is still feeding the animals. I walk over to her. "I didn't get a chance to show you this before. Here's my wages for working the harvest," I tell Mother, handing her both coin purses.

"Two coin purses?" Mother inquires.

"Yes, this one is my wages," I tell her. I open my second purse and pour a few gold coins into my hand to show her. "This is from John. I tried not taking it, but he insisted as a thank you from his family for helping him."

"You need to give this back. His family will need it during the winter as well. You didn't help him for the money," Mother answers.

"I tried, but he insisted. We can keep and use it if needed. I worked so we would have money for supplies and other things during the winter season. We always scrape by each winter, and having this will be helpful."

Mother looks at the purse of money and then at me. "It's your money; you can use it however you wish."

"I know you are upset about last night, and I will take my punishment willingly, but Jenny and Rox want to show me the festivities throughout the city today. May I go? I promise not to drink so much this time, and I will be more careful," I say, looking down and playfully scuffing the ground with my foot.

"We will take care of her," Jenny yells over.

I watch Mother's sternness with me start to melt away.

"You know I can't say no to you when you talk to me in that voice and act that way. I have to figure out how not to be taken in by that. Go. Have fun. We have work to do tomorrow, and while you are out enjoying yourself, I will think of your punishment."

I hug Mother. "Thank you."

I start walking backward toward the road, asking, "You two coming?"

Jenny and Rox run to me. The puppy tries to run with Jenny and Rox, but Mother picks him up and tells him. "No, no, you stay here. It's best if you don't go. Those three might get you in trouble, and we don't want that."

CHAPTER 4
NEW EXPERIENCES

"So, what are we going to do today?" I ask them.

"The archery contest is held in the main square. That's always a big draw. One of the city guard archers enters each year and has won it three years in a row. He's incredible," Rox explains.

"Around the archery competition, vendors set up tents to sell different goods. I bought this small dagger a few harvests ago," he says while handing it to me.

I take the dagger out of its sheath. The weight feels well-balanced, and the blade has decorative engravings. "It's nice," I say, handing it back to him.

"What about you, Jenny? Is there anything you want to see or do?" I ask, nudging her side a bit.

"I love going to the dances to dance and hear music. I also like watching the street performers."

"I don't think I have ever danced," I state.

Jenny looks at me wide-eyed and says, "I will fix that. Dancing is so fun. Even Rox likes it."

"I have to admit it's fun dancing, especially when dancing with pretty girls," Rox adds.

"We'll have to see if Jenny can get me to dance," I say playfully.

When we reach the city, everyone is setting up for the day. We walk to a wooden announcement board filled with event flyers. The flyers showcase the celebration's events, including music, dances, and street performers. I also notice a flyer about the Red Jackets.

I turn to Rox and Jenny, pointing to it, and ask, "Is this connected to the assholes from last night? They were wearing red jackets."

"Yes, they are a new radical group aiming to effect change in and around the city. They have been stirring things up lately and have gained popularity over the past few months, mainly with trouble-makers and residents who truly dislike the people of High Rock. They speak about equality and the balance of power and wealth between the two parts of the city. I do not support them because they inspire violence and bring out the worst in people," Jenny explains.

"That's enough about the Red Jackets. Let's walk around and see what we see," Rox tells us.

Leaving the announcement board, we go to the central square and pass a street vendor peddling a sweet wine drink with fresh berries.

"Come try my drink. The berries add extra refreshment," the peddler says to us.

I look at my friends, wondering if they want to try it. They nod, and I tell the vendor, "Three, please."

The vendor greets me with a smile and places a bunch of berries into three goblets. He crushes them with a wooden stick and pours light pink wine over the crushed berries. He explains before handing us the drinks, "That's one silver now, and if you return the goblets, I will give you three copper back."

I hand over a silver coin and tell my friends, "Make sure you keep your goblets. I want to get three copper back."

They laugh, rolling their eyes.

Walking through the city enjoying our berry wine, one shop window catches my attention. I walk over to take a closer look. I see a variety of armor and clothing on display and notice two things that grab my attention: Brown leather shoulder armor and a pair of deep brown leather pants with small brass adornments going down the legs. I look up at the shop sign to make a note of it. *Not Your Man's Armor*, which puts a smile on my face.

Jenny asks, "Do you like anything you see?"

"The shoulder armor and the leather pants," I say, pointing to them.

Rox motions us to move on. As we get closer to the square, we hear music and crowds of people. Exiting the alleyway, we're greeted by a massive crowd walking around in every direction. I can see the archery contest area ahead of us, and there are many other stages through the square with different activities. I've never experienced anything like this. Why doesn't Mother ever want to come to this?!

"That's the musician from last night at the Dragon Tail," I show Jenny and Rox, pointing to her playing on a stage near us.

Rox runs over to the stage I was pointing to.

I look at Jenny, and she tells me, "Rox has a thing for her."

"Ohhhh," I said, understanding why he was so excited that she was playing at the Dragon Tail last night.

Jenny and I catch up to Rox, who is already gazing at her.

I lean down and whisper to him, "You should talk to her when she takes a break."

Rox shakes his head and tells me, "She is so lovely. I am not. There's no way."

"You don't know that," I retort, pushing him forward playfully.

As we listen, she notices us and smiles, not skipping a note as she plays. As she finishes the song, she jumps off the stage in front of us.

"You're the one who got into the fight last night. Are you alright?" she asks, wiping her forehead with a cloth.

I answer, *[In Elvin] "I'm fine. Just a little bruised but nothing bad."*

Looking surprised, she greets me, *"Nice to meet you; I'm Lindsey Tornrin. It looks like you know how to defend yourself. You put those asshole Red Jackets in their place."*

"I lost control and didn't mean to do that. Anyway, you see my friend here. He really enjoys listening to you play but is very nervous to talk to you. Would you be up to having a drink with him?" I reply, moving my eyes from her to Rox.

Lindsey looks at Rox and back at me and winks. *"Sure, he's kind of cute."*

I turn back to Rox and Jenny. Their mouths are wide open as they look at me.

"You speak, Elvin?" Jenny asks.

"Yes. Don't you?"

Turning to Rox. "Lindsey was wondering if you want to join her for a drink?"

I take his goblet quietly to ensure I get my copper coin.

"You're welcome, by the way," I tell him.

Rox's face instantly changes from confusion to excitement as Lindsey takes his hand and escorts him to the tavern for a drink.

"My job is done. Let's find something to do so these two have time to talk," I say to Jenny as we watch them walk away.

Jenny smiles, grabs my hand, and pulls me toward the other activities. "Nice job, matchmaker."

Walking through the city, Jenny and I stop to watch various street performances. While doing so, I finish Rox's and my drink and hook the goblets on my belt. As we reach the edge of the central square, we notice a large crowd around one performance. We get closer to see a performer demonstrating his abilities of strength and agility by doing handstands, placing spectators on his shoulders, and striking a board that raises a metal piece that rings a bell high above it. I move Jenny and me closer to the front to see the performance better.

"Do you think you could do that?" Jenny asks, referring to the bell.

"Not sure. I never tried."

"Ladies, would you like to try?" the performer asks, motioning us to join him.

I quickly lift Jenny and place her on my right shoulder in front of everyone, which completely surprises her, and she screams.

"Do you mean like this?" I ask him.

"Please put me down," Jenny demands.

I place Jenny down gracefully. I get a look of disbelief from her.

The performer continues motioning me to join him, but I wave to let him know I don't want to. Jenny pushes me towards the performer. I look back at her. Her arms are crossed, and she has a smile on her face.

I look back to the performer. "I guess I'm joining you. What do you want me to do?"

"Shall we see if this young lady can ring the bell?" he asks the crowd.

Everyone cheers for me to try. The performer hands me the large mallet.

"Strike the board as hard as you can; the metal ringer is heavier than you think," he explains.

I walk over to the board and look it over. I grip the mallet with both hands, raise it above my head, and swing down on the board, which sends the metal ringer into the bell. The crowd cheers for me, and I return the mallet to the performer.

"I'm stronger than I look," I tell him.

Before returning to Jenny, I drop a coin in his chest, indicating to the audience they should do the same.

As I make my way to Jenny, a small, thin boy with blond hair stops me. "Are you stronger than a giant?"

I squat down to meet him at his blue eyes. "I don't know, maybe? What's your name?" I ask him.

"Forge."

"I'm Kyra, and this is Jenny."

Jenny waves to Forge.

He's pretty dirty, and his clothes look rough with holes. I look down at his feet, and he's barefoot.

Where's your mom or dad?" I ask him with concern.

"Don't have any," he replies.

At this moment, I realize he's a Forgotten, children left to fend for themselves on the streets of the city.

"I'm sorry. Do you need anything? Have you eaten anything today?" I ask.

Forge shakes his head. "No leftovers. We haven't eaten in days."

"We?" I inquire.

Forge points to a small girl off to the side of us. "My little sister, Ophelia."

Seeing her and this little boy upsets me. I look up at Jenny, who has been watching us.

"Let's fix that," I tell Forge. Do you want to get something to eat? My treat."

Forge nods his head at my idea. I take his hand and walk over to his sister, who has been watching us the whole time. When we reach her, she grabs Forge's hand quickly. I think she is nervous. She's just as thin as Forge. She might be three or maybe four years old. Under all the dirt and grime, I can tell she's a cute little one with braided brown hair tied with a blue bow.

"Your brother and I were thinking of getting some food together. Would you like to join us?" I ask.

"She's nice, Ophelia. We need to eat," Forge tells his sister.

Ophelia nods, squeezing her brother's hand tightly. I look around and see a tavern with large wooden tables and benches outside of it for the celebration.

"Do you know what you are doing?" Jenny asks.

"I do. They're hungry, and I am going to feed them. Let's get something to eat," I tell everyone.

We walk to the tavern and sit down, waiting for someone to serve us. The two children look nervous and are wiggling in their seats. A tavern maid comes to our table and asks, "What can I get you?"

"Four plates of food, please," I tell her.

She looks at me and then the children. Seeing them, her tone changes from upbeat to negative.

"Is there an issue?" I ask, looking at her sternly.

"We don't serve their kind," she informs me.

"What do you mean their kind? Do you mean children?" I retort.

I toss my purse on the table. "I will be paying for their meals, so there shouldn't be any issues. Right?"

The tavern maid steps back and heads inside flustered. Looking at Forge and Ophelia, I see them fidgeting in their seats and looking around. I'm sure they are not used to this and feel exposed.

"You're safe with us," I tell them, rubbing Forge's head, hoping to relax them.

I look over to Jenny, who has a worried look on her face. I make sure she sees me, and I wink at her, which makes her smile slightly.

It doesn't take long before the tavern maid brings out four plates of food and asks, "Is there anything else?"

"I think we're good," I tell her.

Looking at the children, they have already started to attack the food in front of them. Within a few minutes, both plates are empty. I push my plate towards Forge, and Jenny does the same with Ophiela. They dig in just as fast as their first plate, clearing them just as quickly. They must have been starving. After finishing his second plate of food, Forge lets out a good burp, which makes Ophiela giggle.

Jenny also chuckles and tells Ophiela, "I know someone who does that, too. Can I ask where you sleep and stay?"

"Under the bridges."

"Are you warm enough staying there?" Jenny asks.

"We keep each other warm," Ophiela says.

Even though I grew up not having much, I was lucky compared to these two. My mother loves me, and I always had a roof over my head every night, and I never went to bed hungry.

"Why don't you stay at one of the centers?" Jenny asks.

"Centers are worse than the streets. We ran from one last season. We be fine," Forge tells us, looking at his sister.

Looking at Jenny across the table, she seems a little sad. I watch her place her arm around Ophelia. I see this hit a chord with her.

A group of kids, all dressed like Forge and Ophelia, run up to us.

"Forge!" one of the kids calls to get his attention. "We have possible leftovers."

Forge stands, and Ophelia follows her brother's lead. I can tell she sees Forge as her protector and goes where he goes.

"We must go. Thanks for food. It best we eat in long time," he says.

Both Jenny and I stand as well.

As Forge passes me, I take his hand and tell him, "If you or Ophelia need anything, I live in the valley by the Western Pass. Just take the Western Road all the way."

"You different lady. Most don't see us," he answers.

As they join their friends, Ophelia turns back and hugs Jenny quickly before joining the other kids, and I hear them ask Forge, "Who's that?"

Forge answers, "They nice and bought us food. The dark-haired one is very strong."

Jenny takes my hand and tells me, "You are something."

"I've heard of the Forgotten, but I never met one. I don't think I can ever be the same now. It's so sad." I tell Jenny, staring at the group of children running down the street, laughing and joking with each other as if nothing is wrong.

"It is one of the darker sides of this city. Children born from mothers who work in brothels or children of poor families who give them up," Jenny says. "Time to find Rox and a little fun."

I nod and place a few coins on the table to pay for the food, and we start to walk back to the main square.

Walking back, we hear music playing nearby, and Jenny pulls me towards it. Within a few moments, I see a large crowd of people dancing. Knowing she will ask me to dance, I try to slow us down. Jenny starts to pull me more aggressively.

"Come on, let us join the dance," she says.

"I don't know, remember, I haven't ever danced before," I explain, slightly panicking.

"You will be fine. Trust me. It will be fun and cheer us up," she persists.

Walking into the dance area, I stand there as everyone moves around us.

Jenny grabs my attention. "Watch and follow my lead."

She bows, and I do the same. She spins around once, then raises her hands and claps them above her head.

"Your turn, but go in the opposite direction. It is pretty easy," she instructs me.

I repeat what Jenny demonstrated for me. Jenny places her arm into mine, and we spin around. She unlocks our arms and repeats her first movements. We then repeat this over and over again as the music plays. As we dance, I see her smiling as she twirls around me. Occasionally, we switch partners, but we always end up back with each other. I have to admit it; dancing is fun. As the music ends, everyone claps and bows to their partner. Jenny hugs me and kisses my cheek, which causes me to blush.

"Thank you for the dance. It has been too long since I danced," she says, breathing deeply.

"What have you two been doing?" A voice next to us asks.

Looking over, Rox and Lindsey are walking over to us.

"Kyra had her first dance," Jenny proudly informs them.

"You're first dance. Did you like it?" Lindsey asks.

"I was nervous in the beginning, but I did like it. What have you two been up to?" I ask.

"Not too much. We talked for a while and started to walk around looking for you two, and now we're here," Rox explains. "Lindsey and I are going to watch the fireworks tonight on the Eastern Wall. Do you two want to join us?"

Jenny and I look at each other and smile. Lindsey gives us a subtle cue not to join.

"You two should enjoy that together. We will find something to do," Jenny answers.

As we talk, a tram goes over us, which causes me to look up.

"I have always wondered what riding one of those would be like. I bet you can see the whole valley from within one," I say out loud.

"You have never ridden the tram before?" Lindsey asks me.

"No, I never have."

"You two have a lovely day and time tonight," Jenny tells Rox and Lindsey.

While still looking at the tram, I'm suddenly pulled off balance as Jenny pulls me through the square. Trying not to trip, I shout back to Rox and Lindsey, "Have a good time."

"Where are we going? We were talking to them," I ask.

"We are going to ride the tram!" she says excitedly.

"Can we do that? I thought you had to live or work in High Rock to ride the tram," I answer quickly.

"Yes, silly. Anyone can ride it. You just have to pay," she informs me, continuing to pull me forward.

"Pay?" I ask.

"How do you not know this? You will see. Pick up the pace," Jenny tells me.

Making our way through the square toward the tram station, I remember my dream of a girl pulling me through the city. Jenny's blue dress is similar to the one in the dream, and even her hair is the same. Why didn't I connect the dots on this earlier? Well, at least I figured out what that dream was about.

As we continue towards the station, we fight through the crowds as we go against the flow of people. Walking through the main entryway of the station, I am greeted by an immense space with multiple platforms and hundreds of people moving about. Looking up, I see a network of giant gears, wheels, and pulley systems, all moving together. In the middle of the station is a large platform above everything. That is where they control the trams. People work together, pulling and pushing different levers that engage and disengage the gears and wheels moving the trams up and down. It's a mechanical marvel of machinery and engineering.

"Come on, stop looking up. We need to grab the blue tram," Jenny tells me.

"I can't help it! I've heard about this place my whole life. Seeing it in person, it's incredible," I tell her, continuing to look up. "How do they keep it running during the winter when the aqueducts freeze over?"

"During the winter, the city opens an underground aqueduct that supplies water to the station to keep the central tram working as it goes all the way to the top. All other trams are stored in the station until warm weather returns," Jenny answers.

We start walking up a set of metal stairs with very ornate railings, still fighting the flow of people. After two flights, we exit the stairs and walk out to a platform where people are waiting.

"We made it. I can see the blue tram coming down now," Jenny says, breathing a little heavily.

I watch as the tram descends from High Rock. As it enters the station, it stops at the platform we are standing on. This is the first time I have seen one of these up close. It looks to be made mainly of wood that has been painted blue, but I see metal framing between the wood panels and windows. A worker unlocks the tram's door and opens it. People pour out, discussing what they hope to buy and see at the celebration. After a moment, the same worker yells, "All aboard!"

Jenny escorts me to the tram and places two copper coins into a collection box that a worker is monitoring.

"The money is used to help keep it working and pay the people who work here. If the city did not charge, it would have stopped working years ago due to wear and tear and required upkeep. Come sit down here with me. I like sitting on this side going up and the other side going down," she tells me.

I sit beside her on one of the long wooden benches. Jenny indicates I should sit next to the window to look out more easily.

"Where are we going in High Rock?"

"I want to show you where I live."

"Sounds fun. How long does it take to get to your home?"

"Not long, maybe ten minutes or so. When I was younger, I used to walk it, but it takes about an hour to go up or down. The tram is much faster and easier."

As everyone else gets in and sits down, I notice a family sitting across from us. The children are standing on the bench seat, looking out the window excitedly. One of them is holding a giant pink fluffy thing on a stick. Every once in a while, the little girl pulls a piece off and eats it. I see the father take a piece as well, which causes the little girl to scrunch her face with discontent. He smiles and tells her, "Sorry, it is so good."

"What are they eating," I ask.

"Spun sugar on a stick. It is very sweet and fun to eat. Vendors can make it any color they want with food dye. It all tastes the same, but I prefer the blue ones. I think blue tastes better. No matter the color, it has the same effect. Look at the little girl's mouth. You never had spun sugar?" she asks.

I look at the little girl and notice her bright pink mouth, which makes me smile.

As the doors close, I see the workers lock them, and the tram starts to move up and out of the station. It feels very odd, and I grab Jenny's hand tightly.

Jenny laughs slightly and tells me, "You will be fine."

Looking out the window, I can see the whole city below. Everyone looks like little colorful dots moving around. After a few minutes, the tram slows down and stops to let people get on and off. After everyone is seated, the doors are locked again. The tram starts to move with a back-and-forth sway. I don't like this part of the ride at all. I am not used to the motion I'm feeling. Jenny squeezes my hand back to give me comfort.

"I can't believe you live up here. From this vantage point, you can see the whole city, the valley, and the mountains. When I was little, I always imagined what it would be like up here," I tell her.

Jenny smiles and says, "It is not as great as you think. While it has advantages, there are things I do not like or agree with that are all too common up here. It is a constant game of one-upping each other, and the people from High Rock tend to treat people from the Lowlands poorly as they feel they are below them somehow. This is why I prefer to spend as much time as possible in the lower portion of the city."

It doesn't take long before I feel the tram slow down and come to a stop.

"This is where we get off," Jenny tells me, standing.

CHAPTER 5
HIGH ROCK

Exiting the tram, I see all the buildings built of lightly colored mountain stone. Off to the left of us is one of the great aqueducts with water flowing out of it. As the water exits the aqueduct, it creates a waterfall that falls hundreds of feet below into one of the holding pools that supply water to the city and valley. I can smell the mist in the air and feel a breeze on my face. I can see the valley and fields we worked in for the past few weeks. I can see further into the distance than I have ever seen before.

"It's so amazing up here. I can't believe you live up here," I tell Jenny.

"It will take us about ten minutes to get to my home. Do you want to go?" she asks.

I am intrigued by the idea of seeing her home. I want to see how it is different from mine. "Sure."

"Come on, we need to go this way then," Jenny explains, gesturing to me in a direction.

As we walk, I continue taking in the sites around me. There are tree-lined walkways with benches facing the valley. As we continue walking, I see steps leading up to a different level of High Rock. We go up the steps and head down another tree-lined walkway. It doesn't take long before Jenny stops and turns to me.

"This is my home."

We are standing in front of a large wooden door with a golden metal *M* attached to it. Next to the door are small trees in stone pots. Flowers are growing in window boxes under each window.

"Let us use the side entrance. I do not like using the front door that much, as it lets everyone know when I am home," Jenny tells me.

As we walk through the side entrance, "No one is here today. The Harvest Celebration is one of the few times a year when the staff has off," Jenny mentions.

When I enter, I see a large table in the middle of the kitchen and crate after crate on the floor. Looking past the crates and table, I see a fully stocked kitchen with a large fireplace for cooking and ovens next to it for baking.

"I guess we got our winter food supplies today," she says, moving around the crates.

Looking at her family's kitchen, I am taken aback. "Your kitchen is bigger than my whole home," I tell her.

Walking through the kitchen, Jenny grabs an apple from a basket and tosses it to me. "Since we did not eat, I thought you might like one."

I bite the apple, which causes juice to run down the edge of my lower lip. These must have just been picked from the orchard. I forgot how good an apple can taste when it's this fresh. Over the winter, we store our apples in our storage area in the back of our home. We cook with them because they get mealy or soft after a few months.

With a mouth full of apple, I answer, "Thanks!"

We pass through a set of double doors and enter a long hallway lined with paintings and gilded mirrors on the walls. The floor is a wooden floor laid to create artistic patterns. Walking down the hallway, we pass a room filled with books from floor to ceiling.

"You have a library!" I announce excitedly.

"I spend a lot of time there since my parents are not around much," she replies.

"What do you mean they are not around much?" I ask, looking all around.

"My family is so focused on being seen as important that they spend much of their time around specific people who can help them. They give very little value to the people that make their lives easier. For example, they treat Rox's mother poorly most of the time. This upsets me, as she is the sweetest person I know. Sometimes I imagine myself leaving this place and making my life somewhere else," she tells me.

Continuing to the end of the hallway, we enter a large open area with a staircase winding up the wall. Jenny heads up the stairs and motions for me to follow her.

"Is that the front door we just passed?" I ask.

"Yes, the house has two hallways on top of each other with rooms on each side."

At the top of the stairs, we reach a landing and the upstairs hall-way. Walking down, we pass one bedroom after another.

"Which one is yours?" I ask.

"The first one. I will show you if you like, but first I want to show you where I spend most of my time during the warmer weather or when I have to think. Only Rox and his mother know I spend time there," she tells me.

We walk about halfway down the hallway, and Jenny opens a door on the left. I follow her through the doorway and up a set of stairs that lead to another door. When Jenny opens the door, we're hit by sunlight that blinds me for a second. Jenny continues, and I follow, shading the sun from my eyes. As my eyes adjust, I see we are on a small roof area. Jenny sits down on the edge of the roof, dangling her legs.

"Come sit with me," she says, patting the spot beside her.

Sitting beside her, I look out at the valley and city below. It's so quiet and calm here, even with the celebration below in the city.

"You come here to think and be by yourself?" I ask.

"I have been coming out here a lot lately. After Rox and I would come home from the fields, I would sit up here before going to bed. I was excited to show you my home, but as we sat on the tram, I thought it might not be the best idea. I started worrying about what you might think," Jenny says quietly as she looks down, tapping her heels on the side of her home.

"About your home?" I ask, looking at her.

"People who are not from High Rock think we are spoiled. I was worried you might think of me this way," she explains.

"Your home doesn't make me think any differently of you. I can't imagine having such a grand place to live in, but it's also fascinating. As you saw, my home is much smaller. I'm pretty sure we have you beat on open space, though. We have the whole valley; you have a walkway." I answer, trying to make her feel a little better.

She looks at me, smiles, and then leans her head on me as we look at the city and valley below us.

After some time, she asks, "What shall we do?"

"I don't know. You invited me up here. Do you have any taverns or other places we can go?"

"No taverns. Let us go in and see if we can find something to do," Jenny answers, standing up.

As I stand, she offers me her hand.

"Why, thank you. Such a gentleman," I jokingly tell her.

She looks at me and states, "Gentlemen do not look like me."

"They do not," I chuckle.

We head down to the hallway, and I ask her about the paintings hanging on the walls. "Are any of these family members?"

"Every one of them, at least that is what I have been told."

Jenny enters her bedroom and sits at a desk. I look around and start to touch a few things on her dresser and nightstand. Her room is so different than mine. I look at her bed, which is twice as tall as mine and has pillow after pillow on it. I look at her, smiling while pointing at it.

"Go ahead. It is just a bed," she states.

I jump in the air, twist around, and land in the center of her bed. As I lie there, sinking into her bed. "Ohhh—that's soft! My bed is stuffed with straw. I think yours might be made of clouds."

She chuckles and replies, "I never thought of it as clouds, but I like that."

I sit up and look at her. "What are we going to do? Rox is with Lindsey. Do you want to stay here, return to the celebration, or something else?"

"Remember when I said we could talk later? Now that it is just us, let us talk. Are you good with that?" she asks.

I think for a second, remembering the events in the barn.

"I guess so," I answer hesitantly.

Jenny starts to open up to me. "Over the past weeks of getting to know you, I have started to like you much more than a friend. You are so different than any other girl I have ever known. There is some-thing about you that draws me to you. I think you might feel the same, but I am unsure."

Hearing Jenny's confession surprises me but reassures me that my feelings toward her are reciprocated. "I have also started to have feelings for you. When I am not around you, I'm always thinking about you. Your kiss in the barn overloaded my brain ... in a good way," I try to explain to her.

She looks at me for a moment, then walks over. She leans down and places her hands on my thighs. As she does this, I can smell her perfume, and my heart starts to pound. She kisses me softly, and I return her kiss. While kissing, Jenny moves her hands to the back of my head and runs her fingers through my hair, pressing our mouths firmly together. I draw her into me more as our kissing intensifies. She caresses my side, causing me to laugh and squirm for a second. She pulls back and smiles.

"Ticklish, are we?" she asks.

Looking at Jenny, I see her cheeks are flush, and based on how my face feels, I am sure mine are as well. Jenny pushes me playfully further into her bed. She crawls on top of me, and I wrap my arms around her. As we are about to kiss again, we hear a door close and people walking up the stairs.

"Shit! My parents are home!" she jumps out of the bed.

"Can you go into that room and hide there? I am sorry, but if my parents see you up here, it will cause a fight." Pointing to a door.

Jumping off the bed, I scrabble to the door she pointed to and enter it. I don't want to cause any trouble for her. I close the door behind me and realize I'm in a bathroom.

"She has her own bathroom," I say quietly to myself.

I hear Jenny moving around her bedroom, quickly opening something. A voice calls out to her, "Jenniver, are you home?"

"I am in my room, Mother. I am trying to pick a dress for tonight but cannot decide."

Should I wear a black, green or maybe a purple one? Maybe I should stay in the one I am already wearing. I do not know," Jenny yells out.

"Pick any. You look lovely in them all. We are having some people over for a party tonight, and I would like you to join us," her mother requests, sounding much closer this time.

"Tonight, I have plans to watch the fireworks with a new friend," Jenny informs her mother.

Watching fireworks sounds fun. I continue to listen in, leaning against the door.

"The best views are from our patio, bring your new friend. I want to meet them. Do we know their family and what part of High Rock they are from?" her mother asks.

"I do not think so. They are new to the city. I thought it would be nice for me to show her around."

"Your father and I would like you to be at the party tonight, so please bring your friend," Jenny's mother insists.

"Wait, the staff is off today. Who is going to make the food and help with the guests?" Jenny asks.

"We requested our staff to work this evening and will pay them extra. Keep your current dress on; it accentuates your green eyes. Please have the staff make your bed; it looks like they forgot to make it. Your father and I will be resting before the party."

"Hello, child. How are you today?" I hear her father ask.

"I am good, Father," Jenny answers as she continues her performance.

I hear Jenny's mother and father leave and walk down the hallway. Is she going to ask me to go with her to this party? I don't know how I feel about this. I'm comfortable around her, but being thrust into a situation like this makes me nervous. I step back and sit on the edge of her stone tub, looking at the door. It opens slowly, and Jenny sticks her head in.

She smiles and asks, "How do you look in a dress?"

"I don't think I should go to this party. I won't fit in and will not know anyone besides you."

"Do not worry about knowing anyone. You will be with me." Jenny reassures me.

"Why do I have to wear a dress? I think my current outfit is nice."

"I am sorry, but your outfit will not work. Women from High Rock wear their most expensive dresses to parties. If you show up dressed like that, it would cause a stir," she explains.

"Let me think about a dress for you," Jenny says, tapping her foot and looking up. "I have an idea. You can wear one of my mother's dresses. She is about your height."

"How will we get a dress from your parent's room when they are resting there?"

"That is easy. She stores old dresses she has not worn in years in one of our guest rooms. I am sure she would not recognize one if you wore it. She is always buying new outfits to follow current trends. Let us go pick one out for you," she explains softly, ensuring her voice does not carry.

"I'm not sure how I feel about this, but I will do it for you. You're lucky I like you so much."

"Thank you. I will make it worth your while."

"Let's find me a dress, Jenniver," I say as I walk past her. "I can't believe I have to wear a dress to this party."

Jenny squints her eyes at me. "Do not call me Jenniver. Only my mother calls me that."

She catches up to me as I get near the door. She pokes her head into the hallway to see if it's clear.

"Come, it is just across the hallway," she whispers.

We walk softly across the hallway and open the guest room's door. Like Jenny's room, it's decorated with finer things, such as an oversized bed with an intricately carved wooden headboard. Instead of the light colors of Jenny's room, the colors in this room are darker with reds and browns. Against the far wall is a large wooden cabinet with multiple doors. Jenny gestures to close the door so we can keep our mission a secret. Jenny opens every cabinet door, exposing dress after dress of different colors and styles.

"I think you are more of a simple dress type of girl," she says, laughing softly as she looks through all the dresses, sliding them from one hand to the other.

"You're loving this, aren't you?" I ask.

"Maybe a little bit. I wonder what you look like in a dress."

She pulls three dresses out of the closet.

"Let us try these first to see what cut and length looks best on you. I am good at sizing dresses to body types," she informs me.

I walk over to the bed where she laid the dresses. There's a green one with gold accents, a brown one with big round shoulders, and a simple red one with a decorative design that looks like flowers at the base of it. I strip down and step into the green dress, pulling it up on me. It's heavy compared to my clothes. How do women wear these? Even Mothers' outfits have to be lighter than this.

I walk over to a full-length mirror in the room to see how I look. I can't get over what I am seeing. "I look silly," I announce to Jenny.

"First, let me synch it up before we make any decisions."

Suddenly, the dress gets tight as Jenny pulls the drawstrings on the back of the dress. I grab my chest. "Not so tight. You're making it hard to breathe, and you're squishing me."

"Welcome to dress wearing. Now, let us see what that looks like. Well, the height is good. It is a little baggy in the hips, but not too bad. Let us try the red one next." Jenny tells me, releasing the drawstrings. I can breathe again when she does this as the dress falls to the floor.

"You do this every day?" I ask while putting on the red dress. This one ends just above my knees and feels more natural to me. There's nothing lavish about it. It fits my shoulders, and my legs and arms are free compared to the green one. Like before, Jenny pulls the dress's drawstrings, and we look in the mirror.

"I think we found you a dress. What do you think?" she asks.

"I am not sure."

"You look great. Now we have to find shoes since your boots do not go with the dress," Jenny says, looking at the cabinet.

Jenny goes through her mother's shoes in the cabinet's base and pulls out a few pairs. While she does this, I notice a black leather corset in the cabinet. I put it around my waist and look at myself in the mirror.

"How does this look with the dress?" I ask.

"Hmmm...let me see," Jenny says, walking over, holding a pair of simple black shoes. She ties up the corset on me and looks over my shoulder. "I like that combo. Look at you combining outfits to make them look new and different. Mother would never do this. I feel even more certain now she will not realize this is one of her dresses. Try these shoes on. I think they should fit you and they have no heels. I was unsure if you could walk in heels," Jenny tells me, placing the shoes by my feet.

I slip my feet into them and walk around the room. "They feel like slippers more than shoes. They wouldn't last more than an hour in the fields," I say.

"They are not meant for working in," Jenny answers, laughing at me.

Jenny spends a little time adjusting the dress and corset on me, tightening the drawstrings and pulling on parts of the dress to ensure everything is correct. She steps back and nods with approval. "You look pretty. I love your dark hair and how it matches the black accents and shoes. I will put these other dresses away while you hide your clothes under the bed. Then we can go downstairs to the library and wait for the party to start," Jenny tells me.

Even when I was little and wore traditional girl outfits, no one ever called me pretty. It feels nice that someone thinks of me this way. "You think I'm pretty?"

"I do," she answers, touching my nose with her finger.

As we descend the stairs, I instinctively flip my legs over the railing and jump to the landing below. Jenny looks at me with her eyes bugging out of her head.

"I didn't make any noise," I said.

"Please do not do that type of stuff here. If someone saw you, they would realize you are not from High Rock," she tells me softly.

"I'm not from High Rock. I'm from the valley," I reply with a smile.

Once we get into the library, I'm amazed at how many books there are. We have five books at home, not including my grandmother's journals. "How many books do you have?" I ask.

"More than I could read in a lifetime."

I walk over to one of the walls of books to read the titles while touching the book spines with my finger. While moving through the room, I can smell the books. I love it. I continue reading the book titles until I come to a ladder. It's attached to a rail system that allows one to go up and move through the room at different levels. I climb the ladder and push myself down the wall, sliding past rows of books. I push the ladder back the other way and slide back, stopping near Jenny, who is already sitting at the table in the center of the room.

"Having fun, are we?" she asks.

"This room is amazing. I would spend all my free time here reading."

Stepping off the ladder, I notice a book that's a bit taller and older-looking than the others around it. I pull it down to take a closer look at the cover. There's a crescent moon embossed on the cover. I sit down next to Jenny and open it. It's written in Elvin, *The Dark Ones*. I'm intrigued and start to read.

I feel something touch my leg softly, which startles me. I look up, and Jenny is looking at me. "Good book?" she asks.

"Yes, it's about the origins of night creatures, where they come from, and which ones are the most dangerous. Have you ever heard of a Screecher?" I ask.

As I explain the book, Jenny has a blank look on her face. I guess she doesn't care about a Screecher. I look out the window, and the moons are high in the sky. We must have been here for a while.

"The guests have already arrived. My mother knows we are in the library. We can walk out and join them whenever we want. Get ready to hear some boring conversations," Jenny tells me.

Entering the dining room, I see the table has been set and decorated with flowers up and down the center. The wall sconces are glowing, and the chandelier's light crystals create a warm light filling the room. We continue toward a set of double doors that lead to a patio lit by various lanterns and the moon's light. Entering the patio, we see people dressed in formal attire talking and drinking with each other. Jenny is right; every woman is wearing a dress. Jenny's mother calls to us, "Jenniver, come here, and your friend too."

Walking over with Jenny, I start tugging at my outfit. I'm feeling pretty uncomfortable in it, and the thought of meeting her mom is adding to my anxiety.

"Hello, Mother. This is Kyra Everwind, my new friend," Jenny informs her mother.

"Come here, child. Let me look at you," Jenny's mother motions to me to get a closer look.

"Hello," I say nervously.

"Well, look at you. How old are you, and where do you come from, my dear?" Jenny's mother asks me.

"Seventeen, and I live in the—" I start to say, but Jenny stops me.

"Remember, her family just moved to High Rock. They live several levels down as it is their first home here," Jenny finishes my sentence.

"That is right, you mentioned that before. Silly me. Welcome to our home, Kyra. I hope you have a nice time this evening. Please have something to drink. The meal will be ready shortly. Our cook has made various dishes for us to try this evening," Jenny's mother explains.

Jenny grabs my arm and pulls me away, heading straight to a table filled with glasses of different wines.

"Sorry, I did not mean to cut you off before. If you said the valley, it would have caused a scene. The idea of me hanging around a Lowlander is unacceptable," Jenny informs me.

I grab one of the many glasses of wine and hand her one. I drink mine, not putting it down until it's gone. Grabbing a second one of a different type, I repeat this process.

"Slow down. It might be a long night," Jenny insists.

"I think I am going to need a few more of these to get through this party," I tell her.

We hear a voice calling Jenny's name, "Jenniver, glad to see you. You look lovely tonight."

"Could tonight get any worse," Jenny groans.

I turn and see a young man walking toward us. "Who's that?" I ask.

"Jeremy. He has been trying to get under my dress for years. My mom has been trying to get us together for the past year or two because his family is on a higher level than us," Jenny tells me quietly.

I look at her and ask, "Does he know?"

"Nope," she answers quickly.

This should be interesting. As Jeremy gets closer, I see he's a few years older than us. He has brown hair tied back in a ponytail, and he's dressed in a vest with gold trim and dark pants. I also see a gold chain attached to his pocket. He most likely has a pocket watch.

"Hi, Jenniver. How are you? It has been a while since we last saw each other. Who is your friend?" Jeremy greets us.

"It has been a while. Please call me Jenny. I have been good. This is Kyra. We met a few weeks ago and have become good friends pretty quickly," Jenny answers with a playful tone.

"Nice to meet you, Kyra. You are tall," Jeremy says.

"That's how I am. Can't help it," I say matter-of-factly.

"Jenniver, I thought we could talk tonight and catch up. Your mother asked me to come this evening. She said you were asking about me the other day. I think your mother is playing matchmaker again," Jeremy explains while he laughs slightly.

"I am sure she is. She thinks I need to be married before leaving my teen years, or no one will want me," Jenny answers frustratedly.

"Shall the three of us sit and talk?" Jeremy asks.

"Let's do that," I answer, looking at Jenny.

Jenny's eyes widen as Jeremy turns and walks over to a table just off to the right. I lean in and whisper, "If I feel uncomfortable being here, you should too."

While we follow Jeremy to the table, I squeeze her butt, causing her to smile. "That is not fair," she says softly as we walk.

The three of us sit at the table, and Jeremy asks me, "Kyra, I do not remember seeing you around. How long have you been in High Rock?"

"Not long. It feels like my first day at times," I answer, sipping my third glass of wine, which I am starting to feel. I enjoy playing this game, as I can tell it's driving Jenny a little crazy. She's squirming in her seat a tiny bit.

"That explains your pronunciations and wording. It reminds me of a Lowlander or someone not from High Rock. I have been here my whole life. What does your family do?" he asks.

I know I shouldn't get upset about his last statement, as I asked Jenny a similar question yesterday, but for some reason, it bothered me when he asked me the question. I have to let it go and move on. I don't want to cause any trouble.

"We produce ointments, soaps, and elixirs. Some years are better than others," I answer, trying to make what my Mother and I do to earn some extra money sound more significant than it is.

"What do you do for fun?" he asks.

Hearing this question, I want a good answer to make Jenny react. What can I say? "I do lots of things for fun, but I have my favorite," I answer suggestively.

Jeremy smiles, and I feel a sharp pain in my shin as Jenny kicks me under the table. I might have taken it a bit far with that last comment.

We hear the announcement from the house that the meal is ready, and we should all come to the dining room.

"Shall we go to dinner?" Jeremy says, holding his hand out to Jenny.

Jenny and I get up, but Jenny doesn't take Jeremy's hand, which bothers him a bit.

When we enter the dining room, I notice everyone else has already taken their seats. Jenny's parents are sitting at each end of the table, and there are three open seats next to each other near her mom. Jenny shows me where she wants me to sit and sits beside me. Jeremy sits next to her.

Jenny's father gets up and raises a glass to everyone. "We are pleased to have our friends with us again during the Harvest Celebration. Our cook has created new food dishes, so please enjoy the bounty in front of us."

Everyone claps and starts to partake in the feast consisting of roast pig, chicken, and many different vegetables and other dishes.

I whisper to Jenny, "I bet you picked some of these, and I threw them in the cart."

Jenny again kicks me under the table.

"Auch, stop kicking me," I whisper.

"Someone might hear you," she says under her breath.

Looking at all the utensils in front of me, I don't know which ones to use. I look at Jenny, who quietly shows me which fork and knife to use. Usually, I would use my fingers or a spoon to eat. I grab some of the vegetables and start eating quietly. An elf across from us occasionally looks at me, making me self-conscious. Am I doing something wrong? Did I use the wrong fork or something?

When he finally speaks to me, he asks, "What is your name?"

I look at him, chewing and swallowing quickly. "Kyra."

"Do you have Elvin blood in your veins?" he asks.

I look at Jenny, and she shrugs her shoulders slightly. I return my attention to the elf and ask, "Why do you ask?"

"I noticed the slender nature of your face has Elvin characteristics."

"I don't think so. Maybe I have a distant relative, but to my knowledge, I don't," I answer.

"He leans to who I believe is his wife and tells her [*In Elvin*], *"Another one that taints our bloodlines. She has elf blood in her and does not even realize it."*

Even though he tried to be quiet, I heard what he said. I look at him, and he sees my expression of disdain.

[*In Elvin*] *"You shouldn't judge people by their blood but for who they are,"* I say.

Taken aback by my comment, he leans in and asks me, "You speak, Elvin. Who taught you?"

Jenny grabs my hand under the table, knowing I am starting to get upset.

"My mother taught me. She thought it would be important for me to be fluent in languages," I explain.

Looking around the table, I can see the other guests starting to notice our exchange. Hoping to change the focus, Jenny's mother announces, "How is the food, everyone?" Some guests jump in and tell Jenny's mother the food is delicious, but the elf keeps his focus on me.

"Does it matter if I have elf blood in my veins?" I ask him.

"It does. Our bloodline is sacred," he retorts.

The anger continues to grow in me. Looking around the table, everyone knows about the developing situation. Jenny is looking at me, shaking her head ever so slightly to stop. I don't want to cause trouble, but I don't know how to stop this exchange. I take a deep breath and close my eyes for a second. When I feel calmer, I focus back on my adversary and speak as calmly as possible, "Kindness should be given to all, even the ones with closed minds."

The elf is quiet for a second and asks, "How do you know of the words of Kelwrek? Most humans would not know of this."

"As part of my studies, I read different books in the languages I was learning. Kelwrek was one of my favorites. I would read his teachings at night before bed," I answer.

He sits in his chair silently for a while. I watch his expression change slightly. It wasn't as stern as it was before. "I apologize for my behavior. I am older than you think and sometimes stuck in my ways. For centuries, I have seen my race decline, which frightens me. Our race was once the most powerful in Ingenterra. We had cities so grand that everyone envied us. Now, we only have a few of them left, and our place in the world is becoming smaller and smaller," he explains.

Not expecting this change from my combatant, my anger starts to fade, and I become less tense. I loosen the grip on my thigh, and Jenny rubs my hand slightly. I grab my glass of wine and raise it to him. "To good life and harmony, the greatest gift."

He raises his glass to me and says, "You have studied elf lure."

The dinner lasts a few more hours, and the tension from the earlier conversation is gone. Most likely due to the glasses of wine we are drinking. I also notice that Jeremy has been trying to place his hand on Jenny's lap occasionally, which she quickly removes. We have had our hands on each other's laps all night. Jenny would softly caress my thigh every so often with her finger, sending chills up my spine. I think she was doing this to get back at me from earlier.

"Shall we all move to the patio? The fireworks will be starting shortly. I hear they added new colors this year," Jenny's mother announces.

When everyone gets up to go outside, Jeremy stands quickly, helping Jenny up by pulling her seat out as she stands.

Leaving the table, Jenny asks, "Kyra, would you mind joining me? I must relieve myself and would like your help with my dress."

"I will be on the patio; see you both in a few moments," Jeremy says, walking out with everyone else.

"Let us get out of here," she whispers to me.

"You don't have to use the bathroom?" I ask.

"No, I just want to get out of here. If I have to deal with Jeremy any longer, I will go crazy. He kept trying to place his hand on my leg during dinner," Jenny mutters.

Once in the hallway, we head straight toward the main entryway and out of the house. We start laughing as we walk down the walkway.

"That was fun," I say sarcastically.

"Sooo fun. Sorry about Mr. Indrarren. He's 350 years old and has a chip on his shoulder. I am surprised how you turned it around. That is a first," Jenny explains.

"Why do your parents invite him to their home?"

"Status is everything. Hanging out with people of a higher status raises your status. Mr. Indrarren is near the highest level in High Rock. He has been here for over 200 years and has tremendous wealth. His home makes ours look tiny and simple," Jenny explains.

We continue walking, and the wind starts blowing. Jenny moves closer to me. Is she cold? To think of it, my legs are getting cold. Dresses have so many things that don't make sense. Thinking of my exposed legs, I remember my clothes under the bed.

"My clothes," I blurt out.

"Do not worry, no one will find them," Jenny says, with a chattering sound.

"You're cold. We should move down to a lower level where it's warmer. Where's the closest tram?"

"Just up there. That one will take us down to the city level by the Eastern Gate."

"Let's go."

We pick up our pace, getting to the platform area quickly. Looking up and down, I don't see the tram. The wind blows again, and Jenny leans into me closer. I wrap my arms around her, trying to keep her warm. As we wait, I hear people walking toward us, laughing and talking. I look down, trying to see who it might be, but it's too dark. I look harder; suddenly, everything brightens up, and the darkness fades away. I can now see them walking toward us. This is similar to what occurred in the alley, but this time I think I made it happen, but I don't understand how or why I can do this. As they get closer, I can see a group of young Lowlanders talking and drinking from bottles. When they arrive, they look at Jenny and me.

"Checking out High Rock?" I ask.

While trying to get a peek at Jenny, one answers, "We decided to come up and see what might be happening here. So far, it's pretty boring. Who's your friend there? Is she alright?"

"She's just cold. I'm trying to keep her warm until the tram returns," I answer.

"Wait, do I know you?" One of them asks, looking at me.

"I don't think so," I answer.

"I know I know you from somewhere. It will come to me," he says, scratching his head.

I look up and see the tram descending, which relieves me.

"I know! You're the girl from last night's fight at the Dragon Tail!

The one who took out those Red Jackets," he excitedly expressed to his friends.

"I think you might have the wrong person," I state.

"I'm sure it's you. Your hair and face look like hers. Come on. Just admit it."

I look up again and see the tram is getting close but not close enough.

"You're right. It's me. I don't want people to know, that's all. I don't like fighting," I tell them.

The group gets excited with my answer. "Why are you up here? Are you from High Rock? You're dressed like you are," one asks.

"My friend invited me up, and we're heading back down."

While attempting to move closer to Jenny, another suggests, "Since she lives in High Rock, maybe she can help us Lowlanders out."

I move Jenny behind me to protect her. I'm confident this is going to get physical.

I tell Jenny softly, "Step back when I tell you."

"How about we go our separate ways and call it a night? We don't want any trouble." I tell him, leaning in to intimidate him. Looking him in the eye, I begin feeling like I did last night in the fight. "If you want trouble, I am happy to show you what I am capable of."

He steps back with a frightened look and tells me, "No trouble here. Have a good night."

He turns to his friends. "Let's get out of here and leave these two alone."

Everyone in his group is confused by his answer, but they turn around and walk away from us.

At this point, the tram arrives, and I quickly escort Jenny to it. Jenny hands the attendant two coins as we sit. A few moments later, the doors close, and we descend the mountain. Now, out of the cold, Jenny stops shivering.

"That was close," I said.

"That happens all the time here. People come up wanting to see what High Rock is like. Most often, it is just curiosity. Sometimes, it gets violent. The violence has become more frequent since the Red Jackets formed," she explains.

Jenny rests her head on my upper arm like she has done so many times before and closes her eyes. "I am tired and a little drunk. What time is it?" she asks, yawning.

"Not sure, the moons are pretty high still. Maybe eight or nine."

"Can we go back to your home and rest?" Jenny asks, yawning again.

"If you like, it will take about an hour."

As the tram descends, I watch the fireworks exploding in the distance. I think of Rox with Lindsey and hope they are having a good time together. As the tram enters the station, I nudge Jenny. She's asleep. I stand and nudge her again. "Come on, time to go."

She gets up, rubbing her eyes, and walks with me, staying close to me as we make our way through the city. The sounds of celebrating can be heard all around us. People are laughing and seem to be having a merry time with each other. Exiting the city, we take a side road that connects to the Western Road. Walking home, I think about what has transpired today. How is this going to work? She's from High Rock; I'm from the valley. The two don't mix. I also can't stop thinking about what happened in her bedroom. I never experienced anything like that before, and how it made me feel. I look at the twin moons of Adian and Adelynn. They say when they shine this brilliant, good fortune can fall from their light onto you. I hope this is true.

Jenny yawns deeply.

"Hop on my back. I will carry you the rest of the way. I can tell you're exhausted."

Jenny jumps up on my back, and I lock her legs with my arms, pulling her tight to my back. She rests her head on my shoulder, and I feel her settle in as we return to my home.

Reaching my house, I open the door slowly, trying not to disturb

Mother, who is most likely asleep. I close the door as quietly as I can. Turning around, I see the puppy greeting us, sniffing my feet.

"Don't wake Mother. Go back to sleep, little one," I whisper to him.

"We're here. Time to get off," I tell Jenny.

We quietly climb up the ladder to my room. Jenny quickly makes her way to my bed and lays down. I move her legs so I can sit.

"Today might have been my best day ever. Thank you," I tell her.

Not hearing a response, I turn and see Jenny is already asleep. I exhale and smile. I lie down beside her and close my eyes, thinking to myself. Not a bad way to finish off this day.

CHAPTER 6

THINGS CHANGE

I roll over, hearing people talking. It's Jenny and Mother below. I get a little nervous about what they have been discussing. I move ever so slightly, which makes the bed creak, and the conversation stops below.

"Kyra, time to get up. We have guests, and you are being rude. Come down and talk with us before we start our chores," Mother says.

I sit up and place my hands on my lap.

"Coming down," I announce, yawning.

Standing, I realize I am still wearing the dress from last night. I go white with fear. What is Mother going to say? She hasn't seen me in a dress since I was four. I move to the loft's edge and look down at them. They are both sitting at the table. I start my descent and can feel Mother's eyes looking at me.

"So that's the dress you let her borrow," Mother says.

"Yes, she looks pretty in it," Jenny adds.

As I reach the bottom, I turn and look at Mother. She smiles and laughs out loud. "Sorry, sorry. I'm not used to seeing you in a dress. You look lovely, truly," she tells me while chuckling.

I roll my eyes, sitting at the table. I pour a glass of water and drink it down. "I might have had too much wine last night. My head hurts," I say.

"What did you think of the celebration in the city?" Mother asks.

"It was unlike anything I have experienced before," I reply, yawning. "I'm guessing you know about the dinner party."

Looking at Jenny, I say, "We need to find out how Rox's date went."

Jenny rubs her hands together and replies, "Yes, we do. We need to get all the details."

I see Mother made eggs and pork belly. I guess she likes Jenny, as she doesn't cook new food in the morning unless it's for a special reason. Breakfast is generally bread with leftovers. As I think of leftovers, I immediately think of Forge and Ophelia.

"Have you ever met a Forgotten?" I ask Mother.

"I have seen them, but I haven't met one. It makes me sad to think of those children. Why do you ask?"

"Yesterday, I met a little boy and his sister. They were so skinny, and their clothes were so worn. They hadn't eaten in days, so I made sure they had something to eat. I don't understand how we can allow children to live in the city's streets like they do. It really upset me. What caught me off guard was how happy they seemed," I reply, picking at the pork belly in front of me.

Jenny tries to change the subject. She can tell it is putting me in a down mood.

"While you were sleeping, I insisted several times that I want to help with the chores, but your mother keeps saying no," Jenny tells me.

"Thank you again, but you should go home to your family. I am sure they are worried about you," Mother interjects.

"I can help here for a while and then go home. It is the least I can do as a thank you for your hospitality. I will need a change of clothes, as I am pretty sure this outfit is inappropriate for field work," Jenny says, looking down at her dress.

"You're persistent. I still have some of Kyra's clothes from before her growth spurts. We could see if some of those clothes fit you. Kyra, please change and start your normal chores and meet us by the fruit trees. We need to pick them clean and store fruit in the storage area," Mother instructs me.

"Can I have a little food before we start?" I ask.

"Sleepers don't get to eat," Mother tells me. "Come, let's find you something to wear that's more appropriate to today's activity," Mother tells Jenny, taking her hand and walking her to her room.

As they walk away, Jenny smiles and sticks her tongue out at me playfully. I shake my head and go up to my room to change out of the dress. I carefully place it on my bed and chuckle as I look at it. I grab some clothes hanging on my clothing hooks and head back downstairs. When I reach the bottom, I hear Mother and Jenny laughing from Mother's bedroom. This might be trouble. I grab a piece of pork belly and devour it while heading to the barn. I say hello to Smoky and give him a few face rubs and fresh hay to eat. I look at our pig, which has gotten big and fat over the past few months. He'll give us much-needed meat over the winter.

I grab the feed and throw it throughout the yard while calling out to our chickens and other animals. Looking over to our fruit trees, Mother and Jenny pick apples, laughing as they work. Yes, this is going to be trouble. Walking over, I see they picked the apple tree pretty much clean and have now focused on the pear and walnut trees.

"Please take the apples to the root cellar," Mother tells me.

Carrying the first basket of apples seems lighter than the last time I did this. Opening the door, I step down and place the basket on the floor. All the fieldwork must have made me stronger. I repeat this process a few times until all the baskets of apples are stored away.

"The apples are all set. Should I take the pears next?" I ask.

"Yes, and do not stack them on top of the apples. We don't want bruised apples again," Mother reminds me.

"You won't let that go, will you? Three seasons ago, I did that with a few baskets, and you still bring it up every harvest."

I take a bite from one of the pears they just picked. "I think they need more time on the tree. This pear is pretty hard," I announce.

"It is best to pick them now, as they will ripen in storage over the winter. We will make jams and other things with them," Mother informs me.

As Mother and Jenny continue picking fruit and nuts, I realize I'm reprising my role as a transporter again by moving all the fruit and nuts to the root cellar. I guess I am made for this type of work. Walking back to Mother and Jenny, I see the sun is past midday.

"Do you need to get going soon?" I ask Jenny.

"I would rather stay here, but I should get going. I am sure my parents are wondering a little at this point," she tells us.

She pats her hands on her legs. Would you mind if I freshen up before heading home?" she asks Mother.

"Not at all. There's a wash basin in the house. Remember, your dress is hanging in my room," says Mother.

"Mother, I'll put the tools away and walk Jenny back to the city to ensure she gets there safely. I'll help with the rest of the chores when I return," I say.

While walking back to the barn, I can't stop looking at Jenny. Once in the barn, I put away the feed bucket and tools. As I hang the last tool, I'm hit with cold water.

"Ahhhh!" I scream from the shock of having cold water tossed on me.

I turn around and see Jenny standing there with an empty bucket of water. She's smiling at me devilishly.

"Why did you do that?" I ask, screaming.

"You said you would walk me back, and you are dirty. I thought I would help you clean up," she says, grinning ear to ear.

"Really ... I see you are still in your dirty clothes. I think payback is fair game, don't you?" I say, walking toward her while I flip my wet hair back.

"No, no, stay away!" she exclaims while backing up from me.

I take the bucket from her hand and fill it with water from the trough.

"You better not do that," she warns me.

I think for a second and drop the bucket on the ground.

"That is better," she says smugly.

Instead, I pick her up, holding her in the air in front of me.

"Wait, what are you doing? No. Please do not," Jenny says, laughing.

I step into the trough and sit us both down in the cold water.

"Doesn't that feel good?" I ask sarcastically.

"It is freezing!" Jenny screams, trying to get out. I pull her back down and kiss her.

"I am mad at you," she tells me between kisses.

After a bit, she stops telling me she's mad at me, and we're just kissing.

We hear the barn door open, and I look past her head and see Mother standing at the door looking at us. She turns and walks away.

"Wait, Mother, wait," I yell out.

I jump out of the tub to chase after her and tell Jenny, "Get changed. I'll be right back."

Exiting the barn, I see Mother standing in the yard, looking out at the valley.

I walk up behind her and ask, "Are you upset or mad?"

"About you and Jenny? No. I figured there were feelings between you two. There is a glimmer of something when you talk about her," she answers.

"So you're fine with Jenny and I being more than friends?" I ask.

"Just be careful. I know you are of age, but it's hard for a mother to see their child growing up and being intimate with someone. I've known this time would come, but I guess I wasn't expecting it to be now," she explains.

I hug my mother from behind and place my head next to hers. "I'll be careful. I wasn't expecting this, but it feels good."

"I know. Being with someone you care about does feel good. Help her get ready and take her home. I am sure her family is wondering where she is."

I walk back to the barn, thinking it went much smoother than I thought it would. Jenny has already changed and is sitting on the stool. She has a worried expression on her face.

"How mad is she?"

"She's not mad. She figured there was something between us."

"Really? I am surprised. My mother has not accepted who I am."

"I'm so lucky she's my mother. She has always accepted me for who I am. Come on, we should get going."

We both leave the barn and see Mother walking to the house. Jenny runs up to her and hugs her. They talk for a second, and Jenny then returns to me.

"What did you talk about?" I pry.

"I thanked her for her kindness and understanding. I also told her that she passed those qualities on to you. Also, your mom said she will have a few chores waiting for you when you return."

Walking back to the city, we don't say much to each other but enjoy our time together. Approaching the Western Gate, Jenny looks up at High Rock and then at me. "I do not want to say goodbye, but we have to for now," she says sadly.

I answer with a bit of anxiousness, "When do you think we will see each other again?"

"Not soon enough. I have to assess the damage caused by our leaving the party. It might be a day or two. By the way, your mother is amazing if I did not tell you that already. Please tell her I think highly of her. I know my parents are not that accepting," she tells me, looking at me with wet eyes.

I grab her and hold her tight. "You have to get going. I will see you soon."

As I release her, I watch her walk away through the gate. How can I feel so much for someone that I have only known for such a short time?

~

The past few days have been the longest of my life. I am glad I have chores to help us prepare for the winter season. This keeps me busy during the day, but the evenings are different. I'm going crazy thinking about Jenny and how I want to be with her. Today's even worse as we finished our chores early and we are having our main meal early. Sitting at the table, I pick at my food, looking mopey.

"You will see her soon, don't worry," Mother says.

"When?" I ask, continuing to play with my food.

"When she can. Like you, she has obligations. Now eat," Mother orders me.

"I know; I just miss her."

Poking at the stew with my spoon, we hear a knock at the door. I look at Mother, who is as surprised as I am. She walks to the door and opens it.

"Are you Kyra Everwind? I have a package from Jenniver Morant," says the person at the door.

I jump up from the table. "I'm Kyra."

The person hands me the package.

"One second," I tell him, running over to my coin purse to get him a copper coin.

"Thank you, and good day," he says, walking away.

I look at the package. There's a note tucked under the ribbon that holds the package together. I pull the note and see a wax seal with a "*M*" embossed on it. I also smell the faint scent of Jenny's perfume coming from it. Opening the package, I see my clothes that we hid under the bed. I smile. I place my clothes on the table and head to my room for privacy to read the note.

Sitting on my bed, I break the wax seal and open the note.

Kyra,

I am sorry I have taken so long to reach out to you. After getting home, I had to smooth things out with my parents. My mother was quite upset that we left the party. Because of this, I must stay home for two weeks, and I am not allowed to go out at all unless it is to accompany my parents. I am spending most of my days in the library, trying to keep busy, but you are always on my mind.

I am sorry to say it will be at least another week before we can see each other. I look forward to when we are together again.

Jenny

I hold her note to my chest. I need to see her. Being away from her is too hard.

I yell down, "Mother, I'm going to see Jenny."

I jump down from my room, not using the ladder, and grab my things running out the door. I start picking up my pace and run as fast as possible towards the city. I make it through the Western Gate in no time. As I walk to the tram station, I notice the remains of all the festivities, with confetti on the ground and people taking things down. Looking up at High Rock, I try to see if I can see Jenny's home, but I can't. Entering the station, I go to the platform that Jenny and I had taken a few days prior. Waiting for the tram to arrive, I am surrounded by people. Most of them seem to be Lowlanders, but a few are High Rock residents based on how they are dressed.

I look over and see the blue tram approaching. My heart beats faster, knowing I am closer to seeing her. When the tram stops, the station workers open the door, and people exit. When the tram is empty, everyone is given the go-ahead to board. I pay my copper coin and sit in the back corner. As the tram ascends, I realize I might have been hasty in going to see Jenny. How am I going to see her? Her parents won't let me in. I'm not dressed like I was before. Plus, she's not allowed to see anyone. I shake my head; I will figure it out when I arrive. When the tram stops and the doors open, I run to her house. I hope that I get to see her.

While running, I see a group of people walking toward me and realize one of them is Jenny's father. I look around quickly and duck behind a few potted trees so he doesn't see me. Once they are out of earshot, I hear a familiar voice.

"What are you doing?" someone asks from above.

I look up, and Rox is sitting on a wall above me.

"Rox, how are you?" I ask excitedly.

"I'm good, but you still haven't answered my question. What are you doing?"

"I'm here to see Jenny," I answer quietly, hoping no one sees me.

"That's why are you hiding. You're silly," he tells me, jumping from the wall. "Her parents punished her, and she can't leave the house for another week," he explains.

"I know I got a note from her. I had to see her anyway."

"I helped her get your clothes and the messenger to deliver them to you," he informs me.

I pick him up and give him a big hug, telling him, "You don't know how crazy I have been going the past few days. I was driving Mother nuts."

"You're kind of crushing me," he tells me.

I lower him, stand back quickly, and tell him, "Sorry."

"It's alright. We can take the back entrance so that you look like a worker. No one will think any different," he says.

"What about her mother? She knows what I look like."

"Her mother is gone for the day, and she won't be able to see you as the same person since you are dressed so differently," he tells me, motioning me to follow him.

As we walk, I ask, "What have you been doing for the past few days? Is anything new or exciting?"

"Not really, just helping a friend out." He stops and turns to me with a serious face. "Jenny is my best friend and means so much to me. I don't want her to get hurt. Something is different this time. I've never seen her like this. So don't take this lightly. Please don't break her heart! I don't think she could take it. She puts up a good front and seems confident, but she has a fragile side to her that only a few are aware of."

"I won't. I feel the same. A few weeks ago, I never thought I would feel for anyone as I do for Jenny. I am also scared of being hurt."

We stand there in silence for a moment, looking at each other. I look up and see we're at Jenny's home. I follow Rox as he walks down the side of the house and enters the kitchen.

"Mom, this is Jenny's new girlfriend. I'm going to help her see Jenny," he tells his mother.

"She's in the library again," Rox's mother informs us.

I follow Rox, but he stops me. "What are you doing? What if someone sees you? Wait here for a second," Rox orders me as he pushes through the door.

"Rox tells me you're from the Western Pass area. I believe a friend of mine still lives there, but I haven't seen her in years. I miss her greatly," she says, continuing to prep food.

"Really, what's her name? I might know their family," I answer inquisitively.

I hear the door open and Jenny talking. "What is so important in the kitchen?"

As she enters, we lock eyes, and she runs up and hugs me. "You are here!"

"I got your note. I couldn't stay away," I say, embracing her.

"Look at these two. What are we going to do with them?" Rox asks his mother.

"Not sure, but be careful. Jenny, you know what your parents would think and their plans. This doesn't go along with it," Rox's mother explains.

"What plans?" I ask.

"Remember Jeremy? Do not worry about that. I will work that out. What stinks is that I can not leave my house. What are we going to do?"

"We'll figure it out. I can come back every few days until your punishment ends. We'll have to figure out the best times based on your parents' schedule and how much Mother needs me. Do you know where and when your parents will be for the next few days?" I ask Jenny.

"Not really, but they come and go all the time," Jenny answers, frustrated.

"Your parents will be out most of today and most of tomorrow. They have evening plans with a family up two levels the day after tomorrow, but they will be here all day the following day," Rox's mother explains.

"How do you know this?" I ask.

"I have to prep the meals. They need to let me know if they will be here or not," she answers.

"I love you, Elsa," Jenny tells Rox's mother.

"Do we hang out in the kitchen or go somewhere else?" I ask, looking at Rox and Jenny.

Rox's mother slides a plate of cut vegetables for us to snack on and tells us, "Stay here. I will not pay any attention to you."

Jenny and I look at each other and ask Rox simultaneously, "Tell us about your date!"

Rox looks at us as he is about to take a bite of a carrot. He pulls the carrot away from his mouth and smirks. "After you two left us, we enjoyed the celebration until she had to play again. I asked if I could watch and listen, and she said she would like that. She even played a song for me. I could listen to her for hours. I love how she moves when she plays. After she finished her last set, I escorted her to the Eastern Wall to watch the fireworks. While watching the fireworks, I felt her hold my hand."

Jenny and I hold onto each word and ask in unison, "And?"

"As we watched the fireworks, I moved closer to her. When the fireworks ended, I asked her if she would like me to escort her home, which she did," he continued.

"Where does she live?" I ask.

"Why would you ask that?" Jenny shouts, slapping my arm playfully.

She goes right in and asks, "Did you kiss her?"

Suddenly, Rox gets quiet and looks at his mother.

Jenny mouths, "Well, did you?"

Rox nods a few times, smiling.

"We've seen each other every day since the celebration before she performs in the taverns. Even though she's a lot older than me, we seem to enjoy spending time together," he tells us.

"How old is she?" I ask.

"Seventy-five this year," he answers.

Jenny and I do a double take on the last thing Rox said.

"Ohhh ... right, elves age very slowly. How does it feel dating an older woman?" Jenny asks, laughing.

"I don't have a problem with older women when they look like she does."

Jenny slaps Rox's arms lightly at his comment. In return, he smiles back at her.

The three of us catch up, talking and laughing about the dinner party and how Jenny helped with the chores at my place.

Looking out the window, I see that the sunlight is fading. I feel Jenny grab my hand, and I look over to her. I could tell that she was not ready to say goodbye.

"Jenny, your mother is going to be home soon. It would be best to go to your room and look like you were productive," Rox's mother says, moving pots around.

"Rox, can you help me move this large kettle to the cooking hook? I think the two of us can do it," she asks.

"I can do it," I tell her.

I walk over, pick up the pot with one arm, and lift it onto the cooking hook in the fireplace.

"You're strong!" Elsa tells me.

"Glad I can help," I reply.

"I do not want you to leave. This is the happiest I have been in days. It is so boring being here. Even Rox is not here to keep me company now that he has a girl," Jenny says.

"Rox, make sure Jenny's friend gets down from High Rock. Come back right away so Jenny knows," Elsa requests.

"Mom, don't you know Kyra can take care of herself? You should have seen how she took care of three Red Jackets the other day! I don't think there is anyone stronger in Mountain Side. Come on, let's go. I will get you to the tram stop. I think you can handle the rest," Rox says, jumping down from the countertop.

I turn to Rox's mother and tell her, "Thank you for everything."

When I do, I notice she's staring out and not blinking. I wonder what she's thinking about. Jenny stays next to me, trying to stop me from leaving. I turn to her and say, "I will be back."

Jenny hugs me one more time.

"Come on, break it up, you two," Rox says, grabbing my arm.

Before entering the walkway in front of Jenny's home, Rox looks around to make sure no one is coming and motions to me that it's clear.

"I am happy things with Lindsey are going well," I say.

"Me too. I was planning on seeing her tonight. Want to join us?"

"I better not. I have to get up early and help Mother. Plus, I know how we are together; one drink will become two and then three. We are not the best at monitoring each other," I tell him, rubbing his head as we walk.

"We are not, and can you not do that? It messes up my hair. As promised, here we are at the blue tram stop."

I squat down and hug him. "Thanks for everything. I am so happy I have you in my life."

Looking over his shoulder, I see the tram arrive, and people start getting off. I notice one of them is Jenny's mother, and I turn my head down.

I must have had an expression on my face because Rox asks, "What's wrong?"

I whisper, "Jenny's mother is coming this way. What if she sees me?"

"Play along," he quickly responds.

"Rox, is that you over there?" Jenny's mother calls to him from a distance.

"Yes, Mrs. Morant," he answers.

Jenny's mother asks, "Who is this with you?"

"She's a friend who helped me with some packages. She was about to head back down. Thanks for helping," Rox says, handing me a coin.

I take the coin from Rox and nod. I head toward the tram, trying to hide my face.

"Wait, do I know you?" she asks.

I change my voice slightly and say, "I don't think so, ma'am. See you later, Rox." Without looking back, I continued walking to the tram as quickly as possible without trying to look like I was rushing off.

As I walk away, I hear her say, "She looks so familiar."

Entering the tram, I face away from their direction. I hear a knock on the window. I turn instinctually and see Rox smiling, giving me a thumbs-up. We dodged it this time, but we have to be more careful. The last thing I want to do is cause more trouble for Jenny. I feel a bit of relief and anxiety at the same time. Why do we have to sneak around? I want to be able to see her when I want. It shouldn't matter if she is from High Rock and I am not. I feel a bit frustrated as I descend from High Rock.

CHAPTER 7

THE TRUTH IS REVEALED

"I'm back," I announce, entering the house.

Mother has been cooking; I can smell the aroma of herbs and potatoes filling the house.

"That smells good. What is it?"

"Just a simple potato soup. You seem to be in a better mood. I'm guessing you were able to see Jenny. I hope you didn't cause trouble," she says, stirring the pot.

"No trouble. I even got to see Rox, and I met his mom as well. She seems nice and is willing to help when she can. Which reminds me, I plan on returning tomorrow, but I will finish my chores before I leave."

"I was going enact the punishment from the other day, but I might let it slide this one time. I know not seeing Jenny has been difficult for you. I know how it feels when you want to be with someone but you cannot. By the way, let me look at the cut above your eye. How does it look?" Mother asks.

I lean over, and Mother holds my head to look at it. "It's healed! I can barely see where it was," she tells me, astonished.

"Really?"

I get up and walk over to the mirror in Mother's room. She's right; it's healed. There's only a faint scar now. That's not normal. I guess it wasn't as deep as we thought it was.

"Sit down and have some soup. You haven't eaten much over the past few days, and I know your normal appetite," Mother tells me, serving me a bowl of soup.

Taking the bowl in both hands, I breathe in the aroma, which makes me even hungrier. Mother is right; I haven't eaten much over the past few days. I grab a spoon and dig in ravenously.

I mumble, my mouth full of potato, "This is so good. Thank you for the reprieve on my punishment."

"Please swallow before you speak."

"By the way, Rox's mother mentioned she's from the valley and was friends with someone in our area. She hasn't seen them in years, though."

"That's terrible; maybe we know them. Did you get this person's name?" Mother asks, serving herself some soup.

"No, but Elsa said she misses her greatly," I add.

"Elsa?" Mother says softly while holding the wooden spoon over the pot of soup.

"Yes ... what's with the blank look, Mother? Elsa had that same look when I left Jenny's place."

"Nothing, let's enjoy our meal," she says, serving herself some soup.

I could tell Mother was hiding something.

"Do you know Elsa?" I ask hesitantly.

"Why do you ask that?"

"Your reaction to her name tells me a different story than your answer. One thing you taught me well is how to read people."

Mother puts her spoon down and pushes the bowl of soup away.

"I'm the friend Elsa is referring to."

"What happened? Why did you stop seeing each other?" I ask inquisitively.

"I'd rather not say as it brings up many other memories."

This conversation is upsetting Mother, which is not my intention. "I'm sorry. I didn't mean to upset you," I explain.

"Can you lock up the barn while I clean up here?" she asks, taking our bowls away.

"You didn't eat anything, and I'm not finished," I answer.

"Do what I ask," Mother tells me firmly.

Not expecting that tone, I get up quickly and head to the barn. While securing the animals, I wonder what might have caused Mother's reaction. When I get back inside, Mother is lying on her bed. She looks deep in thought.

I walk over and lie beside her, placing my head on her shoulder, "I'm sorry. I didn't mean to upset you."

"This reminds me of when you were little. You used to love sleeping next to me, she reminds me. I am sorry, too. Hearing Elsa's name brought back memories I hadn't thought of in a long time. When I met your father, things between us changed. Elsa tried to understand, but she couldn't get past our relationship. She decided it would be best for us not to be friends anymore," Mother explains.

I sit up quickly, looking at her. "My father!"

"What does my father and Elsa have to do with you not seeing each other?" I ask intensely.

Mother gets up from the bed and goes to the table.

"Come here, child. This might take a bit. Let us have some tea while we talk."

I sit at the table, repeatedly tapping my fingers, waiting for Mother to explain what she told me. "The tea can wait. You can't say something like that and make me wait," I say.

Mother settles into her chair, and I can see she is trying to find the words. She looks pretty nervous, which I have only seen a few times.

"It was about nineteen years ago, I think. The sickness that spread through the valley was ending, but it took so many from us. It didn't matter if you were from the city or the valley. Somehow, I was spared, but I didn't feel lucky. The sickness took your grandparents, as you know. I was seventeen and living here alone, trying to keep things going but struggling. The nighttime was the worst, as I had little to keep me busy. To help pass the nights, I started studying your grandmother's journals to recreate some of her recipes for soaps and ointments to use and sell. One day, I stopped by a home near the city's Eastern Gate with my latest batch of soaps. I asked a small girl in front of her house if she wanted to buy some. When she approached me, I realized she wasn't a little girl but a halfling about my age. She was interested in my soaps but didn't have any money. She was kind and offered me a cider, as it was a rather warm day. Drinking our cider, we talked and realized we greatly enjoyed each other's company. From that day on, Elsa and I became close friends. She would come over and help me with my housework, and I would do the same at her place. She taught me how to cook and make bread, which you have enjoyed. Before Elsa, I couldn't make a basic soup."

While Mother recalls her relationship with Elsa, she gets emotional, and her voice starts wavering.

"What happened? Why did you stop seeing each other?!"

"A few months after meeting Elsa, I was gathering herbs in the meadow in the Western Pass one evening. I noticed the grasses and flowers had been trampled. As I continued further into the meadow, I noticed bodies of goblins. Something or someone had slayed them. I was terrified and started to run back home. As I ran, I noticed someone leaning against a tree. I couldn't tell if they were alive or dead, so I walked up cautiously. When I got closer, I saw it was a soldier, and he was wounded."

"Mother, why haven't you ever told me about this?"

"Let me finish. This is hard for me and will also be hard for you. I have thought about how I would tell you this since you were a baby," she says, placing her hand on mine.

As I look at her, I see this is hard for her.

"The soldier was badly wounded but alive. I decided to help him. It took all my strength to get him down from the meadow to the barn where I could attend to his wounds. While attending to his wounds, I realized he wasn't human. He was something that most would fear. Somehow, I wasn't scared of him, though. Maybe it's because he was so weak, or I didn't perceive any danger when he spoke to me. Over the next few days, he started to improve. I went to check on him one evening, and he was gone. A few days later, he started reappearing every so often to check up on me. I think he saw himself as my protector for saving him. Each time he visited, we would talk more and more. As time passed, we developed stronger feelings for one another. We were surprised and excited when we learned I was pregnant with you. When Elsa found out about who your father was, she could not handle it and decided it would be best for her not to see me anymore. That was the last time I saw Elsa—the winter you were born," Mother tells me as a tear travels down her cheek.

I sit there in shock. I can't believe what I was just told. I don't want to consider it. How is this possible, I think to myself.

"Kyra?" she asks gently.

After a few moments, I look at her. She reaches out to my hand, but I pull away.

"Tell me. My father, what is he?" I ask.

Mother doesn't answer immediately but finally tells me, "Vampire."

Hearing her say vampire causes me to go catatonic. How is this possible? They are evil and vile creatures that feed on the living. This can't be happening. I finally look at her.

"I'm a monster," I tell her, as tears start welling in my eyes.

"No, my child. You are not a monster," Mother says, trying to comfort me.

"How can I not be?" I ask, running out of the house, trying to escape what I was told.

I'm a monster. That's why she kept me isolated for my whole life. She's afraid of what I might do and to whom.

"Wait, don't go! I know you are scared," she pleads from the door.

Running toward the mountain pass as fast as possible, I make it to my favorite place I always loved running through when I was little. Looking around, breathing heavily, I see that most of the flowers are gone due to the colder weather that has started settling in. I walk through the meadow, touching the tops of the tall grass with the palms of my hands, trying to soothe myself, if that's even possible. Walking, I realize this is most likely the meadow that Mother mentioned. I see a tree to my left. I sit down and lean against it, looking out at the valley. I close my eyes, trying to understand everything that was just told to me. I take a couple of deep breaths to help calm myself down. After a while, I feel calmer. I decide to rest there momentarily before heading back down. I shouldn't, but I feel bad that I ran from Mother. I know we have to talk, but I'm unsure how. I look up and close my eyes to think.

When I open my eyes, I'm in front of the castle. Why am I dreaming of this now? I enter the castle as I have done many times before, and I hear the man's voice again.

"This way," he calls to me.

"What do you want? You never tell me anything!" I yell out.

"Come this way. No harm will come to you," he tells me repeatedly.

I move through the central hallway of the castle that leads me to him. Pushing the doors open, I'm hit with a blinding light. This is new; all my other dreams about him have been in darkness. As my eyes adjust to the light, I see the lavish room clearly for the first time. It's full of people talking and enjoying themselves. Music fills the room. I can now see the portraits on the walls and the fresco on the ceiling. In the distance, I see the man clearly for the first time. He gestures to me to come closer. Walking toward him, I pass by people wearing masquerade masks moving in ways that don't seem natural to me. One of the portraits grabs my attention. It's of a young woman about my age. She reminds me of a younger version of Mother. When I get a few feet away from him, I look him over. He's dressed in a dark blue noble's coat with gold accents along the sleeves and edges, which complements his slender features. His long white hair frames his elegant and motionless face. All these features don't hide that he is formidable and shouldn't be trifled with.

"The portrait is of your mother," he says calmly.

Continuing to look at him, I notice his eyes for the first time. They are light blue and match the color of my blue eye. Is this my father? All those dreams were of him? I step back, uneasy.

"Why am I dreaming this?" I ask quickly.

"I don't know why, but I expect you want answers."

The dreams were always the same, but this one is different. What has changed? Is my mind starting to connect things?

"Find me, and I will give you all the answers you need."

I hear the music stop and look to see why. Everyone in the room is moving closer to me, swarming around me. They are trying to touch me and grab me.

"He awaits for you," they start to say over and over again.

"Stay away! Get back!" I yell at them.

I wake up breathing heavily. A second later, I turn, emptying my stomach unexpectedly. I cough and wipe my face, removing the bits of vomit from the corners of my mouth. I lean back against the tree and try to regain my composure. Looking up, the twin moons illuminate the meadow and the valley below. In the distance, I can see the city and hints of light going up the cliffside where High Rock is. Everything I know is different now and will never be the same. I get up slowly and start to make my way back down. I know I have to talk with Mother as I am sure she is truly upset with herself.

While making my way down the mountain pass, I think about the dream and past dreams, and then it hits me—Jenny! How am I going to explain this to her? Should I even try? My brain starts to go over every possible outcome. Jenny understands and still wants to be with me. She's terrified of me and leaves me. She calls the city guard to report Mother and me, and they take us away. My brain is about to explode, thinking of all these scenarios.

Exiting the pass, I see the light coming from the windows of my home. Entering the house, Mother is leaning on the table with her head resting on her arms. Next to her is the small chest that belonged to my father, which she keeps under her bed. I remember pulling it out from under her bed once when I was little. When I did this, I got in trouble for touching it. I never touched it or thought about it again until now.

"Hi," I tell her, standing in the doorway.

She picks up her head and runs over, telling me, "I am sorry. Please forgive me."

"I'm scared, but we have to talk," I answer. I walk to the table and motion for her to sit with me.

I watch Mother rubbing her hands in her lap, which shows me how concerned and worried she is. I never told Mother about my dreams and how they give me insight into my future. She has always been concerned about others finding out about my strength, and I didn't want to burden her with this.

"I have been hiding something from you as well. For as long as I can remember, my dreams mean something. I didn't want to worry you more than you already do. For years, I have been dreaming of a man in a castle. He is shrouded in darkness whenever I have one, and when he speaks to me, it never makes sense. He would say we should talk, but when I get close to him, I would always wake up."

"What does that have to do with tonight?" Mother interjects.

"I'm getting there. I went up the mountain pass to think. While up there, I realized this was the meadow where you and Father met. I sat under a tree, trying to understand all this. I fell asleep and had another dream of this man, but it was different this time. Instead of being in darkness, it was full of light. For the first time, I realized the man in my dreams could be my father. In the dream, I was told to seek him out for answers."

I'm trying to read Mother's facial expression. Her face is still, and she isn't moving.

"Mother, did you hear what I said?"

She looks up at me and takes my hand. "I did. Maybe it's your mind trying to understand everything, or maybe he's reaching out to you. I don't know."

I move my attention from Mother to the chest on the table. I pull it over to me to look at.

"It's locked," she tells me.

"You don't know what's in it?" I ask.

"No. All I know is that before he left, your father gave this to me and said that only you could open it. I tried to open it for years, but with no luck."

Looking at the chest, I see the crest of the wolf and moons from my dreams on the lid. I rub my thumb over it and hear a clicking sound from within the chest. I look up at Mother.

"Has it ever done that before?" I ask.

"No."

I lift the lid, and a sealed letter rests on the chest's contents. Looking more closely at the wax seal, I see the imprint of an *A* in it. I pick up the letter and turn it over to show Mother.

"What does the *A* stand for?" I ask.

"Aaron," she says. "His name is Aaron."

I turn the envelope over and break the seal.

My dearest Kyra,

I wish I were there to be part of your life, but unforeseen circumstances have forced this upon our family. I am truly sorry for any pain this has caused you and your mother. Within this chest are two things I gift to you. The first is my brooch with my crest. My crest shows who and what I am, a creature of the night, but its true meaning is only known to a few. I hope you find the true meaning of our family crest. I have also left you my throwing weapons. They have served me for over two hundred years and have no equal. They are forged of a rare material only known by a few. The blades of these weapons will never need to be honed, as the material they are made from, once forged, becomes almost unbreakable. The material also has unique properties that allow it to become an extension of the user. When you master them, they will serve you in ways you can not imagine.

I am sure you have many questions. I can give you these answers. Head south and out of the valley to find me. I will leave clues to help guide you to me. I look forward to the time when we are together.

May kindness fall on you,
Your Father

I place the letter down on the table.

"What did it say?" Mother asks.

"Not what I was hoping for."

I pick the brooch out of the chest and look at it. I rub my thumb over the raised carving of a wolf and the moons. I place it down and pick up one of his weapons. It's much lighter than I thought it would be. It's not metal, but something different. The weapon has intricate carvings all over it, including the blades that are facing down. In the center of the weapon, I notice runic carvings that go around what looks to be a button. When I press the button, the blades swing out, startling me so that I almost drop the weapon. Grabbing an apple from the basket on the table, I test the weapon's sharpness and easily slice through the apple with no resistance. I can imagine what would happen if the blade came in contact with a body part. I press the button again, and the blades close down. I place it back in the chest with the brooch.

"What am I supposed to do? My whole life has just been turned upside down," I say, dropping my head on my crossed arms.

"I don't know, child. You are still who you are. That has not changed," Mother tries to reassure me.

"I don't know." Wiping my nose and eyes on my arm. "My head hurts from my last dream, and I'm exhausted emotionally. How am I going to see Jenny tomorrow?"

Mother looks at me. "Get some rest and see her tomorrow. I know that being around her gives you happiness. If you can't, I am sure she will understand."

"I won't break my promise to her. I can't do that to her. Maybe you're right, and some sleep might help."

I get up and walk over to hug her. She hugs me back harder than usual. I know this is rough for her as well. Reaching the ladder to my room, I stand there for a moment. I don't want to be alone tonight. I turn and walk into Mother's room and lie on her bed. "Can I stay with you?"

"Of course. I will join you shortly," she replies lovingly.

I lie on the bed, curling up into a ball and closing my eyes, hoping I don't dream tonight. I can't take any more.

CHAPTER 8
A SURPRISE GUEST

Feeling my pillow shift slightly, I open my eyes to realize I'm resting my head on Mother's shoulder. Turning to look out the window, I see morning has arrived. I swing my legs over the side of the bed and rest my hands on my knees. I feel like I didn't sleep at all, even though I woke up just a second ago.

Collecting my thoughts, I feel Mother softly rubbing my back. "How do you feel? You were restless and talking in your sleep throughout the night. You finally settled down when I held you."

"Drained, I kept seeing Father's image and thinking about the dream. Maybe that's what caused my restlessness and talking. I'm going to wash up and start the morning chores," I tell Mother as I stand and stretch.

Grabbing the wash basin, I fill it with water from the bucket next to it to wash up.

"Kyra, I have a question for you. Does Elsa know who you are?"

I stop scrubbing my face and remember Elsa's expression.

"I think she does," I answer, splashing water on my face.

"You're going to have to tread lightly if Elsa does realize you're my daughter. She will be weary of you," Mother warns me.

"I'll be careful," I reply, drying myself off.

A new level of anxiety starts coming over me. How am I going to see Jenny and Rox if Elsa knows? Will she allow me to see them? Will she tell people about me? I head to the barn to tend to the animals so Mother doesn't have to worry about them while I am gone. As I get close to the barn door, I see it's unlocked and open slightly. I enter the barn and hear rustling in the back by one of the stalls.

"Hello? Who's in here?" I ask.

My heart is pounding, wondering who or what is making the sound. It wouldn't be Jenny or Rox. The plan was for me to see them later today. Plus, they wouldn't hide in the barn. Continuing to look around, I notice a shoe poking out.

"Hello, I see your shoe. What are you doing in here?" I speak out.

Elsa steps out in front of me. She looks nervous and maybe a little scared.

"Elsa, what are you doing in the barn?" I ask again.

"Hello, Kyra. I arrived just before sunrise. When I got close to your house, I panicked and hid until I could work up enough courage to knock on your door. Last night, when Rox said your name, I realized who you might be," Elsa tells me, crossing her arms and rubbing her elbows.

"Come to the house. I know Mother will love to see you," I tell her, gesturing her to come.

Elsa walks toward me cautiously. I can tell she's frightened. "You don't have to worry, Elsa."

As we leave the barn, I yell over to the house, "Mother, please come out. An old friend is here to see you."

Mother walks out and looks at us. She stands in the doorway looking at Elsa before she runs over and drops to her knees, hugging her.

"I missed you so! I am so glad you are here," Mother says.

"I missed you as well. I'm sorry for not being there for you and your daughter," Elsa says to Mother.

"You two should talk. I need to tend to the animals," I tell them.

As I head back to the barn, I look back and see both of them hugging each other.

~

So that Mother and Elsa have time to talk, I take my time in the barn. Once finished, I close Smoky's stall and give him a little head scratch before heading to the house. Entering the house, I see Mother and Elsa talking at the table with tea cups in front of them. They seem to be in good spirits.

"We good here?" I ask.

"Getting there," Mother replies.

Elsa turns toward me. "Kyra, I need to tell you something so you understand my position. When I heard Rox say your name last night, it surprised me. It brought a flood of memories and emotions that I hadn't thought of or felt for a long time. After you left, I spent the rest of the evening thinking about your mother and our time together all those years ago. We left things unsettled because I was terrified of your father and you. A child of a vampire could only be evil. With that said, Rox helped me gain perspective on this situation. That's why I came today."

"What do you mean? He gave you perspective," I ask.

"Rox noticed I was pondering something intensely after you left and asked me what I was thinking about. I asked him about you as I wanted to understand who you are. He wondered why, and I said it's a mother's prerogative to know who their child is friends with. Rox told me what you did to help save the foreman you worked for during the harvest and how all you cared about was his safety. This gave me insight, and I was able to see things differently. Your mother told me you learned about your heritage last night and how you took it. I am to blame for this, as it forced your Mother to tell you about your father even if she wasn't ready to. While I am still very uneasy about all of this, I feel you are good at heart, but I will be watching to ensure my son and Jenny are safe. They are precious to me," she explains.

Listening to her, I understand her thoughts and why she feels this way. I still don't understand what I am, and everything we are taught about vampires tells us to be afraid of them and that they are evil.

"What else did he tell you about me?" I ask, becoming vested in Rox's thoughts of me.

"Not too much. Just bits and pieces about conversations you had and how Jenny is very taken with you," she says. After taking a sip of tea. "Honestly, I haven't seen Jenny so happy in a while."

Hearing this last bit of information places a smile on my face that both Mother and Elsa couldn't help but notice.

"Go clean up and see her," Mother orders me to my room. "Wear that dress from the other day. You want to look nice for her," Mother says, laughing.

"Mother, stop it," I tell her as I go to my room.

"Dress?" Elsa asks.

"Jenny lent Kyra a dress that was her mother's so she could attend a dinner party the other night. She looked lovely but felt like a fish out of water in it. My daughter is a bit of a tomboy," Mother chuckles to Elsa.

"I can't believe you brought up the dress. I'm not wearing it to see Jenny. What's wrong with my clothes?" I announce from my room.

"Nothing, my child. It was just a sight, that's all," Mother says, laughing even harder.

As I change my clothes, I hear Mother and Elsa continuing to talk. This might be the start of repairing things. I can only hope. I want Mother and Elsa to become friends again.

Looking in the mirror on my dresser, I tell myself, "You can do this. You can find a way."

I grab the sides of the ladder and slide down.

"I'm off. I'm not sure when I'll be back, but it might be late. Elsa, is there anything you want me to tell Rox or Jenny?" I ask, grabbing an apple from the table to eat.

"No. I want to let you know that I promise that they will only learn of you from you and never from me. It is your information to give," Elsa tells me.

"Thank you. I am still trying to understand it myself. I feel overwhelmed."

I head out the door and start my trek to the city to see my friends. As I walk, I hope this revelation about my father doesn't affect my relationship with them, especially with Jenny. I know that I have really fallen for her, and not having her in my life would devastate me.

~

Finding myself heading back to High Rock feels strange. For as long as I can remember, I imagined what it would be like up here, and now I am here again. It's funny how things work out.

I run out of the tram to get to Jenny as fast as possible. Making my way up to her home, I keep thinking about what happened last night and what it means for me and possibly us. Can I have a relationship with her? Is it safe for me to be with her? Before I realize it, I'm in front of her home. I make my way down the side of the house and knock on the kitchen door. A few minutes pass, and I knock again, but a bit harder, and still nothing. I open the door, peeking my head. "Hello. It's me. Is anyone here?" I ask quietly.

The kitchen is empty. I walk in, passing the fireplace, which still has a small fire burning in it. I thought at least Rox would be here. As I am about to push open one of the double doors that lead to the main house, it opens swiftly into me, knocking me on my ass.

"Ouch!" I say as I hit the kitchen floor.

"Are you alright? I am so sorry," Jenny tells me, leaning down to help me up.

After I'm standing, she hugs me.

"I'll live." Rubbing my butt.

"We have the house to ourselves. My parents are visiting Jeremy's family today, and the staff is busy caring for things outside the house." Jenny tells me, grabbing my hand and pulling me through the doors.

As she leads me through her home, I notice she's wearing a short dress I haven't seen before. It's made of a shiny purple fabric, with white lace along the dress's bottom and around her collar. Her brown hair bounces and sways as we walk. She's wearing the perfume from the note.

"Where's Rox? I thought he would be here," I ask.

"Lindsey showed up this morning wanting to see him, and he jumped at the opportunity to be with her. He told me to tell you he is sorry, but he hopes you understand," she explains.

"She came up to see him? I guess she really likes him," I reply excitedly. "Where are we going?"

"You will see," Jenny teases me.

As we make our way up the stairs, I can't help but look up. "How did I not notice the fresco on the ceiling the last time I was here?" I ask her.

"I do not even notice it anymore," she says.

We continue down the hallway, passing by her room and the door to the roof area. We finally reach a door near the end of the hallway next to her parent's room. She opens it, and we walk into a storage room with crates, chests, and furniture covered in cloth.

"What are we doing in here?"

"Having a lot of time with nothing to do is terribly boring. I started looking through this room to pass the time, and I want to show you what I found. Some of it is pretty fun and interesting."

She lets go of my hand and opens one of the chests. "Where is it? I know I saw it in one of these chests. Ah, here it is." Jenny lifts a purple cloak out of the chest.

"Have you seen one of these before?" she asks. "They are fascinating."

"A cloak. Yes, I have seen cloaks before," I answer slightly sarcastically.

"Not like this one," she informs me. Jenny puts the cloak on and twirls for me. "Ready?" she asks.

"Ready for what?"

Jenny places the hood on her head, and she fades away.

"Jenny?" I ask out into the empty space where she just was.

"I am right here. This cloak makes its wearer invisible when the hood is up." I hear Jenny speak, but I don't see her.

As I look in front of me, she starts to fade in as she removes the hood from her head.

"That's amazing. I have heard of items like this, but I haven't seen one in person," I tell her.

"I think this might come in handy for us if we have to sneak around," she tells me. "Plus, I can do something like this."

She pulls the hood back over her head and fades away again. The next thing I feel is her lips on mine. I grab the space in front of me, pull the hood off her, and she fades back in.

"I prefer to see you when I'm kissing you," I tell her.

Jenny looks at me, smirking slightly. She then takes the cloak off and places it on a crate.

Maybe now is the time I tell her. We're alone, and we won't be interrupted. "I want to talk to you about something," I say timidly.

"Sure, what is on your mind?" Jenny asks, opening another chest.

I stand there silent. Should I tell her? I don't know. What if she pushes me away? I don't think I could take it. "Never mind, it can wait. What are you looking for?" I ask, skirting my initial thought.

"I was looking for a ring I found the other day, but can not find it. Maybe my parents took it," she says, placing her hands on her hips.

"Is there anything else you wanted to show me here, or should we do something else? Maybe the library?" I ask.

"I can not spend another second in the library. I have been in that room for almost a week now. I need a break from it. This punishment is getting to me," she replies. "Let us go to my room and figure something out."

As she walks past me, I smell her perfume again; it's lovely.

Walking toward her room, I grab her hand and feel her fingers wrap around mine. As we enter her room, I pull her towards me to steal a hug from her. "I hope this continues," I whisper to her.

"Me too," she tells me, hugging me back.

"Let us sit on the balcony outside my room. It's a pretty view, and we can talk and just be together," she suggests, leaning back from me.

We pass through Jenny's room and through a glass door that leads to a balcony. On the balcony, there is a small table and two chairs. Sitting down, I notice the tree canopy leaves from the patio below have started to change color. They have bits of yellow and orange on their tips. In a couple of weeks, the tree will be a brilliant yellow with hints of orange and remain this way throughout the winter season, hence its name, the Golden Sun.

I look back at Jenny, who's looking at me.

"What?" I ask.

"Nothing," she replies.

"There's something. What is it?"

"I remember the first time I saw you. I was in the cart with Rox, and I looked over and saw this tall girl determined to work the harvest. You had an aura of confidence when you walked over and lifted the test sack. When you lifted it, I knew I had to get to know you. When you offered me some of your food at the end of the first day. I was more determined than ever to get to know you.

"If you were so determined to get to know me, why didn't you talk to me earlier?" I ask, leaning on my elbows.

"I do not know. Nerves, maybe?" she responds, touching my arm lightly.

The feeling of her touching me this way always sends tingles up my back, causing the hair on my arms to rise. I think about the last time we were in her room and how she made me feel. I grab her hand, holding it, and look at her. The tiny freckles that dot across the brim of her nose and cheeks. Her green eyes sparkle in the light. Letting go of her hand, I touch her face while leaning in to kiss her.

"Where did that come from?" she asks, smiling at me.

"Not sure; I was looking at you and had to kiss you."

Jenny stands, grabbing my hand to escort me back inside.

"Where are we going now?" I ask.

"I want to lie with you."

She turns around, and I see she is starting to undo her dress slightly.

Seeing this, I become incredibly nervous as we walk towards her room. I want to be intimate with her, but I've never been intimate with anyone. I'm not really sure what to do.

"I—I've never been with anyone, but I want to be with you. I'm just not sure what to do," I say nervously.

She turns and looks at me. "We can do as much or as little as you want. I want to be with you and show you more of me, but only if you are comfortable."

Hearing her tell me this, I pull her close to me, softly grab her face between my hands, and kiss her. In return, she kisses me back.

CHAPTER 9
FAMILY

Lying in her bed, Jenny adjusts herself by draping one of her legs over me. "How do you feel?" she asks.

While rubbing her lower back with my thumb, I say, "I'm feeling euphoric and energetic all at the same time. I keep wondering if you enjoyed yourself. I know I haven't felt this close to anyone before, and just laying with you in this bed adds to this experience. I can't imagine any other place I would want to be."

"I know there is no other place I would want to be than right here with you," she tells me, nestling her head into my shoulder.

I wrap my arm around her and start to caress her arm with my finger.

"Are you hungry? I know I am, "Jenny asks.

"Yes, I'm pretty hungry. Is that normal after being with someone?"

"If you do it right," she answers playfully. "Let us get something to eat. We can always come back up here afterward."

"I'm good with that," I tell her, sitting up.

As I get out of bed, Jenny grabs me and pulls me back down.

"On second thought, food can wait," she announces as she tickles me, which causes me to tense up like a steel rod.

Squirming, I scream, "Stop it! No! Stop it! You are in so much trouble." I try to regain my composure. Eventually, I grab her hands, holding them away from my ribs. She tries to move them toward me, but she can't.

I look at her. "My turn," I say devilishly.

"What are you going to do?" she asks with a scared look.

"You'll see," I announce, pushing up from the bed with my elbows and legs, lifting us into the air. I twist us around in the air, placing Jenny under me as we fall back into the bed.

"I would like to inform you that I am not ticklish," she tells me calmly.

"Let's see if that's true."

I start to move my hands to her sides, tickling her, but she doesn't squirm or laugh. She's really not ticklish.

"That's not fair!" I proclaim.

"I told you, but I do like you on top. Let us get something to eat now. I look forward to us continuing this later," she teases me.

I straighten up and look down at her. "Fine."

I jump out of bed and grab my clothes on the floor. "You coming?"

"I am just admiring the view."

Before dressing, I pick up and toss one of her undergarments on her face. She pulls it off quickly, smiling back at me. After getting dressed, we head to the kitchen to find something to eat and drink.

Looking around the kitchen, all I see is a fruit basket and bread on the counter.

"I wonder if Elsa has made anything. She generally keeps her homemade jarred food in the cupboards over here," Jenny says, opening them.

"It looks like jars of jam and a few other jarred vegetables. I think she is getting ready for the winter. By the way, I meant to tell you this the other day. Your mom's bread reminds me of Elsa's bread," she says.

"It's the same," I reply, realizing I let something slip.

"What do you mean, they are the same?"

"Grab the jam and bread. I found some cider over here," I answer, placing two glasses on the large wooden table in the middle of the kitchen.

I don't want to tell Jenny everything about my heritage yet. However, maybe I can start by telling her about Mother and Elsa.

"Something happened last night that you are going to find very interesting. When I got home, I mentioned Elsa to Mother. I learned Elsa and Mother were friends years ago but drifted apart. Also, when Elsa heard my name, she realized who I was. She came to visit us early this morning," I tell Jenny, filling our glasses. "Small world, isn't it?" I look at her and smile nervously.

"Wait! Elsa and your mom were friends? How could you not tell me this already? Why did they drift apart? You have to give me more."

"My understanding is they met after the great sickness. Mother was selling her soaps around the city, and she met Elsa. They quickly became friends and did almost everything together," I explain, sipping on my glass of cider.

"What caused them to drift apart?" she asks, cutting two slices of bread and spreading some jam on them.

"My mother met my father one evening while gathering herbs in the mountains, and they quickly started spending time together. Long story short, I came along about a year later."

"I knew it, a love interest. Keep going," Jenny tells me, sipping her cider.

"I guess it didn't go well when Elsa met my father. It caused a rift between her and Mother," I explain, taking a large drink of my cider to calm my nerves.

"What was the issue?"

How am I going to explain this? I can't blurt out that Elsa was afraid of my Father because of what he is and represents. "Something about his background. After their first meeting, Elsa and my Mother stopped seeing each other."

"There is more there. There has to be. We should investigate and find out all the details," Jenny says, taking a large drink of cider.

"I don't know. I think they are trying to fix things. We should let them try to reconnect and not pry."

"You are no fun," Jenny tells me, eating a little bread.

"Speaking of parents, when are your parents coming home? I don't want to cause trouble for you, and it's getting dark," I say, drinking the rest of my cider.

"Not sure. You are not going anywhere. I have you to myself and want to keep you here as long as possible," she states frankly.

Looking at her, wanting the same, I refill our glasses with cider.

Over the next couple hours, we have several glasses of cider as we talk about our childhoods. We realize that despite more differences than similarities, it doesn't matter. Before we knew it, we were utterly intoxicated and ate most of the bread and half the jar of jam.

"Should we go back to your room and rest?" I ask.

"Rest? I can think of better things we can do," Jenny mumbles.

She's even cuter when she's drunk. Her cheeks are flushed, and her eyes have a dazed look, but somehow they still sparkle. Making our way out of the kitchen, we sway and fall into each other. Getting upstairs was much more of a challenge than it should have been.

In the doorway, Jenny rests one arm on the door jam and one on me and looks at me. "Thank you for helping me to my room. I am sure I would have fallen asleep midway up the stairs."

"No problem. I am happy to hold you and help you up the stairs," I say, smiling at her.

"I think I am falling in love with you. When we are together, I feel whole. When we are apart, I feel empty," she confesses to me.

I'm overwhelmed by what she just told me, and my heart is

pounding with excitement. I place my hand on her chest, and I can feel her heart beating quickly as well.

"I think I'm falling in love with you as well. When we are not together, all I can think about is being with you."

Jenny grabs me and holds on to me. I can't help but do the same. Holding her just feels right.

"Come on, let's get to the bed so we don't have to worry about the spinning world around us," I say.

As we sit on the edge of her bed, we stare out into her room. I think we both just realized what happened.

"I mean it. What I said before," I tell her.

"Me too." Jenny returns my affection while squeezing my hand.

How can I feel so strongly for someone in such a short time? Is this what Mother felt toward Father?

"What now?" I ask.

"I am not sure. I have never thought of or told anyone I loved them. Knowing we feel the same feels awkward and exciting all at once," she tells me, leaning her head on my shoulder.

"Jenniver, we are back. We need to talk to you," Jenny's mother says from the main entryway.

"Shit! Stay here. I will go down and meet them."

Jenny springs from the bed and runs to the door but stops suddenly. She turns around and runs back to kiss me. "Stay here."

"How are you going to talk to them while you're drunk?"

"Do not worry. This is not my first time."

I look at her, realizing this is a true statement.

While waiting on the bed, I hear Jenny greet her parents. I try to listen to their conversation but can't hear much. It sounds like the greeting has become an intense conversation. Jenny is getting louder, even though they are moving away from the main entryway. I get restless and start to snoop around her room. Her dresser has a hairbrush, nail file, and perfume bottle on top of it. I pick up the perfume and smell it. It's the one she is currently wearing. Opening her armoire, I see several dresses, skirts, and other accessories jammed into it. How can one person have so many outfits? I have three tops and a few pairs of pants, not including my undergarments. I turn around and make my way to the bathroom. I can't imagine having a bathroom inside the house, let alone my own personal one. The idea of not having to leave the house in the middle of the night to relieve myself sounds so luxurious. Thinking of this, my bladder reminds me of all the cider I drank earlier. I look at the toilet and think, why not? As I empty my bladder, I put a mental reminder in my head that I have to talk to Mother about upgrading our outhouse. Having a porcelain seat is much nicer than a wooden slab.

After finishing up, I head back to the bedroom door to see if I can hear anything, but I don't. I wonder how long this is going to take. Quietly opening the door to the hallway, I stick my head out, and when I don't see anyone, I walk toward the landing and lean over the railing to see if I see or hear anything. I don't, so I return to Jenny's room and lie on her bed. As I lie on the bed, I smell hints of her perfume, which causes me to turn my head and smell her pillow. I am so weird, I think to myself. Hearing Jenny's voice starting to come from her balcony, I get up and walk over to the door, keeping myself hidden inside.

"What do you mean it is decided?" I hear Jenny yelling.

"Lower your voice," I hear her mother tell her.

"I do not care if I am loud. You made this decision without me, and it is about me," Jenny answers, even louder than before.

"Listen, your father and I have decided that you will marry Jeremy. Combining our two families will strengthen both families for a long time."

Hearing the word marry causes a panic to come over me. Jenny can't marry Jeremy. She doesn't love him. She loves me.

"I will not marry him! I do not like him. Daddy, please!" she pleads to her father.

"You will marry him! That is final. The wedding will be in three weeks," Jenny's mother tells her.

"Three weeks!? That is why you have been visiting their home so much lately. You have been planning this for a long time and kept me out of it. That is why you invited him to the party the other week. I am so glad you have my best interest in mind—or should I say your interest, Mother?" I hear Jenny yell at her mother before she runs off.

I hear her Father say, "That went as well as I thought it would. I hope you know what you are doing. You knew this was not going to go well. We know that Jenny ..."

Hearing stomping coming up the stairs, I turn my head, and then the door flies open. I stand there looking wide-eyed at her from across the room.

"Did you hear that?" Jenny asks.

I nod, trying to figure out what to do or say.

Jenny walks over to her bed and pulls a clothing case from under it. She fills it with clothing and odds and ends from her room.

"I can not be here anymore. She does not understand me and only thinks of herself and her status," Jenny says, frantically closing the case.

Jenny looks at me and asks, "Want a roommate? I will earn my keep and help with anything at your home."

"Are you sure you want to do this?" I ask, grabbing her hands.

"Yes. For a while now. I was on the verge of leaving, but this is the final straw."

"Your parents are downstairs and will see us. How are we going to leave?"

"I do not care if they see us together," she says, squeezing my hands.

We head down the stairs to the front entryway, and before we make it to the bottom landing, we see her parents.

"What are you doing, and who is this?" her mother asks firmly.

"Seriously, Mother?! Look closely!" Jenny tells her as we continue down the stairs.

"You are the girl Jenny invited to our party. Why were you upstairs and dressed like that?" she asks.

"Yes, ma'am," I answer.

"You still have not answered me, young lady. Where are you going with her?" Jenny's mother asks, grabbing her arm as we reach the bottom of the stairs.

"I can not be here anymore. I try to please you and Father, but I can not anymore. You do not even know your daughter and what she wants," she explains, trying to free her arm. "Let go of me!"

"Dear, please let go of her. Jenny, calm down," Jenny's Father asks of everyone, trying to separate the two of them.

"No, she is going to do what I ask of her," her mother tells her husband.

Seeing Jenny struggling to get free and in pain, I push between them and lift her mother's fingers off of Jenny's arm, allowing Jenny to back away from her mother.

"This is not your concern; please leave," she tells me.

"I love her, Mother," Jenny interjects, grabbing my hand.

"What do you mean you love her?" her mother questions.

"You refuse to accept what you already know," Jenny tells her mother. "I will never be able to love Jeremy. I am already in love with Kyra."

Jenny storms to the front door and opens it. Before leaving, she stops and looks up slightly.

"Goodbye, Mother. Goodbye, Father."

Jenny walks out, and I follow closely behind. When I pass through the doorway, I look back and see her parents standing in the foyer, staring at us in shock.

"Are you sure you want to leave it like this?" I ask, trying to catch up to her.

Once we are out of sight, Jenny stops and drops her clothing case.

"Are you alright?" I ask.

"Hold me, please," she says, crying.

I wrap my arms around her, trying to comfort her.

~

Mother is attending to something in the fireplace as we enter the house.

"Hello," I announce our arrival.

Mother turns and says, "Nice to see you again so soon, Jenny."

"Nice to see you as well, Miss Everwind," Jenny greets Mother.

"Is something wrong, my dear? You look upset. Were you crying?" Mother asks, walking over to her.

Mother holds Jenny's face between her hands, looking at her.

"Go upstairs and settle in. I will be up in a second," I tell Jenny, handing her the case.

Jenny hugs Mother before she makes her way up to my bedroom. Mother looks at me intently.

"I'll explain later. She didn't know where else to go," I say as I also head to my room.

Jenny is curled into a ball facing away from me on the bed. I lie down next to her and rub her shoulders. She turns and buries her face into me as she starts to cry again.

I wrap my arms around her, hoping it comforts her, but I don't know if it's helping. After a while, I notice she's no longer crying. She's asleep with dried tears on her cheeks. I carefully get off the bed and pull a blanket over her. I head down to talk to Mother, who is reading one of my grandmother's journals at the table.

"Jenny looked very upset," Mother says with concern.

"She is, and I think with good reason," I reply, taking a seat. "When did Elsa leave?"

"She left a while ago. She wanted to check up on her family since she hadn't seen them in a while. What happened to cause Jenny to be so upset?" Mother asks, closing the journal.

"Jenny's parents told her this evening that they arranged for her to get married to someone she does not love. Her parents have already planned the wedding to take place in three weeks. She had a large argument with her parents, resulting in her packing up and storming out of her home," I answer, picking at the bread at the table.

"What is she going to do?"

"I'm not sure. She asked if she could stay here. I hope that's fine."

"I have no problem with her staying with us." Changing the subject, Mother asks, "Have you told Jenny about last night?"

"I told her about you and Elsa with bits of information about Father; I couldn't find the courage to tell her everything about him."

"You look like you are holding something back. What is it?"

"We expressed our love for each other. Neither of us has felt this way before, and it feels a little scary."

Mother looks at me for a good long while before saying anything. "The heart feels what the heart feels. It's getting late. We can all talk more in the morning. I recommend you both talk this through. While she disagrees with her parents, I am sure they are concerned about her. They should know that she is at least safe. It's up to you to tell Jenny about your Father when you are ready. I recommend that you tell her sooner rather than later. Secrets have a way of coming out; it would be best if she hears it from you. Goodnight, my child."

"Thank you. I am going to stay up a bit."

Mother gets up from the table and kisses the top of my head before heading to her room.

I turn my attention to the fireplace and stare at the glowing embers of red and orange, thinking about all that has happened. Before the harvest, my world consisted of my Mother and our daily chores. Since then, I have found friends, learned about my Father, and fallen in love for the first time. Navigating all these changes will be a challenge.

As the fire starts to die out, I quietly climb into bed, careful not to wake Jenny. I snuggle in next to her, wrapping my arms around her. She shifts, snuggling into me more. Before closing my eyes, I whisper to her, "I love you. I really do."

∽

Hearing Mother downstairs, I open my eyes and check on Jenny. She seems to be sound asleep still. Slipping out of the bed, I quietly make my way downstairs.

"Morning," I whisper to Mother.

"Jenny?" Mother asks.

"Sound asleep. She might sleep all morning, not sure," I reply, hugging Mother.

"I'm going to the barn to tend to the animals. When Jenny wakes up, she might want to talk to you about things. Is there anything else you need me to do while I'm outside?" I quietly ask.

"No, I will watch over her. We will have something to eat together when you come back in. Now go and get back soon," she tells me, pushing me toward the door.

Walking to the barn, I look out at the valley, and it looks like it will be a beautiful day. The sky is already brilliant blue with many white fluffy clouds throughout it. I get straight to work caring for the animals and their stalls. Before returning to the house, I pump fresh water from the well to fill the watering trough. Entering the house, I see Mother starting to serve food, but I don't see Jenny.

"Is she up?" I ask.

Mother shakes her head and says, "Go check on her."

I climb up and sit beside her, placing my hand on her shoulder. "Are you awake? Mother has made food."

"I am not hungry and feel terrible," Jenny mumbles.

"Come on, get up. Staying in bed will not help," I tell her, pulling the blanket off her.

Jenny pulls the blanket back up quickly, trying to enforce her will.

"If that's how you want to play this," I say. I pick up one side of the bed, causing Jenny to roll out of bed and onto the floor with a thud.

"I can not believe you did that. You are so mean," Jenny scowls at me.

"I understand you're upset, but staying in bed is not going to solve things. Come downstairs and have food with us. From there, we will see how we work through this," I insist.

Heading back down the ladder, I announce, "She'll be down in a minute."

Sitting at the table with Mother, we see Jenny starting her descent.

"Morning, Jenny," Mother says, placing a bowl of stew on the table for her.

"Morning Miss Everwind. Your daughter can be forceful at times. She rolled me out of bed onto the floor. You should talk to her about that."

"That's between you two, but I remember doing something similar to her a few years ago. Please eat," Mother replies. "Kyra informed me of the events that happened yesterday. Do you know what you are going to do?"

Jenny sits quietly, holding a spoonful of stew over the bowl before answering.

"I do not know. I have all these feelings, and they conflict with each other. I am so mad at my parents, more so my mother than my father, because I know it was she who set this whole marriage up. She is always trying to figure out ways to improve her status. At times, I feel more like a tool for her to benefit the family's status than a daughter. Jeremy is nice enough; however, I do not love him. The bigger issue is who I have chosen to be with. My mother has known for a long time who I am and has chosen to avoid it and not accept it. At the same time, I do not want to lose them. I am scared I might have to, so I can be happy. This has been a struggle I have been facing for years, and this may be the breaking point. The most important people in my life are Rox, Elsa, and now your daughter," Jenny continues, "I know this is very sudden, and I am asking a lot of you.

Could I please stay here until I can figure things out? I promise to help with anything that is needed around the house."

"You can stay as long as you need," Mother tells Jenny, holding her hand.

"Really!? You do not know how much this means to me," Jenny says, full of gratitude.

"Let us enjoy this meal together, and we'll figure out the details later," Mother answers.

CHAPTER 10
HAPPINESS

Looking out the window, a fresh blanket of snow fell overnight. Turning my head, I see a mass of brown hair.

"It's time to get up," I whisper.

"A few more minutes. You kept me up late last night after going to bed," Jenny responds, half asleep.

"Are you complaining?"

"Not complaining, just tired," Jenny answers, turning to rest her head on me. "I need a few more minutes."

"It snowed last night. It looks peaceful outside," I say, playing with her hair.

Jenny picks up her head, looks out the window, and moves in to snuggle with me, placing her head on my shoulder. "Pretty—Sleepy-time," she mumbles.

"Come on, we need to get up. Remember, Rox, Lindsey, and Elsa will be visiting, and we need to help Mother get things ready," I remind her.

As I sit up, Jenny's head flops onto the bed.

"You suck. I was enjoying that morning snuggle," says Jenny, speaking like a toddler. "Should I make bread or something else to help your mother?"

I remember Jenny's last attempt and how tough the bread was. Mother and I could barely chew it, and even the pig had trouble eating it. Baking is not in her wheelhouse. "Maybe not; I don't think our teeth could handle your bread," I jokingly say.

"Just because we could not cut my last loaf of bread with a knife, it does not mean it was bad," she replies, right before grabbing and starting to tickle me.

I immediately seize up and begin to squirm. "Stop it! You know this drives me crazy," I plead, trying to get away from her.

"I know, that is why I do it. It is your birthday, and I wanted to give you birthday tickles. Happy birthday," Jenny says, looking devilish.

I can't believe I'm eighteen today. It seems like it wasn't that long ago that I turned seventeen.

Jenny kisses me and walks to the window. Due to the cold chill in the air, she wraps her arms around herself to try to keep warm. I walk up behind her, flustered and red-faced, but I place my chin on her shoulder and wrap my arms around her.

"I always enjoy seeing fresh snow clinging to the trees and blanketing the ground. It is so calming and peaceful," I say while enjoying the view out the window.

"It is pretty, and it is cold. I am freezing standing here," Jenny says, quickly grabbing clothes to put on.

We both get dressed. I finish first since I don't do anything special with my hair. Jenny's long, wavy hair takes extra time to get ready. I descend from our room and head to the barn to tend to the animals. While I'm in the barn, I'm sure Jenny will get the fire going to warm the house and get it ready for cooking.

Entering the house, I stamp my feet and announce, "Looks like we got another foot of snow. If this continues for the rest of the winter season, we'll have snow until the growing season."

"Close the door. You are letting the cold in. Come sit with us for our morning meal," Mother insists.

"We're having the tarts? I thought we would save those for later," I say, surprised, sitting at the table.

"I plan to make a cake for your birthday. You only turn eighteen once. Jenny said she would like to help me."

I look at her and then at Jenny, who is looking at me, squinting her eyes.

"I am helping, not making," Jenny says.

I lean back in my chair and let out a slightly loud breath of relief. The next thing I know, I'm hit in the face with a small towel. "What was that for?" I ask.

"You know," Jenny tells me as I pull the towel off my face.

"Enough of that, you two. Speaking of behavior, I know what it's like to be young, but if you could wait a little while so I can fall asleep first, I would appreciate it," Mother requests of us.

Jenny and I go wide-eyed, and our faces flush with embarrassment. I can't believe Mother had to listen to us last night. I'm so embarrassed.

"Sorry Miss Everwind. Your daughter just attacked me," Jenny says, breaking the awkward silence.

I look at her while holding my tart in front of me. I can't believe she just said that, and in front of Mother.

Mother bursts out laughing. "You are just as guilty as she is. I believe you did the same to her the other evening. All I am asking is that you two be a little more discrete. Maybe when I'm not around," Mother asks of us. "Also, I told you, please call me Lily."

Jenny looks down at her tea as if she was caught doing something she shouldn't have done. I'm glad Mother didn't walk in on us when we were in the barn the other day. That would have been very awkward.

"Shall we get started? Our guests will be here in a few hours," I say, trying to change the conversation.

"Yes, let us get started," Jenny says, understanding my goal.

Mother gives us our marching orders. "Jenny, please grab the flour, sugar, fruit, and cold fat from the backroom. Kyra, please get us a fresh bucket of water and clean up the table so we can work at it."

While they are making my birthday cake, I try to sneak a taste here and there. Each time, Mother slaps me on the hand. She gives Blacky a few pieces as he lies by the fire to stay warm. He lucked out, following me home that day. Mother adores him.

As we finish getting everything ready, Mother says, "I'm going to freshen up and take a bath before our guests arrive."

I look at Jenny, laughing slightly.

"What?" she asks.

"I'm curious. How are you covered in flour while Mother has none on her?" I ask, pointing to her clothes and face.

"Well, I guess I am very into helping. Come on, we should change as well. I get to wear a dress today. I am excited as it has been a while," she tells me, patting her clothes and wiping the flour off her face.

We head to our room, and I sit on the bed while Jenny picks out a dress. "Which one do you think I should wear? The blue or green one?" Jenny asks, laying both dresses on the bed next to me.

"Whichever one you like. You look great in both."

"What do you plan on wearing? Your brown pants and blue top?"

"Most likely, those are my nicest clothes," I say while lying back on the bed.

"Please, do not lie on my dresses. You will wrinkle them," Jenny shouts at me.

"Sorry," I say, sitting up quickly.

"You seem distracted again. What is on your mind?"

"Nothing," I say softly.

Ever since she moved in with us, things have been amazing. Every once in a while, I think about telling her everything, as I don't want any secrets between us. However, I chicken out every time because I don't want to ruin what we have. I know she loves me, but dropping the vampire father thing on her might be too much. I couldn't bear losing her.

"Let's get ready," I say, getting off the bed.

Jenny must have decided on the blue dress, as she's placing the green one back on the wall. I watch Jenny as she removes her top. Seeing her topless, I can't help myself, so I walk up behind her and kiss her neck softly. She loves to tickle me and drive me crazy, so I do this to drive her crazy in a different way.

"You are incorrigible. We do not have time for that," she tells me, arching her head slightly while placing her hand on the back of my head.

"Mother's in the barn washing up, remember. It's my birthday."

"True."

She turns and pushes me onto the bed and her dress.

"Your dress," I say.

"I will wear the green one," she informs me.

Mother seems nervous, pacing back and forth, waiting for our guests to arrive.

"Do you think we should make something else?" she asks, adjusting a few things on the table.

"I think we're fine. It's Rox, Lindsey, and Elsa. All they care about is being together with us," I answer.

"I see them," Jenny announces, looking out the window.

"Come, let's greet them and get them out of the cold," Mother instructs us, opening the door.

We walk out to greet them, and they wave at us and yell, "Happy birthday!"

Jenny runs up and gives all of them a hug. I give Rox a fist bop and Lindsey and Elsa a hug. Mother hugs Elsa and Rox and looks at Lindsey as it's the first time they have met.

"You must be Lindsey. I have heard so much about you," Mother says.

"Hello, Miss Everwind. It's nice to meet you finally," Lindsey answers, hugging Mother.

"Thank you for the birthday wishes. I'm sure you are all cold from the walk. Let's get inside where it's warm. Mother and Jenny made a cake for us to enjoy," I say while motioning everyone into the house.

Back inside, I check the water that was already heating in the fireplace, and it's hot. I pour some into our teapot with some wild mountain tea and let it steep. Our guests remove their outer garments and seat themselves at the table. Lindsey places her violin case next to her.

"Do you bring that everywhere you go?" asks Jenny.

"It's always by my side," Lindsey replies, rubbing her hands together to warm them up.

"Her side, her bed," Rox adds.

I look at Rox, squinting my eyes slightly. "Bed?"

He looks up at me, and a smile appears on his face. Jenny whispers something to Lindsey, which causes Lindsey to giggle and nod.

"What did you just whisper to her?" Rox asks.

"Nothing," Jenny replies, sitting back in her chair.

As we all settle at the table, Mother brings out the cake. "I hope everyone likes it. Shall we sing to my little girl?" Mother asks as she places it on the table.

"I'm not a little girl anymore," I say.

"You will always be my little girl, no matter how old you get."

Mother starts to sing, and everyone jumps in, which causes me to hide my face in my hands, hoping it ends soon. I never like being the center of attention, so I can't wait for them to stop singing. As the song ends, they clap for me, and I am grateful the singing has ended.

Mother cuts pieces of cake for everyone, but hands me the first piece. It's a layered cake with fruit between each layer and powdered sugar on top.

"This looks really good. Thank you both for making it," I tell Mother and Jenny.

"Lindsey, I have heard so much about your playing. Would you mind playing something for us later? It's been years since I heard music," Mother says.

"It would be my pleasure, Miss Everwind. Thank you for the cake," Lindsey replies.

"Please call me Lily; Miss Everwind sounds so old and formal. I'm only in my thirties," Mother says. "Elsa, I think you might remember this recipe. We made this cake during our first harvest together."

While enjoying the cake, I can't help but feel happy seeing everyone laughing and having a good time together. Who would have thought I would be this happy six months ago? Finishing up our cake, I notice Jenny sneaking up to our room. She returns and places a small box in front of me.

"Happy birthday," she says.

"I told you no gifts. I just want a simple day with my family and friends."

"Be quiet and open it," she insists.

I open the box, and inside, there's a small rustic-looking bracelet with a small polished red stone in the center. I take it out so everyone can see.

"Try it on. I know you do not like jewelry, but this just seemed perfect for you," Jenny tells me.

I put it on. "I really like it. It's definitely for me. Rough and a little shiny at the same time," I say jokingly.

Looking back at everyone, I see Rox and Mother placing gifts on the table. "What are you all doing?" I ask.

They all say, "It's your birthday."

I squint at everyone briefly before asking, "Fine, which one should I open next?"

Lindsey pushes their gift over. "This is from the three of us."

I open the gift. It's brown leather wrist guards. "Look at these," I say as I take one out and try it on immediately. I twist my wrist around, seeing how it looks on me.

"Thank you," I tell them.

Mother slides her gift over to me. "I hope you like it."

"I'm sure I will."

Her gift is wrapped in brown paper with a ribbon around it. I pull the ribbon and tear the paper to expose a new top. "Did you make this?" I ask.

"I made it while you were working the harvest and late at night when you were sleeping," she explains.

I take a closer look at it. It's really pretty, with detailed stickwork throughout it. What really draws my attention is the needlework in the upper portion of the top. Mother creatively stitched a subtle *K* within the design.

I get up and hug her. "I love it and you, Mother."

"Thank you all for the gifts. You didn't have to, but I do appreciate them all. How about a little music?"

Lindsey takes her violin out and starts to get ready to play by plucking at the strings and making a few adjustments by turning the knobs on the neck of the violin. "Any requests?"

"I wouldn't know what to ask for. Please play what you like," Mother says.

Lindsey moves next to the fireplace, which casts its warm light on her. She starts playing a soft and slow song that fills our home. As we listen, I look over at Jenny. As the light from the fireplace bounces on her face, she looks more beautiful than ever. As Lindsey pulls the last note out and stops, we all clap. I look at Mother, who's wiping her eyes.

"Is something wrong?" I ask Mother.

"No, that was so pretty it made me cry."

Mother gets up and walks over to Lindsey. [In Elvin] *"Thank you for the lovely song,"* she tells Lindsey, hugging her.

Lindsey hugs her back. "You're welcome. I forgot you speak Elvin. Shall I play more?"

"Please, maybe something with a little energy," Mother answers.

Lindsey uses her bow to tap the neck of her violin, creating a beat. We clap along with the beat while she plays. We continue to enjoy her playing song after song. Eventually, she takes a break to have tea.

Looking outside, the sun is starting to get low in the sky. The one downfall of the winter season is the lack of sunlight. It rises late and sets early, so our guests will leave soon to have daylight to head back to the city.

"I'm sorry, but we should start heading back as it will be dark soon. This was lovely seeing you all, especially you, my old friend," Elsa tells Mother.

"Thank you all for coming. I can't imagine a better birthday than this," I say to everyone.

Lindsey puts her violin away while Elsa starts to bundle up. Rox and Lindsey help each other with their coats and gloves.

Jenny walks over to Rox and hugs him."Miss you and hope to see you soon."

She then whispers something into his ear.

"I won't," he replies.

Jenny then hugs Lindsey. "See you soon, and don't forget what we talked about."

"What did you talk about?" asks Rox.

"Nothing, help your mom," Lindsey tells Rox, as Jenny and her giggle again.

Elsa walks over to Jenny. "My dear. You seem happy."

"I am. I have all that I need," Jenny replies, hugging Elsa.

"After you left, your father came to me asking about you. He knows we are close and thought I might know how you are doing. I told him that you were safe and doing well. I didn't give any details about your location. The other day, he gave me this letter, hoping I could get it to you. Do with it as you like," Elsa explains, handing Jenny a sealed letter.

Jenny takes the letter and looks at it for a second. "Thank you."

As we walk them out, we all say our goodbyes a few more times. Right before our path meets the Western Road, they turn and wave goodbye one last time. Walking back to the house, Jenny is quiet. I know she's thinking about the letter. Upon entering the house, she heads to our room, and I see the light crystal get turned up. I help Mother clean up to give Jenny some space. After cleaning up, I go up and check on her. She's sitting on the bed with her back against the headboard, holding her knees with the letter in one hand.

"Is everything alright?" I ask, sitting down next to her.

She hands me the letter.

My Dearest Jenniver,

Elsa was kind enough to tell me you are safe and doing well. I assume you are with your friend. I know you are upset about the marriage, but we thought we were doing the right thing. All we wanted is to ensure your future is secure and you will not want for anything, as this has been a tradition of High Rock for centuries.

Since you left, your mother has not been the same. She was initially upset and mad, but it changed to something else. For the past several months, she has not been going out. Instead, she sits in your room for hours, holding items that belong to you. I know you will not believe this, but she truly misses you. I would be grateful if you could find it in your heart to come home and talk to your mother, hoping we can work through this. I would like to see my little girl again. I miss you more than you could ever imagine.

Your loving Father

I look up at her as this letter is truly heartfelt. "What are you going to do?" I ask with concern.

"I do not know. I did not realize she was this way. She has always been so strong. What do you think I should do?" Jenny asks, rocking a bit.

"It's not my decision to make," I answer, placing the letter on the bed.

"Lily, we can use some of your wisdom," Jenny calls down to her.

"What can I help with?" Mother asks from below.

Mother works her way up the ladder and sees Jenny on the bed. She goes right to her and sits next to her.

"What's wrong, my dear?" Mother asks.

I hand Mother the letter, which she reads quickly. Mother looks worried as she looks up from the letter.

Jenny asks, "What should I do?"

"Based on what I read, it might be an opportunity for healing with your family. Family is the most important thing. Like our family here," Mother tells Jenny.

"You see me as part of this family?" Jenny asks, looking at Mother.

"Of course, my child. This is your home now. Over these past months, I have grown to love you deeply," Mother tells Jenny.

Jenny leans in and gives Mother a long hug, which Mother returns. "I love you too," Jenny replies.

"It's getting late. If you decide to visit your family, it can wait till tomorrow. You two get some sleep. Sleeping on things always adds clarity," Mother tells us.

Mother makes her way down the ladder, and I see her smile at us. "Night."

"Come on. Let's get ready for bed. We don't have to sleep," I say to her.

Jenny gets off the bed and starts to get ready, and I do the same. We crawl into bed and pull the blankets up. Like always, Jenny lies down next to me, resting her head on my shoulder and holding me. I lean over and turn the light crystal down to a low glow.

"If you go, do you want me to go with you?" I ask.

"I do not know. Maybe, but it also might make it harder if you are there. I do not know if I will be there for a few hours or days. Can you hold me? I want to feel you tightly next to me tonight," she asks.

I wrap my arm around Jenny, hoping it helps comfort her as we fall asleep.

I'm on my knees, sobbing intensely. I'm holding out my hands, which are covered in blood. What is going on? Shop windows are smashed, and people are panicking, running in all directions.

I call out, "Mother, Jenny! Where are you?"

I start to panic as I can't seem to find them. I try to stand, but I can't. My legs won't allow me.

"Mother, Jenny, where are you?" I scream!

I sit up quickly, breathing heavily in a cold sweat. I look over, and Jenny is looking at me.

"Are you all right? You woke me up talking in your sleep. What were you dreaming about?" Jenny asks with concern.

"It was a nightmare. I was in the city, and everyone around me was panicking and running from something. The city was in chaos. My hands were covered in blood, and I couldn't find you or Mother."

As I collect my thoughts, I look outside. It's still dark. "What time is it?" I ask.

"We have hours before dawn. It was just a dream," Jenny tries to comfort me while patting the bed, encouraging me to lie back down next to her.

As we lie in bed, I loop some of her wavy hair around my finger and glide it down her cheek. As I do this, Jenny grabs my finger and holds it softly.

~

I have been looking at the ceiling for hours now, thinking about my nightmare. Is it a warning or just a bad dream? I know it will mean something eventually. I look out the window, and morning is just starting to make its presence known. I see slight indications of the mountains against the brightening sky.

"Morning," Jenny says quietly.

"Morning. You're up early," I reply, rubbing her arm slightly.

"My brain started thinking a while ago, but my body is tired still," she says.

"About your seeing your family?"

"Yes, I decided to see them today," she answers while snuggling into me.

"Do you want me to walk you to the city at least?" I ask, scratching her scalp lightly.

"That would be nice," she answers. "Please do not stop that scratching. It feels good."

"You were restless last night. Did you sleep much?" Jenny asks, rolling on her back while rubbing her eyes.

"No, I never fell back asleep. I can't stop thinking about the nightmare."

"It was just a dream."

"Dreams are different for me. They tend to have a meaning or purpose. I never know the meaning at first, but it always becomes clear at some point," I explain to her.

Jenny sits up and leans over me to turn up the light crystal. "What do you mean? Are you saying your dreams come true?"

"They give me insight into things to come."

"Why am I just learning of this now? This seems like something I should know about," she tells me in a slightly upset tone.

"I'm sorry; I don't know why we never discussed this. My dreams for the past few months have been pleasant. I didn't give them much thought. Maybe that's why," I reply.

I see Jenny is confused and maybe a little hurt that she's just learning about this. I feel the urge to tell her everything now.

"I ... I've wanted to tell you something for a long time, but I've been worried about what you might think."

"That you have dreams that give you insight?" she asks skeptically.

I wish I didn't bring this up. With the recent events about her family, now's not the time. However, I need to say something. She deserves the truth.

"No ... there's something else, but now is not the right time. You need to focus on your parents. If you come back, I will to tell you everything," I explain worriedly.

"What do you mean if I come back? Why would you think that? Even if things go well, I do not plan on moving back in with my parents. My place is with you," she assures me.

"They're your parents. It sounds like your mother needs you."

Jenny straddles me, resting her hands on my shoulders while looking at me intensely.

"You are my family. This is where I belong. I plan on coming back as soon as I can. We can talk when I return and only when you are ready," Jenny reassures me.

I hold her face between my hands, looking at her.

"How can I be this lucky?" I ask.

"I do not know, but I guess you lucked out. Shall we get up? I am so hungry. All I ate yesterday was a piece of cake and a tart. While delicious, I need a little more than that, plus the sun will be up shortly," Jenny says as she kisses me and dismounts me to dress.

I get out of bed to dress as well. As Jenny brushes her hair, I stick my head in her way to look at my hair in the mirror. To smooth it out, I run my fingers through my hair.

I head downstairs to get the fire going. Reaching the bottom of the ladder, I give Blacky a little rub on his head, wishing him a good morning. Within a few minutes, I have the fire roaring and place our large pot over the open flames. I tiptoe past Mother, who is still sleeping, to head to the back storage room. I grab a piece of cured pork belly from our pig we slaughtered a few weeks back and a few potatoes. Heading back to the main room, Mother stops me.

"What are you doing?"

"Sorry, I didn't mean to wake you. We couldn't sleep and decided to make something to eat. Should we make you some, too?"

"Don't burn the pork belly. I will be out in a bit. Between you and Jenny, the odds of not burning it are not good," Mother says, half asleep.

I stand there thinking she should make it if she has that little confidence in our cooking. Mother's not wrong, though. Between Jenny's baking ability and my lack of cooking, we have a high chance of making a terrible meal. Continuing to the table, I cut the potatoes into small pieces along with a small wild onion we had in a bowl on the table. I place the pork belly in the pot. As it sizzles in the pot, it fills the house with its fantastic smell. After a bit, I add the potatoes and onions and stir everything together.

Jenny slides down the ladder and leans over, taking a deep inhale.

"Smells good," she says.

"When did you learn to do that?" I ask, pointing to the ladder.

"I do not know; I just did it. I guess I learned watching you all these months. It is much faster this way."

Mother walks out, putting her hair up. "Morning, you two. Is there any tea left from last night?"

"Morning," Jenny replies, pulling out a chair for her. Jenny opens the teapot and shakes her head.

"Kyra said you both couldn't sleep. Have you been thinking about your mother and what you plan on doing?"

"Yes, I will go see them today after our morning chores. It should not be more than a day or so."

"Take all the time you need. We will be here for you when you return. Also, don't worry about the chores. We can handle them. Go be with your parents," says Mother.

"Kyra, you're burning the food because you are more interested in our conversation than watching what you are doing. Nothing is worse than a burnt meal," Mother tells me, winking at Jenny.

Jenny and Mother set the table, and I watch our meal, ensuring it does not burn any more than it already has. When the meal is ready, I serve it up. While it's not to Mother's ability, it's not that bad.

After eating, I look out the window to see that the sun has come up. It's a bright, clear day. The sky is a brilliant blue, with not a cloud to be seen.

"You two should get going. I will clean this up," Mother tells us.

Jenny grabs the leather coat Mother made for me a few years ago. It fits Jenny perfectly. She grabs her scarf and wraps it around her neck. I put on my winter jacket and scarf as well. Jenny walks over to Mother, hugs her, and kisses her cheek. "I will see you soon, love you," she tells her.

Mother looks at her and me and smiles. "I love you too, my dear. Be safe."

Jenny and I head out, and a chill is in the air. We walk, following the tracks our friends made in the snow yesterday.

"Have you thought of what you will say to your mother?" I ask.

"I plan on talking with my father first to understand everything better before seeing her. Depending on what he says, I will figure it out. I know it is going to be tough," she replies. "It is so peaceful out here this morning. The snow is dampening all the sounds. The only sounds I hear are us walking and talking. It is like our own little world out here. I like it this way. Only you and I," Jenny tells me, pulling us closer together.

Walking up to the Western Gate, we look up at High Rock.

"I can not believe it has been months since I have been there. It feels weird," Jenny says, squeezing my hand.

"Do you want me to go with you or stay close by?"

"I need to handle this on my own. Go home and be with your mom. I hope to be back home with you soon. Rox and Elsa are around if I need anything," Jenny reassures me.

She leans on her toes and kisses me. "I love you."

"I love you too. Be safe," I reply.

"Always," Jenny says, winking at me before she enters the city.

Before disappearing from my sight, she turns and waves to me one last time. I breathe in and out deeply and start my way back home. I have an off feeling that I can't shake. I'm worried about the conversation we need to have when she comes home. I can't put it off anymore. She needs to know the whole truth about me. She deserves to know, no matter the outcome.

CHAPTER II

MY WORLD CRUMBLES

Mother and I are sitting at the table, and I have been picking at my food. Jenny has been away for a few days now, and I keep wondering how things are going with her parents and when she will return. I miss having her next to me at night; waking up alone is just as bad. I know she will return, but it can't come soon enough. I have spent most days and nights trying to figure out the best way to tell her everything. Maybe I start with the dreams about my father and how I have had them for years. I can bring in the important details about him depending on how she takes this. I think this is a good plan, but I don't know. Would it be better to blurt out everything as quickly as possible?

"I've decided to tell Jenny everything when she comes back. I can't put it off anymore," I tell Mother.

"It's for the best. I know you have been scared to tell her, but I am sure it will not change how Jenny feels about you. It might shock her at first, but she's strong and knows who you are," she answers, sipping her tea.

"I know, but I'm worried she will see me differently," I reply, pushing the food around my plate.

"I have confidence in you two. I wasn't sure when I first met Jenny, but now I have no doubt you two are meant to be," Mother assures me.

As I'm about to eat something finally, we both hear horns in the distance. We get up from the table and rush outside to see what's happening. In the distance, smoke is rising from the city.

"Something is very wrong. I have to make sure she's all right," I yell, running down the pathway.

"Wait, it might be dangerous. You don't know what's happening," Mother yells back at me.

"I'll be careful, but I need to go," I insist, running as fast as possible toward the city.

Running, I feel the cold air fill my lungs, and my chest hurts. I keep pushing forward as my only thought is of Jenny. As I approach the city, I notice houses have smears painted on their doors. I realize it's the symbol of the Red Jackets I saw on their flyer during the Harvest Celebration. Reaching the Western Gate, I see it's closed, and the guards are lying on the ground, and they look to be unconscious. Looking through the gate, the city seems empty. What's going on? I need to get into the city. I step back, look around, and see the tree I sat under on the first day of the harvest. It's taller than the city wall and has a large limb extending just shy of the wall. Why not, I think to myself. I run over and climb up the tree as quickly as I can. When I reach the limb that extends to the wall, I step out on it using the limb above me for balance. I get about four feet from the wall when the limb above me stops. I dash and jump out of the tree as high and hard as possible, crashing onto the pathway atop the city wall.

"Not the most graceful landing," I tell myself out loud.

I see all the guards on the wall are also asleep. I try to wake one of them by shaking him, but he doesn't. I try another, with the same result. They must have been given something. I grab a sword from a guard just in case. Working my way to the Western Tower, I pass more unconscious guards. I make my way down the spiral stairs to the door that leads out to the city. I open it slowly to ensure it's clear and run down a side street, trying to avoid being seen. As I make my way to the main square, I hear people yelling, and I eventually see Red Jackets looting and destroying shop windows. Jenny was right; they aren't out for change but to cause chaos. How is this equality when they are looting the city? Reaching the square's edge, I see a large crowd with a group of Red Jackets standing on a stage. The leader is speaking to the crowd. I'm about to move closer when someone touches my shoulder.

I quickly turn, ready to strike, but stop. "Forge!" I say, shocked, seeing him.

"Not safe here. We hide under the Eastern Bridge. Join us." Forge says, trying to take me with him.

"I can't. I am looking for my friend, who was with me when you and I met. Have you seen her?" I ask intensely.

Forge shakes his head.

"Sorry, no. Do you know where she was?" he asks.

"She was up in High Rock with her family."

"I heard they took people from High Rock and moved them to the square over there. I hope she not there. They doing bad things to them. I have to go. I need to find my friends," Forge tells me before he runs off.

Hearing this, my heart sinks. I have to find Jenny even more so now. Running out from my current location to my next hiding spot, I hear the Red Jacket on the stage more clearly.

"For as long as we can remember, High Rock has governed over this city with little thought to us Lowlanders. No more, no more, we say. Now is our time, and we will take what is rightfully ours. Our pain will no longer benefit them. You, in front of me, will now know what it means to feel the pain of others," the man preaches to the crowd.

I scan the crowd and see they look to be from High Rock, just as Forge said. They are scared and holding on to each other.

"We are going through your homes and taking what should be ours. Some of you even thought you could try to stop us, which was met with unfavorable results," he continues. "Bring the ones who resisted so we can show what happens to anyone who resists this change."

I watch as men, women, and children are escorted onto the stage. Their arms are tied together, and some of them have been beaten. My heart drops in horror watching Jenny being pulled onto the stage. One of her eyes is swollen shut, and her face is bruised. I head toward Jenny in shock while not taking my eyes off her. They hurt my Jenny. I push through the crowd until I am next to the stage. I'm about to jump onto the stage when Jenny sees me and gestures to me not to with her hands. Her outfit is torn, and she looks frail and in pain. From her eye, which is not swollen, I see a tear travel down her face.

"These troublemakers thought they would resist us," the Red Jacket continues to speak.

The crowd screams and yells, "Don't hurt them. Some are children."

The Red Jacket paces behind the people on the stage while looking at the crowd.

"Yes, some are young, but in a few years, they will be like all the others from High Rock. Take this one," he says, grabbing Jenny by her shoulders.

As he touches her, every muscle in my body tenses up with anger. Don't touch her.

"This one killed one of my men when we entered her home. For this, we punished her," he announces to the crowd. "While I admire her spirit, we had to let her know who was in charge. We killed her parents in front of her. Even then, she resisted us and fought back. Maybe it's time for her to meet her family in the Everlife," he tells the crowd.

"No!" I scream.

"Who said no?" the Red Jacket asks, looking around. After a moment, he focuses on me. "You said no. Why? You're a Lowlander like us. You know they don't think highly of us. What is so important about this one that makes you care for her?" he inquires.

He places his face next to Jenny. "Why does this one care for you? Does she mean something to you as well?" he asks her.

Jenny looks at me with tears traveling down her face. "She does not, and I do not know," she answers.

"Well, that's settled. She doesn't know you, so what does it matter if she lives or dies?" he says.

"What should we do here? Should we save this one or reunite her with her family?" he asks the crowd.

"No!" the crowd cries. "Let her live! Let her live!"

The Red Jacket again leans and whispers something to Jenny, and I see her eyes widen for a second. A moment later, she falls to the stage floor. In the man's hand is a blade covered in her blood.

"No!" I scream, leaping onto the stage. I push the Red Jacket away from her, and I tear the ropes, freeing her hands.

"You'll be fine. You have to be," I tell her as my lips quiver, touching her face softly, trying to stop the blood with my other hand.

"I am sorry. I promised I would come back to you," she softly speaks.

"We're together like you promised," I tell her.

I feel her hand touch my face, and I hold it there. I look into her eyes. "I love you. Please don't leave me. Please don't leave me," I tell her, sobbing.

I see her head shift slightly, and I feel her arm go limp in my hand. Looking at my hand, which is covered in blood, I realize my nightmare's meaning has been revealed. I start to cry out loud, repeating, "No, no, no!"

I grab Jenny with both arms, holding her closely, sobbing. My heart is pounding in my chest from the agony. I feel a rage unlike any other building in me towards the man who took her from me. It keeps swelling, becoming almost unbearable until I scream in agony, filling the square. When I finish my scream, I realize something is different. It's like it was in the tavern, but much more intense. I think my vampire side has taken hold of me, and I want it to. All I want to do is kill the man who took my Jenny from me. I look at Jenny and place her down carefully. Standing, I turn and face the man who took her from me.

"I'm going to rip you apart, as well as anyone who tries to stop me! You took the one thing that meant more to me than anything!" I scream at him.

The man is scared and starts to back away from me. As I move toward him, one of his men tries to strike me down with his sword. As he swings, I grab his arm, stopping him. I squeeze, and I feel his bones snap, causing the sword to fall to the stage as he screams in pain. I toss him off the stage and continue toward my rage's primary target.

Unexpectedly, I feel a sharp pain in my back and front. I look down, and a blade is sticking out of my stomach. I grab the blade quickly and turn to face the person who placed it within me. He has a look of fear in his eyes as I reach behind me and pull the blade out.

"Let's see how you bleed," I tell him, grabbing him and tearing his throat out with my mouth. His blood sprays on me. When it hits me, I taste it, fueling my rage even more.

I drop him, and he falls to the stage, bleeding out. I turn to look for the person who has taken my Jenny from me and see him trying to get away through the crowd, but the crowd of people is making it hard for him. I leap off the stage, landing a few feet from him. I grab him from behind and twist him around to look at me.

"She did nothing to you. All she did was defend her family. You took her from me!" I scream at him.

The man yells for help, but no one seems to be coming to his aid.

"It looks like your friends are too scared to help you," I taunt him.

Embracing who I am ... an executioner serving a sentence of death. I bite down on his neck, piercing his skin with my teeth. I feel his life's energy flowing into me as his blood enters my mouth. As I drink from him, I feel the pain from when I was stabbed go away. I drink faster and faster. The taste is intoxicating. I can't seem to stop. I keep drinking more and more. With each pull of blood, I feel him go limp in my arms while I become stronger.

"Let go!" I hear Jenny.

I pull away and look around.

"Jenny?!" I say frantically.

Seeing her body on the stage, I drop him and return to her. As I near the stage, I hear the man trying to yell at his men, "She's a monster! She must die. Look what she has done."

I stop a few steps from the stage, hearing this. I look down and see a sword on the ground, and I pick it up. I walk back to the man who's holding his neck and on the verge of passing out. I raise my arm and swing down on him with all I have. When the sword connects, it slices down from the side of his neck, severing his hand and continuing through to his lower torso, almost splitting him in half. When this happens, a pulse of energy leaves him and disperses through the city. I turn to his followers and yell, "I will do the same to you. Go, or I will kill you all!"

The few Red Jackets that remain run away out of fear. I turn my attention back to Jenny and carefully pick her up. Her head moves to one side, and I panic, as I don't want to hurt her. I carry her off the stage.

"Can someone help me? I need a healer!" I beg you.

Everyone is backing away from me, scared.

"Why won't you help her!?" I scream.

"You're a demon!" Someone yells at me. "Stay away from me."

"Please help her. I beg," I ask everyone as they run from me frightened. My emotions are out of control. I see a temple off to the side of the square and rush over to it. I kick the door down and enter.

It's dark, and I don't see anyone.

"Is there anyone here? I need help. Is there someone here who can help? She doesn't deserve to die. Please save her!" I yell out into the dark.

I hear a voice from the darkness, "This is a temple for worship, not healing. Please leave."

"Is there a cleric or healer here that can save her?" I plead.

I look into the room's darkness and see a small woman hiding.

"Please help her. I can't live without her."

The woman walks out of the darkness towards me.

"You're not going to hurt me?" she asks.

"No, please. Can you help her?" I ask, in a panic.

"I lost most of my magic years ago. I don't think I can help, but I can see she is something special to you. Place her on the floor here," she instructs.

I place Jenny on the ground, keeping my face hidden. I don't want to frighten this person. I hold Jenny's hand, as I can't let her go. It's still warm, and I squeeze it.

She looks at Jenny's wound and places her hands over her. She starts to chant, and her hands begin to glow. The glow slowly grows, spreading over Jenny. I feel the energy emanating through the hand I am holding of Jenny's. It feels warm and soothing. The glow continues to intensify until it suddenly starts to pulse and fade until it's gone.

"I'm sorry, I don't seem to have enough magic left in me," she tells me sadly.

"Please try again," I plead with her.

She starts again. As before, her hands glow, but the glow fades even more quickly this time.

"I'm sorry, but I don't have the magic left in me to heal her. I'm truly sorry, but I can't help her."

The lady stands and, after a moment, steps away from us.

"That's it. You can't do anything else? Is there anyone else you can think of?" I ask, sobbing over Jenny.

"I'm sorry, but no. Sometimes, magic can't help, even though we want it to. Her wounds were severe, and she had already passed when you brought her here," she tells me.

I collapse on top of Jenny. My life has come crashing down on me.

~

The pain of losing her is too much for me. As I was crying, I felt myself start to feel normal again. My vampire side must have gone away. I force myself to go to the door and open it just enough so I can stick my head out. The only thing I see are the bodies of the Red Jackets that I killed earlier. I go back inside and pick up Jenny to take her home.

Walking home with Jenny in my arms, I'm almost catatonic. Walking up the path to home, I see Mother running towards us.

"What happened? You're covered in blood. Are you hurt?" she asks, in a panicked state.

"They killed her, Mother," I tell her, starting to sob.

"Who did this? What about Rox, Lindsey, and Elsa?" Mother asks, very concerned.

"The Red Jackets did this. I don't know about them. They might be safe," I reply.

"Come, come inside," Mother says warmly, holding me as we walk inside.

I place Jenny on Mother's bed and kneel on the floor, holding her hand, which has gone cold.

"She's gone. I don't know what to do, Mother. How am I to survive without her? The pain is too much for me."

"I know you are in pain, but we must ensure she can travel to the Everlife. In the morning, we will bury her next to my parents. We need to ask the gods to watch over her." Mother says, placing her hand on my shoulder.

"Gods! They took her from me. I don't want anything to do with the gods," I retort.

"I know you're upset, but the gods can protect her in the Everlife. Come be with me while I get things ready for her," she says.

"No, I can't leave her," I answer, holding onto Jenny.

I watch Mother head to the back of her room. She comes out holding white sheets with a few other items. I turn back to Jenny and touch her face.

"I am so angry. What am I to do now? How am I supposed to continue without you?" I ask her. I rest my head on her, crying.

Throughout the night, I remember everything we experienced together, from the first time I saw her to our first kiss in the barn and everything between and since.

I feel Mother place her hand on my back. "I know you don't want to do this, but we have to," she says softly.

I'm exhausted and can barely move, but I know it's time to say goodbye. I'm sure my eyes are swollen and red from crying throughout the night. I stand slowly and turn to Mother. I reach out to hug her but almost fall into her from exhaustion. Mother helps steady me.

"What do we need to do?" I ask.

"I'll prepare Jenny for her journey. Please take care of her resting place next to Grandma and Grandpa."

Walking out of the house, I head to the barn to grab a shovel. Entering the barn, I pass Smokey, who nudges me with his head.

"Not today, boy," I tell him.

I grab a shovel and head to the tree where my grandparents are buried. I clear the snow and start to dig. Every time the shovel pierces the ground, my heart aches. Each shovel of dirt feels like it weighs more than it should. Once Jenny's final resting place is ready, I place the shovel against the tree and head back to the house. Entering the house, I see Jenny wrapped in white sheets.

"I cleaned her and wrapped her," Mother tells me.

"Thank you. I know this is hard for you as well."

I walk over to Jenny and pick her up, knowing this is the last time

I will feel her in my arms as I carry her outside. Carefully placing Jenny into her final resting place, I kneel and uncover Jenny's face. "She looks like she's just sleeping," I tell Mother.

"I don't know when, but I will see you again. I promise this," I tell Jenny.

I place the sheet back over her face and stand next to Mother, taking deep breaths as I feel my throat getting tight. Once again, I am on the verge of crying.

Mother steps forward slightly and looks up to the sky.

"Please take this good and gentle soul and watch over her—"

I hear Mother's voice start to shake as she starts to cry.

"She has brought much happiness to our family, and we wish you would watch over her as she deserves your protection." As Mother says this, a breeze blows around us.

"I think they heard me," she says, looking up.

Mother picks up a handful of fresh dirt and places it on Jenny. I lean down and do the same. We both stand there looking at her and holding each other, crying. After a bit, I pick up the shovel and cover Jenny as carefully as possible. Even in death, she deserves to be treated kindly.

Mother shows me a grave marker and explains, "I made this for her from stone wood, so it will never rot. I wrapped it in colorful twine, as I know Jenny loves colorful things."

"It's lovely. Thank you," I reply while placing Jenny's grave marker.

"I'm going to stay here awhile; you don't have to stay. I will come in when I'm ready," I tell Mother.

"I'm here for you," Mother says, hugging me before heading to the house.

I stay with Jenny, unwilling to leave her. I have moments of uncontrollable sobbing, which turns to anger. As the sun hits just past midday, I hear familiar voices in the distance, "Kyra, Kyra."

I see Rox, Elsa, and Lindsey running up the pathway. I run towards them, excited to see them.

"How are you?" I ask, hugging all three of them at once. We were so worried about you.

"We escaped the city and hid in the woods but never found Jenny or her family. We can't get answers from the city guards either. Do you know anything?" Rox asks, scared.

I look at them and get a knot in my throat as I don't know how to tell him.

"I ... I don't—," I try to say.

"Why are you covered in blood? What is it? Tell me!" Rox demands.

I see Rox looking past me as his face goes white.

"No, no!" he yells, running over to Jenny's grave.

Elsa and Lindsey, in shock, hold their hands in front of their mouths.

"Jenny?" he asks, looking at me as I meet him at her grave.

"I went to find her when I saw the smoke coming from the city. The Red Jackets had already captured her. They said she fought back and even killed one of them. For this, they murdered her parents in front of her. They killed her in front of me just as I got to her. I tried to save her, but I couldn't. I'm sorry, so sorry I couldn't keep her safe. Please forgive me?" I ask, dropping to my knees next to him.

Rox places his arms around me, crying, and I wrap my arms around him, trying to comfort him as well.

CHAPTER 12

THE AFTERMATH

I've been in an emotionally numb state for the past few weeks. When I'm not messing up my chores, I spend most of my time lying in bed, holding Jenny's pillow or one of her dresses, imagining she is next to me. At night, when I try to sleep, I hope I dream of her, but most times, I wake up crying because I dream of the events that led to me losing her. Mother always rushes up to comfort me, but it does little good. When Mother asks me for details about what happened in the city, I can't give them. I tell her reliving it hurts too much. While true, I just don't want to explain what I did and how. All I felt was rage when my vampire side erupted out of me. I felt how powerful it made me, and I didn't fight it. I wanted to punish all of them for what they did. Now, I am terrified of this side of me. I don't ever want it to come to the surface again.

"Kyra, you have to get out of bed. It's almost midday, and Rox will be over anytime now," Mother orders me from below.

"Don't want to," I yell down.

"You better be ready when he arrives. Do I have to roll you out of bed?" Mother asks me with conviction.

"I don't want to see anyone." Turning over in bed while holding Jenny's pillow tightly.

I'm filled with guilt that I couldn't save Jenny; because of this, we don't have her in our lives anymore. I miss Rox, but when I see him, the guilt worsens.

"Do you think you are the only one who's hurting? Jenny would want everyone to move on and try to be happy. You know that," Mother says while making noises on purpose to get me up.

I know she is right, but it's hard to hear it. I force myself to sit up and rub my face to motivate myself to get ready. I peek at myself in the mirror. The site is pretty terrible. I look sickly because I haven't eaten much in the past few weeks. Jenny would tell me to get my act together if she saw me this way. I scratch my head, and I smell myself. I definitely need a bath. I get out of bed and grab some clean clothes.

"You win. I'm going to bathe before he gets here," I announce, stepping onto the ladder.

"That's good. I'm sure the unpleasant odors have been coming from your room."

I look at her knowingly and head to the barn. Stepping outside, the cold air hits me. It should be warmer, with planting season coming in a few weeks. Entering the barn, I fill my bathtub with water and get in. I jump up as the water is freezing. I should have brought some hot water from the house. I settle back down, dealing with the cold water. As I bathe, I see the scar from when I was stabbed by the sword. I touch it, knowing it will remind me of that day and how it was able to heal so quickly.

Getting out of the bathtub, I towel off and dress quickly. Sitting on the bathtub's edge, drying my hair, I think of when Jenny asked me about my hair and changing it. Maybe I should grow it out, as I haven't cut it in a few weeks anyway. My bangs are now falling just past my nose.

Entering the house, I join Mother at the table. "I'm sorry, Mother. I don't know how to move forward. I miss her so much."

"I understand. I felt the same when I lost my parents. However, we have to find a way, whatever it is," Mother tells me, cutting a piece of bread for me. "Please eat something. You haven't eaten much over the past few weeks, and it's showing. You look thin and a little sickly. You have to eat."

"I just don't have an appetite."

We hear a knock at the door, and Rox opens it. "Can I come in?" he asks.

"Yes, of course. Please sit with us," Mother replies.

"How are you doing?" I ask him.

"I still have moments of sadness. Having Lindsey and Mom helps a lot. How about you? You don't look that great. Are you sick?" he asks. "I wanted to give you a little space, but I had to see you," he tells me, placing a red box on the table.

"Honestly, I'm struggling. What's that?"

"High Rock was declared to be safe again. Mom and I went up the other day to get our things from the house. While we were up there, I remembered this. Jenny gave this to me the day after the Harvest Celebration and told me to hold on to it for safekeeping. She said it was a gift she wanted to give you later. I'm sure she would want you to have it now," Rox explains, pushing the box to me.

My hands reach out, shaking. "What is it?"

"I never opened it."

I pull the box closer to me and rub my hand over the top of it softly. I lift the latch and open the lid. Inside is a note in Jenny's handwriting. Below the note, I see the leather shoulder armor and pants I saw in the store window all those months ago. I pick up the note and start to read.

I saw how you looked at these and knew you would never purchase them for yourself. You deserve them, and I want to give them to you.

Sincerely,
Jenny

I place the note back in the box and close the lid. "Sorry, I need a moment," I tell both of them, getting up from the table. I walk outside to get some air and collect myself because I am on the verge of losing it. I only get a few feet from the house and stop. My eyes fill with tears thinking of her.

I feel a hand placed on my side. "Kyra," Rox says.

I turn and kneel, hugging him, not letting go. "I miss her. It hurts so much," I say.

"I know. I miss my best friend and our talks. Sometimes, we would talk all night and be exhausted the next day. Do you know how many late-night talks we had about you? If it was you that Jenny lost, wouldn't you want Jenny to be happy?" Rox asks.

"I know, I know, but it's easier said than done," I answer, starting to collect myself.

"We will get through this. We will have good days and bad days. That's why we are here for each other ... to help when needed, " Rox states as I step back from him.

"Thank you for being such a good friend. So you two talked about me a lot?" I ask, bumping him a bit, trying to lighten the mood.

Rox chuckles. "She told me about how ticklish you are."

"What?! She told you about that," I screech, reaching for him.

Rox dashes away from me, and I chase after him. I forgot how quick he is and how hard he is to catch. We both begin to laugh as I try to catch him. This is the first time I've laughed in weeks. We eventually fall to the ground, tired and winded. That burst of movement exhausted me from the weeks of not caring for myself. I toss a pebble at him lightly, which he bats away easily.

"Stop by the Dragon Tail to see Lindsey play tonight. I know she would like to see you."

"Can you stay for a bit? Maybe have a little food with Mother and me. I know it will make Mother happy to see me eat, and I'm suddenly hungry."

"I'd like that. I thought I smelled fresh bread."

We get up and head to the house, walking side by side.

Sitting cross-legged on my bed, I run my finger over the edge of the decorative accents of the box from Jenny. I open it and then place the note on the bed. I pull the shoulder armor out to examine it. It's lighter than I expected, and the craftsmanship is fantastic. Every part is adjustable to fit different body types. I place it on the bed and pull the pants out to look at them closer. I rub my hands on them and realize how soft they feel. I examine the brass accents going down the legs. I'm not ready to try either item on now. As I put them away, I notice the light catches on something at the bottom of the box. I reach in and pull out a locket. It's a silver locket with a small red jewel in the center of it. I open it and see a tiny etching of Jenny in it. I grasp the locket with both hands while closing my eyes. I put it on and hold it close to my chest.

"I miss you," I say out loud.

I finish putting the rest of the items away and place the box under my bed for safekeeping. Seeing Rox today helped me, and I want to see him and Lindsey tonight. I head downstairs and walk up behind Mother, who's reading one of her journals. I embrace her in a hug from behind.

"What was that for?"

"Thank you for being supportive and pushing me today. Spending time with you and Rox lifted my spirits. I'm going to the city to see Rox and Lindsey," I explain.

"You seem to have a bit more energy this evening. Please take your jacket. It's still cold, and I don't want you freezing. Make sure you eat something while you are there. One piece of bread does not count as a meal. Please be careful, even though the Red Jackets have been taken care of," she tells me.

I grab my jacket and head out. Mother's right, it's cold. I put my jacket on. The cold air feels good on my face as I walk. The air is crisp, and the light of the moons is casting throughout the valley. The mountain peaks are almost shining due to how the moonlight is reflecting off the snow.

Entering the city, I see a large number of guards patrolling. The streets are full of people, and tension is still in the air. As I get close to the Dragon Tail, I hear a familiar song being played. Before entering, I stand outside for a few minutes, gathering the nerve to go in. I hold the locket between my fingers, take a deep breath, and tell myself, "You can do this. She would want you to be happy."

I reach for the door to open it.

PART TWO

MOVING FORWARD

CHAPTER 13

TRYING MOVING ON

For the past few months, I've been doing better and trying to live as Jenny would want me to. My numbness began to fade, I started going out more, and my appetite returned, all of which made Mother happy. However, more recently, I felt myself slipping backward, and it's getting worse. I don't want to worry everyone, so I'm putting on a facade to make everyone think I'm doing better. The only time I feel somewhat normal is when I'm around Rox. He's the only person who can still make me laugh or smile.

Tonight is a special night for Rox and Lindsey, and I want to support them. Tonight is Lindsey's largest show ever, and they spent weeks promoting it. The Dragon Tail is the fullest I have ever seen, and everyone seems to be having a great time listening to her and her band. Luckily for me, Rox reserved a prime table near the stage for us.

"She's amazing tonight," I yell at Rox so he can hear me over the crowd.

"Yes, they are playing extremely well tonight. They were nervous when they saw how full the place was. I told them that they always play great and should not worry about the size of the crowd."

Lindsey and her band play the final note of a song and bow. Everyone claps and cheers.

"We'll be back in a bit. We need a quick break and a drink," she announces to everyone.

Lindsey jumps down from the stage and sits with us. "I'm glad you could make it, Kyra. How's it going?" she asks, kissing Rox and hugging me.

"Today is a better day, I think," I answer.

"That's good. How's your mom? Good, I hope."

"She good. She's been busy with stuff around the house and working on a new ointment to help with joint aches. I think she's using a mountain flower she read about in one of my grandmother's journals," I answer, swirling the ale in my mug.

"Do we think all this effort will pay off?" she asks Rox.

"Based on the numbers, we should pull in a nice profit. Looking around, it looks like the tavern is also doing well," he says.

Lindsey takes my mug and drinks it dry. "Thanks for the drink. Time to get back on stage. Can't let the fans down," she tells me before jumping back on stage.

I look at Rox and turn my mug upside down.

"I'll get you another one. She was thirsty, and mine was empty," he says.

I swing around as Lindsey and her band start to play again, which gets everyone clapping and dancing. As we watch, Phil from last year's harvest comes over and asks me to dance with him. I try to brush him off, but Phil can be very persistent. Giving in, I let Phil escort me to where everyone is dancing, and we start to spin around each other. When the music stops, Phil hugs me, and we all clap for the band. Lindsey and her band begin to play their next song, which is slow and more for listening than dancing.

"Good to see you, Kyra. How long has it been?" he asks.

"It's been a while. Thanks for the dance. I haven't danced—" I get quiet. Remembering the last time I danced was with Jenny.

"You alright? You look deep in thought, suddenly," he says, placing his hand on my shoulder.

I snap out of it. "Sorry, just thinking about someone."

"Can I buy you an ale or something? I'm parched," he says, gesturing to the bar.

"I would like that. Someone drank my last one on me, pointing to Lindsey."

Walking to the bar, Phil asks, "Do you plan on working the harvest this year? I'm sure John will have you back in a heartbeat. You are equal to at least three workers."

"I don't think so. I need to work on a few things."

"It's still a while away. You might feel differently by then. Cheers," Phil says, handing me an ale.

"What's his name? Ro … Rox, right? Is he working with the violinist?"

"Yes, they're also a couple."

"Lucky him. Where's your other friend? The three of you were inseparable."

Hearing him ask about Jenny causes a lump to form in my throat. I don't like talking about her because it always depresses me knowing she's gone.

"We lost Jenny in the riot," I answer woefully.

Phil lowers his head. "Shit, I'm sorry. I didn't know. I was working in the southern portion of the valley when the riot happened. When I came back, I heard about it. Those Red Jackets got what they deserved. Do you need to sit?" he asks, pointing to an open spot on a bench.

"No, I'm doing the best I can. It's been hard. Jenny and I became much more than friends; she became part of my family," I explain while wiping the corner of my eye with the back of my hand.

"I'm sorry. Sorry, I keep saying sorry. Ahh. Do you want to change the topic and have some fun? Maybe darts?" Phil asks, trying to turn things around.

I nod, and he places his arm around me as we head over to the dart area where a few of his friends are. "You all know Kyra. She needs to have fun tonight, and we will make sure she does. Standard rules? The winner has to buy the next round in the hopes the loser has a chance to win." Phil says, grabbing a set of darts and throwing the first one.

"Not bad. Your turn, Kyra," he announces.

Phil and I go back and forth for the next few games, winning and losing. We get pretty drunk as we play, which has been my norm lately. Every time I go to the city, I tend to drink too much; it helps distract me from thinking about Jenny.

Looking at the dartboard, or should I say, two dartboards that overlap each other, I ask Phil, "Which one should I aim at?"

"The middle one."

"There's no middle one; there's a left one and a right one," I clarify, laughing.

"You pick. If you get anything higher than ten, you win; anything lower, I win."

I blink a few times, hoping my vision will clear up, and it does. I throw the dart and miss the dartboard entirely. "You win," I tell him, raising my arms to celebrate his victory.

"I get to hold onto my title. It's going to be a rough morning tomorrow, though, and my wife is going to kill me for sure. I'm sorry, but I have to get home. I hope to see you soon, old friend. Think about working the harvest. I know I would like to see you there, and I'm sure John would want you back as well," he tells me while hugging me goodbye.

"I will, and take care," I answer, returning his hug.

I watch Phil walk through the tavern, trying not to bump into the tables and chairs as he leaves. Looking over, I see Rox and Lindsey at their table. They're talking and counting the money from tonight's performance.

"I might have had one too many ales with Phil," I tell them as I sit down and place my head on the table. "How did you do?"

"We did great. Between the tips and the bar cut, we earned almost a hundred and fifty silver coins. After we pay the band, we should have a nice profit," Rox says excitedly, stacking and organizing the coins.

Surprised, I raise my head, "Wow, that's a lot. You two seem to be making a lot of money lately. What do you plan on doing with it?"

"We have plans, but we still need to figure things out. Until then, we want to keep it quiet," Lindsey tells me.

"You sounded great tonight, Lindsey," I tell her.

"It looks like you had a fun night as well. Maybe too much fun?" she says, placing her hand on my head and rubbing it.

"I did. Phil is always good for a good time," I answer.

As soon as I finish talking, I feel sick to my stomach and run outside, where I projectile vomit into the alley. Leaning forward, I place my hands on my knees. I take a few deep breaths and spit to clear my mouth. I look around, wondering if anyone just saw me. I head back in and sit down with my friends again.

"You alright?" Rox asks.

"I definitely had too much tonight. I will be feeling it tomorrow."

"You mean today. It's only an hour or so before morning. Do you want to sleep at our place?" Rox asks.

"No, I don't want to intrude on you two. You should continue celebrating when you get home," I tell them, smiling.

Lindsey slaps my shoulder lightly and says, "You are too much, and I agree."

Hearing Lindsey's comment, Rox picks up his pace, gathering and securing the coins in a money purse. "Shall we go?"

Walking out of the Dragon Tail, I point to where they shouldn't walk to avoid my vomit.

"Maybe you shouldn't drink so much," Lindsey tells me.

"I know ... you're right. I need to be better," I confess.

We hug, and I watch them head down the alley. I turn and head in the opposite direction toward home. Walking through the city, I pass a few people here and there who look like they might have had a similar night as I. Arriving at the central square, I see High Rock and the lights of homes dotting the cliff face. The tram station is a few hundred feet in front of me, and a tram is entering the station. I walk toward the station so I can grab a ride up. I want to watch the sunrise from High Rock. Entering the station, it's dead quiet. I go up to the central loading platform, where only station workers and a few people are looking to get home from a late night out. Luckily enough, the blue tram is already here. I hand the attendant a copper coin and sit down by the window. As soon as I sit, I regret getting on the tram as memories of my last time in High Rock return to me.

I don't know what compelled me to come up here, but I'm standing in front of Jenny's old home. The outside of the house looks nothing like I remember. All the plants and trees that were perfectly shaped and cared for are dead or almost dead. The windows and the front door are boarded up. Seeing her home in this state really upsets me, and I run over to the door and frantically rip the boards off. When the door is free, I touch the golden *M* on it, thinking of her. I turn the door's handle and push. As the door opens, it produces a loud squeaking sound. Looking in, the house is a mess. Dust, dirt, broken glass, and papers cover the floor.

I hear birds flapping above me, so I look up. The fresco looks damaged by water leaking in from somewhere. Moving my eyes to the landing, I stop and see Jenny leaning on the rail, smiling at me. When I reach for her, she vanishes from my sight. I know it's my mind playing tricks on me, but I have been seeing her occasionally, which worries me. I don't dare go upstairs to her room, as it will be too much for me. I only want to have good memories of being in her room.

Walking down the hallway, I pass the library and see all the books are gone except for a few lying on the floor. The Red Jackets and looters did a good job robbing the house and taking what they wanted. I continue to walk through the house and into the dining room, where the doors leading to the patio are smashed. The landscaping in the back is just as dead as the front, except for the Golden Sun tree. Why did I come here? I have to get out of here. This isn't helping me at all. I walk back inside, heading towards the front door. Off to the side, I see a dark stain on the floor that I didn't notice when I came in. Walking over to it, I realize it's dried blood. Is this where her parents were killed, and they beat her? Kneeling, I touch it and start to cry, thinking of what happened to them here.

"I'm sorry. I couldn't protect her," I tell her parents.

I wipe my face to clear my tears and notice some have fallen on the stain. Rubbing my finger on one of these spots, I see the blood has become wet again, and I look at my fingertip. Seeing the blood, pulls at my other side to place it in my mouth. As the blood hits my tongue, my vision flashes, and I see Jenny's parents holding each other. They're terrified, as Red Jackets are tormenting them. Jenny is on the ground, looking at her parents. Her face is swollen and bloody. My attention goes back to her parents. One of the Red Jackets behind them draws his blade and slits their throats. I step back in horror, tripping, causing me to fall, and pulling me out of the vision. I run out of the house as fast as I can. What just happened? That was terrifying. I didn't want to see that. I didn't want to ever see that. After a few hundred feet, I started to slow my pace and eventually stopped. Did I see Jenny's parents' memories? It was more than a memory. I could feel what they were feeling. They were terrified. I could also feel their love and concern for Jenny. I now know they truly loved her.

Getting lost in those memories, I miss the first and second stops. When the tram reaches the third stop, I get up and walk out. I've never been to this level in High Rock before. The wind is blowing hard, causing my eyes to tear slightly. Thankfully, the air is not too cold. There is a bench off to my right facing out to the valley. I head over to it to watch the sunrise. I know it will be soon since the sky is already turning orange at the horizon.

Sitting there, someone asks, "May I join you and watch the sunrise?"

"If you like," I answer, looking up.

"Mr. Indrarren," I say, surprised to see him.

"You remember me. I wasn't sure if you would, Miss Everwind," he replies, sitting beside me. "What brings you up here? It's late, or should I say early. You have a long walk back home, do you not?"

"I didn't want to go home just yet."

"How are you doing? I know of the events that have transpired," he softly says.

Staring at the horizon, I see the sun starting to peek out. "I'm alright ... no, that's a lie. I'm not."

Why did I tell him how I was feeling? I barely know him. We had one interaction a while ago, which wasn't the best. How is this going to help?

"Love can be a strange thing. It can bring great happiness but also great pain and sadness. I knew you and Jenniver were more than friends the night I met you," he adds.

I face him, as this caught my attention.

"How? You just met me that evening?"

"It was not you so much, but Jenniver. I noticed the small things she did throughout the meal. From pointing out what utensils to use to how she held your hand under the table throughout our meal. I became curious about you, and you surprised me," he tells me, tapping his walking cane.

"Can I ask you something?" I ask.

"Please do."

"You seem different. Softer, in a way. I was expecting another heated discussion."

Looking up, he says, "Recent events have made me look at things differently. This city did and does need to change. The Red Jacket's methods for change were horrific and inexcusable. I hope we can learn and implement the necessary changes to live together in harmony. I started meeting with a few people who have influence within the city. I hope they will be open-minded."

I think about his previous comment as we sit there watching the sunrise. Has he ever lost anyone before? I need to know. He might be able to give me insight into how to move on.

"Have you ever lost anyone who meant more to you than anything?"

He didn't say anything immediately, but I could tell he was thinking.

"Being the age I am, I have experienced many things. One of them is the pain of losing someone, and it feels like your world has ended. I was married to the love of my life for almost a hundred years, and it was not nearly enough time. One day, she started to cough slightly. We did not think much of it at first, but it became progressively worse until she became bedridden. Nothing I or the healers did helped. Within two weeks, she was gone. I was devastated and filled with grief. I became bitter and withdrawn as everything reminded me of her. She was everything to me. She made me laugh and drove me crazy all at the same time. I finally realized that to get over her, I needed to change my routine and environment. I decided to close up my home to travel and experience the vastness of our world."

"Where did you go?"

"While the valley seems to go forever, it is just a tiny part of the Kingdom of Tailte. There is so much to see and experience. Eventually, I settled on the Southern Coast in the city of Madrina. It is a beautiful coastal city with a warm, dry climate. The surrounding waters are aqua-blue, and ships come and go all day and night. They even have skyships that dock there. While there, I met Rina, the woman you saw me with at the dinner party. She is quiet and the opposite of my first wife, but she is just as kind. She taught me to enjoy life again. Over time, we fell in love. Eventually married and came back here."

"How long have you been married to Rina?"

"Going on fifteen years now," he answers, tapping his walking cane.

"Everything reminds me of Jenny. I even see her occasionally, and then she's gone."

"Maybe you should travel like I did. It could make it easier for you to heal. At the very least, you would experience our beautiful world. Something to think about," he suggests, standing. "I should get back to Rina. We always have our morning meal to ensure we start the day together. Good morning to you, Miss Everwind. I hope you find your way again."

(In Elvin) *"Thank you,"* I reply.

I look at the morning sky, now filled with orange and red hues. I should be getting back home. Mother will be wondering where I am.

During the walk home, the effects of playing darts with Phil show themself as I empty my stomach several more times. I have to remember that playing darts with Phil is fun, but it has terrible consequences. Walking up the pathway to my house, Mother is outside feeding the chickens, and Blacky is chasing after them. I wave. "Sorry, long night."

"I guess so; you look terrible. Is that vomit on you? Clean up, get something in your stomach, and help me with the chores."

I continue to the house and go to my room, collapsing onto my bed.

A few minutes later, Mother comes into the house. "Get down here. You don't get to sleep. Your behavior over the past few weeks has been unacceptable, and it's getting worse," she yells up to me.

"Can we talk later? I'm tired and want to sleep," speaking into my pillow.

"What would she think of you being this way?!"

Hearing her say this angers me. I jump down from my room and land right in front of her.

"I don't know. She might be upset with me, but she is not here anymore to tell me," I bark at Mother.

Mother steps back from me. She seems afraid.

What am I doing? I feel terrible about what I just did. I know she is just watching out for me.

"I'm sorry … I didn't mean to scare you. I … I don't know what to do. I have been trying, but I can't get past this. I'm lost without her Mother. I see her everywhere, from the brush on our dresser to her dresses hanging on the wall. I even see flashes of her standing in front of me every once in a while. Mother, I'm broken, and I don't know how to fix myself," I tell her, crying.

"I didn't know. I thought you were doing better. We all did," Mother answers, hugging me.

I was at first, but recently, I started to slip back to how I was feeling when I first lost her. I thought it would be best for everyone if I pretended I was doing well. I'm still so angry and sad she's not here."

"What can I do to help you? I wish you had told me." Mother hugs me tightly, and I hold on to her. As we embrace each other, I remember my conversation with Mr. Indrarren.

"I think I need to leave," I answer.

Mother pulls back, looking at me, "Leave? What do you mean?"

"Someone gave me some advice, and I think I agree with it. If everything here reminds me of her, it might be the only way to get over her. I can also try to find Father to get the answers I need. His letter said to travel south."

"All your friends and family are here. When would you leave?"

"I don't know. Soon."

"I can't imagine you not being here. What am I to do without you?"

"I know you don't want to hear this, but it might be my only option. I can't keep going the way I'm going. I'm afraid of what I might do."

~

Looking over my bed, I think I have all the items I will need for my journey. At the bottom of my backpack, I place a change of clothes, including the new shirt my mother made for me. On top of the clothes, I place rations of apples and homemade travel cakes. Mother gave me one of the valley maps my grandfather made when they first came to the valley. I don't know how accurate it might be, but it's better than nothing. I secure this in an inside pocket. On the outside of the backpack, I attach a blanket.

Next, I count the coins in my coin purse. I should have enough to last a long while, having never spent any of the gold that John gave me.

"Kyra, can you come down? I want to talk to you," Mother calls up to me.

"I need a second."

I swing the backpack onto my shoulder and head down to Mother. As I descend, Mother sits at the table with her hands on Father's chest. Before I join her at the table, I place my backpack by the door for tomorrow. I can't believe that I will be leaving in the morning.

"What is it?" I ask.

"Please sit. I don't understand why leaving will help you, but I want you to find what you need to be happy again. That is the most important thing for me. Your father left these to you for a reason, and I know what they are capable of. It would be best if you took them with you to protect yourself. The brooch might be able to help you find him. Please promise me you will be careful and come home to me."

"I know you don't understand, but I must do this. I don't know how long I will be gone, but I hope not too long." I say as I lean over and hug her. "I promise. I will be back as soon as I can."

Looking at myself in the mirror, I laugh slightly. Jenny knew what she was doing when she bought those pants. I grab the brooch, pin it on, and clip Father's weapons onto my belt. I am as ready as I will ever be. Heading downstairs, I grab my backpack from where I left it by the door, but I don't see Mother.

"Mother," I yell out.

"Outside," I hear her reply.

Walking out of the house, I see Mother, Elsa, Rox, and Lindsey standing together. Seeing them all together makes my stomach turn. Since I decided to leave, we have spent almost every day together, but saying goodbye will still be hard.

"Hi, everyone," I say, trying to keep it light.

They all run over. I can see that everyone is sad, and I don't want to make things worse by crying, as I know it will cause them to cry as well. I drop my backpack and hug Lindsey.

"Thank you for being a friend. Please try to keep Rox's ego in line. It doesn't have to get any bigger than it is," I tell her.

"I will, and be safe. I hope you come back soon," she tells me with an unsteady voice.

I kneel and hug Elsa. "Please help Mother when you can. She puts up a good front and says that she's fine, but if there is anything you can do while I'm gone, I will be most grateful."

"You don't even have to ask," Elsa replies.

At this point, the knot in my throat is making it hard to talk. How am I going to get through this without crying?

"You, my friend," I start to say, getting choked up and stumbling on my words. "You ... you make sure you take care of this lovely lady next to you. You won the grand prize with her. When I return, we will have lots to talk about," I tell Rox, hugging him deeply.

"I see you're wearing the gifts from Jenny and us. I'm glad. I will miss you, my goofy friend."

I stand and look at Mother. All I can do is hug her and hold onto her tightly. "I love you."

Hugging Mother, I feel a nudge at my leg. I look down, wiping my eyes.

Picking up Blacky, I say, "Make sure you take care of Mother. She will need you to protect her."

Placing him down, I pick up my backpack.

"I love you all," I say, grabbing them for one last group hug. Walking down the path, I turn to look back one more time. I see Mother holding onto Lindsey, crying. Elsa and Rox wave to me. I have such a knot in my throat and am tearing up. I know this might be the opportunity I need to move on and find myself again. Only time will tell.

CHAPTER 14

NEW FRIENDSHIPS

Using my grandfather's map, I'm staying on the Southern Road. It looks to be the most direct way to the Great Passage, which connects the valley to the Midlands. Each day offers new majestic views. The rolling landscape is filled with forests and wildflower fields. Lakes and rivers fed by melting snow from the mountains provide me with fresh water.

Today, I came upon a quaint village by a lake. I see the lake on my grandfather's map but not the village. This village must have been settled after he drew the map. Standing on the crest of a hill, I see an open-air market. Knowing I am low on rations, I put the map away and decide to go to the market. It would be nice to have some social interaction. It has been a while since I last spoke with anyone, and I've been talking to myself more than I should.

Entering the village, I'm greeted by buildings made of timber and stone. The roofs of every building are fully covered with moss. Some of the roofs even have small flowers growing within the moss. It's quite pretty to see how nature and these buildings live together. Continuing to the center of the village where the market is, I notice a wooden statue of a woman holding a golden ball in her hand, which is raised high into the air. I look to see if I find a plaque or something that tells me who this might be, but I don't see any. Turning my attention to my original goal, I walk to the market and look for supplies. People are walking around, talking to each other about various things. Every so often, a few of them look at me and speak to the person they are next to, which makes me feel a bit uncomfortable. I don't blame them, as I am an outsider. Continuing through the market, I find a fruit vendor. Looking at what's available to buy, I see a variety of apples and pears that look delicious.

"How much?" I ask.

"Copper each, my love," answers the lady, working the cart.

"I'll take three of each," I say, handing her the coins.

I stow away the fruit in my pack but keep one to eat on the spot.

"Thanks," I say with a mouth full of apple.

"Haven't seen you before. New to the area?" she asks, organizing her fruit.

"Traveling through. Been on the road for a while," I tell her.

"Where are you traveling to? Any place in particular?"

"No particular place, just traveling south to work through a few things."

"Welcome to Lake View. We are a bit of a tight-knit community, but we're friendly. You might have noticed that some people are looking at you. Pay them no attention; they don't mean anything by it. I'm Martha."

"Kyra," I answer back.

"I wish you safe travels, and may the gods be with you," Martha warmly tells me.

"You as well."

Looking around the market, I notice a fish vendor across the way. When I get to his stand, I see dried and smoked fish hanging on hooks. This is perfect, as it will last a while.

"How much for the smoked or dried fish?" I ask.

"Smoked is five copper, and dried is three copper," he informs me.

I lean in and smell the fish. The smoked fish is more pungent than the dried fish. I will get dried fish, hoping it doesn't stink up my backpack.

"Two dried," I request.

He quickly takes down the fish and holds out his hand for payment. I drop six copper into his hand, and he hands me my purchase. I stow it away with my other supplies.

Nothing else is grabbing my attention around the market, so I decide to rest by a tree next to the water's edge. Sitting under the tree, I finish my apple and watch fishermen casting their nets into the water. This place is calm and relaxing compared to Mountain Side, where everything is crowded and busy, with people moving in every direction. I hear laughter to my left and see a group of children swimming and jumping off a tree limb extending over the water. They look like they are having a great time together. Watching them, I remember how I used to climb the tree by our home. I would hang upside down from its limbs with my legs and talk to Mother as she worked below. This always made her nervous, as she feared I would fall. After a while, she started calling me her little monkey, as I could climb almost anything. I just had a natural talent for it.

After a short rest, I get going, as it's already past midday. Walking out of the village, I see a broken cart and its owner trying to fix it. One of the wheels has fallen off, and he's struggling to get it back on. I run up to offer some help.

"Can I help?" I ask him.

He looks up at me with a defeated and tired look.

"I've never seen a wheel pin fall out of a wheel assembly. I can't get the wheel on and lift the cart simultaneously," he explains.

"No problem; I can help," I say as I grab the back of the cart and adjust my hands to ensure a good grip.

"I would be most grateful. I will lift the cart so you can—" he tries to tell me.

I didn't let him finish his thought as I lifted the cart. "Is this good?"

He's staring at me, holding the wheel and the pin.

"Do you mind? It's getting a little heavy," I tell him with a slight sense of urgency.

"Sorry." He places the wheel on the axle and inserts the pin, locking them together.

I lower the cart, and when I feel its weight sitting on the axle, I let go and slap my hands together a few times to clean them off.

"Have a good day," I say as I continue on my way.

"You too, and thank you," he shouts after me with gratitude.

I get up the road a little before I hear the cart and man come up behind me.

"Thanks again for helping. If you hadn't come by, who knows how long I would have been stranded? You saved my day. My family was expecting me a while ago," he explains.

"No worries. Glad I could help," I reply, continuing to walk.

"What's your name? I don't remember seeing you around here before."

"Kyra. I'm not from here; I'm just passing through."

"I don't have much, but I need to repay you for helping. Have you eaten today?" he asks. "I'm sure my family will welcome you for a meal."

"You don't have to. I'm glad I was able to help."

"I always pay my way. Please join me and my family for a meal," he persists.

I stop walking and look up at him. I haven't had a sit-down meal since I left home. The idea of a hot meal does sound good. I look at him closely, trying to get a read on him. Can I trust him? He's on the younger side but older than me. He may be in his mid-twenties. I can see he works hard based on his hands and tanned skin. He seems to have a kind face framed by brown hair that falls to each side. Mother has always told me to trust my gut.

"Just a meal," I state cautiously

"Maybe some conversation," he says, chuckling.

I think about the offer and go with my gut. I'm confident I could easily overpower him if he tries anything.

"A meal, and then I will be on my way," I tell him.

"Great, my home is just over the hill. My kids are going to be excited. We never have guests. Do you want to jump up here with me?"

I play it safe and jump into the back of the cart to keep my eyes on him.

He smiles before giving the horse the go-ahead. "I'm Orlan."

"Nice to meet you, Orlan."

As we make our way up the hill, I take in the views of the lake, the village, and the surrounding fields of wildflowers that cover the rolling hills. In the distance, I notice several homes with pathways leading to the village. At the crest of the hill, I see a small cottage nestled by some woods with a small brook next to it. Like the buildings in the village, the roof is covered in moss. I also see two children running around and a woman walking up from the brook with a bucket under her arm.

"Is that your home?" I ask.

"Yes, that's home with my family outside."

Pulling up to his home, Orlan is greeted by his children running up next to the cart.

"Father, what took you so long? Mother was starting to get worried," the boy says.

"A wheel fell off, but Kyra was nice to help me get it back on," Orlan answers his son. "As a thank you, I offered her a meal with us."

Pulling back on the reins, the cart comes to a stop, and I jump out. In front of me is a little girl giving me the once-over.

"Hi," I say to her.

I see Orlan smile as his wife walks up to us. I can tell she is not pleased, but will go with the situation. She is a little shorter than I, with long dark hair in a ponytail. Her blue eyes have an intensity to them. I'm pretty confident she's the one in charge of this family.

She approaches me and introduces herself, "I'm Mileena."

"I'm Kyra. I can be on my way if it is too much trouble."

"It's fine. Thank you for helping Orlan. We're having hare for dinner. Do you eat hare?"

"I'm grateful for a hot meal."

I look back at Orlan, who is holding his little girl.

"How's my sweet Iris?" he asks, hugging and kissing her. "Has Emery been playing with you nicely today?"

The little girl gives her father a big nod. She's no more than four years old. I think her brother might be a year or two older. Iris resembles a child version of her mother, and Emery looks like his father.

"Children, play over there while Father puts the cart and horse away. We will be eating shortly," Mileena tells her children.

Orlan lowers his daughter to the ground and pats her bottom softly as she runs off after her brother.

"Can I help with anything?" I ask everyone.

"You can help me with the cart and horse. We can talk before the meal," Orlan says.

I quickly walk to catch up with him as Mileena intimidates me. I am pretty sure Mother would like Mileena as she is so protective of her family.

I help Orlan put the cart and the horse away, and we sit down on a few hay bales to watch the kids play.

"I can watch them play for hours. It reminds me of when I was a child, not a care in the world. That's how I met Mileena. We used to play together as children. She grew up just over there," he tells me, pointing between two hills in the distance.

"By the way, where are you from?" he asks, continuing to watch his children.

"Up north, Mountain Side, to be exact."

"Wow, that's quite a distance away. Why are you traveling by yourself?" he asks. "Most women wouldn't do that."

Not wanting to go into too much detail, I tell him, "I needed to get away and figure some things out. Someone gave me the idea that maybe if I travel, it might help me work through things."

"Fair enough," he replies.

Looking around, I notice one of the walls has crumbled.

"What happened there?" I ask, pointing at the crumbling wall.

"It's been like that for a while. I need to rebuild it, but finding the time is hard between everything else. At least I have the first row of stones in place," he explains.

Iris runs up to me and takes my hand. "Can you play with us?"

I look at Orlan, and he nods.

"What are we playing?" I ask as Iris pulls me off my seat.

"Emery is the dragon, and we have to catch his tail. First, we find him and then pull his tail off," she says excitedly.

I smile and tell her, "Let's look for our dragon."

I start looking around with Iris to find the dragon. It doesn't take long before I see Emery hiding behind a tree.

We squat down, and I whisper, "I see the dragon. He's hiding behind that tree. Go that way, and I will go this way. We will flank him and take his tail."

Iris runs off quickly in the direction I told her to go. We surround Emery from both sides. When I get behind him, I see he has a ribbon attached to his pants. I see Iris is in position, and I give her the go-ahead. She runs in and steals the ribbon from her brother.

"We caught the dragon," she yells excitedly.

"Your turn. You be the dragon," Emery tells me.

"Yes. Please be the dragon," Iris pleads, bouncing energetically, handing me the ribbon.

"Should I be a scary dragon or a silly dragon?" I respond.

"Scary dragon!" they both shout at me in unison.

I loop the ribbon around my belt and run from them to hide. I climb up a tree and hang upside down like I used to do as a child, so they can easily see me. As I wait there, I watch both of them looking for me, but they're looking down more than up. As they move closer to me, I hear something rustling in the woods around them. They continue to move towards me, and the rustling sound is following them. I look back at the cottage and see Orlan by the house, gathering firewood. My heart is pounding as I know something is about to happen.

The children look up and yell, "We found you!"

Just as they yell, a large boar in the underbrush bursts out, rampaging toward them. When the children turn and see the boar, they scream and run as fast as they can away from it. I jump down, placing myself between them and the charging beast. Grabbing one of my weapons, I activate it and charge at the boar, tackling it to the ground. As we roll and fight each other, it's trying to gore me with its tusks. I stab it repeatedly with my weapon until it stops moving. I roll away from it and stand up, breathing heavily, looking at the children.

"You are safe now," I say, trying to comfort the children.

Orlan and Mileena rush over to us. Mileena picks up Iris, who is crying, and Orlan comforts Emery, who's holding onto his father's leg.

I ask them, shaking, "Are they hurt?"

"No, thanks to you. Are you injured?" Orlan asks.

I shake my head. "I don't think so."

Looking at my hands covered in the boar's blood, I feel my heart start to pound. I feel the monster wanting out at the sight of blood. I fight it as I don't want it to show itself. I need to get away from here.

"Come, let us all return to the house," Mileena tells everyone.

I don't move as I try to keep my other side at bay. Orlan walks over to me. "It's over; please come with us," he tells me.

I follow them carefully, keeping my distance. I feel the monster inside of me wanting to take hold. What am I going to do? I don't know what will happen if it takes hold of me. When we get to the cottage, I hesitate to enter their home.

Orlan places his hand on my shoulder to guide me into his home. "Come in; you're welcome in our home," he says.

"Iris and Emery, clean up and work on your studies in your room until I call you for the meal. We must take care of our friend," Mileena tells her children.

She walks over and hugs me. "Thank you for saving my children."

I stiffen up, afraid of what I might do. Don't hug me! Stay far away from me. I don't know if I can keep it at bay.

She instructs Orlan, "Please get me a damp towel so we can clean her up."

Looking down at my hands again, my heart pounds even harder. I now smell the blood and feel my other side about to take hold. It wants out. My hands shake more as I try to fight it and step back from them. I only get a step away before Mileena grabs my weapon so that she can wipe the blood off my hands. As she is cleaning my hands, the smell of the blood lessens, and I'm able to push my other half away. That side of me hasn't come out since I lost Jenny. Back then, I wanted it because of my anger toward the men who took her from me. Now, I don't ever want it to come out again, as it scares me.

"Thank you. You don't know how much that means to me," I tell her.

"It's the least I can do. Please sit at the table and relax. The meal will be ready shortly," Mileena tells me.

I sit down and quickly use the towel to clean my weapon so I can put it away. The smell of blood emanating from the towel attracts my other half, like a bee to a flower. I toss the towel away from me. With the scent further away, I feel better and in control of myself again.

"I'll hang the boar to prepare it for slaughter. It will make a good meal for us tomorrow. We shouldn't waste it," Orlan informs us as he walks outside.

Mileena is busy preparing our meal. I take a moment to look around their home, which is similar to mine. There is one large main room with a fireplace in the middle for cooking and heating. I'm sitting at what I think is their prep area and main eating table. I also see a small desk under a window and a wash area in another corner. I see Iris and Emery peeking from a doorway as I look over to the two rooms at the back of their home. That must be their bedroom; I'm guessing the other one is Orlan and Mileena's.

"I can help. I know how to set a table." I turn my attention to Mileena.

"No, please sit. I need a minute, then I plan to sit with you," she answers, placing the dinnerware on the table. She then sits next to me.

"I'm so grateful for what you did. My children are my life. Why would you put yourself in such danger? That animal could have easily killed you," She says, looking at me.

"I don't know, I just reacted," I answer, rubbing my locket between my thumb and forefinger.

Mileena takes my free hand. "Is everything alright?" she asks, showing concern.

Looking at her, I answer, "I think so. I'm not hurt if that's what you mean."

She reaches for a pitcher on the table, pours a large glass of light pink liquid, and hands it to me.

"I think you might need this. I know I do."

I take the glass and take a sip. It's a fruity wine, and it's delicious. I quickly start gulping it down, spilling some out of the sides of my mouth. Placing the glass on the table, I look up at Mileena as she stares at me with wide eyes.

"I guess I needed that," I say with a chuckle.

"I guess so," she says.

"Mommy, can we come out?" I hear Iris ask from across the room.

"Yes, but please don't bother our guest. She still seems a little shaken," she tells them.

Emery and Iris come running from their room and sit across from me.

Jokingly, I say to the children, "Some game of catch the dragon."

Orlan enters the house and announces, "The boar is taken care of. It's a big one. Once it's smoked and dried, it will give us meat for a while. Kyra, I brought your backpack in with me. I'll leave it right here." As he sits at the table with us, he pours himself a large glass of wine. "What a day."

Mileena places a platter of roasted hare and vegetables on the table. It smells and looks amazing. Wisps of steam come off the plate, and I can smell the spices she used. My mouth starts watering, and I think about how it will taste.

Mileena sits beside me, "Please eat; you've earned it."

Even though I could eat that whole hare myself, I take a few vegetables to my plate as I don't want to take too much. Orlan looks at me, rips off one of the hare's legs, and places it on my plate. "Please eat."

I give the serving fork to Orlan, and he serves his family. When everyone has something to eat, we all start to eat quietly together. The hare is seasoned well, and the roasted vegetables are just as good. I don't recognize the seasonings, but I like them.

"What's the crest on your brooch?" Orlan asks.

"It's my father's crest," I answer.

The children lean over to look at it. I take it off to show them. Mileena offers me a refill, and I gladly hold out my glass.

"Is your family of noble descent?" he asks.

"No, far from it. I grew up in a small house outside Mountain Side," I reply. "The food is delicious. Thank you again. I've been living off the land and buying things here and there when I can. Otherwise, I have been eating travel cakes."

"Travel cakes? I like cake," Emery states.

I look at him. "This is not the cake you are thinking of. They are made of flour, fat, and some salt. They are hard and have no taste, but can fill a belly when needed. My mother made me a bunch of them before I left. You can try one if you like. I have them in my bag."

"Maybe later, finish your meal," Mileena tells her son.

"You're not missing anything. Trust me," I tell Emery.

"Where do you plan to go next?" Mileena asks.

"I don't have a plan besides heading south toward the passage. How far is it from here?" I ask them.

"The Great Passage is about a week's ride from here. On foot, maybe two weeks, depending on how fast you travel. You plan on leaving the valley?" Orlan inquires.

"It's one of the reasons I'm traveling. I was told of things outside the valley that I want to experience and find myself again, and maybe someone else."

"How can you find yourself?" Emery asks.

I smile a little; this would seem odd to a child.

"How can I explain this? Have you ever been so sad or upset that you didn't feel like your normal self?" I ask him.

I see Emery thinking. After a few moments, he answers, "Last year, our dog died, and it made me very sad. I didn't want to play or do much for a few days, but Iris, Mommy, and Daddy helped me feel better."

"I lost someone that I loved very deeply, too, and I am still feeling sad because she's no longer with me. As I travel, I hope to find things that make me happy, which might lead to finding happiness again. At least that's the plan."

"Is it working?" Iris asks.

I haven't thought about how I have been feeling lately. All I know is that today is the first day I haven't felt lonely, and I have smiled more today than I have in weeks. "You know, I might have found a little happiness … today, to be exact," I say to Iris.

"It's me. Mommy tells me that I make everyone smile," Iris says with a big smile.

A smirk comes across my face, and I look at Mileena.

"It's true, she makes everyone smile," confirms Mileena.

Iris gets up from the table and sits on Orlan's lap while resting her head against his chest. "Daddy, can you play for us tonight?"

Orlan rubs the top of Iris's head. "When we're done with our meal, I'll play."

How he interacts with her reminds me of how my Mother cared

for me when I was little. I was more like Emery than Iris, but Mother always had a lap for me to sit on and was ready to hug me any time.

"I hope you like music. It's how we spend many an evening," Orlan says.

"I would like to hear some music. I have a friend who plays back home," I tell everyone.

Mileena motions to see if I am done with my meal before taking my plate.

"I am, thank you," I tell her. "How can I help to get ready for the music?"

"We just have to move the table to the side of the room so the kids can dance while I play. It takes Mileena and me a few hard pushes to move it," Orlan informs me.

"I got this. Where do you want it?" I ask.

Orlan points to where the table should be moved. "It's pretty heavy and doesn't slide easily on the dirt floor. We can do it together," he says.

I grab the table's edges with both hands and lift it. Holding it in front of me, I move it to the location where I was just shown. I turn back to Orlan. "Good?" I ask.

Everyone is looking at me, but Orlan adds. "That explains the cart and the boar. How strong are you?"

"Pretty strong," I tell them, smiling.

The children move the chairs out of the way so that there's an open space in front of the fireplace. Iris runs to a corner, grabs a lute, and brings it to Orlan.

"Play the fun song. I want to twirl," Iris requests, brimming with energy.

"Alright. Ready?" he asks his daughter.

Orlan starts to strum the strings and moves his hands up and down the neck of the lute, making a fun and cheerful sound. Iris begins to twirl and dance. Her brother does the same. Watching them dance as the fire's light casts on them, I see how happy they are. Mileena joins in by clapping her hands to the beat. She starts to speed up her clapping, which causes the children to twirl faster and faster until both children fall on the ground laughing as the song ends.

Iris gets up and pulls me to the open area. "Dance with me."

"I don't know if I can dance like you; all that twirling might make me sick."

"Show me how you dance?" she asks.

I think back to dancing with Jenny and how she taught me.

"We need music with a beat like this." I start clapping my hands together to give Orlan the beat. He quickly begins to play something that we can dance to.

"Watch me, and then you do the same but in reverse," I tell Iris.

I bow to Iris and turn in a circle. Once around, I raise my hands and clap above my head. "Your turn, but in the opposite direction."

I watch Iris mimic what I did and see her thinking about each move. I realize that's what I must have looked like when Jenny taught me this dance. When she finishes the last move, I walk around her. Once facing her again, I repeat the initial moves.

"Walk around me and do the same," I tell her.

I grab her brother and help him learn the dance as well. In no time, both of them are dancing together. I step away to watch them, feeling like I accomplished something.

Orlan plays song after song, and the children dance, adding new moves to what I taught them. They even occasionally pull their mother and me in to dance with them. As the last song ends, I look out the window and see it's dark outside.

I should be going. I need to find a spot to rest for the night.

"Thank you for the time with your family. Do you know if there is an Inn or a place where I can rest for the night? I can pay," I say.

Orlan stands, and Mileena walks over to me. "There's an Inn in the village, but you are welcome to stay with us tonight. You can take one of the children's beds. They can sleep together, as they do that every once in a while anyway."

"No, I can't do that. I don't want to burden you. You have been so kind to me already. It's no trouble for me to walk back to the village," I answer.

"You are no burden. We owe you more than a meal and some music," Mileena insists.

Iris runs up to me. "Stay, please! You can sleep in my bed. I have a teddy bear you can use to make you feel safe." Her eyes are filled with conviction. I'm pretty sure those brown eyes get her everything she wants.

"Alright, just for tonight. Then I have to get going in the morning," I tell her.

I look at my hosts and ask, "Does she always get her way?"

"Pretty much. She's also good at playing the two of us against each other," Mileena shares.

"Come on, you two, time for bed. It's late," Mileena tells Iris and Emery.

Emery and Iris walk over to hug their parents goodnight.

As they walk by me, Emery tells me goodnight. Iris motions me down to her. I kneel, and she hugs me as well. I hug her back. This little girl is so sweet.

They walk to their room, and I hear them jump onto a bed.

"Don't sprawl like last time. Keep to your side." I hear Emery tell Iris.

"Want to help me move this back?" Orlan asks, holding one side of the table. I quickly grab the other side of the table, and we place it back where it was earlier. I grab two seats and swing them under the table; he does the same with the rest of the chairs and sits down.

"Please sit," he says.

"It seems our daughter has taken a real liking to you. From what you said earlier, aside from the boar attack, it sounded like you had a good day today," he says, pouring three glasses of wine. "Come sit with us, my love," he calls to Mileena, who is cleaning up the kitchen.

Mileena sits down next to Orlan, and we toast to each other.

"To be honest, today has been one of the best days I have had in a long time," I answer before sipping the wine. "By the way, this wine is delicious."

"Thank you. I make it out back. We sell it to the inn in the village. That's why Orlan was there today," Mileena tells me.

We sit for a while longer, drinking wine and enjoying conversation with each other. Eventually, we all decide it's time to go to sleep.

I walk to the back room and see Emery and Iris sleeping in a bed together. Emery is on his side, and Iris is on her back, arms and legs spread out and draped over her brother. I chuckle at this site. I sit on the empty bed, undo my shoulder armor, take off my wrist guards, and finally, my boots. When the air hits my bare feet, it feels incredible. I wiggle my toes for a moment. As I lie down, I feel a lump under me. I sit up, pull out Iris's teddy bear, and place it next to my items. It's a small bed, but it's better than the ground, which has been my bed lately. I adjust myself till I feel comfortable and close my eyes. I feel myself about to fall asleep when someone crawls into bed with me. I open my eyes, and it's Iris. She snuggles in next to me with her teddy bear and seems to fall asleep quickly. What should I do? Should I take her back to Emery's bed? I don't want to wake her. Ultimately, I wrap my arm around her and close my eyes.

I wake up to the sounds of Iris running around the house. Sitting up, I stretch. I haven't slept that soundly since leaving home. Having a bed to sleep in is so much better than the ground. As I lower my arms, Iris slams into me, hugging me.

"Morning, Kyra," she tells me.

"Morning," I reply, hugging her back.

"Looks like you had a visitor last night. When we woke up, we went to check on everyone, and she was sound asleep next to you," Mileena tells me.

Feeling awkward, I explain, "She climbed into bed with me as I was about to fall asleep. I didn't know what to do so—."

"It's fine. She trusts you," Mileena reassures me.

Not wanting to overstay my welcome, I start gathering my things up.

"I should be heading out. Is there a wash basin I can use to freshen up before I leave? It's been a while."

Mileena points to the corner where I saw the wash area from yesterday.

"Where's Orlan and Emery?" I ask as I walk to the wash area.

"He's working on the wall, and Emery is with him. They won't be in for a while, so you will not have to worry about them seeing you as you wash," Mileena informs me.

I take my shirt off to wash myself. While washing, I look up, and Iris is standing in front of me.

"You look like mommy, but different, why?" she asks me.

I'm not fully awake, and this girl asks me why I look different from her mom. "I'm sorry, I don't understand," I say.

Iris points to my arms and stomach.

Realizing what she's talking about, I smile. "Growing up, I had a lot of hard chores that made me strong, like chopping wood and clearing the fields. Would you believe I was skinny when I was your age, almost twig-like? If you help your mom and dad with chores, you might get muscles like mine," I tell Iris.

Mileena is smiling as she watches us interact.

I rub Iris's head. "Go find your brother and play."

Iris runs outside, and I finish washing up quickly, as I don't know when the boys will be coming in.

"Staying for breakfast?" Mileena asks.

"That would be nice. It smells good. What is it?"

"Boar," she says, smiling at me.

"I feel out of place, not helping. Is there anything I can help with?" I ask.

"No, I'm good. Maybe Orlan can use your help. Tell him the food will be ready shortly," she says, continuing to prepare the meal.

When I get outside, Orlan is lifting a stone and is about to place it within the wall.

"Let me help," I announce, running over.

I hold the stone in place so he can grab some mortar to secure it.

"Thanks. Having an extra set of hands helps. At this rate, this will take weeks to fix," he tells me.

"How long have you been working on this?" I ask.

"Few weeks. It's slow going since it's just me," he answers.

Looking over the crumbled wall, I realize that I can help him. I've fixed a portion of our house's wall, and this one should be no different.

"I can help you, and if we work together, we can get this done in a few days," I say.

Orlan turns to me. "What about heading out? Don't you need to get going?" he asks.

"I have time; I'm in no hurry. Let me help you. You can use the extra set of hands, and I am strong enough to make things easier. What do you say?" I extend my hand out for a shake.

"Sounds good." He agrees, shaking my hand.

"Mileena wanted me to tell you the morning meal will be ready soon," I say.

"I'm starving, and let's let everyone know you'll be staying a few extra days. I know someone who will be excited," Orlan says while we walk back to the cottage together.

CHAPTER 15
THE FESTIVAL

"Got it?" I ask.

"Yes, that's perfect," he answers.

"Do you two want a drink and something to eat?" Mileena shouts over to us.

"Please. The sun is beating down on us today," I answer.

Orlan jumps down from the ladder and greets Mileena. "How's my love today?"

"Kids have been a handful. They are full of energy because they are excited about later," she answers.

Mileena is about to hand me a glass of water when I notice Emery running out of the cottage with Iris chasing him.

"Those are not yours to play with. You'll get in trouble," Iris yells at Emery.

Looking at Emery, I see he has my weapons in his hands. I dash over so that I am right in front of him, which causes him to run straight into me, knocking him to the ground.

I put my hand out, waving my fingers toward me. "Give those to me. You might get hurt," I tell him.

"I just wanted to play with them," he says.

Mileena stampers over and picks Emery up off the ground while handing me my weapons.

"That does it. You're coming with me," she angrily tells him.

Feeling very out of place, I look up at Iris.

"What's going to happen?" I ask Iris.

"Mommy is going to talk to him and give him a punishment," she says.

"Ahhh. I've gotten a few of those growing up. Let's sit down with your dad."

Iris takes my hand as we walk back over to join Orlan, who has been watching the situation unfold while enjoying his sandwich.

"Emery is getting in trouble with Mommy," Iris tells Orlan.

"I saw," he answers.

Sitting on a hay bale, Iris jumps into my lap and grabs half of my sandwich. "Mmm ... good."

"Did you just take half of my sandwich?" I ask.

Iris looks at me with a devilish look as she chews. She jumps off my lap, grabs the other half of my sandwich, and runs away laughing.

"Come back here, you little thief," I yell at her playfully.

I chase her around the yard, trying to get the remainder of my sandwich back. The whole time, we are laughing. This little girl is so quick and nimble. She reminds me of Rox. I eventually catch her, pick her up, and swing her around playfully.

"I got you, you little thief."

I place her down, and she hands me back half the sandwich.

"You earned it," she tells me.

"Iris, come inside and let them be," I hear Mileena say by the door.

Iris heads inside, eating half of my sandwich. I walk back to Orlan, who's smiling at me.

"She's gotten to you," he says.

"What do you mean? We were playing with each other," I answer.

"There's more than just playing happening there. Even I can see it. I'm surprised you don't," he replies.

I look at Orlan, as I don't understand his last comment.

"What do you mean?" I ask.

"Iris makes you happy. I've noticed every time you are with her, you're smiling or laughing. I guess she has been good for you," he tells me.

Sitting there digesting what he just said, I realize I have felt more like my old self over the past few days. I chuckle a little and look at him.

"I guess so. Iris might have been the medicine I needed," I answer.

Looking down at my weapons, I say, "I should practice with these. A few days ago, against the boar, was the only time I've used them, and not correctly. I need to figure out how to use them properly."

"You don't know how to use them?" Orlan asks.

"Not really."

I grab them and walk toward a large tree until it is about twenty feet from me. I activate the blades and throw one straight at the tree. It bounces off. I throw the second one, and I miss my target completely. Behind me, I hear Orlan chuckling.

"Stop laughing," I say, embarrassed.

I retrieve them to try again. Again, I fail to get either of them to stick into the tree. What am I doing wrong? I should be able to throw them like throwing knives.

"You're terrible."

"I'm trying. I bet you couldn't do any better."

"Try throwing them sideways. They remind me of a boomerang," Orlan suggests.

I look down at them. He's right; they have that shape. I pivot my arm slightly to throw it sideways. When I do this, it feels more natural than how I was throwing it before. I wind up and launch it, and it hits the tree, sticking in. I jump excitedly.

"Better, but you threw it oddly. Try an overhand throw and twist your body simultaneously," Orlan suggests.

I look back at him, squinting my eyes. I will try his way, as he was right last time. I flip my hand over and look at my target. I wind up and launch it at the tree. It slices through the air, humming, although it misses the tree. A second later, I hear the humming sound getting louder as the weapon comes right back at me. Not knowing what to do, I hit the ground to avoid being hit by it. I get back up and see Orlan wide-eyed. My weapon is just past his head, stuck in a bale of hay.

"Shit! Sorry! Are you alright?" I ask.

"Maybe you should put those away for now. I want to keep my head."

"I will. I think you're right about how to throw them. It sliced through the air. Did you hear the sound it made?" I ask, pulling it out of the hay.

"I did hear the sound, especially when it whizzed by my head. Come on, we are getting close to finishing this wall. We can play later."

Placing the last stone, Orlan secures it with mortar, and we slap our hands together in celebration.

"I'm so glad it's done. We did, in a few days, which would have taken me weeks. Thank you for staying and helping," he exclaims.

Standing on the ladder, I wipe the sweat off my brow. I jump down, grab our bucket of drinking water, and pour it over my head. "That feels amazing."

Orlan looks at me and then turns his head, looking away.

"What? Do I have something on me?" I ask.

"No, but your shirt is wet, and I'm trying to be a proper gentleman," he states nervously.

"What?" I look down and see what he means.

"Sorry!" I exclaim, crossing my arms over my chest as my face turns red.

Iris, Emery, and Mileena emerge from the cottage and walk over to us. Mileena is wearing a bright red skirt with a cream top and holding a change of clothes. The children are also dressed in nice outfits.

"Daddy, can we go to the festival now? It will be dark soon, and we want to see the lanterns being lit," Emery says.

"Why are you all wet?" Iris asks.

"I was hot, so I dumped water over my head. Did Emery say festival?"

Mileena explains, "There's a festival in the village to celebrate the growing season. Everyone looks forward to it each year, which is part of the reason the children have been hyper today."

"We were so focused on finishing the wall, I almost forgot about the festival. Come with us; you will have a nice time. We have to clean up first." Orlan says with urgency as he takes the change of clothes Mileena had been holding for him.

"Kyra, please come. We can dance and wrap the giant pole with ribbons," Iris requests.

"That does sound fun. I have to wash up and change quickly," I tell them as I turn around to run inside. After washing up, I dump my backpack on the bed and put together an outfit, including the shirt Mother made me. It seems like the right time to wear it. It doesn't take me long to get ready, and I run out to rejoin everyone else.

Orlan has already changed and has the horse and cart ready. I didn't think I was that long, but maybe I was. The kids are in the back of the cart already, and Mileena is sitting next to Orlan.

"Come on! Hurry up!" Iris yells at me.

I run over and jump in the back with the children. Orlan gives the horse the go-ahead, and we're off.

"Tell me about this festival. What is there to do?" I ask everyone.

"Throughout the village, paper lanterns are hung from the trees and buildings. When night starts to fall, we light the lanterns and release them into the air. The lanterns symbolize the sun's light and warmth, which nourish the land and enable our crops to grow. There's also music, food, drinking, and games for everyone," Mileena explains.

"Will you dance with me?" Iris asks.

"Yes, I will. How can I say no to you?" I reply, rubbing her head.

As we approach the village, it looks like everyone from the area is already at the festival. Before Orlan can stop the cart, Emery jumps out and runs into the village.

"Stay close, and come when I call for you," Mileena yells after Emery.

I jump out, pick up Iris, and place her on the ground. Looking around, I see lanterns hanging everywhere. Orlan and Mileena take Iris's hand, and we walk in together. Music is playing, and people are laughing. It reminds me of the Harvest Celebration back home, but much more quaint. As we enter the village center, I notice long tables where everyone can gather. Many of the vendors from the market are giving out treats. Off to the side, there's a giant pole with colorful ribbons attached to the top. People are dancing around it while holding a ribbon in their hands. As they dance, the ribbon wraps around the pole.

I lean down. "Is this the dancing you wanted to do with me?" I ask Iris, pointing to the pole.

She nods a few times at me.

Suddenly, we hear cheering and thumping sounds to the right of us. Looking over, I see a large crowd of people watching something. "What's going on over there?" I ask.

"That's the stone throw," Orlan answers. "Come on, let's check it out."

"You two have fun with your rocks. Iris and I will find a treat to eat," Mileena tells us.

Reaching the stone throw contest, I see a rather large man with dark hair and a beard holding a sizable stone in his arms. He runs up to the throw line and launches it as far as he can. It thumps when it hits the ground, and everyone cheers for him.

"Is the goal to throw it the furthest possible?" I ask.

"Yes, it's a pretty easy game, but very competitive. Bets are placed on each throw. How far do you think you could throw it?" Orlan asks.

"I don't know, at least that far, but I don't know how heavy the stone is. Not all stones weigh the same."

"Orlan, who's your friend?" I hear.

I turn and see the man who just threw the stone.

"Want to help me make a little money?" Orlan asks me quietly. "Play along."

Orlan turns to the man approaching us and says, "Zurth. This is Kyra. She has been staying with us and helping me fix the wall you promised to help me with."

"Did she. Lucky for me. I should buy you a drink for getting me out of that project," he tells me.

"If you like," I answer.

"That last throw wasn't your best. Getting old, are we? I bet Kyra can beat you," Orlan eggs him on.

Zurth looks at Orlan and then at me before he laughs out loud. "Do you really think she can beat old Zurth?"

"Ten silver she can," Orlan counters quickly.

"I am happy to take your money. Let's get this over with," Zurth waves at me to join him.

"You can beat him, right? If I lose, Mileena will not be too happy," Orlan tells me.

"No pressure, thanks," I say to him as I walk into the competition area.

Zurth picks up a stone. "It's simple: Run up to the line and throw it as hard as you can; whoever throws it the furthest wins. Since I'm holding one, I will throw first."

I nod and watch. Zurth runs up the line and throws the stone in the air. It travels a good way, maybe twenty feet or more. The crowd cheers and claps for him.

"Your turn," he tells me.

I pick up one of the stones. I look up, and Zurth has a confused look on his face. I bet he thought I would have trouble picking it up. I run up to the line and throw it as hard as I can. As I watch the stone moving through the air, everything seems to slow down. I hear the crowd cheer when it lands far past Zurth's throw. I look over at the crowd cheering, and for a second, I see Jenny among them.

"That was great!" Orlan says, running up to me.

I try to look around him to get another look at Jenny, but I don't see her anymore. My mind must be playing tricks on me again.

"What are you looking for?" Orlan asks, turning to look over his shoulder.

"I thought I saw someone, but it's impossible," I answer.

Zurth walks up to us and hands Orlan his payment. "I would have never expected you to do that. What's your name again, strong lady?"

"Kyra, Kyra Everwind," I answer.

"Come on, I owe you a drink," Orlan says, tapping his heavier coin purse.

Walking back to the center of the village, I think about why I saw Jenny. At home, I thought it was due to my state of mind. I have been feeling better and even more so since I met Orlan and his family. My mind is in better shape, so it can't be that.

"Kyra." I look down and see Iris; her face is covered in chocolate and something else.

"Look at you. It must be pretty tasty if you look like that," I tell the messy little girl.

"Chocolate-covered cookies. She hasn't figured out how to eat them without getting covered in chocolate yet," Mileena informs me. Turning to Orlan, she asks him, "How much did you lose?"

I look at her and then Orlan. "We won."

"Really?! He never wins. How much?" she asks.

Orlan pats his coin purse. "Ten Silver."

Mileena quickly takes the purse. "I'm keeping this safe."

"How will I buy things if you have my money?"

Mileena looks at Orlan, and I lean over. "You might want not to push this. I've seen that look before, and it never ends well for you."

"Good call," he confirms with me.

I turn my focus to the chocolate monster next to me. I wipe my finger on her face and taste it. "Mmmm. I didn't know you tasted so good."

Iris giggles and starts to wiggle her very sticky fingers at me.

"Umm, stay away from me with those. You will get me all sticky, and I don't like to be sticky," I tell her.

She starts to run toward me with her contagious laugh. I run around a nearby table to get away from her. We do a few laps around the table until I turn and pick her up.

"Gotch you." I'm holding her away from me while she giggles and wiggles in my arms.

"Hello there again," I hear a voice directed towards me.

I turn to see Martha, who sold me fruit when I first arrived in Lake Shore. "Hi. One second, let me place this sticky monster down. Ask your mom to clean you up."

Iris walks over to Mileena, who starts to wipe her face and hands.

"Stuck around," Martha says.

"Yes, but I will be heading out tomorrow."

"How do you know Iris and her family?"

"The day you met me, as I was leaving the village, I came across Orlan, who was having trouble with his cart. After helping him fix it, he offered me a hot meal as a thank you. One thing led to another and I've been staying with them since," I explain.

"I guess you visited at the right time then. I hope you enjoy the festival," she says.

"I hope you enjoy the festival as well," I reply.

"We got all of us something to eat and drink," Orlan tells me as they pass by. "Come join us."

"Go eat and enjoy yourself. I am glad you can enjoy our festival," Martha tells me.

"Thanks. It was nice seeing you again. Take care."

I join Orlan and Mileena at a table. In front of me is a plate of steaming hot sausages and a few potatoes. I pick up one of the sausages with my fingers. It's hot. I take a bite and chew carefully, trying not to burn my mouth. The seasonings and texture are so different from what I'm familiar with. "What's the seasoning in these sausages? It's sweet but also herby. I think you use it in your cooking as well?" I ask Mileena.

"That's Golden Stalk. It's a wild plant that grows in this area. We cook with the berries and leaves. The berries are very tart when fresh, but when you dry them, they become sweet. That's what you're tasting in the sausage. It's good, right?"

Taking a second bite of my food, I smile at her and nod. As we eat, I realize Iris is no longer around us. I look right, left, and then under the table, as I wouldn't put that past her to hide there.

"She's over there with the other kids," Orlan tells me.

I spin around and see Iris and Emery playing and laughing with several children.

"I overheard some of your conversation with Martha. You plan on leaving tomorrow?" Mileena asks.

Turning back to Mileena, "Yes, now that the stable wall is finished, I should be on my way."

"We are going to miss you, and I am pretty sure there is someone who is going to take it pretty hard," Orlan tells me, looking out at the kids.

"I'm going to miss you all. Your kindness has meant so much to me. The time I've spent with you has helped me feel like my old self. I feel I'm in a better place because of you all."

Raising my mug, "To good fortune and friends," I toast them.

Mileena and Orlan crash their mugs into mine. "To good fortune and friends."

While eating our food and reminiscing about our time together, I notice people lighting the lanterns. As each one is lit, the festival is filled with a warmer and warmer glow. A sense of happiness fills the air as everyone looks upon them.

"Pretty special seeing them all lit, don't you think?" Mileena asks.

"Yes, it's pretty amazing. I love how they cast their light over everything," I answer.

"Wait till we release them," Orlan says.

We are all standing in the center of the village, each holding a lit lantern. One of the village elders holds their lantern high over his head and proclaims, "We offer this small token of warmth and light in the hopes of a fruitful growing season." As he looks up, he releases his lantern. His lantern floats higher and higher from the small fire that warms the air within it.

Everyone else releases theirs, so I let go of mine and watch it join the rest. This moment feels magical, watching all the lanterns glowing warmly and rising in the night sky. Looking at Mileena and Orlan, I see them holding each other and watching the lanterns rise above us. Within a few moments, they catch the wind and travel over the lake, and we can see their reflections in the lake water. Some children run after them but stop at the water's edge. Iris and Emery don't move as they look exhausted from all the activities they have participated in, and the sugar has worn off.

"That was special; thank you for sharing this with me," I say.

"Glad you enjoyed it. Shall we get home? These little ones look wiped out," Mileena says.

Walking to our cart, Emery and Iris can barely keep their eyes open. They keep rubbing their eyes, showing how tired they are.

Suddenly, Iris says, "It looks like your jewelry."

I turn to Iris. "What looks like my jewelry?"

Iris points to a lantern hanging on a building next to us. I walk up to it and see a painted wolf with moons that match my brooch. It's not a perfect match, but it's close. I step back and see the building where the lantern hangs. It's a spice shop.

"Go in. We'll wait out here," Mileena says.

I walk into the shop and see rows of open bowls filled with spices. The smell of all the spices is almost burning my nose.

"Is there anyone here?" I ask.

"One second," I hear from the back of the shop.

A moment later, a woman about my mother's age walks up to me. "How can I help you? Looking for a particular spice?" she asks.

"I noticed your lantern out front."

"It's been in my family for years. It's not for sale if that's what you're asking. Everyone wants to buy it, but I can't sell it."

"I'm not interested in buying it, but could you tell me about the painted design on it?"

"My mother made it when she was young. Why do you ask?"

"The wolf and moons match my father's crest. Is your mother here? Could I talk to her?"

The woman lowers her head slightly and then straightens up. "I'm sorry, but my mother passed a few years back. I don't know much about the lantern except that she said a man who wore a pin with a wolf and the moons helped her. To honor him, she made the lantern. Do you think it's your father's crest?"

"It could be, but I'm not sure."

"Is there anything else I can help you with? Maybe some spices or elixirs?"

"No, thank you." I nod and turn around to rejoin my friends.

Walking out, I look at the lantern again. Is this one of the clues Father said he would leave behind for me to follow? It has to be his crest. Her mother made the lantern, not him, but maybe it's a start. If so, he was here at some point, even before he met Mother.

I walk over, and Emery is leaning on his mom asleep. Iris is doing the same with Orlan.

"Did you find anything out?" Orlan asks.

"It could be my father's crest on the lantern. She said her mother made it based on what she remembered of a pin worn by a man who helped her."

"Well, it's something, right?" Mileena says.

"I guess. I was hoping for more. Perhaps a location or something to point me in the right direction. This searching for him seems like a game that might lead to disappointment. Shall we get going? I could use some sleep myself. I have a long day of travel tomorrow," I tell them.

Everyone, including me, doesn't have a happy expression. I lean down and give Emery a fist bump to say goodbye. "Protect your sister. That's what big brothers do."

He nods.

Looking at Iris, I can tell she's pretty upset. She's leaning into Mileena's leg, pouting. I go to my knees so we can look at each other eye to eye.

"What's with that face?" I ask her.

"Do you have to go?" she mumbles.

"I do, I'm sorry. I will visit you on my way home since I have to come back this way," I tell her.

"When?" she asks.

"I don't know. But I promise to visit you and your family when I return this way," I say, trying to comfort her.

"How do I know you will keep your promise?" she asks.

"I always keep my promises," I answer, touching her cheek.

She doesn't believe me. How am I going to convince her and make her feel better? I notice the bracelet from Jenny and take it off. "See this bracelet. It's very important to me. It was given to me by someone whom I love greatly. Can you protect it for me while I'm gone? You can give it back when I see you again."

Iris takes the bracelet from me and hugs me. "You have to come back. You promised."

I get up and extend my hand to Orlan. "Thanks for everything."

"Get that hand out of here. Be safe, and good luck." He leans in and hugs me.

I turn to Mileena.

"I packed up a few things for you along the way: some dried meat, fruit, and a few other things. Please visit us if you are in our area again," she tells me, handing me the package.

"Thank you," I reply while hugging her.

I stow away the supplies in my backpack and swing it onto my shoulders.

"Goodbye, and thank you all again for everything," I say, holding back my emotions.

As I turn and walk away, I hear Iris yelling as she runs towards me. "Stay with us!"

I turn and kneel quickly, resting my hands on her shoulders. Mileena is walking towards us, but I put my hand out to let Mileena know I will take care of this.

"I have to go. It makes me sad too, but I have to," I explain to her.

"Why, we have so much fun together," she tries telling me between sobs.

"You are so special, you know that. You know how I know this?" I ask her.

Iris shakes her head, wiping her nose and eyes.

"Because of you and your family, I feel a little more like my old self than I have in a long time. Before meeting you, I was sad a lot, but now I am not so sad. You must have been my happy medicine, but I must leave. I still need to do things and get even happier. Go to your mom," I tell her.

I watch Iris slowly walk back to her mom. Mileena picks her up in her arms. I look at my new friends for a moment and then turn to continue my journey.

CHAPTER 16

THE SEARCH CONTINUES

It has been nearly two weeks since I left my friends in Lake Shore. As I've continued southward towards the Great Passage, I've encountered a few villages and small towns where I've looked for more leads about my father. Despite not finding any leads, I am determined to continue forward.

Along the way, I've been practicing throwing my weapons each day. I was so excited the first time I caught one. After I caught it, I had to check that I still had all my fingers. From then on, my confidence in using the weapons grew; they even began to feel like an extension of myself. When I throw them now, they slice through the air, making a humming sound that I have grown to like. Most recently, I've figured out how to control them so they return to me as quickly or as slowly as I want. It almost feels like they are attached to me via invisible elastic lines. All I know is that I am getting very good at using them, and there is no chance that Orlan will laugh now.

Looking out at the mountains, the sun is setting behind them. A little way from the road, a Stone Tree is in bloom. Stone Trees are unique. They look dead until small pink flowers appear, signaling they are ready to bear fruit. In a good bloom, only a few pieces of fruit grow per branch.

As I admire the tree, I think about the possibility of enjoying this rare delicacy. It is just a small walk through a knee-high field of grass to get to the clearing where the tree is. This might make a good campsite for the night if the ground is dry. Walking off the road, I use the Stone Tree as my guide to the clearing. I discover it's a little paradise when I get to the clearing. The sound of rolling water from a stream is soothing and will provide me with fresh water. Moss covering the ground will make for a soft ground cover on which to sleep. I immediately get a drink from the stream since I have been thirsty all day, and no matter what, I haven't been able to quench it.

Stone trees grow incredibly slowly, and this one is quite tall. I'm guessing it is well over a hundred years old. When I knock my knuckles on the tree's hard trunk, it sounds more like I'm knocking on stone than wood. I look up, and I'm in luck. The tree has fruit, and they look like they are ready to be picked. I'm excited; I drop my pack and climb up to pick some apple-sized fruit. When I reach the first one, I pick it and quickly take a bite. The tough outer skin is slightly bitter, but the flesh below it is sweet and firm. I have only tasted this a few times as a special treat. The fruit is hard to come by and is generally expensive if you find it in a market. I finish the one I'm eating and place the pit in my pocket. I pick two more before jumping down to get my campsite ready.

I pull out my map to see where I am once the campfire is burning well. Based on the map, I am less than half a day from the Great Passage. I can't believe that I'm almost out of the valley. I put the map away, along with one of the stone fruits. While eating the other one, I watch the daylight vanish. In the distance, I can see the dancing lights in the northern sky. Back home, I would see them easily, but I am so far south now that they are barely noticeable. Watching them, I think of everyone back home, especially Mother. I wonder how she is doing. I am sure she is worried about me like I am of her. I know she didn't want me to leave, but I'm not sure what I would have done if I hadn't. I was falling deeper into my hole, and I was starting to have thoughts of joining Jenny. I know this would have destroyed her. Since leaving, I haven't thought of this, plus my time with Orlan's family helped me more than I could ever imagine.

Finishing my fruit, I place the pit with the other one in my pocket. I'll drop them on the ground on my way out tomorrow, hoping they take root. Before turning in for the night, I head to the stream to wash my hands and face and get another drink because I am still thirsty. Settling in by the fire, I place the largest piece of wood I found on top of the fire to help burn through the night. I pull out my blanket; it has been colder at night than I thought. I rest my head on my backpack and close my eyes.

I feel like I am running faster than I have ever run before. It almost feels like I'm hovering over the ground as I chase after something. I can hear its heartbeat and smell the animal. Leaping over some brush, I see a small fawn trying to run away from me. When I land, I tackle it to the ground. It screams in fear at being caught, and before it screams again, I bite down on its neck and start drinking from it. As I pull its blood into my mouth and start swallowing, the taste is indescribable. It's warm, rich, and sweet. I bite down harder and drink faster and more ravenously until I feel the fawn stop resisting me, and it goes limp in my arms. I release my mouth from its neck and exhale, feeling satisfied.

Hearing the sounds of the stream, I open my eyes and see the sun shining down on me. Getting up, I stumble toward the stream to splash water on my face to help me wake up more. I feel extra tired this morning from the dreams I had. Leaning over the water, I see my reflection. My mouth is covered in blood. I stare at it for a few seconds, and then I start to splash water on my face, frantically trying to wash away the blood. As I do this, I remember my dream, or what I thought was a dream. I stand and look around. I see something lying by the water's edge. I run over and see the fawn from my dream. Its neck was bitten and is covered in blood. My dream wasn't a dream at all? I must have transformed in my sleep and hunted last night. This terrifies me, as I realize I don't have control over this as much as I thought I did. What if this happened when I was with Orlan's family? Iris climbed into bed with me a few times while I was there. It could have easily been one of them instead of this fawn. I couldn't live with myself if I ever hurt any of them.

Realizing this, my nerves and emotions get the best of me. I fall to the ground on my hands and knees and empty my stomach, spraying red below me. Seeing the ground covered in the fawn's blood, I feel my other side rising within me. It desires the blood, even though it was in my stomach a second ago. I try to get up and walk away from the blood, but when I do this, I start to feel myself transform quickly, and I lunge at the blood. Somehow, I suppress the transformation, falling to the ground. What is happening to me, and why now? The only conclusion I can come to is the desire for blood is growing. Maybe that is why I was so thirsty yesterday, and no matter how much water I drank, I couldn't quench my thirst. I must figure out how to deal with this soon, as I don't want this to happen again. Hopefully, since I fed last night, I'll have time to figure something out. The last time I drank was when I lost Jenny, and that was a while ago. It should be at least that long.

Gathering up my things, I kick dirt into the smoldering remains of my campfire to ensure it's out. Looking up at the deep blue sky and fluffy clouds, I can at least be grateful for a lovely day weather-wise. Walking to the road, I drop the stone fruit pits from my pocket and step on them to push them into the ground. Turning onto the road, I continue heading south. As I travel, I feel I am more awake and aware of everything around me. I'm also full of energy. Is it the fawn's blood making me feel this way?

CHAPTER 17

THE TRADING POST

As the day progresses, clouds gather, and the blue sky turns grey. I was hoping it wouldn't rain on me, but I started feeling the first drops around midday. At first, it wasn't terrible, as it was a light rain, but within a short time, it turned into a downpour. With no signs of shelter, I am forced to continue.

Through the pelting rain, I start to see the silhouette of the Great Passage in the distance. Eventually, the rain lightens up, and I pick up my pace, hoping to find some shelter before it rains heavily again. Every part of me is soaked, and my teeth are starting to chatter. I now see more of the passage opening with its sheer cliffs and giant figures carved into each side of the opening.

Trudging through the muddy road, I come across a sign. I wipe the water from my eyes so I can read the sign. *Trading Post Inn* with an arrow pointing towards the Great Passage. Having a roof over my head is a needed comfort. I start to double-time it as I can see the clouds gathering again. They look like they will release the next round of heavy rain shortly.

I come across another sign for the inn, pointing to a road to my left. I head down the road, thinking of a warm, dry place and a bed.

Walking down the road leads me through some woods, then to a clearing where I see the inn. It's much larger than I expected, with multiple levels and chimneys dotting the roof lines. Continuing towards it, I notice the inn's stone and wooden beam construction and a very large open stable full of horses and carts. When I reach the inn's main door, the rain picks up again, and I quickly enter the inn. I have had enough of the rain.

Upon entering, I'm greeted at the front desk by a dwarf with a gruff demeanor. He pushes up his eyeglasses and asks, "Room? Meal?"

"How much for a room?" I reply, walking up to the desk, dripping water everywhere.

"Ten silver per night. If you want a bath, that's an extra two copper. A hot bath costs five copper. Towels included. Meals and drinks are extra," he informs me.

What's with dwarfs? Why are they always so gruff? Ten silver is more than I want to spend, but the thought of a hot bath entices me too much. I inadvertently get the desk wet when I drop the coins on the desk. The dwarf looks at me and grabs a towel to wipe the desk dry while taking the coins.

"Room eighteen. Up the stairs to the second level. You can't miss it. I'll have our servant girl get your bath ready. Meals are served after sunset," he tells me, sliding my room key to me.

Walking through the inn, I immediately think of the Dragon Tail. It's rustic, with large wooden beams that span multiple levels. The inn has an immense central fireplace and lanterns throughout to light it. Against several walls are paintings of landscapes as well as people. Continuing through the main room, I notice all sorts of patrons sitting and enjoying a drink with each other or playing games at tables. Making my way up the stairs, I get to the upper level and walk down the walkway that overlooks the main room below. Seeing a door with eighteen carved into it, I try my key and open it. Entering the room, there's a large bed against the far wall next to a fireplace. Grateful that a fire is already lit, I walk over to it quickly to feel its warmth and warm my hands. I see a window on the outer wall and a dresser with a light crystal lamp. There's a wooden bathtub in one corner with water pipes next to it. I sit on the bed and bounce on it several times to test it out. I remove my waterlogged boots, turn one over, and watch water pour out. I repeat this with my other boot. I remove my armor and place everything by the fireplace to dry. I dump my backpack out to see if any of it is wet. Thankfully, nothing on the inside got wet. Unfortunately, my blanket is soaked from being attached to the outside. I squeeze the blanket, removing as much water as possible, and hang it by the fire to dry. I hope it dries by morning.

"Maid service to get your bath ready." I hear a knock at the door.

"Come in," I answer.

A servant girl, maybe a few years younger than me, enters with stacks of towels, a sponge, and soap. She walks over to the bathtub and takes a key attached to a chain from around her neck. She inserts it into a lock, turning on the water faucets to fill the tub.

"How hot would you like your bath, ma'am?" she asks.

Hearing someone call me ma'am sounds strange. I'm not that much older than she is, and I would only do that when talking to an elder.

"Please call me Kyra. Hot enough to warm up my cold bones," I reply.

"Yes, ma'am, hot," she says in return.

I watch her adjust the water amounts, and she fills the tub quickly. Running water in our house would be a real luxury and a time saver. Going to the barn to get water from our well is not the most convenient, and it can be terrible during the winter. Looking over at the steaming water, I start to get excited. I can't wait to soak in it.

"Please get undressed. So I can give you your bath," she explains to me.

I do a double-take at what she just told me. "Excuse me. Can you say that again?"

"Please undress so I can give you your bath," she repeats.

"I can bathe myself."

"No, ma'am. It's part of the service you paid for. If I don't, I will get in trouble with the owner. Please, ma'am," she persists.

I stand there feeling very awkward. What do I do? Do I undress like she asked, or stay here and tell her to leave? The last time someone bathed me was Mother, and I was around two or three. I don't want to cause trouble, and I'm glad it's a girl. I undress, placing my wet clothes by the fire to dry. When I turn around, trying to cover myself, the servant girl looks at me oddly.

"Can you please look away? You're making me feel even more uncomfortable," I request.

"Sorry, ma'am. Please take off the locket as well."

Holding my locket, I tell her, "This never leaves my neck."

"Yes, ma'am, please get in. It's ready."

I quickly walk over, trying to cover myself the best I can. I get into the bathtub just as swiftly and feel the hot water burn slightly as it hits my skin.

"Ouch, ouch, that's hot," I say.

The servant girl quickly turns on the cold water and mixes some to cool the water. I lower myself into the water and hold my knees to my chest, trying to keep my front covered. The next thing I know, the girl is scrubbing my back, and it feels great. It's almost like a massage. I start to close my eyes as I enjoy the scrubbing. She moves to my neck, which feels even better, and then pulls one of my arms out to wash it. She moves around the tub and grabs my other arm to wash it. When she finishes with my arms, I feel her grab one of my legs, which forces me to lean back and grab the side of the tub. This girl is on a mission to get me clean. It doesn't take her long to wash both legs.

"Ma'am, can you stand so I can wash your front?"

I grab the sponge out of her hand and hold it tight to my chest. "I'll wash my front. You can go. I will make sure you don't get in trouble," I tell her.

She looks at me briefly, "Yes, ma'am."

She stands and walks out of my room. When she closes the door behind her, I slip down in the hot water and breathe out. When she was washing me, I felt like I was three years old again, and Mother was bathing me. I chuckle for a second and finish washing myself. I do a final rinse-off by fully dunking below the water before settling in for a soak. The water feels fantastic, splashing it slightly. I rest my head on the back of the tub and watch the fire.

I must have soaked too long; my hands and feet have turned wrinkly. I get out and towel off. The towel is so soft, much softer than the towels at home. I head to the bed and put on a dry outfit. Turning to my items drying by the fire, they are looking pretty good. They should be dry in a few hours. My boots are steaming because they are too close to the fire. I examine them. Thankfully, there is no damage, and they are almost dry. I put them on, and they are warm and feel nice on my feet. I look out the window and see it's still raining. I am so glad I am not sleeping outside tonight. I hear my stomach growl, telling me I need to get some food. I grab my purse and weapons and head downstairs.

Heading down the walkway, I hear the sounds of laughter and mugs clanging echoing through the inn. I look over the railing and see that the main area is bustling. As I walk down the stairs, a bard and a lady of the tavern pass me. Reaching the lower level, almost every seat has been taken. While looking for a spot to sit, a tavern maid moves in front of me and asks, "Table or bar?"

"Table, and if possible, in the corner. I like a wall to my back," I answer.

She nods and escorts me to a small, empty table in the corner.

"Food, Ale, Cider, what will it be?"

"Cider, and what do you have for food?"

"This evening, we have roast elk with root vegetables."

"I'll have a plate of that as well," I reply, as my stomach growls loudly.

"Sounds like you need a double portion," the tavern maid jokes. "I'll be right out with your food and cider."

I feel uncomfortable, as I don't know anyone here. Most look like travelers, but they all seem to know each other. Ladies of the tavern walk from table to table, trying to persuade patrons to join them upstairs for their services. They're dressed up, trying to look their prettiest.

The tavern maid returns quickly, placing my meal in front of me and the largest cider I've ever seen.

"That's huge! How am I going to drink that? It looks to be three ciders worth," I tell her, chuckling.

"All our drinks are that big. Eight copper," she tells me.

I reach into my purse and hand her the coins, and she leaves. While the staff isn't the friendliest, they offer quick service, and the food smells amazing. I clear my plate and make a good dent in the cider quickly. Sitting at the table, digesting my meal, one of the ladies walks over to me.

"How are you tonight?" she asks pleasantly.

"I'm fine; how are you?" I answer.

"I'm good. Can I join you?" she asks, pulling a seat out.

As she settles in, she moves her hair back behind one of her ears, and I notice she's an elf. She's quite pretty, with long brown hair tied in ribbons. Her blue eyes draw you in against her fair complexion and oval face.

"Make yourself comfortable," I say, hesitantly straightening up in my seat.

"I don't think I've seen you before. I'm Madeline, but everyone calls me Maddie." She extends her hand out to me.

"Kyra," I say, shaking her hand.

"That's an interesting name. Where are you from?"

"Mountain Side," I reply, reaching for my cider.

Her eyes light up. "Are you from High Rock? I hear that place is amazing with the aqueducts and waterfalls."

"No, I'm from outside the city. The waterfalls are pretty, though. Why are you asking me so many questions?" I ask, placing my cider down.

"No reason, just getting to know you. What brings you here? It's a long way from Mountain Side," she says, reaching for my cider.

I grab my cider, pulling it closer to me, and tell her, "Traveling and looking for someone."

She looks at me with one eye slightly closed. "Who are you looking for? I know almost everyone in this part of the valley. I might be able to help," she continues, asking me even more questions.

"See this crest." Pointing to my brooch. "Have you ever seen this before?"

She leans over to look at it and shakes her head. "Sorry, I don't know that. It's pretty, though. Do you want to buy me a drink so we can get to know each other better? I'm really thirsty."

"Why would I buy you a drink?" I ask, taking another sip of my cider to tease her.

"You're a tough one. Since we were being so nice to each other, I thought it would be better if we were both drinking. Come on, one drink. Trust me, I'm fun," she tells me, placing her head in her hands and leaning on the table while looking at me.

I pass her my cider since I don't want any more. She takes it and drinks it down in seconds. "You made me work for that," she tells me, followed by a loud burp.

I smile, which she catches.

"You can smile?" she teases me.

"At times, but only recently," I let some truth slip through.

"Why is that? Did something happen?"

"I'd rather not talk about it. I should get going. I plan on leaving early tomorrow to make it through the passage by the end of the day. Nice meeting you, Maddie. I hope you have a good night," I say, pushing my chair out.

"Don't go. We're finally starting to talk." She grabs my hand.

Pulling my hand away quickly, I tell her, "Please don't."

She looks at me, realizing she might have touched a nerve, which she did.

"Sorry, I didn't mean to upset you. Who was he? You kept rubbing the locket around your neck the whole time I was here. Is that who you're looking for?" she asks.

I hadn't realized I was rubbing it. This has become a habit when I am feeling uncomfortable or worried.

"She's none of your business," I answer sternly.

As I'm standing there looking at her, one of the other patrons walks over to us.

"Maddie, if she's not interested, join me. I could use some company tonight," he says, intoxicated.

She looks at him. "Not now, I'm busy here."

"Come on, I have plenty of money this time," he tries to convince her.

Maddie tries to brush him off, but he gets annoyed with her and grabs her arm.

"Stop. I told you not now." Maddie raises her voice to him as she tries to remove his hand, but she can't.

"She said she didn't want to go with you. Take it easy; you're hurting her," I tell him, removing his hand from her arm and pushing him away from us.

"Stay out of this. I know what she likes. Money and I have it," he tells me, pushing into my space and trying to get back to Maddie.

"Don't," I order him.

"What are you going to do?" he taunts me.

I don't plan on hurting him, but I want to prove a point quickly. I lift him off his feet, look over, and see a clothing hook. I place him on the hook where he dangles, kicking his feet in the air and reaching behind, trying to get off it.

I step back and tell him, "Hang there for a bit and think about how to treat people."

I turn back to Maddie, who is covering her mouth, but I can see she's smiling. "That was amazing. How did you pick him up like that?" She asks me, grinning ear to ear as she walks over to look at the man hanging on the hook.

"None of that here. Get him down," the gruff dwarf yells from the front desk.

I walk back over to the dangling man. "Are you going to behave?" I ask him.

"Just get me down," he answers.

I grab him and lift him off the hook. "Remember, be nice," I tell him.

He walks back to his table, where his table companions laugh at him.

"Thanks for that. Sometimes, they can get a bit physical," she tells me.

"Have a good night," I say to her.

I head upstairs, not wanting to deal with anything else tonight. I make it about halfway to my bed after entering my room when I hear knocking at my door. I shake my head, as I am pretty sure it's Maddie. She seems like a person who does not give up until she gets what she wants.

"Maddie, I'm not interested. Please leave me alone," I tell the door.

I hear the knock again and open the door quickly.

"Maddie—" It isn't Maddie. It's the servant girl from before.

"Mr. Storm would like to talk to you," she tells me.

"Who's Mr. Storm?"

"Please come with me. He doesn't like to wait," she informs me.

"Really." I don't like the idea of being summoned. What am I, one of his workers? Exiting my room, I follow the servant girl back downstairs. A man gestures to me to approach him, and I walk over and stand in front of his table.

"Mr. Storm, I presume?" I ask.

"Ankin Storm, if you like to know," he says. "Please sit." He pushes a chair toward me with his feet.

"I'd rather stand," I reply, being stubborn.

"Your choice. I watched what you did for Maddie." Gesturing for me to sit again.

Maddie brushes past me and sits down next to him. "Sit, Kyra. We don't bite."

"Maddie tells me you're looking for someone. Your brooch might be a way to find them. May I see it?" he asks, holding out his hand.

I look at him closely and realize he's also an elf. He has an air of confidence, which I have come to be used to with elves now. Even Lindsey has a bit of this, but her sweetness shines through. He has a similar complexion to Maddie and the same blue eyes and hair color.

I sit with them, but my guard is up. I hand him my brooch and watch him carefully.

"Lovely. It's very old. The craftsmanship is exceptional, and the design is exquisite. How did you come to own it?" he asks, handing it back to me.

"It was my Father's," I reply, pinning it back on me.

"I don't know the crest, but I know someone who might. If he doesn't, he can research it for you. He always gets the answers," Mr. Storm tells me.

There might be someone who knows the crest or can help me. This piques my interest. "Why are you willing to help me?" I ask.

"Because you helped my sister," he replies, swirling his glass of wine.

I would never have guessed these two were brother and sister. It is not common for ladies of the tavern to be related to the owner.

"I didn't do anything, but thank you. Where can I go to find this man?"

"Very good. It's about a two-day journey from here. You'll have to head through the passage and continue to the city of River Song. Look for Historical Records in the city's eastern section. The shop owner is Ryker. Tell him I sent you. It will cost you for any needed research," he explains.

My mood and thoughts of Mr. Storm change, and I become less annoyed.

"Thank you," I say.

"I always pay my debts. We're even now," he answers back. Maddie, walk our guest back to her room and ensure she is cared for and happy … whatever she might like."

Maddie gets up and pulls me out of my chair. "Come on."

"I can walk myself to my room. You don't have to escort me."

As Maddie pulls me through the tavern, I hear someone behind us. "Make a fool of me, will you?"

Turning, I see the person I placed on the hook coming at me with a blade in his hand. I push Maddie away and reach for one of my weapons, activating it. I slice up at my attacker's hand in one motion. The man looks at me, wondering what happened.

"Did you drop something?" I ask him.

He looks down and sees his hand on the floor holding the blade and screams. Grabbing his bleeding stump, he runs out of the tavern in a panic. I scan the room, ready for what might be coming at me next. I see everyone looking at me for a second, but then they return to what they were doing like nothing happened. I shake my weapon, trying to remove the blood from it quickly. When I do this, I get a whiff of the blood, and it causes me to close my eyes and inhale deeply. It's so inviting and intoxicating. I open my eyes and shake my head to snap myself out of it. I quickly put my weapon away to mask the smell. Even though I fed last night, I can't believe how much I wanted to taste the blood. It's getting worse with each exposure. How long can I go before I can't hide my other side?

"That was amazing. What type of weapon is that?" Maddie asks, running up to me.

I don't want to answer her. I continue walking to my room to be alone. Maddie stays right next to me the whole time.

"Thanks for escorting me upstairs. I have it from here," I tell her.

"Alright," Maddie turns with a smile and heads downstairs.

I shake my head as I lock the door. I get ready for bed. This will be the first time since leaving home that I can sleep in with just my undergarments.

I turn and scream, "Ahhh!" Maddie's standing in my room. I jump back. "How did you get in here!? I didn't even hear you. I even locked the door!?"

"Master key. Benefits of knowing the owner," she says, grinning, dangling the key at me.

"I heard you were fit, but the description wasn't as good as seeing it in person."

"Maddie, can you go? I want to sleep."

"Sure, not a problem," she says, walking over to the bed while undressing.

"No, that's not what I meant. Why don't you get this, for the love of the gods?" I ask, getting frustrated.

I walk over, pulling her dress back up, and escort her out of my room. I want to get to sleep. Plus, I'm worried about the blood I just smelled. What if I do something to her?

"Wait, wait. Brother wants to make sure you're taken care of and happy. Don't you like me?" she asks in a worried tone.

Hearing the tone in her voice, I stop and ask, "What will happen if you don't stay?"

"He might get mad," she answers, with a slightly scared tone.

"What happens when he gets mad?"

She doesn't have to tell me anymore. I notice a faint bruise on her face. How does or why would a brother want to treat his sister like this? Against my better judgment, I relock the door and hope nothing happens.

"You can stay for however long you think is the right amount of time to make your brother happy, but that's it," I explain to her.

I climb into bed, pull the blankets over me, and hold them tightly to create a barrier around me. Lying in the bed, I feel Maddie looking at me, standing in the middle of the room.

After a few minutes, I tell her, "Get over here, but stay on your side of the bed."

I hear her run across the room and jump into bed, which causes me to bounce around a bit.

"Please tell me you have your dress on," I ask.

"You have your dress on," she repeats to me jokingly.

I reach behind me and feel her. There's no dress. I shake my head and close my eyes, pulling the blankets tighter around me.

"Please stay on your side of the bed," I tell her.

"Who is she, the one in your locket?" Maddie asks.

I open my eyes, but I don't answer for a while. Finally, I say, "Jenny."

"What made her so special?" Maddie asks quietly.

"She just was ... Goodnight. No more talking." I close my eyes.

"Night," she says, and I feel her roll over.

I start to wake up, hearing the birds outside my window. When I adjust my head on the pillow, I feel someone adjust next to me. "Maddie!" I sit up quickly and look at her. She's sound asleep. This elf is crazy. I don't think she's all there. I shake her to wake her, but I'm greeted with a hand motioning me to stop. Placing my hand over my eyes, frustrated, I can't help but smile. I'm still tired, so I settle down to see if I can get more sleep. Lying there, I feel Maddie turn over and snuggle into me. Feeling her next to me at first shocked me, but it also felt nice. I take her hand and pull her arm over me.

"You're nice. Most are not as nice as you are," she tells me, half asleep.

"Why do you do what you do?" I ask.

"It's all I know."

I spin around and face her. "I'm sure you know more than this."

"I'm not smart, but I'm pretty. At least that's what everyone tells me," she answers, looking at me.

"You're more than this, and you are pretty," I say, slightly touching her face.

Maddie smiles and touches my face. She leans in and kisses me. I pull back, surprised. Why did she kiss me? I didn't want her to kiss me. Looking at Maddie, she's biting her lower lip slightly, making her look irresistible. All I feel is how much I want her in this moment. I can't help myself. I kiss her back. Maddie pulls me closer to her, intensifying our kissing.

Lying on my back, breathing heavily, Maddie flops beside me.

"It's been a while," I tell her, staring at the ceiling with a flushed face.

"You look like you needed that," she tells me.

"What does that mean?" I ask, looking at her.

"You were so tense and serious last night," she answers, lightly laughing.

"You were driving me nuts. All I wanted was to sleep, and you wouldn't leave." I poke her sides a bit.

She lets out a giggle. "Don't do that. I'm ticklish."

My eyes get huge, and I quickly mount her and tickle her.

"Ticklish, are you?"

"Yes, please stop! Stop," she pleads, wiggling under me.

Victory is finally mine, I think to myself. Unexpectedly, I'm filled with guilt. I get off her and sit on the bed, holding my knees.

"Why did you stop? What's wrong?" she asks, sitting up.

"Guilt," I answer in a soft tone. "Jenny, the person in my locket. She loved tickling me, but when I tried to tickle her, nothing. It was so unfair. Do you know how many times she tickled me and how much I would give to be tickled by her again?" I explain. "When you said you were ticklish, I just acted. I feel guilty now."

Maddie slides in next to me and holds me.

"Part of your service?" I ask.

"No, not part of my services," she says, squeezing me tighter.

Maddie left a bit ago to let me be alone and collect my thoughts. Eventually, I get ready and head downstairs. Walking down the last flight of stairs, Maddie is waiting for me.

"I thought I would walk you out and give you this, holding out a drinking pouch. Good service is important, brother tells me," she says.

"You don't have to give me that," I answer, meeting her at the bottom of the stairs.

"I know, but I want to. It's not water. It's something our brewmaster and I have been working on." She tosses it to me.

I catch it and swing it around my shoulder. "Thanks."

It's still early, so the inn is quiet, with just a few people talking to each other at tables. Most everyone is still sleeping off last night. Heading to the front desk, I ring the bell and place my room key on the desk. "Returning my key," I say, hoping someone will hear me from behind the curtain.

The dwarf appears from behind the curtain, drinking a steaming cup of tea. "Hope we met your expectations?" he asks, taking the key.

"You did," I tell him.

Heading to the door, Maddie continues to walk with me.

"You don't have to walk with me."

"I want to," she answers.

It doesn't take long before we're at the Southern Road. In my hurry to get out of the rain yesterday, I didn't notice the Great Passage was so close to where I turned to get to the inn. I couldn't see the scale of it yesterday either, due to the weather, but I can see it clearly in its grandeur today. The passage has immense vertical rock faces on both sides that rise high up into the sky. At the entrance, each side has a figure carved into it that spans from the base to almost the top. One is a warrior holding a sword and shield, and the other is a mage wielding a staff. I can tell by how the figures were depicted and the mosses growing on them that they were carved in ancient times. Carving them into the rock face must have taken incredible time and effort. The passage walls extend down the Southern Road as far as the eye can see.

I feel Maddie grab my hand, and I turn toward her.

"I guess this is goodbye," I tell her.

"I don't like goodbyes. How about until we see each other again?"

She leans up and kisses my cheek.

"You are a strange one. Take care," I tell her, hugging her. "Till next time."

CHAPTER 18

RIVER SONG

It's midday when I take a break by a group of large rocks. I think I'm about halfway through the passage and should be able to make it out by nightfall. Sitting, I hear my stomach growl. Realizing I haven't had anything to eat all day, I reach into my backpack, looking for something. I pull out my last travel cake. As I hold the cake in my hand, it starts to crumble. Being as old as it is, I'm surprised it was whole for the short time it was in my hand. Looking at the pieces and crumbs in my hand, I put them in my mouth and chew, thinking it's better than nothing. My mouth goes dry as every bit of moisture is sucked by the stale crumbs. Eventually, my mouth produces enough spit so I can swallow it. I brush off my hands of any extra crumbs and continue on my way.

Walking through the passage, I feel tiny compared to the vast rock faces to my left and right. They seem to go up forever and don't stop until they touch the sky. The passage is mainly bare except for bits of vegetation and small bushes here and there, compared to the lush, green valley I left this morning.

As evening sets in, I walk out of the passage, and in front of me is the Midlands. It resembles the valley, with its rolling hills and woods, but no mountains on either side. Looking around, there's an outcrop of large boulders that might make an excellent place to rest for the night. The largest of the boulders has an overhang that creates a natural covering from above. As I inspect the area, I see signs of old campsites. I start a fire using bits and pieces of leftover wood from old campfires and a few fresh pieces from the surrounding area. I poke the fire and place the largest piece of wood I found on top of it to burn through the night.

I lean against one of the rocks and watch the sky as dusk fades to night. I can't believe how far I have traveled already. Wishing I had something to celebrate this moment, I remember the drinking pouch that Maddie gave me. She said it wasn't water, so I'm guessing cider or wine. I take a big swig of it and instantly realize it's none of these. The taste and burn in my mouth causes me to spray the drink almost instantly. When the spray hits the campfire, it ignites, creating a fireball that rises above me. I feel my face to see if it singed any of my hair. I start to laugh at the events that just unfolded, thanks to Maddie. I take another taste, knowing what to expect this time. It burns the whole way down to my stomach. Is she trying to kill me? The taste reminds me of burnt wood and sugar. I don't find it very pleasant, so I put it away and settle in for the night.

Mr. Storm's directions to River Song were spot on. Walking up to the city's main gate, I cross a stone bridge with a river flowing under it. Looking over the edge of the bridge, I see the river enters the city through a low archway just a little ways down. As I'm about to enter the city, guards at the entrance stop me.

"What's your business here?" They ask.

Looking through the gate, I turn back to them.

"I'm looking for a business called Historical Records," I tell them.

One of them steps toward me and starts investigating me with their sword, trying to get a look at what I am carrying.

"What are those?" he asks, pointing to my weapons.

"Those are to protect me if needed."

"Open your backpack," he orders.

I don't want any trouble, so I quickly remove my backpack, place it on the ground, and open it for them to look in. The guard pokes around in it for a second.

"You're good, proceed," he tells me.

Not wasting any time, I head into the city, closing up my backpack as I walk. I see the river that entered through the city wall. It cuts the city into two parts with several arching bridges allowing people to easily cross from one section of the city to another. The buildings are similar to the Trading Post. They are constructed of large wooden beams and stone. Remembering what Mr. Storm told me, I take the first main road to the city's eastern part. Not knowing where I am, I stop at a fruit and vegetable vendor to get directions. Plus, I'm hungry and can always eat an apple.

"Afternoon. How much for the fruit?" I ask, striking up a conversation.

"Apples and peaches are two copper each, and vegetables are three copper for any two. If you buy more, we can work out a deal," the man tells me.

"I'll take three apples and three peaches. How much?" I ask, looking them over.

"Eleven copper for six," he answers.

"Ten copper," I counter.

He places his hand out, motioning his figures towards him. "Deal."

I hand him the coins and ask, "I'm looking for Historical Records. I was told it's located in the city's eastern section. Do you know where?"

"I do. What's it worth to you?" he asks.

I pick up another peach.

"Full price." Smiling at him.

"Head down this street and take the second left. It's on the right side, just down a little way."

I flip him the two copper and take my fruit. As I leave, I immediately take a bite of the peach. It is sweet and juicy. I finish it while making my way down the street. It isn't long before I am standing in front of Historical Records. The shop has a charming look, with a large front glass window and the shop's name hanging on a sign just over the door. Looking through the window, I see stacks of books throughout the shop. Opening the door, I hear a bell ring above me, which startles me. As I close the door, the smell of musty old books and dust hits my nose. I wipe my finger on the top of one of the book stacks, which shows how covered everything is with a thick layer of dust. Mother would be beside herself, seeing how dusty this place is. Meandering through the store, I step carefully as books are even on the floor. I might accidentally knock a stack over if I bump one.

"What can we do for you?" I hear someone ask me.

"Hello. I'm looking for Ryker. Mr. Storm from the Trading Post Inn said he might be able to help me," I announce.

"One second, I will get Mr. Ryker," the voice tells me.

Once at the store's counter, also covered in books, I wait for Mr. Ryker. Within a minute, I hear footsteps coming toward me. From behind the counter, the top of a head scurries toward me. The figure adjusts something behind the counter, and an elderly gnome with crazy hair and spectacles on the brim of his nose rises in front of me.

"So Ankin said I might be able to help you. What did you do to get his favor?" he asks.

"I helped his sister with a matter," I answer, looking at him between the piles of books.

"So what do you need answers on? I'm busy." He pushes his spectacles up on his nose slightly.

I take my brooch off and hand it to him. "Can you tell me anything about this, specifically the crest?"

He reaches for a magnifying glass on the counter to examine it.

"Well, it's old, very old. I'm guessing a hundred years or more.

The artistry is exquisite. Whoever made this was a master jeweler. Ah, I have found the jeweler's mark," he tells me.

"So you know who made it?" I ask.

"No, but knowing this will help. If you like, we can look into this more. This one intrigues me due to its age. It will take at least a few days, and I say fifty gold coins should cover it," he tells me.

Hearing fifty gold shocks me. Why so much? I have to talk him down on the price, as I don't have that much money.

"I'm sorry, but I can't afford that. What about ten gold?" I counter.

He changes his focus from the brooch to me. "It takes time to research these things, and time is money, my dear. Fifty gold will get you the answers you want. My skills don't come cheap, but I always get answers."

He hands my brooch back to me. "When you can pay the price, I will be here."

I want answers or clues, but I can't spend that much. I will probably sleep outside the city tonight, as I shouldn't spend money on another room. Leaving the shop, I accidentally hit a stack of books, causing it to topple over. I momentarily look at the books on the floor before leaving the store.

Walking through the city, trying to figure out my next move, I hear cheering and yelling. Looking over, I see a large crowd. At least they're having a good time over there. Being curious, I head over to see what all the excitement is about. I force my way through the crowd to see what everyone is watching. When I reach the front, I see everyone looking down into a fighting pit below street level. I lean on the railing to look at the action below better. The stands are filled with every type of person yelling and screaming for more. They all seem to be holding pieces of paper, which means this is a betting pit. I look to the fighting area, and I see two people dragging an unconscious person out of the ring by his arms. He seems to be pretty beaten up. On the other side, I see the largest man I have ever seen walking out of the fighting area. He has to be at least eight feet tall and almost four feet wide at his shoulders. He must have giant blood in him to be that large.

Turning to the person beside me, I ask, "What's happening?"

"That poor chap thought he could win the prize money," he tells me.

"Prize money?" I ask, becoming much more interested.

"Five hundred gold if you beat the champion," he says, pointing to the giant.

"How does one enter for a chance at the prize money?" I ask.

"That's easy. Just go down to the fighting area and walk in. The only rule they have is no weapons," the man says before looking at me. "They won't let you participate if that's what you're thinking of doing."

"Really, why?" I ask

"No woman has ever entered the ring." He turns his attention back to the ring below.

Hearing this made me want to try even more. If I win the prize money, I will have more than enough to pay Mr. Ryker, plus I won't have to worry about having enough money for the rest of my travels. I have to try. What's the worst that can happen? I make my way through the crowd and head toward the stairs leading to the fighting area below.

Descending the stairs, I hear a man calling out to the crowd, "Is there anyone willing to try for the prize money? Come on, Slainar is starting to wear out after the last fight. Is there anyone?"

When I reach the edge of the ring, I drop my backpack and take a deep breath before entering.

"Hold on, we have someone," the announcer yells out, walking up to me. "You want to fight Slainar? Are you sure? He won't take it easy on you."

"Five hundred gold if I win, correct?" I confirm with the man.

He points over to a small chest full of gold coins. "If you win, it's yours. Are you sure?"

I nod.

"Everyone, this young lady wants a chance at the prize money," he announces.

I hear a mix of chuckles and cheers from the crowd. I look around the crowd and see papers being passed around and collected. I am pretty sure they're placing their bets that I will lose. I hope to prove them wrong.

"Careful, he might want to kiss you instead of fighting you," someone from the crowd yells.

I look over, and Slainar is walking over. When he gets a few feet from me, he stops and looks down at me. He's even larger up close. This might not have been a good idea. I could get hurt if I'm not careful.

In a deep voice, he tells me, "A woman. Might be fun. I promise not to hurt you too badly."

"Thanks," I tell him.

The announcer leans over to me and asks, "What's your name?"

"Kyra," I answer, starting to bounce up and down and pull on my arms to loosen up.

"Let's give it up for Kyra and hope Slainar doesn't hurt her too much. Odds have been set at eight to one, and betting is now closed," he yells to the crowd as he steps out of the ring.

As I stand in front of Slainar, I have to look up to meet him eye to eye. I can't believe how he towers over me. His grey eyes almost look kind, but I can tell he is wild and has no problem hurting people. Lowering my eyes, I can't help but notice his chest and how it bulges out along with every other muscle on him. His arms are larger than my thighs. It looks like he has been doing this for a long time, as he has scars all over his body. He raises his hand to shake, and I see his hands are wrapped in bandages, and his knuckles are stained red. He smiles and tells me, "Good luck."

I smile and nervously return the gesture. When we shake, his hand covers not only mine but a portion of my lower arm. We get one shake in, and suddenly, he yanks me into a close line that hits me so hard that it almost flips me over, causing me to land on my upper back hard. This fight was definitely not the best idea. This is going to hurt afterward.

While the crowd is cheering for my competitor, I catch my breath. I get up and roll my head around to check that my neck is not injured. Looking over, Slainar is facing away from me, raising his arms to get accolades from the crowd. While he's occupied, I walk up behind him and tap him on his back to get his attention.

As he turns, I tell him, "My turn."

I follow this up with a double-fisted uppercut to his jaw, sending him stumbling backward. The crowd cheers, but I prepare for his retaliation, knowing one punch won't do him in. It only takes him a second to collect himself, and he runs at me, hoping to grab me. As he reaches for me, I dash to the side and try to sweep his leg. However, when I connect, my leg stops cold. It didn't have the effect I was hoping for. I flip up quickly to my feet, but he grabs me by my shoulders and lifts me off the ground. I'm at his mercy. What is he going to do to me? All I know is that it's going to hurt.

"You're strong. That punch hurt," he tells me, right before he head-butts me and drops me to the ground.

Lying on the ground, all I see are stars. I feel my face where he connected with his huge, hard head. It's cut and swelling. I must end this quickly, as I don't know how long I can last against this giant man. I jump back to get space between us. I beckon him to continue the fight, which excites the crowd watching us. He shakes his head slightly in disbelief before he stomps over to me. I dash around him and grab his mid-region. I start to squeeze him as hard as I can. I feel him trying to remove my grip, but I have a different plan. I heave with all that I have, and I lift him off the ground and flip him backward onto his shoulders and neck. When he hits the ground, the impact makes a thunderous sound. I twist around again and repeat this motion two more times, slamming him into the ground as hard as I can each time. After the third one, I let go. I'm exhausted from lifting and slamming him into the ground. Standing there, breathing heavily, I wipe the sweat from my eyes along with a bit of blood as well.

After a moment, he gets up slowly. What do I have to do to knock him out? I can tell he's hurt by the way he's moving. I run at him and jump into the air, doing a flying double kick to his chest, which causes him to stumble backward, but he doesn't fall. I jump onto his back and wrap my arms around his neck with all I have left. He tries to pull my arms off. As he tries to shake me off, my legs are flailing from side to side, but I manage to keep hold of his neck. His neck is like a tree trunk, and I can feel him flexing every neck muscle, trying to resist my hold. He eventually stops shaking and goes down on one knee and then another, finally falling flat on his face with me still holding on. After a few seconds, I release the hold. He's breathing, but he's out cold.

I slide off his back and fall to my knees, exhausted. When I get up, the crowd cheers my name, "Kyra! Kyra!"

I raise my arm in victory and stumble over to the announcer and prize money.

"Five hundred gold. Right?" I ask, exhausted.

He nods and looks in shock at what just happened. I grab the chest and almost drop it due to my exhaustion. I lock it under my arm tightly and return to my stuff on the other side of the ring, passing Slainar, who is starting to get up.

"You are a good fighter," he tells me.

"You are one tough fighter, and I never want to fight you again," I answer, trying to help him up.

He extends his hand out again to shake. I look at him cautiously but slowly, meet his hand with mine, and we shake. He then walks away.

Leaving the ring, I grab my stuff and walk up the stairs. Getting up the stairs is a struggle, as my body is spent. When I return to street level, a few onlookers pat my back. I head to Historical Records.

On my way, I hear someone coming up behind me. "Wait up."

I turn, and I see the announcer chasing after me.

"That was impressive. You are the first to win against Slainar. How did you do it?" he asks.

"I don't know; I'm just lucky. I have to be somewhere, picking up my pace.

"I'd like to talk to you about an opportunity," he says, trying to keep up with me.

I yell back, "Not interested."

It only takes me a few minutes to get back to Historical Records. When I enter, I knock over a few more stacks of books due to my current condition. Mr. Ryker is already at the counter with his face buried in a book.

"Back again, so soon?"

"Fifty gold?" I ask.

"That's what I said," looking up at me. "What happened to you?"

"I won prize money to get the gold," I say, placing the chest on the counter.

I open it, count out fifty gold coins, and slide them over to him clumsily.

"Do you need a healer?" he asks, concerned.

"I will be fine. Just need a night's rest."

"That's more than a night's rest, and that's a bit of gold you have there. I recommend placing it in a bank for safekeeping, or if you like, we can keep it safe. We have a vault in the back. We keep our customers' items there while we work on them. I would be happy to place your gold, along with your brooch, in our vault. No extra charge," he explains, gathering up his payment.

I don't know if I can trust this gnome, but I also don't know how to manage this amount of gold. My purse only holds about fifty coins.

"I guess that works. How can you assure me that it will be safe?"

"Our business has been built on trust and good work. I would not tarnish it in any way. You have my word. Your brooch and gold will be safe. Our vault is very secure, with a magic seal; only I can open it," he tells me.

For some reason, I believe him or am too tired. Either way, I push the chest over to him. "How long will the research take?"

"A few days to a week. It all depends if we get lucky. Don't worry; I never let my customers down. Check back in a few days, and I will have an update for you. I'm guessing you're staying in the city now. I would recommend *The Bard's Inn*. It's just down the street from here. It's a good place, the prices are reasonable, and they even offer discounts for staying multiple days," he tells me, handing me a receipt.

"Thanks. I'll be back in a few days for an update."

I stand there for a second, gathering up the strength to move.

I start to walk out and hear him say, "The brooch. I need it for the research."

Walking back, I hand him the brooch, trying not to stumble too much in his store. He said the inn was just down the street, and that's where I'm going for a large drink.

Exiting the store, I'm greeted by the man who was following me earlier.

"I really want to talk to you. Do you have a few minutes?" he asks, walking backward in front of me.

"I don't. I want to have a drink and get some rest," I tell him, trying to avoid him.

"Come on. You cleaned me out. No one has ever won against Slainar before. You owe me at least a conversation to hear me out. The first round is on me. If you don't like what I have to say, then that's it," he tells me.

I stop, which probably isn't the best thing to do, but I can tell he has a desperate look on his face. "Fine, but I'm not agreeing to anything," I say.

"Great. I know of a place down here that serves a great ale. By the way, I'm Brynn Silver."

Walking together, Brynn recaps my fight with Slainar and how the crowd went wild as we exchanged blows. I tune him out because I have no interest in what he is going to offer, plus I don't want to be reminded about the fight. I'm humoring him because he is offering to buy me a drink, and I can use one right now. As we walk, I start to feel my body recovering. My muscles weren't as tired, and the pain was beginning to lessen. Feeling the spot where I was headbutted, the swelling is going down as well. I guess this is one of the few benefits of being half-vampire. I'm able to recover and heal quickly.

"We're here," he announces, approaching a door and opening it for me.

I look up, and the sign above the door reads *Drinks*. This is going to be interesting. Upon entering, the place is pretty dark, with just a few light crystals glowing on the walls. It's pretty full, which generally means it's a good place. There's a heavy smell of pipe smoke and ale in the air. Brynn calls to the person behind the bar, "Two specials."

"I know it doesn't look like much, but the drinks are good. Plus, the price is right. It's where all the locals go for a drink. Let's sit over here," he says, walking over to a table against the back wall.

Sitting down, I lean back in my chair. "So what's this offer that I can't refuse?" I ask.

"You fight for me. Between you and Slainar, we'll win every tournament. You took a close line from him. Most don't get up from that. Plus, you're a woman. That adds to promoting you in fights," he explains.

"Why would I do that? I don't need to fight," I say.

"I would pay you for each fight. Say ten gold per fight," he tries to richen his offer.

The barkeep places two large frothy mugs of ale on the table and walks away.

I grab my mug and blow on the foam before tasting it. It has a slightly bitter note, but it's not bad. I drink a large portion of it down.

"Sorry, I'm just not interested. I hope to only be here for a few days. Then I am off. I have other priorities," I explain to him, placing the mug down.

"Wouldn't you like to earn some extra money for your travels?" he asks, trying to keep the conversation going.

"I just won five hundred gold. How much gold do you think I need to have with me?"

He is persistent, which I respect, but he's not getting it. Plus, I'm starting to feel tired, and I should be getting to the inn to get a room.

"How's your ale?" he asks.

"It's good, but there's a slightly bitter taste afterward that I'm not a fan of."

I take another large drink. Why am I feeling so tired? I look over to Brynn, and I am having trouble focusing. He sounds muffled, like I am underwater.

"You don't look that great suddenly. Are you alright?" Brynn asks.

I'm trying to focus by blinking my eyes. I'm feeling dizzy now. What's wrong with me?

"I guess you're feeling it already," Brynn says.

"What? What did you say?" I ask, trying to look at him.

"You cost Lady Beimaris five hundred gold and more. Slainar said he won't fight anymore because of you. You just walked into something you wish you never did. I am sorry, but I have to protect what's important to me," he continues.

I stand up, realizing that he must have drugged me.

"What do you mean?" I ask. On the verge of falling over, I grasp the table's edge, hoping to keep myself up. How could I have been so careless? I have to get out of here quickly. As soon as I try to move, I crash face-first onto the table. The last thing I hear before passing out is Brynn telling someone, "Let's get her out of here quickly and quietly."

CHAPTER 19
TAKEN

I can hear the people carrying me talking to each other as the tops of my feet scrape the ground. Opening my eyes, I see a stone floor below me. The air is putrid smelling, similar to a sewer but different.

"What ... what's going on? Where am I?" I mumble.

"Quick, get her in the cell and a collar on her. She's starting to wake up," I hear one of them say.

I feel myself being dropped on the ground and something being locked around my neck. The next thing I hear is the sound of a metal door closing and keys jingling before everything goes black again.

Hearing water dripping, I open my eyes, blinking several times. My head feels like I had a long night of drinking. Sitting up, I hold my head and close my eyes due to the pain. After a moment, I look around and realize I'm in a cell. Why am I here? Did I do something that got me in trouble? I stand and stumble into the wall near me. Feeling dizzy, I lean against the wall. Through the cell bars, I see a few small old flame torches and a grate in the ceiling where moon-light shines through.

The air is damp from water leaching from the stone walls, allowing a greenish moss to grow. That must have been the water I heard dripping before. Along with the dampness, the odor of death and rot fills the air, causing me to dry heave. I cover my mouth and nose, trying to mask the smell, but it's useless. I can practically taste it. To see more of this area and better understand where I am, I use my ability to see in the dark. When I do this, I see them. Individuals either pacing or leaning on walls of their cells. Some look to be in terrible shape, with injuries or just neglect. One person, a few cells down, looks like they have died as they are face down on the floor. I need to figure out why I'm here. I'm nervous I did something. Did I transform last night and hurt someone? That couldn't be it. If they saw me drinking from someone, I am sure they would have killed me. This is something else. I reach the front of the cell and grab the bars.

"What am I doing here?" I try to yell, but my voice is almost gone.

Hearing my lack of voice, I rattle the cell door, trying to get some-one's attention.

"Stop it! They will come and punish you and maybe us," someone shoots at me.

I stop rattling the cell door and turn toward the voice.

"What do you mean? I have no clue what's going on. I woke up in this cell. I don't know why," I say in a harsh, scratchy voice.

"We all woke up in these cells and with a collar on," he tells me.

I reach around my neck and feel the metal collar. What is this? I try to take it off, but I can't.

"You can't remove it. No matter how hard you try. It's enchant-ed," he tells me, walking into the light.

I see a fair-skinned man with red hair and green eyes looking at me between the bars. He also has bruises on his arms and face.

"I'm Killian; try not to panic. It won't help. I'm talking from experience."

Hearing him say not to panic causes me to panic, as something is not right here.

"Why am I here?" I ask, walking up to him.

"We're here to fight in Lady Beimaris's tournaments."

"Who?"

"Lady Beimaris runs this place. Somehow, you were unfortunate enough to be selected or, should I say, taken."

My head is still killing me, but I try to remember. The last thing I remember is having a drink with Brynn. Anger starts to come over me instantly. I was careless, and Brynn drugged me.

"What day is it?" I ask.

"I lost track of what day it might be years ago. Time goes by differently down here. We know the seasons and if it's night or day from that grate above, but that's it. Most likely, it's only been a day or two since you were taken, but it depends on the dosage of the sleeping potion you were given," he informs me. "It's late; no one will come here till the morning. You might as well get some rest and allow the last of the potion to clear out of your system. She'll want to meet and test you as the new fighter."

"I don't want to fight," I yell at him, but my voice barely works.

"It doesn't matter. If you don't. You'll die." He tells me, walking back into the darkness of his cell.

I slide down the cell wall. What did I get myself into?

I open my eyes after hearing people talking. I must have fallen asleep, as sunlight is shining through the grate in the ceiling.

"Wake up." The people down the way bang on the metal bars to ensure everyone is up. Looking down, I can see three men who look to be guards. They're wearing leather vests, dark pants, and brown boots. Each seems to have a set of keys and a wooden club. One of them also has a whip attached to his side.

I stand up and wipe the dried tears from my face.

"She was brought in yesterday; she's in the last cell," one of them tells the others.

I move to the back of my cell, knowing they are coming for me.

"Look at you. You're taller than I thought you might be and fairer as well. Lady Beimaris wants to meet you. Don't move and follow my orders," the guard tells me.

A strange sensation starts to come over me. I don't know what's happening as my body becomes stiff, but my mind is trying to fight it. Why can't I move?

"Come here and hold your hands out," the guard orders me.

I start to walk toward him, holding my hands out. I don't want to do this, but my body moves against my will. The more I fight it, the more I start to feel a throbbing pain in my head.

"Are we confused? Everyone is at first. You have to do what we say because of that collar around your neck and the bracelet around my wrist," he says, showing me the bracelet. Your mind will try to resist, but your body can't help but obey." Laughing, like a joke, was just played on me.

When I get in front of him, he places shackles on my wrists. "We heard you were stronger than most. So we want to make sure that you are secured."

"Why am I here? What did I do?" I ask softly because my voice is still not normal.

"Nothing. You were just taken, like all the others. Come on; Lady Beimaris is waiting to meet you. She hasn't been this curious about a fighter in a long time. We don't want to be on her bad side by making her wait. Follow me," he orders me, pulling at my shackles.

Walking out of my cell, we pass the other prisoners, who are looking at me. We head up a set of stairs to a door. When he opens the door, the sunlight blinds me for a second as my eyes are used to the darkness below. After a moment, my eyes adjust, and I see I'm in a large arena surrounded by stands. I'm still trying to resist, but my body keeps going forward. The pain in my head is almost unbearable at this point. I feel like I have the worst headache I have ever had. We continue around the arena's edge to a set of stairs that go up through the stands to the top. From this vantage point, I can see guards are everywhere. We turn and head down a walkway to a set of doors with two huge guards in front of them. I look up and think this might be a private box to watch the fights.

"We have Lady Beimaris's new fighter. She wanted to give her a look over before her first fight," my escorts tell the guards.

They open the doors and escort me in. I keep my head down but scan the room. It's a formal gathering area with different sitting areas separated by carpets and furniture. In the center of the ceiling is an extravagant light crystal chandelier that illuminates the whole room. Throughout the room are several candelabras with burning candles. Facing the direction of the arena, I see a large window that overlooks it. Just in front of the window is a desk with my backpack. To my right is a wall of books and a set of closed double doors.

"Remember, only speak when spoken to. Otherwise, you will regret it," my escort warns me.

As we stand there, I watch someone walk over to the double doors, open one of them slightly, and softly talk into it, too quiet for me to hear.

A second later, the doors swing open, and a woman walks out in a flowing dark silk robe. It only takes me a second to realize I'm looking at a shadow elf, one of the cruelest species in our world. They think every species except theirs is inferior and is meant to serve them. She looks at me as she walks across the room to the desk. Her black-on-black eyes and dark, twisted horns stand out against her white hair and almost white complexion. What's a shadow elf doing in The Midlands? They rarely leave their region. In the room she came from, there's a bed with someone lying in it. That must be her private quarters. When she finally sits down at the desk, she pulls smoke from the smoking stick she has with her.

"You're the one who bested Slainar. I wish I had seen that," she tells me.

"Why am I here? I don't belong here."

"You're here because you took something from me, and I plan on getting it back and much more. Tell me about these; they are quite elegant and unlike anything I've seen before," she says, gesturing to my weapons on her desk. "We didn't realize what they were until one of my men pressed one of these buttons while holding it. He lost two fingers when the blades swung out," she says as she presses the button to activate the blades on my weapon.

"What do you want me to say?" I ask more clearly, as my voice seems to be returning.

"Nothing really, I was curious. They will make a unique wall piece, don't you think?" she states, clicking the button again to close the blades.

Looking past her, I see a wall of weapons that must belong to the others she has taken.

"Let's see what else you had with you," she says, standing and dumping my backpack on her desk.

Seeing my belongings on her desk, I start to squirm.

"Clothes, map, blanket, drinking pouch, fruit. What's this? A stone fruit. Where did you get this? It's been years since I had one of these. I will enjoy this with someone shortly."

I don't respond. All I want her to do is get away from my stuff and let me go.

"You don't want to talk? No worries; you can speak in the arena. I want to see the individual who bested one of my best fighters," she tells me.

"I won't fight."

Pain hits my lower back, and I drop to my knees as my escort with the wooden club strikes me from behind.

"No one talks back at Lady Beimaris," he yells.

"It's alright, she has spirit. I like that," she tells him.

She walks over to me and squats, meeting me face-to-face.

"Let's see what you can do. Put her against Valrig. Reach out to his owner and set it for later today," she tells everyone in the room.

She looks back at me. "See you in the arena. I hope you are as good as I think you are. Till then."

Returning to her private area, she announces, "Burn the rest of her items. It's a pity. The shirt with the needlework was nice, but she won't need it anymore."

"No," I yell, hearing that my belongings will be destroyed.

The guard picks me up aggressively and tells me to go with him, and the sensation comes over me again. Everything I hold dear has been taken from me. Being escorted back to the holding area, I look around to see if I recognize anything in the distance or the surrounding area, but I don't.

The sensation stops, and I can move freely once I am back in my cell and they lock the door. As the guards walk away, one of them tells me, "Good luck against Valrig. You thought Slainar was tough."

I start pacing in my cell, figuring out how to get out of this place. I can run when the fight begins. They won't use the collars then, but the guards around the arena will stop me. Looking down, I see I am rubbing Jenny's locket. They must have missed this when they captured me. I quickly place it under all my clothing and next to my skin to ensure it stays hidden. They are not getting this, no matter what.

"Stop pacing and save your energy," I hear Killian tell me.

"Easier said than done. They want me to fight, and I don't want to. Who's Valrig?"

"A monstrous ogre. He likes to play with his victims before killing them. He makes them think they might win before he turns the tide. Then, he either stomps their head into the ground or crushes their skull between his hands. I'm told he doesn't mind being a slave as long as he gets to fight and kill. I'm sorry, but I don't see you making it through this even if you defeated Slainar," he tells me.

Hearing this, I lean against the wall and think to myself. This is it. I'll finally be reunited with Jenny. The gods have put me through hell; they at least owe me this.

As I wait in my cell, I hear people talking through the grate in the ceiling. It sounds like the arena is filling with spectators to see me fight, or, should I say, my death, as I have been told. It doesn't take long before the crowd above me is excitedly yelling and cheering. Knowing that I am most likely going to be killed, my nerves begin to show. I hold out my hand, and it's shaking.

"Kyra, I hear Valrig has a bad eye. Try to use that if you can," Killian tells me, placing his hand through the bars to shake mine.

I walk over and grab his forearm out of respect for his gesture.

"I hope the gods smile on you," he tells me.

I nod and step back, waiting for the guards to come for me. If I am going to die, I should face it head-on. I don't have to wait long as I hear the door open at the top of the stairs. I watch one of the same guards as before walking toward my cell.

"Stand there and don't move," he commands me.

The collar enforces his will on me. I hate it. The sensation is so painful, as my mind tries to fight it. He gives me another order as he opens the door, "Come this way."

He escorts me to the center of the arena, where he commands me, "Stop."

Looking around, the arena is filled with spectators cheering. Lady Beimaris is looking down at me from her private viewing area. Her extravagant outfit, with layers of fabrics and colors, seems more suitable for a party than a fighting match. She raises a glass to me. Next to her are several other people dressed as she is, most likely fellow enslavers. I get furious at the sight of all these people who came here to see me fight for my life for entertainment and profit.

"Do I get a weapon?"

"No weapons. Lady Beimaris prefers non-weapon fighting as

they are more physical," he tells me. "I have five gold coins on you lasting more than a minute. Don't let me down."

I look at him and sarcastically say, "I hope I don't disappoint you."

Across the way, I see a rather large ogre entering the arena, pushing guards to the side like toys. This has to be Valrig. Everything that was mentioned to me seems to be accurate. He's monstrous. He stands at least three feet over everyone around him. His greenish coloring makes him stand out against the arena's wooden construction. Watching this enormous being, I realize I have little to no chance of surviving this. It didn't take him long to lock eyes on me and head straight toward me. As he gets closer, I notice he isn't wearing a collar. I step back out of fear as I think he is about to attack me.

"He doesn't have a collar!" I announce.

"Don't worry. He won't start until Lady Beimaris gives the go-ahead," my escort tells me.

Valrig stops before me, huffing, and leans down to look at me.

"Good luck. You're going to need it," the man informs me as he leaves the arena quickly.

Standing up close and personal with Valrig is even more terrifying. His tusks stick out five inches or more, protruding from his lower lip. Trying to size him up, I notice his hands and feet are wrapped in bandages like Slainar. I see nothing attached to his belt or the garments around his waist.

"You pretty, I won't hit face too much," he informs me.

As he says this, I notice his right eye is cloudy. So that's the eye, Killian mentioned. He straightens up, steps back, and looks up toward Lady Beimaris.

"Valrig ready," he yells up at her.

I'm unsure what will happen next, but my legs are shaking slightly. Without warning, I hear a gong ring throughout the arena. I jump back to increase the space between us, but he comes charging at me with all his mass, trying to grab me. Luckily, I dash out of his grasp in the direction of his bad eye. I seem to be faster than he is.

"Fast, aren't you? You can't avoid Valrig forever," he tells me.

Realizing he's right, I go on the offensive and run at him and slam his huge chin with an uppercut, causing his head to fly back. I quickly follow this up by grabbing and trying to slam him to the ground. Before I can, he bashes his fists onto my back. I hear cracking in my body as I am forced to the ground. Upon impact, all the air is knocked out of my lungs, and the pain sets in. The next thing I feel is him kicking me in my side, sending me flying several feet away. Rolling to a stop, I try to get up but can't. The pain is too intense, and I start to cough up blood. Within a few seconds, this monster beat me.

Lying on the ground in pain, someone tells me, "Things are not going your way. I know you can win this. You have to accept who you are and use it."

I pick up my head and see Jenny squatting beside me, smiling.

"Why are you not fighting with all that you are? I know it scares you, but it is not your time to die. Promise me you will never give up, no matter what," she tells me as she fades away. I reach for her, but she's gone.

"Jenny."

As I lie on the ground in pain, I think of her and everyone back home, as well as Iris and her family. She told me to use what I have been scared of allowing out. I pick myself off the ground slowly. As I stand there, I close my eyes and breathe deeply. Be who I am and use what I have. I start to awaken the part of me that I have tried to keep hidden from everyone.

"I promise you I will not give up."

I feel myself transform as I open my eyes. Unlike all other times, I am in control of this transformation. Turning to my opponent, I'm ready to continue our fight. When I do this, the crowd cheers, seeing me stand. Valrig looks confused. He wasn't expecting me to get up from his round of attacks. Before he has a second to do anything, I dash at him faster than I have ever moved before, and I lock my hands together and swing from the ground up, connecting with his broad chin. The impact causes him to fly backward and onto his back. Before he can get up, I jump high into the air and drive my knees into his chest. When my knees impact, I hear cracking sounds.

"Payback is painful!" I yell at him.

He yells in pain but swings his large arm at me in defense. I jump off him quickly. Even in my current state, one of his blows will hurt me. He gets up, holding his chest with one arm. He's having trouble breathing. I must have hurt him with my last attack.

"How you get up. Valrig, crush your back. Heard ribs break," he says, in pain.

I run around him quickly, grabbing him from behind. I suplex him to the ground. As I twist away, he gets up and slowly walks toward me. I run and leap at him with a diving double leg kick as I did against Slaniar, but instead of connecting, he grabs me and places me into a bear hug. He begins to squeeze me in his massive arms. I scream in pain, trying to push away with all that I have, but his strength is incredible.

I look down and see his neck and bulging veins. I lean into him and bite down on his neck, piercing his skin with my fangs to drain him. As I drink from him, I feel his blood pulsing through me. It energizes me, and the pain from my injuries fade. As I continue to drink from him, I see flashes of Valrig fighting others but also being beaten by his owner. As with Jenny's parents' memories, I feel his pain and sadness. All he wants is to be free of all this. He isn't as monstrous as I was told, but forced to do what he must to stay alive. When I start to feel his heartbeat slowing and his grip on me loosens, I release my mouth.

I should be able to pull away from him, but he's still holding on to me and starts to squeeze again. I lean back, trying to get some leverage to pull myself out of his grip, and that's when I see his face. I push with my left arm to create some distance between us, and I start striking him with my right elbow and fist over and over again in the center of his face. With each blow, I inflict more and more damage. His face is bleeding, and his lower lip is split wide open, but he's still holding and squeezing me with all that he has. I grab his tusks in each hand and start to pull on them in opposite directions, trying to rip them out. His eyes widen with concern, and he squeezes even tighter, trying to crush me. I pull harder and harder, and I hear a snapping sound. With a final pull, I snap off one of his tusks, quickly burying it deep into his neck and then pulling it out. When I do this, blood sprays wildly from his neck. He drops me and holds his neck, trying to stop the bleeding. I step back, ready to defend myself, watching as blood sprays from his neck. He looks at me and starts stepping toward me, but I move back. After a few steps, he falls to the ground, and I watch blood pool near him.

The crowd roars with excitement as I stand over him.

I drop the tusk and see Lady Beimaris smiling at me. I run in her direction, enraged at what she has made me do. I get a few steps when I feel the controlling sensation pulsing through my body, and I stop, almost falling to the ground. The pain in my mind is starting to build as I try to move. I scream out of frustration. As I struggle to move, Lady Beimaris appears at the entrance of the fighting area and walks toward me, accompanied by her bodyguards.

"Well, well. Aren't you full of surprises? What are you?" she questions me.

I scream at her animalistically. "Allow me to move. I will show you what I am."

"That's not very nice," she tells me with a smirk. "You made me a lot of money today, and I plan to make much more with you. You belong to me now," she tells me coldly.

I scream at her, and with all that I have, I'm able to move one step toward her, which causes her to step backward. When I try to move again, my vision goes white, and I feel myself fall to the ground.

~

Feeling my cell's cold, damp stone floor on my face, I hear someone talking to me.

"Wake up. You survived. How did you defeat Valrig?" I hear Killian ask, surprised.

Opening my eyes, I get up and instantly feel the pain on the back of my head. I place my hand on my head and feel a large bump. I look at my hand to see if there's blood, but there isn't. I lean against the wall of my cell. How has my life come to this? Less than a year ago, I was the happiest I had ever been, and now I am here. The gods don't seem to like me.

"So tell me, how did you beat Valrig?" Killian asks again.

"I made the choice and a promise," I answer.

"I'm not sure what that means, but you lived. That's what's important. Living and the hope of getting out of here one day. Not all of us will make it, but you might have a chance based on what you did today," he explains.

"Living at what cost?" Feeling the back of my head again.

Ever since my vampire side first appeared, I have tried to keep it hidden because I feared what I might do. To survive in this place, I have to accept who I am. I am not human or a vampire. I am something different. I hope to hold onto who I am in this place. Only time will tell.

CHAPTER 20
KILLIAN

How long have I been in this hell? It has to be at least a few months, as I have seen the season change while fighting in the arena. It's also the only time I get to breathe fresh air instead of the putrid smell of the holding area. When I am in my cell, I have learned not to say much because if I do, I'm punished by my captors. Throughout my time here, Killian has been trying to talk to me occasionally, as his other cell neighbor doesn't speak a shared language. I try to ignore him as much as I can, but every so often, I give in. Today is one of those days.

"You're persistent, aren't you?" I ask.

"Talking helps pass the time, and we have lots of time," he answers. "You haven't told me anything about yourself since we first met. What's your story? Where do you come from?"

"Why is that important? I'm just trying to survive this place," I say.

"We're all doing that. It doesn't mean we can't talk."

Knowing he won't stop, I tell him, "I'm from the valley."

"Me too. I'm from the Far North. I belonged to a small tribe near the town of Reyvik. What town are you from?" he asks.

"Mountain Side."

"You're a talkative one. What's with the short answers?" he replies.

He's lucky I'm talking to him at all. "My turn. You said, belonged. What does that mean?"

"I decided to leave my tribe."

"Why?"

"Why would anybody leave everything they know or their family? Love. What else has that type of power over someone?"

"Love," I say quietly.

Hearing him say this word makes me think of Jenny and everyone back home and how much I miss them. I wish I had never left home.

"What's their name?" I ask.

"Silva."

"That's a pretty name. Do you have any children?" I ask.

"Two boys who were a handful back then. They have to be close to ten and eight now. I miss my family greatly."

"How long has it been since you have seen them?"

"I think I have been here for two years, but I'm unsure."

Answering my last question, I see the pain on his face as he talks about his family.

"Tell me about your family. What's waiting for you back home?" he asks.

"I don't want to talk about them. Talking about them is too painful. I'm pretty sure I won't ever see them again."

"You can't think that way. You have to imagine getting out of here and returning to them."

I walk over and sit down, leaning on the bars that separate us, looking at the floor of my cell. Just mentioning them lowers my mood, as if that's possible. "I don't see how; this place is a fortress. I heard the guards discussing getting rid of the fighter two cells down. They tossed his body down a ravine not far from here. That's how we get out of here."

"You're a downer, aren't you?" he states.

"Tell me about the locket. Who's in the locket around your neck?" he asks. "I notice you rub it often. Does it comfort you?"

"How did you know about that? I was sure I kept it hidden."

"You only rub it when it's just us down here. I have eyes," he answers.

"Someone I lost a while ago."

"Tell me about them; I like to know."

I haven't talked about Jenny much since her death, not even with Mother, as I find it too painful at times still. Maybe it would help. Plus, I have a captive audience, and we do have time.

"I was seventeen and wanted to work the harvest back home..."

I'm dropped onto the floor of my cell by two guards who carried me back from my last fight. I can barely move, as I have nothing left in me. I'm confident I have internal injuries from being kicked repeatedly, as well as the stab and slashing wounds that are still bleeding pretty badly.

Lying there, I hear my cell door close, and one of the guards says, "I don't think she's going to make it. Lady Beimaris is going to be upset for sure. I heard she had the owner of the other fighters killed for breaking the rules."

The arena door closes, and I hear Killian move up to the bars that separate us.

"Shit, you're in bad shape. What happened?" he asks.

"She had me fight two fighters at once. I guess she wanted to up the ante. One had a hidden blade," I barely won, coughing up blood.

I crawl over to him and lean against the bars, on the verge of passing out.

I feel him wrap one of his arms around me to hold me up as he wipes the blood off my face with a rag. "That's a deep cut on your face. It looks like it's burnt or something."

"I think the blade was poisoned. It burned instantly as it cut me," I answer. "I don't think I'm going to make it. I'm cold and feel funny."

He holds me tighter as he tells me, "You have to make it; we promised each other to get out of here together. You told me you always keep your promises. I'm going to hold you to that!"

As my eyes close for what I believe will be the last time, I softly say, "I'm sorry. I tried to keep it, Jenny, but I don't think I can anymore. I'm tired and would rather be with you than here."

I feel myself drift, and I see myself and Killian from above. Is this what it's like? Is this what Jenny saw when she died?

Looking at Killian and me, I hear Jenny's voice. "No, it's not your time. Ask him!"

I feel her push me back toward myself and open my eyes. "You're a stubborn one, aren't you?"

"I thought I lost you," Killian says.

I don't want to ask him, but it's the only way I can recover from this.

"Blood."

"Yes, you're covered in your blood," he says.

"No—I need to drink blood," I answer.

"What? I don't understand."

"If I drink blood, it will help me."

"What? Why?" Killian asks, confused.

"It's part of who I am. If I drink blood, it will heal me."

"I don't know what that means, but how do we get you blood?"

"You can give me some."

I don't want to do this, but if I don't, I'm pretty sure I won't make it through the next hour, and I'm pretty sure someone will be angry with me. I don't ever want her to be angry with me.

"I'm not losing you. Do what you have to," he tells me.

"Are you sure?"

"Yes, do what you have to!" he shouts.

I take hold of his arm with the last of my strength and turn it over, exposing the underside of his wrist. Looking down nervously. "I'm sorry if this hurts."

I transform and bite down and start to drink from him. As his blood hits my tongue, the taste of it causes me to drink faster and harder. I close my eyes, enjoying the taste and warmth I'm feeling. As I drink, the pain and exhaustion fade, and my strength starts to come back.

"How much do you need? I'm starting to feel light-headed and dizzy," he says.

Opening my eyes, I quickly pull his arm away from my mouth to force myself to stop. I move against the opposite wall of my cell to give us space. I am breathing heavily due to the rush of drinking from him. I gaze over at him and see him looking at me, holding his wrist.

"Your eyes, they're almost glowing. Are you alright?"

I close my eyes to try to calm myself as the blood has put me in an excited state. After a moment, I open my eyes and look down at a wound on my arm. I watch it close up, leaving a scar where it was.

"I should be alright now. Thank you."

I walk over to him and sit next to him. "So now you know."

"As long as you're going to be ..."

I watch him start to slump and lean on the bars before he passes out. I put my arm through the bars and hold him up so he doesn't fall over. I wish I didn't drink from him, but if I didn't, I wouldn't survive. I am grateful for this, but it makes me nervous at the same time that I might have to rely on this every so often if I am badly injured. I never want to think of Killian as a source of blood. We have grown close over the past few months.

I'm pacing in my cell, listening to the crowd cheering and stomping in the stands through the vent. Today is intense, with the number of fights being held in one day. Lady Beimaris has put together a tournament that has caused a few of our fellow fighters not to return. Luckily, I won my match with only minor injuries. Killian was taken up for his match not long ago. When they escorted him out, something felt off to me, and I could tell he felt it as well. Not knowing how Killian is doing is getting to me. The match has been going on for much longer than any of his previous matches. Suddenly, I hear a large cheer from above as someone has won. I'm rubbing my locket, trying to calm myself, but it's not working. Hearing the door to the arena open, I feel a sense of relief as I will see Killian shortly. I head to the front of my cell, grabbing the bars and looking down. I only see two guards coming down the stairs. Where's Killian? Why is he not with them? Maybe Lady Beimaris is talking to him.

"That fight was crazy. I can't believe he almost won," one of them says.

"Where's Killian?" I yell out.

They stop at the base of the stairs and look towards me.

"Your friend? He didn't make it. They're dragging his body out of the arena right now," the other one tells me.

"What—what did you say?!" I yell, with a tremble in my voice.

"Your friend didn't make it. He lost," the other one says.

Hearing this, I retreat to the far back of my cell and slide down the wall. When I hit the ground, I hold myself. A moment later, I feel my face getting wet from tears, and I start to cry and scream, filling the holding area with my cries of pain. The only thing I cared about in this place that kept me going is now gone. Sitting on the ground, I realize I am now truly alone in this place.

I have been staying in the back of my cell, hiding in the shadows, since Killian's death. My mind is busy with my memories of him and how we spent our time together. My fondest memories are of when we taught each other, like when he was teaching me his native tongue. Most of the time, I made him laugh due to how I pronounced words or how I would mix up words or sounds. Due to his patience and much practice, I finally grasped it well enough to converse with him. In return, I taught him Elvin, which he grasped quickly.

I'm sure my next fight will be soon, as it's been a few days since my last one. The bitch likes to keep me active because I bring in the crowds, bringing her gold in return. Hearing the arena door open, I watch the holding area attendant and a guard walking down the stairs, talking to each other.

"Did she do that?" The attendant asks.

"That's what I heard," the guard answers.

"I can't believe she would rig a fight so one of her fighters would lose. Why would she do that?"

"I heard she made three times the gold when he lost."

"When was this?"

"A few months back. During the big tournament."

Are they talking about Killian? They must be. That bitch made it so my friend couldn't win and come back to me. Processing what I'm hearing, I close my fists tightly and clench my jaw out of anger. I watch them as they talk casually about my friend, making their way towards me. I get up quietly and walk to the front of my cell. I reach through the bars and grab the guard, who's wearing a bracelet. I pull as hard as I can, which causes his head to smash into the metal bars, cracking it open like an egg. Letting go, he falls to the ground, silent as the blood pools by his head. I hear the attendant scream, and before he can move away, I grab his arm and start pulling him repeatedly into my cell. With each pull, he smashes into the bars. When I stop, he's wedged between two bars of my cell. I might have pulled him through the bars entirely if I pulled a few more times. Hearing guards rushing into the holding area, I step back and look at my revenge for Killian. I smile at the carnage I have just caused.

"Back up and don't move!" the lead guard yells at me.

I back up and follow the orders. I watch them attending to my victims, but there's nothing they can do.

"They're gone. She cracked his skull wide open, and he's just broken. Look at him; he's half pulled through the bars," the guard says.

I watch the lead guard reach for his whip. "I wish I could kill you right now, but I can't. I can do this instead. Turn around!"

As I turn around, I hear my cell door open, and then I feel the first strike against my back. The pain is instant and intense. I fall to my knees as the whip strikes me again and again. Within a few moments, I am flat on the ground, shaking in pain, when I hear her.

"That's enough; I think she's learned her lesson. Clean this mess up and attend to her wounds. Those can get infected if not cleaned and bandaged," Lady Beimaris demands.

"You want her wounds cleaned and bandaged?! What about what she did?! My friend is dead!" the guard states, astonished and enraged.

"I don't care. She's more important than he was. Do you hear me?" Lady Beimaris states to my punisher.

I struggle to stand, but I finally get up and face her.

"Look at you. Even in this state, you can stand," Lady Beimaris says.

"I'm going to kill you," I grumble at her.

"Maybe, but not today. Kneel and be quiet. I have to clean up your mess," she answers.

I try to fight her command, but the pain becomes terrible. I give in and kneel on the ground. My head feels like it's about to explode from trying to resist her command. As I look at her, all I feel is rage. I want her to feel the same level of pain that she causes me physically and emotionally.

"Paint a line in front of her cell to show a safe distance to ensure this doesn't happen again. She's becoming more unstable lately, and finding good workers is hard," she says to the guards.

She then turns back to me.

"Try not to cause any more trouble, will you? I'm giving you a week to rest and heal before I put you back in the arena. I want you to be strong enough to keep your record intact. You're a legend in this world," she says, walking out of the holding area.

"I hope you misbehave so I can punish you again," the guard angrily tells me, patting his whip on his belt.

After everyone leaves, I release my anger and pain by screaming. When I do this, I notice the other fighters covering their ears as my screaming fills the holding area. I get up, stumble to a side wall of my cell, and punch it as screaming isn't enough. It hurts, but I punch the wall again. The pain I feel in my hands forces my mind to focus on that instead of everything else I am feeling. I continue to punch the wall over and over again until I notice blood on the wall. I stop and look at my hands. My knuckles are bleeding and swollen, but I feel calmer as my emotions are numb. I move to the back of my cell and slide down to rest. Sitting, I look at my swollen and bloody hands. They are throbbing and burning from the damage I inflicted on them. I hear a scratching sound. I look down and see a rat beside me, exploring my cell. I transform and quickly grab it. Within a few seconds, I drain it and toss it out of my cell. Even though it's only a tiny amount of blood, I feel my body using it. I watch as the broken skin of my knuckles heals. My back doesn't hurt as much, but it's far from healed. I would need twenty rats for those wounds. Luckily, rats are a common thing down here.

PART THREE

REMEMBERING WHO YOU ARE

CHAPTER 21

AN EMPTY SOUL

I almost don't recognize the reflection in the puddle beside me. I see an adult with long, matted hair. A scar that starts above their left eye and ends on their cheek is a reminder of a time when a blade was snuck into a fight long ago. Turning away from my reflection, I rub my locket between my thumb and index finger to calm myself. I have retreated to the darkness, where I don't allow my emotions or feelings to be present. They do me no good in this place. The only thing that gives me comfort is the locket around my neck that I have kept hidden all these years. However, recently, I have been thinking of giving up on life. I'm exhausted physically and mentally from being in this hell. My thoughts keep drifting to purposely losing my next match so that not only does the bitch lose, but I am finally away from this place and reunited with Jenny in the Everlife.

Hearing the arena door open, I look up to see the short, green-skinned parasite of a goblin. With each step, I hear the grating sound of his long toenails scratching the stone steps as he descends. Accompanying him is a teenage boy I've never seen before.

"What is that terrible stench?" the boy asks.

"It's the fighters and the sewer hole. Don't worry, you'll get used to the smell. The first day is the worst," the goblin says, laughing maniacally.

The boy looks to be in his mid-teens with blond hair pulled into a ponytail. He's thin and looks very out of place. He has to be new. He's dressed in street clothing, not the everyday attendant outfit. I can sense there's a bit of innocence to him that doesn't match this place, but that will likely fade over time as he works here.

The smell of this cesspool is getting to him as he starts dry heaving. He grabs a rag from his pocket and wraps it around his face, covering his mouth and nose. I smile slightly, as I know this doesn't work. The stench of this place can't be blocked.

"Why are the fighters kept in cells?" the boy asks as they reach the bottom of the stairs.

"Let's say they didn't agree to be here," the parasite tells him.

The parasite continues to explain how things work down here. "Each morning, ask the fighters to place their bucket outside their cell so you can empty it in the sewer hole over there. Afterwards, place it back where they can grab it. You'll also be serving their food in the evenings. The kitchen brings a pot of food down for you to dish out in these bowls. Each fighter gets a scoop of whatever they made. There's also a bucket of water and a ladle if they ask for water. When they're done, they'll push the bowls out so you can collect and restack them. Got it?"

Watching the boy nod, I can see he has a look in his eyes. It seems that he's surprised at how it is for us down here.

"To ensure they behave, they all wear a collar. These collars require them to follow our orders as long as you're wearing one of these," he points to the bracelet on his arm. "When you have earned everyone's trust, you will get one as well, but don't expect it for a while. Let me show you how it works."

The boy and his teacher walk over to the cell that currently holds the Kalkin, a dog-like species that walks upright from the desert region of Tailte.

"Come here and kneel before us," he orders the Kalkin.

The Kalkin growls at him, exposing his teeth and trying to resist, but he ends up walking and kneeling in front of this devilish goblin who enjoys his work a bit too much.

"You see. No issues. That's how we get them to the arena as well." They continue to walk down the row of cells toward me.

"They're all dangerous, but be extra cautious around the last cell. That cell holds our standing resident. She's been here for ten years and is Lady Beimaris's most valuable fighter."

"She?" the boy asks.

"Don't be fooled because she's a woman. She's deadly. See the blood stain on the wall in front of her cell. That blood belonged to the person you're replacing. A few weeks ago, she attacked him because he crossed the line without realizing it. Within a matter of seconds, she bashed his head and body against her cell and tossed him against the wall. Don't ever cross the red line in front of her cell," he warns the boy.

"Got it. Don't cross the red line," he answers, looking at it.

"It's morning, so it's bucket time. Get to it. I am going to go back up and tend to a few things. I'll be back this evening. Don't get killed."

The boy looks lost and nervous. He looks around, trying to control his fear. Finally, he starts asking the fighters for their buckets.

"Can I have your bucket, please? I don't want any trouble," he says to the fighter in the first cell.

He must think that we might not hurt him if he asks nicely. We are always happy to hand over our buckets that are full of our shit, piss, and blood from our wounds. This would never be the time to hurt a worker.

When he gets a cell or two away from me, I see him remove the rag from his face. I think he realizes it doesn't help. As he walks up to my cell, I see him trying to find me, but I'm in the back of my cell, against the wall in the shadows.

"Please don't hurt me. Can I have your bucket?" he asks me.

I haven't used my bucket for the past day because I haven't eaten or drunk anything. I kick the empty bucket toward him, hitting the cell's bars.

Seeing the bucket is empty, the boy steps back and says, "I'm going to leave it here."

I watch him return to the chair beside the small table holding our meal bowls. He stares out and occasionally looks at the fighters. I stop rubbing my locket as it isn't helping my restlessness. I stand and face the wall, imagining it's my captor, and I start to punch it repeatedly to punch away my restlessness. As I'm striking the wall, I notice the boy walks over to my cell to watch me.

"Can I help you?" I ask between punches.

"No, I just wanted to see you. Are you from the North? You sound like you are," he says, returning to his chair.

I notice he's flinching with every strike I make against the wall. Years of doing this have toughened my knuckles to the point where I don't feel them. After a few minutes, I notice him returning to my cell again. I stop and look over my shoulder. He's past the red line. I dash at him, reaching through the bars and grabbing his throat. I start to squeeze. Even though I don't know him, he's part of this hell. He has a look of panic in his eyes as he knows I am going to kill him. As I am about to crush his throat, he gasps, "Lady ... it's me ... Forge." Gasping for air. "Remember ... I asked if you were as strong as a giant?"

Hearing his words causes memories I have buried deep to flip through my mind. As I remember, I feel something I haven't allowed in years: an emotion. I release him, and he falls to the ground, holding his throat, gasping, and coughing.

"Why are you here?" he asks, coughing.

I step back into the shadows of my cell and slide down the back wall. "Leave this place if you can."

~

Throughout the rest of the morning and into the afternoon, I stay in the shadows. The memories of the day I met Forge keep playing through my mind. Why is he here? I can't help but look at him. He's grown so much since I saw him. He's still skinny, but he's almost a man. I see him watching my cell with a worried look. Every so often, he rubs his throat where I grabbed it. I'm sure it's sore, as I was about to crush his windpipe. I can start to see bruising from where my fingers were around his neck.

It was early evening, and the kitchen was dropping off our food, if that's what you call it. It is a large pot of brown gop comprised of leftover food scraps. Most of the time, it's full of bugs and other things because they never clean the pot. They keep reheating it and adding to what is already there. I watch Forge open the lid and stir. He smells it and almost instantly dry heaves over the pot.

The human fighter in the cell near him walks up to the front of his cell. "Don't vomit in our food. It's all we get," the fighter states.

Forge replies with, "How can you eat this?"

"When it's all we get, we eat it. Otherwise, we go hungry. I saw what happened earlier. Don't let anyone know you know her. If they find out, you will be removed. Do you understand?" the fighter explains to Forge.

"By removed, you mean ..." Forge pauses.

"Yes. Be careful. I'm surprised she didn't crush your throat. You must have triggered a memory. Memories are a bad thing here. This place changes everyone, and not in a good way. She's most likely not the same person you remember. She has been fighting for her life for longer than anyone here," he tells Forge, holding on to the bars of his cell.

This statement is true. I am not the same person I was when I was captured. I don't even know if I could ever be that person again. With every fight, I lose more and more of who I am.

I watch Forge scooping our meals into bowls and placing them in front of our cells. When he gets to mine, he puts a bowl down and tells me, "I wish I had something better for you, but it's what I have to give you."

I stay silent, as I am not sure what to do. I don't want to speak to him, but at the same time, I do.

He leaves the bowl and starts to walk back, but stops after a few steps. He turns back and pulls an apple out of his pocket.

"It's not much, but it's better than that," he says.

He rolls the apple into my cell, and it stops next to me. I look down at it. The last apple I saw was when a guard was eating one as he watched over us years ago. I pick it up and smell it. It's fresh and feels firm. I take a large bite from it. As I chew, the sweet flavor fills my mouth. I almost don't want to swallow to keep the flavor in my mouth as long as possible. Sitting quietly, eating the apple, I feel something on my cheek. I touch my cheek with my finger and look at it. Why am I crying? After finishing the apple, core, and all, I watch Forge intensely for the rest of the evening, wondering how and why he's here. He must have gotten into trouble or involved in something he shouldn't have. Looking at the air vent, I notice the sunlight is no longer shining in, indicating daylight is ending.

"You made it through your first day and didn't die. Good job," Forge's teacher tells him as he descends into the holding area.

"Can I ask a question? How did these fighters get here?" Forge asks again.

"Most are bought or traded. Some are payments or are sold to cover debts," the goblin explains to Forge as he looks at the leftovers in the pot. "Your shift's done. Go to the workers' barracks and get some sleep. Tomorrow is a big day. Lady Beimaris has set up a fight for her prized fighter. Make sure you're here early so we can get her ready."

I see Forge look down at my cell for a second before quickly heading up the stairs.

"What's the rush? Hmm. This looks pretty good," the goblin mumbles, looking into the pot.

I turn my head away and close my eyes. I will be fighting tomorrow. Maybe I'll act on my plan this time.

CHAPTER 22
THE GAMBLE

I adjust myself against the cell wall. We all learn quickly that it's better to sleep upright than on the floor, as the rats can bite your face, and these bites tend to become infected. Speaking of rats, I notice a large one by me. I quickly grab it and transform to drain it of its blood. It's enough to keep the hunger at bay and help me heal. If it hadn't been for the endless supply of rats in this place, I don't know if I would have survived as long as I have. I pass the dead rat to the cell next to me, and the other fighters then pass it to the Kalkin to eat. We learned that he can only eat freshly killed food, as he can't digest any other type. He would have died from starvation weeks ago without the endless supply of rats.

I look up, hearing people filling the arena through the air vent. It doesn't take long before the arena guards enter the holding area with the goblin by their side. They head over to me to escort me up to the arena. I stand, waiting for them to open my cell.

"Come to the front of the cell and stay there," the lead guard tells me. I feel the sensation come over me, and I obey. I don't resist the collar. Years ago, I learned the more you fight it, the more pain you feel.

"Don't move," he tells me as he places restraints on my wrists. "Follow us, and don't cause any trouble. Your opponent will be arriving soon. We need to get you to the arena."

I see Forge run up to us, and one of the guards pushes him back against the wall. "Stay away. We have to be careful with this one."

"I was told I was going to help," Forge informs them.

"Stand there and don't get in our way," one of the other guards tells him.

As I'm escorted out of my cell, I see Forge looking at me closely. The other fighters shake their cell doors and howl as I walk past them.

"Your fellow fighters wish you well," one of the guards tells me as they escort me to the arena above.

Exiting the holding area, the sun hits my eyes. I raise my hands to shade them since it's been more than two weeks since I have seen the sun. As I'm escorted to the center of the arena, the crowds roar for me. Hearing their cheers disgusts me. I see Lady Beimaris looking down at me from her usual vantage point. Even from this distance, I see she's smiling at me like always. I look over to the opposite side of the arena and see a female being escorted out in chains, screaming at everyone around her. She appears to be from the Far North based on her fur clothing, tightly braided blond hair, and blue paint streaked across her young, fair-skinned face. I'm guessing she is in her late teens. She probably doesn't have much fighting experience, but you never know. Either way, I will end this quickly so she doesn't have to suffer as I have.

Her escorts remove her chains, and they run away from her quickly. She finally sees me standing there, screaming at everyone watching her. Yes, I am the one you have to worry about.

The guards remove my shackles and step away. It's only me and the girl in the arena now. She yells at me [In her native language], "*I kill you to survive!*"

I understood what she just said. Is she from Killian's clan? I hear the gong sound through the arena. The girl runs at me and starts to swing at me. She's fast, but I evade and block her attacks easily.

I need to know if she's from Killian's clan.

I ask [In her language], *"Are you from the Northern Tribe by Reyvik?"*

She doesn't answer me, as she's blind with rage and continues to attack me in the hopes of landing a strike. I counter her last swing with a backhand across her face, knocking her down on the ground, which enrages her even more. She gets up quickly and starts swinging at me again. I have to get through to her. I yell at her, *"Stop!"*

She stops swinging and steps back. *"You speak my tongue,"* she states, breathing heavily. *"Are you from the north by Reyvik?"*

I hear the crowd's cheering stop because they don't understand what is happening.

"Not Reyvik, but close to it. How do you know my tongue?" She answers.

"A friend taught me it years ago. When you spoke, I had to know if you were from his clan."

The crowd is starting to boo us, which I enjoy hearing. I look over to see Lady Beimaris is not happy either. She's not getting her money's worth, and the betting will be lower than expected.

"We must fight till one of us is left standing, or we both die, yes? I'm not afraid of dying and will meet death with honor, as it's our way," She says, raising her arms again.

I look at her and breathe in deeply. *"Yes, only one of us will be left standing, and I promised someone I would always be standing. No matter what."*

The girl charges at me. We exchange blows and blocks with each other again. I have to give it to her; she's better than I thought, but she lacks foresight in predicting my movements. After a few more exchanges, I grab her head, which surprises her. She grabs my hands and tries to pull them off her head, but she can't. I'm much stronger than she is, even in my weakened state.

"You won't feel this, and I am sorry," I tell her.

I twist her head fully around, snapping her neck, which causes her to fall to the ground. I stand there looking at this young girl whom I just killed. I hear the crowd cheer for my victory, which is torture. Standing there motionless, I feel the shackles placed on me again, and I'm escorted back to the holding area. Walking past the cells, the other fighters stand at the front of theirs with their heads lowered. We do this out of respect for the fighter who lost their life. I see Forge sitting in the chair as he watches me being placed back in my cell.

As they remove my shackles, one of them tells me, "Lady Beimaris will be down shortly to talk to you. Make sure you behave."

As the cell door closes, I feel rage building inside me. Within a few minutes, the arena door opens, and I hear Lady Beimaris and her escorts coming down.

"The smell. I always forget how badly it smells down here," she announces, quickly getting to my cell.

"Congratulations on your win, but I have to say it was a little boring. What was with all that talking? I was glad when you finally ended it. I could tell she was no match for you. For your next fight, less talking and more action, so we can enjoy it more and make the betting more interesting." She laughs slightly.

Hearing that last remark, I launch at her from within my cell, hoping to grab her through the bars so I can strangle her.

However, she quickly commands, "Stop."

I fall to the ground, holding my head as the pain pulses through it. All I want to do is kill her for all she has done to me and everyone down here.

"I'm glad you still have the fire, but save your energy. I'll be taking you to another arena far from here to fight. They are unaware of your fighting record. I can cash in on you. For now, you have a few days off. Rest up," she tells me before leaving the area with her minions.

I lean against one of the walls of my cell, holding my head until the pulsing pain subsides.

"I have another apple if you like?" Forge asks me.

"Not hungry."

"I keep calling you Lady. I was wondering what your name is. I can't seem to remember it."

"Kyra," I answer, lowering my hands as the pain finally disappears.

"I watched you fight from the door. You're so fast, and it didn't seem like your opponent was a real threat to you. You were able to counter every one of her strikes. I've never seen anything like it before. I ... I was wondering something, though. May I ask what you told her right before you ... ?" he asks carefully.

I take my time to answer. "I told her I was sorry."

I stand and start to punch the wall. "Leave me alone! I don't want to talk." With each strike of my hand to the wall, I try to punch away what I am feeling, but it's not working. Why? It's worked for years, so why not now? Eventually, I stop and walk to the back of my cell, still trying to suppress what I'm feeling.

Later that afternoon, Forge walks back to my cell.

"Want that apple now?" he asks.

I raise my hand out of the shadows, and he tosses it to me. I catch it without looking. Like the other apple, this one is sweet and crunchy. I have missed apples.

As I eat my treat, he starts talking. "I was thinking—the collars and the bracelets. The bracelets seem to be the most important part. Can I ask you a question?"

"I guess."

"A person wearing a collar has to obey a person wearing a bracelet, right?"

"Yes."

I see him deep in thought, bouncing his leg as he thinks and moving his finger back and forth as if he is figuring something out. He turns to me excitedly. "I know how to get you and everyone else out of here."

"What?" I ask, confused.

"I just have to get a bracelet and make sure there's a distraction so we get out without being seen," he tells me.

"How are you going to get a bracelet? Only the most trusted workers are given one. There's no chance you will get one," I tell him doubtfully.

"You'll have to trust me. I know my target." He winks at me.

"Target? Plan?" I ask skeptically.

He runs up the stairs and out of the holding area without answering. How is he going to free us? I don't think he understands what it might take to do this and the consequences if it doesn't work. There is no way out of this place. I stand and start pacing anxiously in my cell. I haven't felt anxious in years. A few other fighters look toward me as they haven't seen me like this before. My mind is going frantic, trying to understand Forge's possible plan. I don't know how it will work, but at the same time, the hope of getting out of this place is almost too much not to think about.

It's not long before I hear the door open again. Forge races down the stairs and straight toward me. I notice the other fighters watching him as well.

"Tonight. Be ready," he informs everyone, sitting in the chair like nothing is happening. We all watch him intensely. How is he going to get us out of here? Eventually, we settle back down to our usual patterns, and even Forge closes his eyes and seems to fall asleep. The door opens, and that parasite goblin makes his way down the stairs and notices Forge sleeping. He quickly runs over to him and kicks the chair to wake him up.

"No sleeping!"

Forge shakes his head, waking up. "Sorry, it's boring down here. Did they bring the food down?"

"Do you see the pot?" he replies sarcastically, picking his teeth.

"No." Forge looks over where it's typically kept.

"Go see where it is. They must be running behind."

I watch Forge run up the stairs and out of the holding area. Waiting for Forge to return, we hear yelling through the air vent.

Suddenly, the door slams open, and Forge runs down the stairs in a panic. "The barracks are on fire, spreading to the southern corner!"

"What! My stuff!" The goblin exclaims, standing.

"Go, I will stay here and watch them," Forge tells him.

As the goblin runs out, Forge bumps into him. "Sorry. Good luck. I hope your stuff is safe."

I watch the goblin run up the stairs while Forge walks toward me, smiling ear to ear.

"What's so funny?" I ask.

"I told you to trust me, "He says, showing me the cell keys in one hand and a bracelet in another.

One thing you might not know is most Forgotten are expert pickpockets. It's a skill we all learn to survive. I was one of the best in Mountain Side," he explains quickly while putting on the bracelet.

He takes a deep breath.

"Here we go. Take off your collar," he tells me.

As with all other bracelet wearers, I feel the sensation. I unlatch the collar around my neck, and it falls to the ground. Feeling the air hit my exposed neck feels incredible. I touch my neck, look down at the collar, and smash it with my foot.

"Shit, that worked! What a flaw in the design," Forge tells me.

I quickly move to the cell door. Forge starts fumbling with the keys to open it, but before he can, I tell him, "Back up!" As I kick the cell door wide open, breaking the lock.

"Why couldn't you do that before?" he asks.

"Standing command. I couldn't whenever I tried, even when no one was here."

We run over to the other fighters. "Everyone ready to get out of here?" he asks.

Forge commands them, "Remove your collars and break them." As everyone removes their collars, he quickly opens their cells.

The excitement in the air is electric as we scramble to the door. With no collars to stop us, we are ready to go through anyone who tries to stop us.

We all nod and head up the stairs, with Forge leading the way. Forge opens the door slightly to see what's going on. He motions to everyone, and we exit. We follow the arena's inner wall in a single file. As we reach the arena's exit, we see the barracks engulfed in flames. I guess this was Forge's plan: have a distraction big enough to keep everyone busy while we escape. It seems to have worked.

"Everyone is focused on the fire. We can head this way and get out of the camp," he tells everyone.

The fighters move past Forge one after another, slapping him on his back as a gesture of gratitude. I watch him turn and look at me. "Come on. Let's go."

"Go with them. I have to take care of something," I tell him.

"I'm not leaving you! We're almost there. What so important?"

I place my hands on his shoulders. "I will meet up with you and the others later. Go, go now!"

I push Forge forward, insisting that he continues without me. He nods reluctantly and runs to catch up with the others. I watch him for a second before I turn back to end this madness once and for all.

Making my way back along the arena's wall, I jump into the stands and head towards her private quarters. Making my way down the walkway, I can feel the fire's intensity, forcing me to look down. Below, every worker is trying to put the fire out by throwing buckets of water at it. Behind them, I see her directing the efforts. I carefully enter her quarters and quickly close the door behind me. I head to her wall of trophies and grab my weapons that she placed there all those years ago. I examine them and activate the blades on each one to make sure they still work. I click them onto my belt, where they belong. I look over and see a cart filled with bottles of spirits. I grab the largest bottle and drink from it. I wipe my mouth and exhale. Looking across the room, I see the double doors I remember from when I was last here and walk over to them. I swing them open and enter her most personal area. Looking around, I see luxuries that were paid for by the pain of others: A large bed with silk sheets, a large wardrobe, most likely filled with her outfits I have seen her wear through the years, and a dressing table with a mirror, jewelry, hair, and beauty items. Turning, I notice a painting on the wall of her with someone. I walk over to get a closer look. It's a young shadow elf boy. They have similar facial features, and her hand is on his shoulder. Is she a mother? How can someone so cruel be a mother? I take my weapon and slash the painting across her face.

How am I going to do this? It could be hours before she returns, plus her guards will surround her. None of this matters, as I can wait for as long as it takes, and nothing or no one will stop me from ending her tonight.

Standing before the painting, I hear yelling coming from the entryway door. I quickly close the doors to her private area.

"Find out how that fire started and tell me when it's out! It's going to cost me a fortune to rebuild the barracks. It's a total loss. I want to know if this was an accident or on purpose," I hear her yell.

I smile, hearing her frustration. I peek through the crack of the doors and watch her walk over to the cart of spirits. She grabs the bottle I just drank from. She pours herself a large drink and drinks it down aggressively. She slams the glass on the cart, looking down at it.

"Lady Beimaris, Lady Beimaris. The fighters are gone!" a guard announces, running into the room.

"What do you mean the fighters are gone?" she questions the guard, raising her head in a scary tone. The guard backs up in fear, as do the others around her.

"We went down to check on them. All their cells are open, and their collars are smashed on the ground," the guard tells her very nervously.

Lady Beimaris goes quiet for a second, then screams and throws the glass she is holding at the guard, but it hits the wall and shatters.

"Find them. Find every one of them!" She screams at everyone. "They can't be far. I'm not losing anything else tonight. What are you waiting for? Go! All of you go! Don't return until you have them!"

I watch everyone leave quickly, terrified of her. As the last one leaves, they close the door so she's not disturbed. I couldn't plan this any better. We're alone, and there isn't anyone here to interfere. I watch her move behind her desk, where she leans on her arms while looking down. After a moment, she swipes the contents off the top of her desk onto the floor. She slams the desk with her hands and screams. I love seeing her this way. She's always in control, and now she's not. She turns and leans against her desk, holding her hands to her eyes, trying to calm down.

After a moment, she looks up at the wall and stares at it for a second. "Wait. Where are they?" I hear her say.

I quickly open the doors and run at her. She turns, but it's too late. I grab her and throw her into the bookshelves a few feet away, as hard as I can. Before she has a chance to hit the ground, I dash over, holding her up and covering her mouth so she can't yell for help.

"I'm going to enjoy this," I tell her.

I toss her against another wall, allowing her to fall to the floor. So that we are face to face, I lift her back up. I slap her face, mocking her, showing her who is in charge now. She's bleeding from her head, and I can see bruises forming on her face.

"Don't pass out on me. I'm not done yet. I want to show you the monster you created—a monster far worse than the one I thought I was before coming here."

She looks at me and barely gets out, "How?"

"Kindness is the reason I am here ... something you know nothing about, and I plan to show you nothing of," I tell her.

I transform, showing her my vampire side up close. As I glare at her, she turns her head. She's afraid, as she knows I am going to kill her. I bite down on her neck and start draining her life. As her blood courses through my body, I see flashes of her laughing and celebrating with others as they watch the fights. I feel her unremorseful excitement and pleasure from watching fighters kill each other in the arena for her profit. Continuing to drink from her, I see other memories of her counting her winnings. All she wants is more and more gold; she will do anything to get more of it.

I bite down harder, which causes her to wince in pain as I drink aggressively from her. My thirst for vengeance and blood seems to be unquenchable. I continue to drink from her until I feel her heartbeat almost stop. I will not allow her to die this way; it's too humane; she deserves to suffer for her actions.

I pull away from her and toss her across the room again. She lands on the cart of spirits. They shatter and cover her and the floor around her with their liquid. She's weak but tries to pick herself up off the floor. I pick up an unbroken bottle and pour it over her to ensure she is covered.

"I hope you suffer as you burn. This is for Killian and all the others."

I tip over one of the candelabras on top of her and watch her burst into flames. She screams as her flesh burns. After a few moments, she drops to the ground, silent. Watching her body burn, I feel satisfied, looking at her charring remains. I see the fire spreading and engulfing the room's walls and furniture. I run out of the room and make my way out of the arena to join the others.

Running through the woods, I catch their scent and follow it, ascending through the nearby forest. I hear a crashing sound and look back. The arena is completely engulfed in flames, and it's starting to collapse. I smile, seeing the warm yellow and orange glow of the fire burning down that horrible place. Continuing through the forest, I see the glow of a campfire in the distance. As I get closer, I see it's them and revert to my human form before entering the campsite. Everyone is sitting around the fire, but no one is talking.

Stepping into the light of the fire, I get everyone's attention, and they look up at me.

Forge runs up to me. "You made it."

"I told you I would." Turning to the fighters, I say, "Lady Beimaris is no more. She's burning with the rest of that place. She will never be able to do this to anyone again."

The fighters look at me briefly and nod. I walk over to the fire to join them. After so many years in the cold and damp cells, it feels comforting to be near the warmth of a fire. Forge sits down next to me. Everyone is speechless while watching the fire under the clear night sky.

CHAPTER 23
PARTNERS

I didn't sleep so that I could keep watch in case any of her minions found us.

As dawn breaks, the forest comes alive with animal and bird activity. I gaze up through the pine trees that sheltered us and see the morning sunlight shining through. Looking over, I see the fighters are beginning to stir.

"Morning," Forge tells me, yawning.

"Morning. Do you know where we are?"

"I think so. I was recruited from River Song, which is about two days to the north of here. The Northern Road should be down there somewhere," he says, pointing easterly.

Learning that River Song is close, I think of Brynn and how he is the last part of my vengeance. I will go there in the hopes of finding him so I can end him as well.

The human fighter walks up to us, and I stand to greet him.

"This is goodbye then," he tells me.

"Good luck," I return, extending my hand.

"I hope you find what you are looking for as well. I'm Brody Warsong, by the way." He grabs my forearm to shake.

"Kyra Everwind."

Brody then turns to Forge. "I don't know how to thank you for what you did, but we'll forever be in your debt. If you need anything, you can find me in Elos on the southern coast," he tells Forge while placing his hand on Forge's shoulder.

I watch Forge acknowledge his gesture. None of the other fighters walk over to us, but they all acknowledge Forge and me, and we do the same with them as they leave the campsite.

"Where are we going?" Forge asks me.

"We aren't going anywhere," I tell him.

"What do you mean, we're partners? We need to stick together," he reminds me.

"I owe you more than I can ever say or do, but we are not partners. Go back to where you need to be, as I have to do something I don't want you to be part of." I try to enforce my will on him. "Thank you, and I wish you good fortune."

I head in the direction that Forge pointed out and descend through the forest. I know Forge is following me as I hear him behind me. I pick up my pace, thinking I will lose him, but he keeps pace. He's stubborn, for sure. Yelling to him behind me, "When we get to the road, you're on your own."

It doesn't take long before we reach the Northern Road.

"I have years of experience fighting to survive. I won't slow you down; don't worry about me," he tells me.

"You're persistent, aren't you?" I shake my head slightly. "We can travel together for now. When we get to River Song, we go our separate ways."

Forge acknowledges, and we head up the Northern Road together.

By mid-afternoon, we come across a body of water just off the road with a path to it. I stop and look down at myself. It's been years since

I bathed, and it shows. I head down the path, thinking about washing off years of filth.

Forge asks, "Why are we going down here? Do you need water?"

"I need to bathe and wash the last of that place off of me. We can set up camp and rest."

As we approach the water, I see a clearing that would make a good campsite for us. I start undressing, dropping my clothes as I approach the water's edge. Walking out into the water, I let my fingers caress the top of the water. When I'm waist-deep, I start to swim out. I flip over on my back and float for a while. The water is cold, but it feels good against my skin. I look up at the blue sky and watch the clouds like I did when I was little. At first, nothing, but then I see a horse-shaped form in a cloud. In another, I see a dragon with its wings spread wide. The two clouds merge, becoming what looks to be a wolf. Looking at this cloud, it starts to change again. The wolf's head turns as if it's looking at me. I see breaks in the cloud where its eyes would be. I begin to feel angry and resentful as the cloud is making me think of my father. He is the reason that I spent ten years in that prison. I wouldn't have been captured if I hadn't gone after the prize money to help me find him.

"Go away. I don't want anything to do with you," I yell at it.

I watch the cloud start to change shape and fade into another cloud. Feeling agitated, I push the air out of my lungs; I sink a few feet below the water's surface, where I stay suspended in silence, closing my eyes. All I sense is the cold water around me and a few faint sounds from above. After a moment, I open my eyes and start to twist and twirl around, rubbing my body all over to remove the last of that dreadful place off of me. When I feel clean, I resurface and take a deep breath. I whip my hair back to keep it out of my eyes and look to the shore. My clothes have been placed on bushes near a fire that Forge must have made. I swim back and start to make my way out of the water, squeezing my long hair.

"You should bathe to get that place off you, too," I tell him.

He looks over at me, then looks down at the ground quickly. His face is turning red.

"What? Haven't you ever seen a naked woman before?" I ask.

"No, not really. I washed your clothes. Would you mind putting them on?" he asks, continuing to look at the ground.

I don't understand the big deal, but I dress to make him feel at ease.

As I place my top on, he asks, "Do they still hurt?"

I pause briefly. "Not anymore," I say while putting the rest of my outfit on. I know he's referring to my scars.

"Did you get them from fighting?"

"Some but not all. Some are from when I misbehaved."

I turn and see he looks pretty uncomfortable. I don't know how to comfort or let him know he doesn't have to worry about them. They are part of who I am now.

"I'm hungry. The last thing I ate was that apple. Are you hungry?" I ask.

"I'm always hungry. What's the plan?"

"I'm sure there are fish in the water and berries around. When my hair dries a bit more, we can look and see what we can find."

"Sounds like a plan. By the way, I kind of like your long hair. Maybe trim it or braid it." He pokes at the fire with a stick.

"I don't know how to braid hair," I share while squeezing more water out of my hair.

"Even I know how to braid hair. I had to braid Ophelia's hair for years until she learned how to."

He drops the stick, walks over to me, and takes a small pocket knife out.

I grab his arm as soon as I see the knife. I stare at the cutting edge of the blade and have flashbacks of the fight when I almost died.

"You're hurting me. I was only going to cut your hair and braid it. I promise," he says, wincing.

I release his arm and slowly lower my arm.

"Promise not to hurt me?" he asks. "I'm just trying to help."

"Sorry, I have been living on instinct for years."

"I get it, but try to relax. I'm not going to hurt you. I promise. How long do you want your hair to be?"

"I don't know."

As I sit there, my heart is pounding. I feel Forge gather my damp hair in his hand. He cuts my hair in a few quick motions and hands me a bundle of hair that's nearly two feet long.

"Hold this."

Looking at my hair, I realize it represents years in hell. I feel him start to braid my hair, and in no time, he says, "Done."

I touch the top of my head and feel my hair pulled tight to my scalp and the braid down to my lower back.

"How is it going to stay?" I ask.

"I used a piece of twine I had in my pocket. I recommend getting a ribbon or hair clasp to keep it braided."

"I hope you like it. Look at your reflection in the water," he says while touching my shoulder.

I recoil slightly.

He returns to where he was sitting and picks up his stick to poke at the fire again.

"Sorry about touching you," he says.

I don't know why I flinched like that, but my body reacted. How damaged am I that a touch causes me to pull away from people? I am still holding the hair that Forge handed me. I toss it into the fire and watch it burn. The smell of my burning hair hits my nose, and the scent reminds me of when Lady Beimaris was burning to her death. I smile slightly, thinking of her death again.

"Thank you for cutting and braiding my hair. I'm sure it's fine. No need to check," I tell him.

"I know you've been isolated and put through hell. However, it would be best if you tried to open up a little and let people you trust back in," he suggests.

"I don't know how to trust people or even trust myself. You saw how I just grabbed your arm and reacted to you touching me. I don't know how or what I might do if someone just came up to me that I didn't know at all," I explain. "I might hurt them or worse."

"Do you trust me? Take it day by day and see what happens. It won't be easy, but maybe you can get back or at least remember the person who offered me and my sister that meal."

"You have earned my trust, but I don't know if I could ever be that person again. She hasn't been around for years."

My stomach growls. Not wanting to continue with the conversation, I stand.

"You said you were hungry, as am I. Let's see what we can find. It might be best to stay here for the night and rest. It will be dark in a few hours, and we can continue at first light."

Exploring around the water's edge, we didn't find much besides a few berry plants that the wildlife mostly picked through. The water has little to no life in it, just waterbugs and a few minnows.

"I've never been to a body of water with such a lack of life," I tell Forge.

"I guess these few berries will be our meal for the night," he states.

"I guess so. Let's hope we find something tomorrow on our way to River Song."

Looking all around, I notice everything goes silent. All the birds and insects have stopped making noises. Forge was about to say something, but I raised my hand to keep him quiet. I hear water moving for a second, and then it stops. I draw my weapons, preparing them as I move us away from the water's edge. I sense something has been watching us and is about to move on us.

"What's wrong?" he asks quietly.

"I'm not sure, but something has spooked the birds and insects. Let's get back to the campsite." I move us back even further.

"You're kind of freaking me out," he says.

Without warning, the water in front of us explodes upward, spraying us. In the center of the water explosion, a serpent rises above us. It shakes and vibrates its webbed frill as it shrieks at us, exposing its pointed teeth and forked tongue.

"That explains the lack of wildlife," I shout. "I'm going to get its attention. I want you to run away as fast as you can."

"I'm not leaving you. I can help," Forge argues with me.

I watch the serpent arch back as it's about to strike at Forge. I raise my arms, waving them repeatedly to get its attention. "Over here!" I scream at it.

It turns toward me, hissing. Its yellow serpent eyes focus on me.

"Run!" I yell at Forge.

The serpent hisses and lunges at me with its mouth wide open, trying to grab me. I dodge its attack and slice down on it with both of my weapons, injuring it. However, it quickly counters my attack by slapping me with its tail. I am knocked to the ground and drop my weapons. As I try to get up, it wraps itself around me and raises me to its head as it squeezes me between its coils. The pressure is incredible. If I don't get out of its grip, I will pass out from having the air squeezed out of me. I push with both arms, hoping I can slip out, but I can't. The serpent tightens its grip on me. I scream in pain, and I feel myself transform out of survival instinct. Feeling the rush of power, I push as hard as possible to give myself a little space between me and the serpent's body, but it squeezes tighter on me. I feel my body being compressed. Is this how it's going to end for me? I survived all those years in the hellhole to end up as a meal.

Realizing I only have a few moments left before I pass out. I grab the beast with my hands and drive my fingers into it, tearing at its flesh. Suddenly, I hear it roar in pain, and it loosens its grip on me, and I slip out of its death grip. Hitting the ground, I gasp for air, and I dash away, grabbing my weapons.

The beast has turned its attention away from me and is now focused on Forge, armed with a slingshot and ready to fire. I realize that I have Forge to thank for my life again. He shot one of the beast's eyes out. This kid is full of surprises.

"I'm not sure what's going on with you, but are you alright?" he yells.

"I'll explain later," I yell back. "Do you think you can hit the other eye?"

"Yes, I just need a clean shot."

I must turn the beast's head in the opposite direction so Forge can take the shot. I dash to the beast's left, throwing my weapons as fast and as hard as I can, repeatedly slicing through its flesh, which causes it to swing its head in the direction of my attacks. I hear a quick whistle sound followed by the beast screaming. It's thrashing around in pain. Forge must have hit his mark and shot the beast's other eye out. Taking this opportunity, I run and lunge at its head and drive both of my weapons into its skull, causing it to slam to the ground. As I am on top of it, pressing my weapons deeper into its head, it breathes its last breath out.

Standing up, I lean forward, holding my side. I'm pretty sure I have broken ribs from being squeezed. I try to calm down, but my adrenaline is pumping through me. I have to calm down, or I might hurt Forge.

Forge runs up. "Are you alright?"

Trying not to look at him, "I think it broke a few ribs."

Forge tries to help, but I push him away. "Stay away, I haven't calmed down yet. I don't want to hurt you."

"You're hurt. Let me help you," he says, puzzled.

I try to calm myself by slowing my breathing and closing my eyes. Every time I breathe, the pain is sharp, and I can't seem to change back. After a few more breaths, I realize he'll see me as I am. I turn to face him.

Watching Forge, he pulls his slingshot back but doesn't raise it at me.

"I saw something happen to you when it grabbed you, but seeing you up close—" he says nervously.

Standing there looking at each other, I feel the pain subside slightly as I start healing. The pain lessens, and I can finally revert to my human form.

"Do you plan on using that?" I ask him.

After a moment, he loosens the tension on his slingshot. "You're not going to attack me, are you?"

"No, why would I do that?" Pulling my weapons from the beast's head. I lean down, rip one of the more prominent teeth out of its mouth, and toss it to him. "For a keepsake."

Moving to the side of the fallen beast, I pierce its shiny blue skin and slice down, removing a piece of its flesh. "Looks like we found our meal," I say, holding it up to Forge.

"I like fish, but this might be different. By the way, I saved you twice now, but who's counting?"

"Add it to my invoice. By the way, you're cooking it if you want something edible," I reply, walking past him.

Sitting around the campfire, waiting for our meal to cook, I can tell Forge wants to ask me questions. He occasionally turns to me as if he wants to ask something, but instead turns his attention back to our meal. I decide to initiate the conversation to make it easier for both of us.

"You keep looking at me. I guess you're trying to figure out what you saw and have questions about me. Before you ask anything, let me tell you this: I accepted who I am long ago and everything that comes with it."

Forge tilts his head at me. "What are you?"

"I'm a half-breed. My mother is human, and my father is not."

"Your father is?"

I don't want to hide the truth from him. He has earned that from me. "Vampire," I say.

Forge's eyes go wide for a second. "How's that possible? They feed upon the living. They're evil and killers."

"I don't fully understand it myself, but life has taught me that not everything is all good or all evil. Good people can do bad things for reasons they feel are right. At the same time, bad people may also do good. I have done some pretty terrible things to survive. Am I good or evil?"

He looks at me, nodding slightly. I think he agrees with my thought, but I am not sure.

"Do you know your father? The idea of a vampire father is unimaginable to me."

Hearing this question causes me to tense up because of my hatred towards him. "No, and I don't plan to."

I watch Forge digest what I'm telling him. He's taking this much better than I thought he would. I think most people would have attacked me or run by this point.

"You don't seem to be holding your ribs anymore. Don't they hurt?"

Looking down, I realize most of the pain has gone away.

"By morning, they will be healed. That's one benefit of being a half-vampire. I heal extremely fast," I say as I toss a stick into the fire.

"What about blood? Do you ever crave blood?"

"All the time; it's gotten stronger over the years. I can control the hunger for a while, but if I go too long, my vampire side will become dominant and demand it. It's only happened once so far, a long time ago. You don't have anything to worry about; I had some the other day," I reassured him.

"Had some?" he asks.

"Let's just say she wasn't going to need it anymore."

Forge starts to dry heave. "Do you mean?"

"I do."

"Now that I don't have an appetite, I think our meal is ready, but I'm not sure what it should feel like when it's cooked." Cutting a piece off a couple of pieces, he tosses one over to me to try. "Let me know if you think it's done?"

I pop it into my mouth and chew, and he does the same. It chews like beef, but not really. It's softer. What's odd is the taste. Looking over to Forge, I see he has an expression that might be similar to mine.

"What do you think it tastes like?" he asks.

At the same time, we both say, "Chicken."

"Want another piece?" he asks.

I nod as I swallow. He cuts more and tosses a large piece over to me.

CHAPTER 24

LETTING IT OUT

orge nudges me to wake me up. "Do you want some?" he asks, chewing.

"Yes," I reply while sitting up.

Rubbing my face to help wake myself up, Forge hands me a piece of meat from last night's meal.

"I think we should finish it up," he tells me.

I take a bite. It's dry and tough from smoking over the campfire overnight. It has a strong smoked flavor now, which is not very pleasant. At least it's something to put in our bellies. As we eat, we look out and watch the morning mist slowly move over the water. Watching the mist and listening to the birds around us, I think of Brynn and what I want to do to him. I hope he's still at River Song so I can get my vengeance. He was the one who initially captured me, and I must end him.

~

Throughout the morning, Forge's talking increased to the point where he was talking nonstop about everything and nothing. I can't take it anymore. I need silence for at least a little while.

"Forge, no talking for a little bit? My ears need a break," I state firmly.

"Am I talking too much? Sorry, when I get to know someone and feel more comfortable around them, I talk more. I guess I feel more comfortable around you."

I turn around and look at him, placing my finger to my mouth.

"Sorry, I'll be quiet."

The silence lasts about twenty minutes before he asks, "What is so important at River Song?"

I roll my eyes and shake my head, but it's a valid question. "I'm hoping to find someone so I can kill him. Also, before I was taken, I left something with someone. I hope to get it back."

"Kill someone, why?"

"He's the reason I lost ten years of my life in that horrid place," I state coldly.

Forge didn't ask or talk to me for the rest of the way.

We are stopped by city guards crossing the main bridge into River Song.

"What's your business here?" one of the guards asks.

Forge speaks up before I get a chance. "My friend here is going to get something she left with a friend before she heads north. I'm here to see my sister," he tells them.

The other guard gives me a look over.

"You look to be a scrapper. You going to cause any trouble?" he asks.

"Only if someone deserves it," I answer.

I see him smile slightly and nod his head. "I like that answer. Go ahead."

Entering the city, I pick up my pace and head toward the fighting pit where I battled all those years ago. When we arrive, the fighting pit is in shambles. Everything is falling apart, from the signs to the fighting area itself.

I look at Forge and tell him, "Come on, I have another place to go. It's just down the way from here."

Forge acknowledges, and we run down the street toward Historical Records. I hope it's there, unlike the fighting pit. To my delight, it is. We enter the store and head straight to the counter while avoiding the stacks of books. This place is still a mess. Reaching the counter, I ring the bell.

A worker emerges from behind the curtain and walks up to greet us.

"Can I help you?" he asks.

"Yes, I want to speak to Mr. Ryker."

"Is he expecting you?"

"He's been holding on to something for me for a long time."

"One second, please." The worker heads behind the curtain.

A moment later, the curtain moves. I hear steps and realize it's Ryker. I see the top of his head coming our way. He steps up and pushes his spectacles up on his nose. "Been a long time. Where did you go?" he asks.

"Do you still have my items?"

"Of course we do. I pride myself on keeping my customers' items safe. Do you have the receipt still?" Holding out his hand.

I shake my head. "A brooch and chest."

"I know what they are. I was hoping for the receipt. I like to keep things in order."

He places a book on the counter and starts flipping through its pages. He stops at a page and slides his finger down.

"Bring out items 4589 and 4590," he yells to the back of the store.

A moment later, the worker from before emerges from behind the curtain and places my brooch, chest, and an envelope on the counter. I briefly look down at the brooch and then focus on the chest. I pull the chest over to me and open it. It's still full of gold coins.

"Whoa, that's yours?!" Forge exclaims.

I don't have a money purse. Do you have one?" I ask Mr. Ryker.

"I can sell you one for two silver," he informs me, and I agree.

I fill the money purse with the gold and tie it to my belt.

I close the chest and tell Mr. Ryker. "This gold is his now, pointing toward Forge. Make sure he has access to it when he needs it. I want to make sure he is taken care of."

"As you wish," he replies.

I turn to Forge. "This is for helping me and the others. Use it wisely. You can trust Mr. Ryker. I need to go now and take care of that other business," I tell Forge, running out of the store.

"Wait, Kyra, wait." I hear, as the door closes behind me.

I head toward the tavern I was taken from, hoping to find Brynn there. As I get close, the rage builds in me. If he isn't there, hopefully, there's at least someone who can lead me to him. I am going to make him pay for what he did to me.

When I arrive at the tavern, my rage is in full effect. Bursting through the door, everyone turns to me. I look around. In the corner, I see a man sitting at a table, passed out. Is that him or just a drunk? I walk over and pick his head up to see his face. It's him. I yell at everyone. "Get out!"

He opens his eyes and looks at me, half-conscious. "Do I know you?"

I look up, and everyone is still staring at me. I transform and yell at them, flipping the table beside me with my other hand. "Get out, or face the same wrath as this man!"

This causes everyone to panic, leaving quickly, tripping over each other.

"You don't remember me?! You don't remember what you did to me?!" I ask him angrily.

"Should I? I did so many things to so many people," he slurs.

Grabbing his shirt, I lift and slam him against the wall. Holding him there, I yell, "I was put through hell for years because of you. I'm going to show you the pain you caused me!"

"Hell, I've known hell daily for years," he tells me.

Looking at him, I can see he means what he is saying, "What do you mean you've known hell every day?" I slam him into the wall again.

"I lost everything because of that monster. I did anything she asked because she threatened to kill my wife and child. Even after everything I did for her, she still killed them. That's when I finally stopped working for her. I would be better off dead, but I am too much of a coward to do it myself. You would be doing me a favor by killing me."

Ready to tear him apart, I realize he was a pawn like I was. I drop him, and he falls to the floor. She has caused so much pain to so many. Killing him might be a gift to him. I'm better off letting him continue to suffer.

"Get out," I tell him.

I watch him get off the ground slowly and stumble out of the tavern.

Standing there, every part of my body trembles with rage. When there's nowhere else for my rage to go, I snap and start to tear the tavern apart. I flip table after table over and throw benches and chairs across the room, causing them to shatter against the wall. I scream out of frustration and anger. When there's nothing left to smash, I start pacing back and forth.

"Kyra, stop!" I hear someone at the front of the tavern.

I see a wall that I am about to punch. Stepping towards it, I feel someone holding on to me. I try to remove them, but they hold on tighter. Looking down, it's Forge.

"Let go of me; I don't want to hurt you," I yell at him.

"No, I'm not letting go of you!"

I scream over and over again, releasing my anger. As my last scream fades, I start to cry, falling to my knees. In the process, I take Forge with me to the ground. He never let go of me.

"Why?" I ask, sobbing.

"I don't know," Forge tells me. "Let it out."

I start to release the years of pain and suffering I endured by sobbing uncontrollably. Eventually, I become silent, and Forge looks at me.

"You alright?" he asks.

"I don't know if I will ever be alright. I'm still so angry, but I don't have anything left in me right now."

As I wipe the tears off my face, I realize I have transformed back into a human while crying.

He helps me up. "You have every right to be angry for what you went through. I know it won't be easy, but you have to try. I'm sure your family and friends back in Mountain Side will help you," he tries to comfort me.

"I'm more broken now than I was when I left home."

"Sometimes things get broken, but often they can be fixed."

Maybe it's possible I can be fixed. Changing the subject, "How did you find me?"

"It wasn't hard. I saw everyone running out of this place. Plus, I heard the smashing of things and the screaming coming from inside. Come on, let's get out of here."

We leave the tavern to find people outside, gossiping about what might have happened inside. They look at me and step back. I'm sure they are scared of me.

"I think it will be closed for repairs for a while," I tell them.

Forge laughs. "Did you just tell a joke?"

Walking through the city, I remember what Forge said about his sister and how she's here. "Your sister is here in River Song. Where?" I ask.

"She works for an inn on the other side of the city as a washgirl for tips. The owner pays her with meals and a bed in the back of the inn. It's a good deal for her, and she seems happy. I visit her when I can. Do you want to see her?"

"No. I was curious, that's all."

When we get near the city's main gate, I stop us. "This is where we part," I tell him.

"Wait. Now?" he asks.

"Yes, it's best this way. Remember, use the gold wisely. You can trust Ryker. He kept it safe for me all this time."

"You forgot these back there. I wanted to make sure you have them," he says, holding out the envelope and my brooch.

I don't know what to do with them. I don't want to wear the brooch, and knowing where my father might be no longer interests me.

"Are you going to take them?" he asks. "They seemed important."

Reluctantly, I take them.

Placing my hand on his head, I rub it like I did all those years ago. "Thank you for everything. I wish you the best."

Heading towards the city's main gate, I hear Forge yell, "I guess we are paid in full now."

I raise my arm to acknowledge him.

On the way out of the city, I notice a supply shop and head in to get some supplies for the trek home.

"Can I help you find anything?" the person behind the counter asks.

"No, I'll find what I want," I answer.

I grab a travel bag that can be swung over one shoulder, flint, and a package of food rations, and then head to the counter.

"How much?" I ask, dropping everything on the counter.

"Let's see. Flint, rations, and the travel bag. That will be five gold pieces," he says. "I also noticed your top is a bit worse for wear. This nice black top looks like it will fit you. It's only twenty silver."

I look at the new top and then down at mine. Mine is on the verge of falling apart.

"Ten silver," I counter.

"Done," he replies.

I drop the coins on the counter and shove everything into my new travel bag, including the brooch and envelope. Finally, heading out of the city, I jog, hoping to make it to the passage before nightfall.

CHAPTER 25
AN EVENING GUEST

As evening approaches, I see my goal in front of me. With the sun still shining on me, I push myself. I reach the passage's entrance just as the last sunlight vanishes from the sky.

Exhausted from the day's travel, I set up camp nestled between rock outcroppings for protection. Settling in for the night, I snack on some food rations I purchased early today and watch the night sky. It doesn't take long before my eyes get heavy, and they close on me.

Before I fall asleep, I hear the sound of a metal chain; I open my eyes. I get up to investigate. Creeping towards the sound, I have one of my weapons ready if needed. The sound is getting louder, indicating I'm going in the right direction. Poking my head around a rock formation, I see a large white wolf trying to free itself from a hunter's trap. Knowing what it feels like to be trapped, I feel compassion for this creature. I want to free it, but how? This wolf can quickly kill me if it gets hold of me with its mouth. I carefully walk over to it slowly. When I get about ten feet from it, it notices me. It starts to growl, snapping its jaws at me violently, warning me to stay away.

"Easy, take it easy. I'm here to help," I tell it.

This wolf is one of the largest I have ever seen. It has to be four feet at its shoulder. I keep eye contact with it and feel myself transform without wanting to. When this happens, I feel a connection with it. I can feel it's scared and ready to defend itself.

I repeat to it, "I'm here to help you. I won't hurt you."

The wolf starts calming down, and I move closer. I'm frightened as well. If it decides to attack me, it could grab my throat and kill me. I see the trap clearly and how the wolf's paw is caught. Its paw doesn't look to be too injured, though.

"I'm going to open this so you can get out. Please don't hurt me," I tell it.

I quickly grab the trap's jaws and pull them apart. The wolf runs away into the night. I lie on the ground, breathing a heavy sigh of relief. The wolf is free, and I'm still alive. I pick up the trap and smash it against a rock so it can't be used again.

When I get back to camp, I lean against my travel bag, ready to get some sleep. Looking past the fire, I notice two eyes watching me from the darkness. I use my ability to see in the dark; these eyes belong to the wolf I freed. It's lying on the ground, watching me. I sit up very slowly, keeping my eyes on it. After a while, it walks into my camp and stares at me. I slowly reach into my bag and pull out a piece of dried meat to toss towards it. It sniffs the food and eats it. Surprisingly, the wolf lies down and continues watching me with its ice-blue eyes. I won't be sleeping tonight, as I don't want to be a possible meal for him. The night wears on, and I struggle to keep my eyes open. It's a few hours before dawn, and I don't know how this standoff will end. We both seem to want to be the victor here.

Opening my eyes, I see the sun is up, and the fire is out. Realizing I had fallen asleep, I quickly look around for the wolf. I don't see it anywhere, and I breathe a sigh of relief. I walk over to where it watched me from last night. I see tracks, so I know I didn't imagine it.

While packing up my gear, I grab a piece of meat to eat for energy for the day. Traveling through the passage, I keep thinking of Maddie and whether she's still at the Trading Post. It would be nice to see her, and I am sure she could put a smile on my face. Throughout the day, I look up often at the cliffs around me. I forgot how majestic the passage is with its rock formations and small trees that cling to the rock, reaching for sunlight.

Just as evening sets in, I exit the passage and enter the valley. Looking out, I see the sign that points to the Trading Post. I head straight for the sign and make the turn up the road. As I walk, I hear a rustling sound just to my side. I see the wolf from last night, which causes me to stop in my tracks. I wasn't expecting to see it again; now it's almost beside me. What am I going to do? It moves closer to me, and I stay completely still. It starts to lick its mouth. I slowly go into my bag to pull out another piece of dried meat. I hold it out for it. My heart is beating out of my chest. Why am I doing this? The wolf cautiously moves toward me, opening its mouth carefully. It grabs the meat from my hand before it steps back to eat it. I think that went well. It lowers its head towards me. I take a chance and carefully move towards the wolf with my hands out so I don't spook it. I get about a foot away from it before it approaches me. When it does this, I feel its fur running through my fingers. I can't help but rub the wolf's fur.

"Good boy," I tell it.

I think it's a boy. I squat and look underneath him to confirm he's a boy while continuing to rub him. He leans into me, which is a surprise. Maybe he's just thanking me for freeing him from the trap; I don't know. I stand up and give him one last rub. As I step away, he's just standing there looking at me. I turn and continue to the Trading Post.

As I walk, I notice he's following me. "What is it with animals following me?" I ask out loud.

Shrugging my shoulders, we continue toward the Trading Post. When we enter the clearing, I see the inn. Smoke is coming from the main central chimney and a few others. From the stables, I hear horses fidgeting, snorting, and neighing. I think they can sense my companion, who's making them nervous.

I look down at him. "What will we do with you? You should—"

I don't get my last few words out before he runs away into the woods. I shake my head at this and wonder if he understood me. This wolf is an oddity, for sure.

Entering the inn, I head to the front desk and ring the bell.

A curtain slides open, revealing a woman wearing a long light blue dress with a dark leather vest on top. Her blond hair is pulled into a ponytail. She walks up to the desk to greet me with a smile, which disappears quickly.

"Are you alright? Do you need help? You're clothes are torn, and it looks like you've been tortured," she says with concern.

I don't want to explain my appearance, so I ask for a room. "I'm fine. Do you have any rooms available?"

"We do have rooms. They are twelve silver per night. Are you sure you don't need assistance?"

I toss the coins on the counter. "I'm fine. Is Maddie here?"

"I'm sorry to say no. She left a few seasons back. Do I know you? You look familiar."

I look at her, trying to see if I remember her, but she doesn't look familiar. "I don't think so."

"I'm pretty sure I remember you; I don't forget faces. It will come to me. Anyway, enjoy your stay. If you need anything, please let me know. We pride ourselves on our services and ensuring our customers' safety and happiness. Room twelve. Second level. If you're hungry, our meals are being served now," she says, pushing my room key towards me.

"A meal would be good," I answer.

The woman steps from behind the counter and looks into the main area of the inn.

"It's already a bit full, but there's a free table in the far corner. Go have a seat there, and I will have one of our servers come over," she instructs me.

Walking through the inn, I go to the table I was shown and sit with my back to the wall. I've always preferred to have my back to the wall, but now I feel even more strongly that it is a necessity to protect myself.

It doesn't take long before a server walks up to my table. "What can I get for you?" she asks.

"Ale and whatever you're serving for the meal," I reply.

The server nods and heads to the bar. Looking around, things haven't changed much here. Everything is what I remember, from the large central fireplace in the middle of the room to the large beams above me throughout the tavern. It doesn't take long before a huge ale, and my food is placed in front of me. Looking at my ale, with its foam head sliding down the side of the mug, I pick it up and take a long drink from it. How long has it been since I had an ale? This might be the worst ale in the world, but it tastes magnificent.

"Five copper," the server says, holding her hand out.

I place a silver coin in her hand. "The rest is yours."

"Thank you," she tells me before walking away.

I look at the plate of food in front of me. It's a mix of meat and root vegetables. I start to eat when one of the ladies of the tavern walks over to me.

"How's your evening going?" She asks me.

"I'm not interested," I tell her with a mouth full of food.

Being in this crowded tavern is making me anxious enough. It's taking all I am to keep my composure just sitting here, eating and drinking. I keep thinking that everyone is watching me. I don't want to deal with this.

The lady from the front desk walks over to us and whispers something into the lady's ear. She nods and leaves.

"Sorry about that, Miss Everwind. I could see you didn't want to be disturbed. I will ensure this doesn't happen again."

I look at her, puzzled.

"How do you know my name?"

"It took me a few minutes, but I finally remembered. I pulled out one of our old ledgers to look up your name. When I saw your name, it all came back to me. I bathed you back then," she explains.

I think back to the last time I was here and the young tavern girl. "Wendy?"

"Yes, ma'am. Sorry, Kyra," she replies jokingly.

"Thanks for asking her to leave. I don't … " I try to say, but stumble on my words.

"May I sit? If not, that's alright," Wendy says.

I nod, and she pulls the chair out.

"I will not pry, but I'm concerned. You're not how I remember you. Is there anything I can do for you?" She asks kindly.

I don't want to tell her anything, but I remember what Forge said about letting people in. "I'm not the same person. I was on a journey to find myself when you saw me last. After I left here, a lot beyond my control happened to me. I was held captive for ten years in a horrid place that no one should ever endure. It changed me."

Wendy looks shocked and dismayed. "By the gods, I am so sorry. Are you sure you are safe now?" she says, reaching for my hands, but I pull away. "I am sorry, I did not mean to scare you. Is there anything I can do to comfort you?"

I shake my head slightly and say, "I appreciate your concern, but I have to work through this. The reason I came back here was to see Maddie. She made me smile, and I enjoyed her company. I was hoping for this again."

Wendy is quiet for a long time. I can see she's deep in thought, trying to find the right words. "The last time you were here, you had a profound effect on Maddie."

"How?"

"After you left, Maddie started to change slowly. Initially, it was small things, but over time, she became more and more independent and defiant toward Mr. Storm. She stopped being a lady of the inn and focused all her efforts on crafting her drink and painting. I don't know if you know this, but Maddie is quite a good artist. Most of the paintings in the inn are hers. I noticed her drawing you a few times in her sketchbooks. I think it's because of you she became who she is now. Like Maddie, I believe you have it in you to adapt and be who you want to be."

I sit there quietly, digesting what Wendy told me. Maddie left this place because of me. Then I remember our conversation about being more. She wanted to be more and did something about it. If Maddie could, I can get through this as well.

"If you're done eating, I'd be happy to show you to your room," Wendy says.

Thinking of a night's rest in a bed for the first time in a long time sounds like a gift.

Wendy stands, extends her arm, and asks, "Shall we?"

I stand and follow Wendy. Walking up the stairs, Wendy stays beside me but keeps a little distance. She understands how to be around me somehow. She is making me feel comfortable. At the top of the stairs, I notice a painting of the inn. It's excellent, with lots of little details throughout. This must be one of her paintings. I notice an *M* in the corner. Wendy stops us at room ten.

"My key is for room twelve. Why did we stop here?" I ask.

Wendy unlocks it and opens it.

"I thought you might like this room better."

I walk in, and it's a fine room with a large bed and a fireplace with a fire already going in it. There's a dresser and mirror. I see another painting and walk up to it. It's a painting of the passage at sunset. Like the previous painting, it's full of details. This painting also has an *M* in the bottom corner, confirming my suspicions about the painting in the hall being one of Maddie's.

"One of hers?" I ask.

"Yes. This is one of my favorites. It's the last one she did before leaving. Her paintings are in the main area of the inn, plus the hallways, but this is the only private room with one. That's why I am moving you to this room," Wendy tells me.

Hearing her tell me this, I can't help but feel gratitude towards her. It's thoughtful of her to give me this since Maddie is no longer here.

"Thank you," I tell her.

"I'm glad you like the room. Please don't hesitate to ask if you need anything. Our staff is here to help," she tells me as she exits the room.

"Wendy, thank you for telling me about Maddie."

"My pleasure," she replies, closing the door.

I look at myself in the mirror and see a worn and tired person who doesn't know her place in the world now. I open the window for fresh air. One thing I appreciate is fresh air. For ten years, all I breathed was foul air. I start to undress and hear a knock at the door. I walk over and open it. Wendy is standing there with bath supplies.

"I thought you might enjoy a soak in a hot bath to relax. If you don't mind, I will draw you one at no charge, and I promise you can bathe yourself this time," she says, walking over to the tub and filling it for me.

Once my bath is ready, Wendy walks out and tells me, "Goodnight. Don't forget to lock up."

"Night, and thank you."

Looking at the steaming water, I strip down as fast as possible. I am suddenly anxious to get in, as it has been over ten years since I had a hot bath. I hop into the water, which is almost too hot, but I don't care. I dunk my head below the water, feeling the hot water all around me. I resurface, grab the soap and sponge, and scrub myself. Washing my hair is the best part. Even though I washed in the lake water the other night, this is different. I'm clean now. I settle in for a long soak, feeling myself melt into the tub.

When the water is no longer hot, I get out. I walk over to the bed and jump in, pulling the sheets over me. After adjusting my head on the pillow, I close my eyes, ready to enjoy sleeping in a bed for the first time in ten years.

Lying in bed, I toss and turn for hours, trying to get comfortable.

Why can't I get comfortable? I finally take the pillow and lie down on the floor. Lying on the floor, my body finally relaxes. The bed must be too soft for my body, as it has gotten used to sleeping on a stone floor. Feeling myself drifting off, I hear a howl outside. I smile; hearing this comforts me, and I finally fall asleep.

When I wake up, the sky is deep blue. It looks to be another nice day. I pick myself off the floor and look at the bed I didn't use. The whole time I was in that place, I wished I had a bed or a mattress to sleep on. The first time I can sleep on one, I can't. I know there is some irony in this. The gods are playing a joke on me, and I don't like it.

I start dressing, and as I'm about to put on my worn top, I remember the one I purchased in River Song. I grab it out of my travel bag and put it on. It feels nice and fits me well. I toss my old top into the fire.

Walking downstairs, my stomach growls as I catch the aroma of something roasting. I see the table I was at last night and head over to it. Before sitting down, I see Wendy at the front desk and motion to her. She quickly comes over to greet me.

"Good morning, Kyra. I hope you enjoyed your bath. I like your new top. How may I help you this morning?"

"You don't know how much that bath meant to me. What am I smelling? I'm starving."

We have pig ribs and chicken. Would you like some?"

"Ribs and a large mug of water."

"I'll be right back with your meal."

Sitting there, I reminisce about the time Maddie sat across from me at this table. She drove me up the wall that night and then in the morning. I hope she's doing well. I wonder where she went. I hope she isn't in River Song, and I missed an opportunity to see her.

Wendy comes back with my food and water. The food smells fantastic.

"I got you a little of both. Please enjoy," she says, walking away.

I dig in, devouring my meal, and drink the water in a few large swigs. With a full belly, I can start on my way. I motion to Wendy again, and she walks over.

"Looks like you enjoyed it. Anything else?" she asks.

"No," I answer, paying for my meal plus a little extra as a thank you for her kindness.

"Thank you, Kyra." She replies while sweeping the coins off the table into her hand.

Before she leaves, I hand her my room key. She nods and takes it.

"Good luck in your travels. I hope you find what you are looking for."

"As do I," I say, extending my hand to her.

She grabs my hand with both of hers.

Walking out of the inn, I see the sun is high in the sky. I hadn't realized that I slept so late. The wolf is nowhere to be found; maybe I'll never see him again. Since it's past midday, I run to make up time.

I cover as much ground as I can each day, only stopping when necessary. That way, I can get home as soon as possible. To my surprise, the wolf is sticking around and has become my travel companion. He shows up when I'm settling down for the evening. Most nights, he lies beside me and rests his head on my lap while I rub his head and neck. I never know how long he will be staying. Sometimes, he only stays with me for an hour and leaves before I fall asleep. Other nights, I fall asleep with him next to me, and he is gone when I wake up. I've grown quite fond of him, as he is my only company and I feel safer when he's with me. I call him Ghost due to his coloring and how he vanishes without notice.

CHAPTER 26

OLD FRIENDS

As I reach the top of a hill, I see Lake Shore. I should be able to see their cottage from here. Peering into the distance, I find it just off to the left. I continue to walk towards their home. As I get closer, I can see there isn't anyone outside, but smoke is coming from the chimney. My anxiety starts to set in, knowing that I promised Iris that I would visit on the way back home. Will it be uncomfortable? How will they react to my appearance? Will I do something that causes an issue? The more I get into my head, the more I realize none of this matters. I made a promise to a little girl that I care for, and I plan to keep that promise. I have to go down there and see if they still live there. It could be a different family, as it has been ten years.

Making my way down the road to their home, I enter the woods just before their clearing to get a better look without being seen. If they don't live there, I can leave without being noticed. I squat down and look through the trees and brush. It's quiet, and I don't see any movement. My stomach growls as I breathe in the aroma of what is being cooked. As I look on, the front door opens, and a teenage girl walks to the wood stacked next to the cottage. When she turns with a few pieces in her arms, I realize I'm looking at Iris. She's no longer a little girl. I watch her go back inside, talking to someone.

Seeing her, my desire to see my friends becomes overwhelming. I head toward the cottage, slowly convincing myself it will be fine. Iris reappears in the doorway when I get a stone's throw away. She looks at me, which stops me in my tracks.

She leans back, and I hear her say to the inside, "Someone's here."

Iris continues to look at me. I don't think she recognizes me.

"You're no longer a little girl, are you?" I ask.

Hearing my voice must have triggered something. She runs towards me and hugs me tightly.

"Where have you been?" she asks excitedly.

As she embraces me, I tense up, but after a moment, I feel myself give in to her and hug her back just as tightly. Feeling her in my arms brings back memories of holding her in my lap and swinging her around in the air.

"Sorry it took so long," I respond.

I step back to take a closer look at her. I hold her shoulders between my hands. She's grown up and is quite pretty, like her mother.

"Who is it?" Mileena walks through the doorway, wiping her hands on an apron. She recognizes me right away and runs over to greet me. "Hello, my long-lost friend. How have you been?"

"It is so nice to see old friends."

Mileena looks at me, and I can tell she realizes things are different with me. Her smile fades slightly, and her eyes focus on my face. "Looks like you could use a rest. Orlan and Emery will be home in a few hours. They are helping a neighbor clear his field today. When they return, we can share a meal like old times."

Iris takes my arm and walks me into their home. I feel as if I'm a stranger in their home. I sit quietly at the table and look around. It looks pretty much the same, with just a few changes here and there.

Iris doesn't take her eyes off me the whole time. I can't believe this teenager in front of me is the little girl I so fondly remember.

I finally get up enough nerve to speak. "You're fourteen now?"

"Almost fifteen," she answers quickly.

"She thinks she's all grown up, and she even has a boy she likes," Mileena tells me.

Iris's face turns a little red. "Mother, why did you tell her that?"

Noticing a pitcher on the table, I ask, "Does that have any of your mother's wine in it?"

Iris grabs a glass and pours some wine for me. "Here, have some."

I take a sip and remember how good her wine is. It's sweet with a slight tartness at the end.

While I'm drinking, Iris is looking at me. "You seem nervous or something."

"I am," I respond hesitantly.

"Why?"

"I've been through a lot since I left here, and I don't want to bother you or your family with it. Just know I am glad I am here with you."

Iris focuses on me, specifically the scar on my face.

She leans in and touches it. "Is this part of what you went through?"

I take a moment to reply, "Yes. I've had this for a long time now."

She continues to examine me carefully; her expression changes slightly when she sees my arms. "Mother!"

I recoil from her, placing my arms under the table, as I don't want to explain. This was a bad idea. I should leave.

"What is it?" she asks Iris.

Iris looks at Mileena, who sees that Iris is upset.

"Her arms," she tells Mileena.

Mileena sits at the table, looks at me, and asks, "I saw them when we were outside. Is there anything we can do for you?"

I'm quiet, trying to hide my arms. I'm not sure what to do.

Should I get up and leave? No, that would worry them more if I just left them without any explanation.

"May I?" she asks, gesturing to see my arms.

I nod hesitantly and place my hands on the table. She takes my hands into hers and examines them. "These look old, but they healed nicely. Is this one a bite?"

All I can do is nod to her questions.

"Are there more than these?" she asks, looking up at my face.

"Yes," I tell her, with a waver in my voice.

"I don't know what happened, but you are safe with us. Is there anything we can do for you?"

"I don't know. I was nervous about coming here to see you again. I was worried about what you might think and what I might do. I'm different now. I'm not the same person I was back then. When both of you greeted me, it brought me back to our time together, and it felt nice. For years, I didn't allow myself to feel anything. In doing this, I became an empty shell of a person."

Iris leans in and hugs me while Mileena squeezes my hands. I can't express how much their compassion means to me.

"When I was looking at your arm, I noticed your hands were dirty, and your clothes could use a wash. When was the last time you bathed? Would you like to?" Mileena asks.

"I would like that. Can I bathe alone? I don't want you to see me."

Mileena turns to her daughter. "Finish your chores outside, and I will join you shortly."

She turns back to me. "I will get your bath ready and get you some clean clothes so we can wash what you are wearing. I think one of Orlan's field outfits should fit you."

Iris heads outside, and I hear wood being chopped. Mileena gets up and prepares my bath while I sit at the table, not knowing what to do with myself.

When Mileena goes into her room, I get up from the table to check out the bath. I feel the water, and it's warm. I look out the window and see Iris chopping wood. I take off my armor and wrist-guards. I start to take off my top when I hear Mileena.

"I didn't mean to. I thought I had time to get the clothes for you and get outside."

Standing there with my top half off, I know she sees the scars on my back from being whipped.

"My dear, I am so sorry. Who did this to you?"

"Someone who will never do it again to anyone. I made sure of that."

I finish undressing and get into the tub to wash myself.

Mileena walks over and places the change of clothes next to the tub for me.

"I will let you be. Call if you need anything," she tells me, walking out.

I wash quickly. Looking over the tub, I see the clothes Mileena left me, a comb, and a few grooming items. Getting out of the tub, I use the grooming supplies to trim my nails and comb my hair to remove all the knots. I don't think I will ever get used to long hair. Short hair is much easier. I dress and go outside to see what everyone is doing. Iris is still chopping wood and working up a good sweat.

"Where's your mom?" I yell over.

"By the brook."

"Need help?"

"No, I got this. I'm sorry I upset you before. Seeing the scars worried me." She swings down, easily splitting the log in half.

I look up at her. "Not bad, and I know you didn't mean to upset me. You're the first friend from my past to see them. I wasn't sure how to react."

She smiles and rolls up her sleeves, exposing some pretty developed arms.

"Someone has been chopping a lot of wood," I tell her.

"I remembered what you said. I wanted to be strong like you."

"You're on your way."

"I think I might be able to take you now," she teases me.

"Really," I state, walking up to the pile of wood she has been pulling from. I pick up a large piece and place it on the chopping stump.

"May I?" I ask, taking the axe from her.

I swing down on the log with one arm, splitting it in two, burying the axe's blade deep in the chopping stump.

I give the axe back to her. "You still have a bit to go. I've gotten stronger since you were little."

"How?"

"I'm just stronger and will always be," I tell her.

She runs at me, laughing, and jumps onto my back playfully. When she does this, I'm transported back to a fight in the arena. Someone is holding me from behind, and I am trying to get them off of me. In a panic, I twist around, knocking Iris off me, and I am about to lunge at her. As soon as I see her, I stop and step back quickly. "I'm sorry. I didn't mean to."

Iris gets up off the ground and runs away, frightened.

"Iris, no, it's me. I didn't mean to."

I stand there upset and start hitting my shoulder, trying to punish myself for doing that to Iris.

Mileena runs up. "What happened?"

"Iris didn't do anything wrong. She was playing with me, and it triggered me. I was back in that place I escaped from. It's my fault. I should get going. I don't want to cause any more issues for your family. It was a bad idea for me to visit you."

"Stay. I'm sure you just startled her more than anything. I am pretty sure I know where she is," she tells me.

"No, let me go to her. I should explain to her why I reacted the way I did. Where is she?"

"Follow the path behind the cottage. You will find her there. It's her special place to think and be alone." Mileena points toward the path.

Heading down the path, I start to hear someone crying. I pick up my pace and see Iris sitting against a large oak tree surrounded by wildflowers and a few large rocks.

I know why she comes here; it's serene. I walk over carefully so I don't scare her more.

"Can I sit?"

I see her nod as she holds her knees.

"I didn't mean to toss you off me like that. When you jumped on my back, something came over me. It felt like I was back in that terrible place. My body and mind just reacted. Being in that place for so long did something to me, and I don't know if it will ever go away, even though I want to forget that place. When I saw you on the ground, it terrified me that I might have hurt you."

"You think you might have hurt me?" She asks, wiping her nose and eyes.

"I know I wouldn't on purpose. I react in ways I might not want to. I have a side of me that might come out, and I can't allow that to happen around you or your family," I explain to her.

"A side of you?"

"There's a part of me that I keep hidden, but this part also allowed me to stay alive all those years. It allowed me to fight when I couldn't anymore. It's strong, but it's dangerous. It's taken me years to understand and control it."

"What do you mean, control it?" she asks, wiping the last tears from her cheeks.

I feel that I have no recourse but to tell her so she understands.

"I want to tell you something, but I'm unsure how, so I will show you." I'm nervous to do this, but I think it's the right thing to do. At least, I hope it is. "Look at my eyes. What do you see?"

"They're two colors like always. Blue and green."

Continuing to look at her, I allow my other side to surface just enough.

Iris's eyes go wide. "Wait, they just turned red and have a shimmer."

I relax and allow my other side to fade away.

"Wait, what happened? How did you do that?" she asks.

"I allowed my other side to come to the surface just enough. A side of me that for years I feared, but I no longer do. When you jumped on my back, it felt like someone was attacking me. My other side could have appeared out of instinct, and I could have hurt you. I snapped out of it when I saw you on the ground."

"How do you have this other side?"

"I was born with it. I didn't know about it until I was a few years older than you. It's the reason for my strength and other things I can do."

"What other things can you do?" she asks.

"I can see in the dark, almost like daylight."

"That can be handy, I bet." She leans her head on me, as she used to when she was little.

"It can be, but it also has a dark side. But let's not talk about that. Are we good?" I ask.

"Yes, we're good. I'll keep this between us. Do you mind if we stay here for a bit? I like it when we're together, just the two of us. I missed you more than you could imagine," she tells me.

"We can stay here as long as you like."

Walking back to the cottage, my curiosity gets the best of me. I want to know more about this boy Iris likes and if he's good enough for her.

"Tell me about this boy you like?"

Iris nudges me as if to say stop that. "I don't want to tell you," she says.

"Tell me. Is he cute? What's his name? You have to give me a few details."

"John," she finally tells me. "I think he's cute, and I really like how his blue eyes sparkle. Every time he sees me, he smiles at me."

"John is a good name. It sounds like he likes you as well. Have you talked to him?"

"We've talked a little, but I am always nervous around him."

I'm in no place to give any advice on relationships now or even in the past, but it doesn't stop me.

"It's alright to be nervous, but don't let that prevent you from getting to know him. One thing life has taught me is that time is precious. Don't wait; you might not have the chance to tell him how you feel. If he doesn't feel the same, move on, knowing you at least expressed your feelings. It does sound like he might feel the same as you."

"Easy for you to say; you're not the one who might get her heart broken."

I pull out the locket from around my neck and open it to show Iris. "This is Jenny. She was everything to me. I lost her a long time ago. I wish I had more time with her so I could tell her everything I felt and wanted to tell her. I lost that opportunity and will regret that for the rest of my life."

Iris looks at the image of Jenny. "She's pretty."

Closing the locket, I place it under my shirt.

"Do you think I should tell John?" she asks.

"Yes, tell him the next time you see him."

We look at each other for a moment, and she nods.

"Come on, let's get back. I'm starving. I've been smelling your mother's cooking since I arrived and haven't eaten anything today. Do you know what your mom is making?"

"Chicken stew."

Iris and I are sitting at the table waiting for dinner. Mileena looks at me from the kitchen, and I nod back at her, letting her know that Iris and I worked it out.

"While you were with Iris, I cleaned your clothes. Your pants are in pretty rough shape. The leather is worn so thin in areas that I don't think they will last much longer. They're hanging to dry in the back. Your shirt came clean, no problem. I think it's best to keep Orlan's clothes," Mileena tells me.

"Thank you. I can pay you for his clothes," I reply to her.

"No need, it's our pleasure."

I lean over the table and look at the pot of bubbling stew in the fireplace. I take a deep inhale, remembering how good Mileena's cooking is.

"I can't believe it has been ten years since we last saw you. How old are you now, twenty-eight?" Mileena inquires. "You don't look more than twenty. What's your secret?"

I haven't thought about how I look, but my appearance hasn't aged that much. I lost my teenage look, but that's about it.

I turn to Iris, who is playing with my hair.

"What are you doing?" I ask.

"Your hair is kind of crazy. Can I braid it? I think you will like it," she says.

"I would like that. I don't know how to braid my hair."

Iris jumps up and pulls at my hair, causing my head to bobble.

"This is going to be so fun. I can teach you. Start by pulling the hair you want to braid back into a tight ponytail. Then, divide the hair into three sections, ensuring you keep it tight. Take the left section of the hair and pull it over the middle section. That is now the new middle section. Take the right section of hair and pull it over the middle section. Repeat this until you run out of hair to braid. Tie it off with a ribbon or clasp. I will make a fancier braid for your hair, which I like to do in my hair. First, I will make a small braid on each side of your head." Iris proceeds to pull at my hair, making the first braid. "Hold this, and don't let go, or I will have to redo the whole thing." She then makes the second braid and hands it to me to hold. "Then braid the small braids into a larger braid with the rest of your hair like this," she tells me as she takes the two smaller braids from my grasp. "Hold this again. I need to get a hair clasp." She runs to her room and returns a second later with something in her hand. She takes my hair and clamps something metal at the end of the braid. "Done."

I walk over to a mirror on the wall and look at myself, turning and twisting my head and body around to see what it looks like. I like this look on me. It keeps my hair organized, and she did it so quickly. I turn back to Iris. "How does it look?"

"It's perfect for you. Keep the hair clasp; I have many. Come braid my hair."

Iris unbraids her hair and scratches her fingers on her head to mess up her hair.

"Try to do what I did," she says.

It takes me a few times, but I finally get it where it doesn't look terrible.

"I think I have it. Don't judge it too harshly," I say playfully.

Iris gets up, looks at the mirror, and chuckles. "Not too bad. Practice will help, but I think you've got the basics down. You'll get better and faster each time you do it." She sits back down next to me. "I'm glad you're here. I missed you. I wondered where you were and what you were seeing." She straightens up quickly. "Sorry, I didn't mean to—"

"I know what you meant. Being with you and your family helps. It reminds me that there is good out there."

The door bursts open. I'm startled and instinctively react by clenching my fists.

I see Orlan and relax. He looks over at me and smiles. "Well, look who finally came to visit. What took you so long, my friend? Emery, do you remember Kyra?" Emery walks in behind Orlan. He's gotten big. He's taller than his father and has to duck his head a bit as he enters.

He looks over to me. "I remember. How's it going?" he asks, muttering under his breath.

"He's a happy one. I thought I had moody already called for," I mutter under my breath to Iris.

"He's always like this lately," she informs me.

Orlan walks over to Mileena, playfully slaps her backside, and kisses her cheek. "How's my love doing today?"

She turns toward him with a smirk. "You know I hate it when you do that, plus we have guests. Behave." She then quickly whispers something to him. He nods.

He turns to me with his arms wide open. "Come here, my friend," he says.

Before I finish standing, he embraces me in a huge hug.

"So nice to see you again. Sit," he says as he joins us at the table.

Emery joins us as well. He towers over his father as he sits next to him. He pours himself some wine and sits quietly next to his father.

"How have you been?" I ask Emery.

Emery doesn't answer and looks at his glass of wine.

"Ooch! Why did you kick me?" he yells, looking at Iris.

"She asked you a question," Iris replies.

Mileena walks over to the table and tells them, "Both of you behave. We have a guest."

Mileena looks at me. "Brother-sister relationships. Always at each other in some fashion."

Not knowing much about this, I sit there watching them scowling at each other.

"What brings you back to our neck of the valley?" Orlan asks.

"Finally heading home."

"Is your time limited with us again?" As Orlan asks me this, I feel Iris hold my hand under the table. I look down at it and then at her. I know she wants me to stay longer, but I can't.

"I can only stay the night. I have to get back home. I need to know how Mother and my friends are. I never meant to stay away this long, and not knowing how they are is tormenting me."

Orlan replies, "I understand. I think I speak for all of us; we wish you could stay longer."

Looking past Orlan, I see his lute in the corner. "Do you still play?" I ask Orlan while motioning to the lute.

"Not so much. Ever since Iris and Emery grew up, they don't dance much anymore. If I do play, it's for myself or Mileena."

As Orlan and I talk, Mileena sets the table for our meal.

"You don't dance anymore? I remember you both twirling and twisting for hours." I look at both Iris and Emery.

"Not so much," Iris answers.

"I can play tonight," he answers.

Mileena parts Orlan and Emery so she can place the pot of stew on the table and sits next to Iris. She begins serving and hands me the first bowl of stew. I raise it to my nose and smell it. It smells even better close up.

I grab a spoon and scoop a full spoonful into my mouth. As soon as the stew hits my mouth, so does its extreme heat. I open my mouth and breathe out, trying to cool it down. "Hot!" I wave my hand in front of my mouth.

Emery chuckles at me. I look at him and can't help but laugh slightly, trying not to spit food out. Eventually, I swallow and say to Mileena, "It's delicious, but next time I will blow on it first."

Everyone looks at me and blows on their spoons before taking their first bite. They all laugh, and Orlan leans over the table, placing his hand on my shoulder. "I missed you."

I smile, and we continue with our meal together. While we eat, they update me on what they've been up to, and I open up a little and tell them about my first time at the Trading Post and Maddie. Everyone laughs multiple times when I describe Maddie's hijinks.

As I finish describing my time with Maddie, Emery tries to probe for details about Maddie and me.

"Some things are private," Mileena says while slapping the back of his head.

As we clean up, we hear a howl outside the door. Everyone turns with concern. Seeing Orlan and Emery charge to the door. I jump up and block them from getting to it.

"He's with me!" I exclaim.

"It's a wolf! Our livestock is in danger," Emery says.

"What do you mean, he's with you?" Orlan asks with concern.

"We've been traveling together. We're friends."

Watching them, I back up to the door and open it. "It will be fine, I promise."

Stepping outside, Iris yells at me, "Don't go out there!"

Ghost is about twenty feet in front of me. I walk up to him and kneel. "Hey boy, they're scared of you. It might be best if you stay away tonight. They're my good friends."

Ghost looks past me at the open door and starts to whine, sniffing the air. I scratch his face and place my arm around him. Looking back, everyone is staring at us from the doorway.

"You see. He won't hurt anyone."

"Stay here. I'll be right back," I tell him.

Making my way back inside, I quickly grab a bowl, filling it with stew. I walk back outside, passing everyone.

"Wait," Mileena tells me.

I turn back and tell her, "He's just hungry."

I sit beside Ghost and give him the bowl of stew to eat. When he's done, he rubs his head against me and licks my face. I look over, and Iris is slowly walking over to me.

"Iris, get back here!" Mileena orders her quietly, trying not to scare Ghost.

"If Kyra says it's safe. I trust her," she answers.

Iris is standing about a foot away from us. I can tell she is extremely nervous. I'm a little nervous, as this is the first time anyone but me has been this close to him. I'm not getting any warning signs from him. "Easy, boy, she's a friend and special to me."

Iris slowly touches his head and rubs it softly. She moves closer and kneels on the ground next to us to rub him more. A smile comes over her face.

"You see," I tell her.

"Mother, he's so soft," Iris tells Mileena.

"That's enough! Please, can you come back here? I am very nervous," Mileena pleads with Iris.

Iris gets up slowly and heads back to her family, smiling.

"You'd better get going. See you tomorrow." Giving him one last rub before he darts off into the woods.

"All good. He was checking on me," I tell them, heading back inside with the bowl in hand.

Orlan closes the door, and they all sit at the table. They all look shocked.

Iris breaks the silence. "That was amazing! How did you two become friends?"

"I freed him from a hunter's trap. He started following me, and we have been together ever since. I think he thinks he's my protector and checks up on me. I like it when he's around."

"Now I've seen everything," Orlan announces, pouring himself a large glass of wine.

Emery asks, "It looked like he knew what you told him. How are you two able to do that?"

I grab my glass and take a drink. "I don't think he understands me, but I feel a connection with him. Sometimes, it does feel like we understand what each of us is thinking. It will be interesting when I get home. Not sure Mother is going to allow him in the house."

Mileena shakes her head. "I'm pretty sure she won't allow a wolf in the house."

I stand and take the dishes to the washing area. As a thank you, I start washing them. Mileena gets up and escorts me back to the table. "No, no, that's not your job. Iris and Emery finish cleaning up while we set up Kyra's sleeping area."

Emery makes a gruff sound and says, "That's woman's work."

Which causes Mileena to reprimand him quickly. "It's family work. Do it."

Mileena and Orlan motion to me. I follow them to Iris's and Emery's room, where I slept the last time I was here. I see there are still only two beds.

"I'm not going to take Iris's or Emery's bed. I can sleep on the floor or in the stable. I don't mind, and I think my body would prefer it. I tried a bed recently, and it didn't go well," I tell them.

"You're not sleeping on the floor or in the stable," Mileena tells me firmly.

"I don't mind," I tell them. "Really."

From the other room, Iris announces. "We can share a bed, I don't mind. My bed is big enough."

I shake my head. "Floor or stable," I tell them.

Iris walks over and sits on her bed.

"There's plenty of room for us," she explains.

They both look at me. "Remember, she always gets her way," Orlan reminds me.

I look at Iris, knowing she won't give in. "I guess," I say reluctantly, shrugging my shoulders.

"It will be fun. We can talk all night if you like," she says.

"I'm not much of a talker," I reply.

"I guess that's settled. You two will share a bed," Orlan says.

We head back to the main room, and Orlan grabs his lute and sits at the table. "Are you still interested in hearing music tonight?" he asks.

"If you don't mind." Sitting down at the table. I watch him pluck the strings and turn the knobs to get it back in tune. He looks up. "Any requests?"

"Play whatever you want," I tell him.

I watch him think for a second before he starts to play. It's a pretty song that invokes happy feelings, making me remember when I was with everyone while Lindsey played for us on my birthday. It seems so long ago, but that was the last time I was truly happy.

As Orlan strums the last note, he looks up. "Not too bad. Little rusty for sure. Another?"

"Please," I answer.

Orlan starts playing a second song. Iris sits next to me and watches her father play. Emery sits across from me and smiles. The cold veneer from earlier is starting to wear away. While enjoying the music, Mileena places a cake on the table. It's topped with berries and a sugary glaze.

"You timed your visit well. I made this cake this morning as a special treat for the family tonight," Mileena tells me.

Not seeing such a treat in years, my mouth starts to water. I try to pick off one of the sugar-covered berries, but Mileena slaps my hand. "Not yet."

Pulling my hand back, I taste my fingers. The sweet taste in my mouth is fantastic. I turn back toward my musical entertainment and listen. Orlan finishes the song, and we all clap for him.

"Berry cake," he announces. "Been a while since she made this. We must have been good, or she's in a good mood. Is this due to last night's activities?"

"Please don't say stuff like that; the idea of you and Mom—" Iris and Emery announce simultaneously.

I can't help but chuckle when I see Mileena and Orlan smiling at each other, as their children are entirely uncomfortable now.

"We don't have to have this tonight," she tells us, picking up the cake.

We all say, "No, we want cake!"

She puts the cake back down and cuts pieces for everyone. I'm more excited about this than any other food I have had in the past weeks. I love sweets. Picking the cake off my plate, I take a bite. It's sweet with a bit of tartness from the berries. The sugar crust feels a little gritty in my mouth, but in a good way. I shove the rest of the cake into my mouth and start chewing for a few minutes with my cheeks puffed out. I look over at everyone as they watch me chew.

"Sorry, it's been a long time since I had something like this," I mumble with a full mouth.

Iris starts to laugh and shoves her piece of cake in her mouth.

"It's good, right?" She spits cake as she speaks.

I know she did this so I wouldn't feel out of place. I have forgotten how to act and use social manners. I have to rely less on instinctive actions and more on thought, so I don't make others around me uncomfortable, as well as myself.

As we finish our cake, we all agree that it is late. Orlan and Emery are especially tired from the fieldwork. We all retreat to our beds.

Emery flops onto his bed and turns over quickly. I look at Iris as she sits down on the bed.

"I can sleep on the floor. It feels weird for me now that you're much older."

"We will make it work for a night," she tells me, looking down. "I know you must leave, but I don't want you to."

I sit down next to her. "I know. I have to be with my family and friends back home."

I kick off my boots, scoot back on the bed, and lean against the wall. A second later, I yawn. I have been so tired lately. My body is telling me to slow down, but I can't until I return home. "It's a little small for both of us, isn't it?" I ask her.

"It is, but I like having you here with me—one second. I have something for you," she tells me.

She reaches into her small nightstand and pulls out the bracelet I gave her.

"Only wore it on special occasions as I didn't want to damage or lose it," she tells me, handing it to me.

I take it and look at it while rubbing the red stone in the center. I hand it back to her.

"Keep it. It belongs to you now. I only had it for a few months, and you have had it for years and have kept it safe. You're the rightful owner."

"Are you sure?"

"I am. It's yours."

She places it on her wrist and hugs me. "Thank you. I will always keep it safe."

"I can't believe how tired I am feeling." Yawning again.

I close my eyes and say, "We will make it work for a night."

There's something about this girl that calms me. She lays her head in my lap and settles in.

"Is this alright?" she asks.

"That's fine," I reply, placing my arm over her.

Feeling something move, I open my eyes and look down. Iris is still using my lap as a pillow. I look over to the window and see that dawn is here. I close my eyes to try to fall back to sleep, but my mind starts to think about leaving and how it will make me feel. I carefully lift Iris's head off my lap and quietly get out of bed, trying not to wake anyone. Sitting at the table, I think about everything that has transpired since yesterday. I still don't have a good handle on my emotions. It might be best for me to leave before they wake up. I quietly gather my things and pack them away. I look over to the desk and grab a few pieces of paper and a pencil to explain why I left without saying goodbye. I stare at the paper for a while and then start writing.

My friends,

I hope you are not upset with me for leaving without saying goodbye. It would have been too difficult for me. Thank you for your kindness and for inviting me into your family again. You can't imagine how much I cherish you all. You don't know how much this time with you, while short, has helped me. This has shown me the importance of family and how family supports each other. I have been away from mine for far too long, and I need to be with them now. I know Mileena will be upset, but I'm leaving some gold as a token of my gratitude for all you have done for me and the clothes. Please use it as you wish to help make your life a little easier. I hope we have the opportunity to see each other again.

Your devoted friend,
Kyra

Grabbing another piece of paper, I stare at it for a long time, trying to find my words. How do I tell her how I feel about her? Eventually, I start writing, hoping the words will come to me.

Iris,

Seeing you again has made me realize that I must find the old me or a version of it. I can't believe you're no longer that little girl who worked her way into my heart all those years ago and, in a way, became a medicine for me. Even during this short visit, I felt your influence on me. Remember to keep that joy and spread it to all. Please don't be upset with me for leaving without saying goodbye. I hope you under-

stand why I did it this way. Just know that you are special to me, and I will always carry you with me.

If you are ever up north, you can find me on the outskirts of Mountain Side just off the Western Road. I hope my crude map below can help guide you. If you ever come, we will welcome you and your family openly. It's the least I can do as you and your family have treated me so well.

With love,
Kyra

I fold the letters up and place the family's letter on the table with a small pile of gold coins, trying not to make a noise. I gather my things and walk back to Iris, who's still sound asleep. I look at her momentarily, taking her in to burn her image into my memory. I place her letter next to her and lightly touch her head. When I do this, she moves slightly. Did I wake her? I hope not. I watch for a moment, and she settles again and doesn't move, continuing to sleep soundly. As I turn to leave, I see Emery sitting up in his bed, looking at me.

"Good luck. I'll make sure she gets it. Mom is going to be upset with you," he whispers.

I walk over to him and give him a quick hug. "Thanks. Keep everyone safe."

Walking out, I close the door as quietly as I can. I barely get a few steps when I hear the door open behind me. Turning, I see Iris standing there holding my letter. She's upset, and I can tell she is on the verge of crying. She runs over to me.

"Please don't go again," she says, tears running down her cheeks.

"I have to. I'm sorry," I tell her.

"Can't you stay a little longer? Please! You're like the older sister I never had. I don't want you to leave," she pleads with me.

I drop my bag and embrace her. "I feel the same. I know this hurts. It hurts me as well, but I have to. You are welcome to visit me anytime. This is not goodbye; it is until we see each other again," I tell her.

I let the hug go and step back.

Iris says, "We will see each other again."

I turn and start walking up the road. Before I get too far, I turn back, wave to her one last time, and yell, "Remember, don't wait; tell him how you feel."

CHAPTER 27
THE REUNION

I'm sure I'm a day's journey away from home, based on the mountain peaks in the distance. I'm almost there. Settling in for the night, I go through my bag to see what I have left for food rations. Digging through it, I see the envelope and the brooch. I pull the envelope out and look at it. Do I even want to know what it says? I should toss it into the fire, as it doesn't matter what it says. I don't have any interest in finding him anymore. As I'm about to toss it into the fire, I stop. What if. I can't believe he still has a hold on me in a way, even if I don't want him to.

I'm resting by the fire when Ghost appears. This time, he has something in his mouth and drops it on the ground a few feet from me.

"What did you bring me?" I get up and walk over to look at it.

He brought a large hare to enjoy for our evening meal.

I pick it up and give him a thank you rub behind his ears.

"Come on, let's get this ready. You get half."

Prepping our meal, I toss the innards to Ghost, who devours them. I hang the hare over the campfire to roast. It doesn't take long before we smell it. Ghost settles in next to me and rests his head on my lap, which causes me to rub his ears and neck automatically. Picking up the envelope again, I must know what's in it. I don't have to act on it. I open the envelope and pull a piece of paper out.

Dear Miss Everwind,

When I first saw the brooch, I knew it was old, but I was surprised to find out how old it was. The jeweler who made it was Aaron Endronn, and his last known work was dated a little over three hundred years ago. There are only a few known pieces of his work, and everyone commands an extremely high price if available. Since this is the first brooch known to have been made by him, the value of it would be hard to estimate.

The crest belongs to an individual known as the Night Wolf. My research indicates that the Night Wolf is thought to be a vampire lord who resides near the coastal port city of Sailtre in the southern region of Tailte. Not much is known of him except that he is allegedly part of a Council of Vampires, which is believed to have influence throughout Tailte. The crest of the wolf and moons is only worn or given to a select few that the Night Wolf feels are worthy.

- Ryker

I lower the letter, feeling lost in a way. I know where he is now. Even before I was captured, I wasn't even close. It would have taken a few months to get to the southern coast. I crumple the letter and envelope and toss them into the fire. My family is Mother, and that is good enough for me. Unlike him, who left us, I know she wants to be part of my life.

I rub my companion a bit more to help ease my emotions as I feel them coming to the surface. I'm glad Ghost is here, as petting him makes me feel better. Rubbing his neck, I start thinking of Mother and how I want to be with her more than ever. I hope she has been alright all these years without me. I know she is strong, but she has a weakness, and it's me. She did everything for me, and how do I repay her? I leave her to try to make myself feel better. Some daughter I am. I look over to our meal and get up to check on it. It seems to be done. I see Ghost standing, licking his chops. I tear our meal in half and toss his half over to him, which he catches in his mouth and immediately starts to eat and rip it apart. As we eat, I decide I will travel through the night to get home by dawn, hopefully. It will be a long, hard night because I will be up for a day and a half, but seeing Mother will make it worthwhile. After finishing my meal, I gather my things and kick dirt in the fire to put it out.

"Ready?" I ask my companion, "Let's go."

As the moonlight fills the valley, I remember how beautiful it is from the rolling hills and surrounded by the high mountain peaks. We start jogging, Ghost pulls away from me quickly, bounding back and forth between the sides of the road. He passes right in front of me at times, and it seems like he's playing with me. I try to grab him, but I miss him every time. This game keeps my energy up through the night. I know if I stop, I will crash and have to sleep. We keep this pace for hours, only to slow down and walk for a bit to give our legs a rest, but we start running again as soon as our legs are ready. One benefit of being in that place for all those years is that my body has been conditioned to survive and keep going no matter what.

It was close to dawn, but this last effort has paid off. In the distance, I see Mountain Side. I pick up my pace with excitement, thinking of Mother.

"We're almost there. It's not much further. Come on, boy."

Looking down, I see he's not beside me but standing a few feet behind me. Maybe he's tired from traveling through the night, and I would understand if he were.

I walk back to him. "Come on. Let's go."

He whines softly at me between pants.

"What's wrong? Are you tired? Did you hurt something?" I ask, leaning down to look at him. As I look him over, I hug him to let him know he's fine. Suddenly, I feel someone hugging me back.

"I am sorry, my child. We have to part ways now, but we should talk," a voice tells me.

Startled, I jump back. In front of me is a man kneeling with long white hair. As he gazes upon me, I am drawn toward his blue eyes. This can't be him.

"Is this real? Did I fall asleep?"

"You are not asleep or dreaming," he tells me.

He stands and looks at me, dressed in the outfit from my dreams. As I look up at him, anger starts to fill me. I turn and walk away, not wanting to look at him. Why is he here now? Continuing towards home, I can sense he is close behind me. With each step I take, I get increasingly angrier. Finally, after walking for a while, my anger hits its boiling point. Stopping abruptly, I drop my bag on the ground and look through it frantically to find his brooch. When I see it, I toss it at him, and it hits him in the chest.

"You can have this back; I don't need it anymore, like you didn't need us! I can't believe you show up now!" I yell. "Where were you when I would have wanted or needed a father? When I lost Jenny and everything I have been through since!"

He starts to move toward me, and I back up, putting my hands up, as I don't want him to get close to me. "Do you know what I went through for ten years because of you?!" I raise my voice even more.

"I am sorry for not being there for you all those years. Please know that it was as hard on me as it was on you. I could not stay away any longer when I learned what had happened to you. I swear, if I had known, I would have come and saved you no matter the cost to me."

"No, you don't get to do that. You don't get to say you're sorry. You haven't earned that right!" I yell at him as tears form in my eyes.

"You do not know how sorry I am."

He continues walking toward me, but I push him back aggressively, almost knocking him to the ground.

"No, stay away. It's too late for that. I don't want or need you in my life. I don't understand what Mother ever saw in you!"

I'm on the verge of losing it when he looks at me and touches my face. His hand is cool and somehow comforting. "You are just as beautiful as your Mother. You were just a few months old the last time I looked upon your eyes."

"I hate you for what you did to Mother and me."

"Hate me if you must, but know I love you," he tells me calmly.

"You don't know how to love. How could you?" I'm still yelling at him.

"I know love because of your mother. She showed me that even a creature such as I can be loved and that I, too, can love. That is why I had to leave you both to ensure you were safe from my kind."

"What do you mean by ensuring our safety?" I interrupt him, trying to calm myself.

"You have the ability to exist in both the living and vampire worlds, which makes my kind very nervous. You seem to have most of our abilities; however, you have very few of our weaknesses. This makes you very dangerous and powerful. I knew at your birth I would have to shield your existence from the council because of the possibility of what you—" he stops suddenly.

He collects his thoughts and continues, "Know that I have always tried watching over you, even if you did not realize it. When I learned of your vanishing, I was frantic and have been using every resource available to me to find you. It was not until recently that I learned of your location and the place where you were held captive. My network of spies informed me that the place must have been protected by a magical barrier to keep it a secret from prying eyes."

My mind and body start to give in, and I lean into him.

"Do not let this or anyone define you. You decide who you are. I know you will get past this pain you are going through. Be around the ones you care for, as they bring out the best in you. The more you are, the more I believe you will heal," he tries to comfort me.

"I hope you are right," I answer.

He takes the brooch and pins it onto me.

"The wolf is truly never alone. It survives because of its pack. Even though the pack might have disagreements, the wolf will defend the pack until its death. You are part of my pack and will always be. Remember that."

Hearing him say these words, I agree with him on this one thing. Family is family, and you will defend it no matter what.

"Mother will be happy to see you. She's going to be mad at you, but I think she misses you more," I explain, wiping the tears from my face.

"I am sure she is. I miss her as well. However, I can't go with you," he informs me.

"What?" I ask, stepping back from him.

"Why? Why can't you come?" I ask, shocked.

"This is as far as I can go at this time. If I go with you, it could expose your Mother to danger. I can not allow that. Both of your safety is paramount to me," he explains.

"I can't believe this. We're finally together, and you can't stay for even a few hours. I have so many questions. Why?" I ask angrily.

"There are limits to what I can do right now, but I am working on it. It will take a little time. Once I convince the council that you are not dangerous, I will be able to spend near-endless time with you and answer all your questions. Until then, I will be watching over you and your mother more than ever. When you need me, I will know and be there for you both. Nothing will prevent me this time, my child. Nothing."

"So this is it? I want to punch you in the face," I tell him, annoyed.

He looks over his shoulder and then back at me.

"Please let your mother know I think of her always. I am sorry for all the pain she has endured over the years because of me," he says, touching my face.

Looking past him, the sky is starting to brighten as dawn

approaches. Not knowing when or if I will see him again, I hesitantly hug him, just in case. "I'm still mad at you."

"I know." He hugs me back.

As we embrace, I start to feel nothing between my arms. I look and see a colored mist move away from me slowly. It then rises and flies away high in the air. Standing in the middle of the road, I try to understand my feelings about what just happened. On the one hand, I am somewhat happy we finally met, but on the other hand, I'm furious at him for not being part of my life. Maybe time will help, as he said. I don't know. All I truly know is that I want to be home with Mother.

I turn and run towards home. Mountain Side is just ahead of me, and I see the Western Road. I turn down it and pick up my pace. The morning sun is shining on the fields, and in the distance, I see my home up on the small hill by the Western Pass. My adrenaline is maxing out, and it's the only thing keeping me going now. Heading up the path, I see smoke coming from the chimney. As I reach the clearing, I start walking to catch my breath. I made it. Looking toward my home, I see the door open, and Blacky runs out straight toward me. I wasn't sure if he would still be with Mother, as he's getting old. When he gets to me, he starts barking and jumping with excitement.

"How are you, boy? Did you take care of Mother? How is she?" I kneel and rub his sides and face to calm him down.

Looking over, I see Mother in the doorway. She's holding her hand above her eyes as the morning sun blinds her. She walks toward me; I pick up my bag and walk to meet her.

"Hello, Mother," I say emotionally.

Hearing my voice, she runs toward me and embraces me in her arms, squeezing me as she has never done before.

"You're here, you're home!" she says, crying.

"I missed you," I tell her.

She grabs my face and kisses it all over as tears fall down her cheeks.

"You're all grown up. What happened to your face?"

"We can talk about that later. Can we go inside?"

Mother nods, and I wipe the tears from her face and mine. She holds my arm very tightly. I think she's worried I might disappear.

I drop my belongings on the floor by the door as we enter the house. It feels like home but doesn't, at the same time. There are hints of smells that bring back memories. Everything mostly looks how I remember it.

"I'm happy Blacky is still here. I wasn't sure if he would be," I tell Mother.

"He's been my faithful companion all this time."

She reaches over and holds my hand. "You can't know how happy I am right now. I was wondering if I would ever see you again."

"I'm sorry I was gone for so long. Things kept me away for a lot longer than I ever expected."

"Your hair, it's so long. When did you start braiding it?" Mother says, touching my hair.

"Somewhat recently."

"Are you hungry?" she asks.

"I'm good. Just tired. I have been up for almost two days, trying to get back here as quickly as possible. How have you been? Are things alright here? I see the fields have been planted already."

"Things are good. The fields keep me busy, and our friends visit me as often as possible," she explains.

Seeing my old chair, I sit down. While I sit, my body relaxes as exhaustion hits me. I yawn and shake my head.

"Is the scar on your face part of why you didn't return until now?"

"Yes, I will explain later. I want to hear more about you and things around here."

"You look exhausted. Do you want to lie down?"

Sitting in my chair, my vision gets blurry, and I can't seem to focus. I blink a few times to correct it, but it doesn't work. I think I'm more than tired. My mind and exhausted body tell me to let go as I have reached my goal. I can't fight it, and I feel my body surrender to the exhaustion.

"Kyra, Kyra," I hear Mother ask me again.

"I'm fine, just … "

I open my eyes, and I'm lying on Mother's bed. Mother is resting in a chair next to me. I sit up, which wakes her.

"How long did I sleep?" I ask.

"Two days."

"Two days!"

"I watched over you. You were a bit restless at times and talked in your sleep. Who's Iris?"

"Someone special who helped me when I needed it. What else did I say?" I inquire.

"Not much, but you were dreaming about something that made you tense up. I saw you clench your fists like you were defending yourself a few times."

I don't remember dreaming. I hope this didn't upset her, as I don't want her to worry about me.

"By chance, do I still have clothes in my room? I should bathe and clean up," I say.

"Your room is just as you left it. I didn't touch anything besides cleaning things every once in a while," she tells me.

I get up and head to the barn, asking Mother, "Can you bring me a change of clean clothes?" In the barn, I fill our tub with water from the well. I feel it, and it's cold. I should have brought some hot water from the house, but I will make this work.

I see Mother enter, holding clothes for me and my old brown boots.

"Do you want me to get hot water from inside?" she asks.

"No, I will make this work," I tell her.

I start to undress, but stop, remembering that she doesn't know. I can't ask her to leave; she will wonder why. I know she wants to help me. No matter what, she will learn of them at some point. Now is no worse than any other time to expose the scars.

I turn to her. "Mother, what you are going to see will upset you. They are part of who I am now."

I continue to undress, and I hear her gasp. Mother runs to me, upset.

"What happened to you?! How did this happen?!" she asks, sobbing.

"I will explain later; I just need to figure out how to," I say to her, a bit shaken.

I sit down in the water. Mother sits down next to the bath, and I start to bathe myself.

"May I?" she asks.

I nod, and she removes my braids and takes the sponge from me. She starts washing me gently, starting with my arms. I think she's nervous, and they might hurt if she uses too much pressure. When she starts to wash my back, I begin to cry as I know this is torture for her. I eventually grab her hand, which holds the sponge. "I'll finish up and meet you back in the house."

"As you wish," she says softly.

I watch Mother get up and walk back to the house, almost in a trance-like state. She's trying to be strong, but seeing me this way has somehow broken her. I finish bathing and dress quickly because I know I have to talk to her about everything.

Entering the house, Mother has prepared some food and tea. I think she did this to keep her mind busy until I returned. Sitting at the table, I look at Mother. She's aged some. She has some grey hair starting to show in a few areas, and she has the beginning of crow's feet around her eyes. However, she is still as pretty as before. Her green eyes sparkle as I look at her.

"I know what you saw was difficult. Try not to think about them," I tell her.

"I don't know if I can do that. I need to know what happened to my daughter."

How am I going to explain why I have these scars and what I did to survive while being imprisoned for all those years? The idea of telling her that I killed people to survive, and more so that I killed people out of revenge, and that I found pleasure in doing it, will crush her. What will she think of her daughter for doing all these things?

"Kyra, please tell me. I need to know."

"I ... I don't know what to say because there is no easy way to say it, and I'm afraid of what you will think of me after I tell you."

"You are my daughter, and I will love you no matter what."

I look at her, and her eyes tell me she will not back down until I tell her everything.

"I was captured..."

Mother leans back in her chair, digesting everything I told her about my time at the arena and how it changed me. After a few moments, she looks up at me.

"What can I do?" she asks emotionally.

"Just be patient and help me when I need it."

She grabs my hand. "Always."

Wanting to change the topic, but Mother beat me to it.

"Did you find your father or details about him?" she asks.

I knew I would have to share everything with Mother when I returned. While I am not happy to talk about it, it is best to get everything out in the open so we can move on.

"I did."

"Found or details?"

"Found. The irony is that he shows up after I decided I didn't want to find or have him in my life. Let's say it was an emotional exchange between us when we met. Only time will tell if we might have a relationship. He has to prove to me that he wants me in his life. He did want me to tell you that he's sorry for all the pain you have faced. However, he can't be with us due to the stupid council he's part of," I explain to her.

I look up and see Mother staring off into the distance. I'm sure she is thinking about him and most likely remembering their time together.

"How did he look?" she asks.

I grab Mother's hand. "He looks like you remember, I am sure."

"Speaking of Father. I need you to know who your daughter is. This might be as difficult as what I told you earlier."

She looks up at me, wiping her eyes. "What is it?"

I push my chair back to give us a little space and look at her. "You need to see the part of Father that lives within me."

I see her adjust herself in her seat. I close my eyes, hoping this doesn't scare her. I look at her and transform. Mother looks at me, reaches out to my face, and touches my cheek.

"This doesn't scare me. You are my daughter, and this is part of you."

"I've learned to control it, but this part of me can still be dangerous."

"You don't seem dangerous to me. I see my daughter, whom I have missed," she reassures me.

Looking at her, I return to my human state and tell her, "I love you, Mother."

"Child, I love you too." Mother hugs me tightly.

I pour myself another cup of tea to ease my tight throat. I offer some to Mother as well, who places her cup out. Filling her cup, I notice a few figurines on the fireplace mantel that I have never seen before.

"When did you get those?" I point to them.

"They were a gift from Rox, Lindsey, and Elsa for my fortieth birthday a few years ago."

Hearing their names perks me up. "How are they? What have they been up to?"

"Elsa moved back with her family to help her mother after her father passed. Rox and Lindsey got married a few years after you left. It was a lovely ceremony. I know they wished you were there for it. All of their hard work has paid off as well. A few years ago, they purchased a concert hall in the city where she performs a few days a week. People from all over the valley come to see her play. The hall is called Tornrin Hall, and it's located off the central square." Mother unloads a large amount of information on me at once.

"I'm sorry to hear about Elsa's father. I'm so happy for Rox and Lindsey. They deserve it. I told him she was special, and he listened. I will visit them soon. First, I want to be with you for a while. I'm sorry for missing so many of your birthdays. I hope we can make up some of our lost time. Tell me more."

Mother and I talk about everything and anything. She tells me about her work around the house and some new ointments she is developing. She has been fortunate that our neighbors have been helping with the fieldwork while I was gone. I tell her about Maddie and Iris's family and how they welcomed me into their home. Before we knew it, it was late into the night. Surprisingly, I was tired even though I had slept for two days. I can also see that Mother is tired. Her eyes are starting to close. I'm sure she didn't sleep much as she watched over me for two days.

"You look tired, Mother. Go to bed. I will clean up here and head up afterward."

Mother gets up and hugs me goodnight. I can't help but hug her back and hold on to her for longer than a goodnight hug should be. "I've missed your touch."

"As have I," she tells me softly in my ear.

After cleaning up, I head up to my old room. It is just as Mother said. Nothing has changed or has been moved. Even Jenny's clothes are still on the hooks. Looking at them, I realize it's time to put them away. I go to the corner of the room and open Jenny's chest. I carefully fold her dresses to stow them away. As I walk past the dresser, I notice her hairbrush, perfume, and a few other items on the dresser. I pick up the brush and see some of her hair still in it. I clean the brush and make a little hair bundle for safekeeping.

I pick up the perfume bottle and open it to sniff it. As the smell of flowers and sweetness hit my nose, I have a flashback of her sitting at the dresser. She turns and giggles at me. I smile at this memory and close the bottle. I leave the brush on the dresser. I will need to use it while I have long hair. Also, I think using it will comfort me as if Jenny were brushing my hair. I take the rest of her items, place them in her chest, and store the chest in the corner.

I look over and see Mother folded and put the clothes I wore home on the chair in my room, along with my travel bag and weapons. I grab the bag and sit on my bed. I pull out my shoulder armor and leather pants. I look at the armor that has saved me more times than I can count, and it shows it. I run my fingers over a portion where I see a bite mark. One of my competitors tried to bite my shoulder but bit down on my armor instead. I gather everything up, including my weapons, and place everything in my chest at the foot of the bed. I get ready for bed and crawl in, hoping I can sleep. I turn down the light crystal and close my eyes. Today was a tough day in many ways, but it was also a good day. There will be many more tough days ahead, but hopefully, there will also be many good days.

CHAPTER 28
RECONNECTING

I sit up. My throat is burning and dry. Why now? It hasn't been that long. I jump out of bed and make my way out of the house quickly. The burning is becoming almost unbearable. Running straight to the barn, I need to drink from one of our animals. I see Smokey. Walking over to him, Smokey moves away from me. I can tell he senses something is different about me.

"It's alright; I just need a little," I tell him, starting to breathe a bit heavier.

Opening the stall, I walk in and caress his neck and face to let him know I don't mean him any harm. "Good boy. That's it."

While I rub him, I transform. I bite down carefully, as I don't want to startle him or cause him any pain while I drink from him. It doesn't take long before the burning in my throat disappears, and I stop. I pinch the small wound I made on him and hold it until it stops bleeding. Being such a large animal, the amount I took from him is no more than when someone cuts their finger.

"Thank you, my friend. I will most likely have to do this every so often." Rubbing his neck and side. "When was the last time Mother took you out for a ride? I bet it's been a while."

I walk Smokey out of his stall and out of the barn. In the distance, I can see the sky is starting to brighten. "Come on, let's see what you still have." I jump on Smokey bareback, and he stampers back some. "I'm guessing Mother hasn't ridden you in years. You always were more of a workhorse than a riding horse."

I give him a nudge while holding onto his mane, and we take off into the fields next to the house. As I ride him through the fields, I let go of his mane and let my arms bounce to my sides like I used to do as a child. Eventually, I close my eyes and allow Smokey to guide me where he wants. Eventually, he stops. Opening my eyes, I see we are at the edge of the Western Road, and in front of us, I can see the sun rising between the mountain peaks.

"Thank you. That meant more to me than you can imagine," I tell him, leaning down on his neck while rubbing it.

I take hold of his mane and turn him with my legs to head back home to let him cool down and rest. Walking back to the house, I think of Rox and Lindsey and decide I will see them today. It will be a tough day, like yesterday, but I need to see them. Entering the house, I can see Mother is still asleep, and Blacky is snuggled next to her. I am sure yesterday was just as draining on her as it was for me. I don't want to wake her, but I want to let her know where I am so she doesn't worry. I am positive it will upset her if I am not here when she wakes up.

Walking over, I place my hand on her shoulder. "Stay in bed and rest. I'm heading into the city to explore and see Rox and Lindsey," I whisper to her.

Mother turns to face me and holds her arms out to me. "Come back soon."

I lean down, and she hugs me.

"I will be back by sunset, I promise."

~

Entering the city feels strange. There are things I recognize, but there are stores and other things that I don't. I look up at High Rock and see the trams are already moving up and down from it. I wonder if anyone moved into her home since I left. Most likely, yes, but the thought of this saddens me. Making my way to the main square, I notice a large tower building under construction. It has multiple spires with platforms coming off each one. My curiosity gets the best of me, and I head over to see what this new building is about. When arriving at the base of the building, stone masons are already hard at work placing and laying stones. One of them turns toward me to get another stone, and I try to get his attention.

"What's this structure going to be for?" I ask.

"It's going to be the new skyship docking station. It will be ready in about six months. It will allow multiple skyships to dock at once for trade and transport," he tells me.

"Skyships have been coming here?" I ask.

"Occasionally, but they can only land outside the city. With this station, it will be easier for them to dock. The hope is to grow our trade route with them," he answers before returning to work.

Things are changing here. Seeing a skyship was one of the items I wanted to see on my travels, but I never did. I won't have to go far now before finally seeing one. I watch the workers briefly before returning to the central market. Continuing through the market, something catches my nose. I inhale deeply, and the sweet smell of sugar and bread fills my nose. Following the scent, I end up at a cart selling a variety of fresh pastries.

"Something catching your fancy? What can I get for you?" the vendor asks.

I look at the pastries: peach, apple, cherry, and spiced nuts.

"I'll take a peach one. How much?" I ask.

"Two copper."

Reaching for my purse, I notice a small girl beside me looking at the pastries. I instantly realize she's a Forgotten, and I squat and ask her, "Which one do you want?"

Doing this startles her for a second, and she backs away from me.

I smile at her and tell her, "Pick one. My treat."

She looks at me confused and then points to a cherry one.

"I'll take a cherry one as well." Handing the vendor four copper.

I offer the cherry pastry to the girl. "Here you go."

She looks at me nervously.

"It's alright. It's yours. I'm going to eat mine by the fountain. You can join me if you like."

She takes the pastry, and I walk to the fountain to enjoy mine. As I sit on the fountain's edge, she walks over and jumps up to sit beside me.

"Thanks," she tells me.

"I used to love these pastries. When I was little, it was the one thing my mom would allow me to get as a treat when we visited the city."

Touching my pastry to hers, we start to enjoy them.

With a full mouth of food, I say, "That's good. I'm Kyra. What's your name?"

Between chewing and swallowing, she gets out, "Emily."

She's devouring the pastry and, in the process, getting it all over her face and fingers. I finish mine not far after she finishes hers.

"Where are your friends? Are they looking for leftovers?" I ask.

She nods, jumping from the fountain's edge, and turns to me.

I chuckle slightly as I look at her.

"Come here," I tell her.

I pull a cloth out of my pocket and wipe her face and hands clean.

"Thanks," she says shyly.

"One second," I say. I reach into my coin purse and hand her a gold coin. "For you and your friends. Buy as much food as you can."

Her eyes light up. "Is this a trick?"

"No trick."

"Thank you." She runs off through the square. Some things

haven't changed since I have been gone. This city needs to fix this. These children need to be taken care of in some way.

I stay at the fountain and watch the market come to life. It might be a good way for me to become more comfortable around people. I watch as the vendors set up their carts of various goods to be sold, and the people buying them. I feel uneasy as the market gets busy with person after person walking by me and sometimes bumping into me. When the market is in full swing, my anxiety starts to rise, but I tell myself this is normal. They don't want to do anything to you. They are focused on selling and buying. It is approaching midday, and it is time to find Rox and Lindsey. Mother said Tornrin Hall was on the edge of the central square. It doesn't take long to find it due to the extravagant sign with gold lettering. I guess they have done well. As I approach the door, I hear music and applause coming from within. Entering the lobby, I see a few people walking around in vests and dark pants. In front of me are several large paintings of Lindsey playing and dancing.

One of the people in vests comes up to me and asks, "May I help you?"

"I want to see Lindsey and Rox," I tell them.

"Mrs. Tornrin is performing currently, and her husband is backstage. May I ask who you are?" he asks.

"An old friend," I answer.

"If you like, you may go in and watch her perform, but it's a full house, and you will have to stand in the back," he tells me.

"How many people are in there?" I ask.

"About a thousand," he answers.

Hearing that number makes me uncomfortable, but I want to see them.

"That's fine," I tell him, walking towards the music.

"Excuse me, do you have a ticket?" he asks, stopping me.

"No."

"Normally, it's ten silver, but five silver will do since you missed a good portion of the show." He holds his hand out.

This is the first time I have had to pay to see Lindsey play. I reach into my purse and pay him, and he then directs me to a door. Entering the theater, I stay by the door. If I become too uncomfortable, it will be easy for me to leave. Standing against the back wall with a few others, I settle in and see Lindsey and her band. She's playing a song I recognize while she dances and moves throughout the stage and between her band members. She is just as pretty and elegant as the day I left. I lose myself in the music, and everything around me fades away. I'm brought back when I hear the audience clapping for her.

The person next to me nudges me. "She's so fantastic, isn't she?"

When the applause calms down, she walks up to the front of the stage.

"Thank you all for coming. Last night, I dreamed about a friend. We think of her often and hope she is doing well, as we haven't seen her in a long time. Because of this dream, I want to close with this final song. I hope you like it."

Lindsey steps back and starts playing. It only takes a few notes before I realize it was the song she played for Mother on my birthday all those years ago. Without realizing it, I walk, not taking my eyes off her. I get about halfway down the aisle before she looks up and stops playing mid-bow pull. After a moment, I nod to confirm that she is indeed seeing me. I am also aware that the audience is now looking at me and then at Lindsey, trying to figure out what is happening. One of her band members walks up to her to check on her, and she hands them her violin and bow before jumping down from the stage and embracing me.

"When, where have you been?!" she asks me, squeezing tight.

As she squeezes me, I stiffen slightly but then relax.

"Just a few days ago," I answer.

Looking up at the stage, I see Rox running out, trying to figure out what is happening. He looks down at us. I raise my hand to wave at him.

"Thank you, everyone! That concludes our show. We hope you

enjoyed yourself. There's a free takeaway as you leave. Our staff will be handing them at the doors," he announces to the audience.

While everyone exits, Rox makes his way to us.

I kneel to meet him at eye level. He has a beard now, but I can still see my friend past it. He's matured some, and he has lost his adolescent look.

"Hi, my old friend," I tell him.

"I don't know what to say or do," he tells me.

"You don't have to say or do anything. When did you grow the beard?" Wiping my eyes a bit.

"A few years back. My beard is not important. Where have you been? We thought we lost you forever," he tells me.

The next thing I know, Lindsey grabs my arm and pulls me towards a door.

I immediately pull my arm free and almost pull her down simultaneously.

"Don't do that," I tell her aggressively.

Rox runs over to help her, and they look at me, trying to figure out what happened and why I did what I did. "I didn't mean to pull you like that, but I don't like being touched in that manner. When you grabbed my arm, I reacted. It's me, not you," I tell them.

"I want to take you to our home to talk," she says.

This is not going well. I'm messing this up; I almost hurt her. I might have to leave, as I don't want them to fear me. Lindsay walks over to me and places her hand on my shoulder. "We just want to talk."

Looking down out of shame, I nod and then look at her.

"Sorry for that. I didn't mean to," I answer.

"It's alright. Come this way." Lindsey turns and holds Rox's hand as they walk to a door on the side of the theatre.

After entering the door, we head up a set of stairs and turn down a hallway. Along the walls are various framed prints of Lindsey's shows, each labeled with the date of the show. These prints show that Lindsey has performed at this level for several years. At the end of the hallway, we come to a door with *Private* carved in it. They walk in. I hesitate to enter for a second, but follow them. Their home is a large open room with areas defined by different furniture within the posts and beams. Some of the walls have paintings. One in particular catches my eye. I walk over to get a better look and quickly realize it's a painting of Jenny. The artist who painted it captured her eyes and how they twinkled. I almost touch it and then pull my hand back.

"We have always kept her in our hearts. Please sit." Lindsey escorts me to a chair.

They sit on a couch facing me. They're both looking at me, waiting. I feel very awkward and upset about what I did to Lindsey.

Rox finally breaks the silence. "What happened back there? We want to understand and know where you have been for the past ten years. We really missed you and were worried about you."

"I'm sorry for pulling you, Lindsey. I didn't mean to. I would never want to hurt you. I just reacted out of habit."

"Habit?" Lindsey asks.

"You haven't said anything yet, but I am sure you noticed my face. My travels didn't go the way I thought they would. They went terribly wrong. That is why I was away for so long."

As I look at them, I can see they are trying to understand and will ask for clarity on what I just said. As I wait for them to speak, I notice movement behind them. A little girl with blond curly hair is peeking around the corner. Rox and Lindsey turn to see what I am looking at, and Lindsey motions for the little girl to come over.

"You can say hi," Lindsey tells her.

The little girl walks over and stands beside Lindsey, holding her dress. She's wearing a white lace dress that ends just above her knees. She seems pretty shy. Looking more closely, I see slightly pointy ears and a round nose similar to Rox's.

"Momma, who's this?" she asks.

I look at the three of them together. I have missed so much not being here, including their marriage and when they started a family.

Why didn't Mother tell me they had a little girl? I am going to have to ask her when I get home.

"This is our daughter, Jenniver," Lindsey says.

They named her Jenniver. Hearing this sends a tingle through me.

"Hi, I'm Kyra. I'm glad to meet you leaning towards her a bit."

Jenniver leans into Lindsey for safety.

"Jenniver, she's an old friend. We haven't seen her since before you were born. She just returned home and came to see us," Lindsey explains to her.

Leaning against Lindsey, she points to my face. "You have an ouchie."

I touch my scar instinctively. "It's fine. It doesn't hurt anymore," I tell her.

"Did you fall?" she asks.

"No, a bad person gave this to me long ago," I tell her.

She looks at me, pondering my answer. "Did they get in trouble?"

"They did," I tell her. "You're very pretty, like your mom."

Jenniver smiles and buries her head into Lindsey. "No, Mommy is more pretty."

I laugh slightly and sit back in my chair. "I think you have your dad's wit," I tell her.

"Jenniver, can you return to your room and practice your lessons? Remember proper finger placement. Grandma Elsa will be over later to play with you. We need to talk to our friend in private," Lindsey tells her.

Jenniver moves to Rox and pulls on his sleeve. Rox leans down so she can hug him, to which he replies, "Thank you, lemon drop."

As she passes me to head back to her room, she asks me, "Maybe we can play sometime?"

"I would like that if it's fine with your mom and dad," I tell her.

I watch Lindsey listen for the door to close.

"She's adorable. I'm so happy for you both!" I exclaim excitedly.

"Thank you," Rox tells me. "You said you were in a place that kept you away. The scar, did you get it at the same place?" he asks.

"Along with others," I push up one of my sleeves, exposing my arm for them to see. I don't want to hide anything from them, no matter how shocking or painful it might be.

"How many?" Lindsey asks.

"More than I want to count. That's why I behaved the way I did before. Being in that place for so long did something to me. I'm trying to fix myself, but it's hard."

They both look at me, trying to find the right words, but struggle. What would you say to someone who just told you they were tortured for years?

Rox gets off the couch and holds my hand while Lindsey leans over to hold my other hand.

"What do you need from us?" Rox asks.

I don't know if it's in my mind or happening, but I feel warmth traveling up my arms and into my chest as they hold my hands.

"I am not sure, but this helps. I guess just being there for me when I need it and understanding if I have moments. I want to get back to being a version of my old self if possible," I tell them.

Trying to lighten the focus of our talk, I ask, "How's Elsa?"

"I see what you are doing. Even back then, you used to try to change the focus off of you. I'll play your game. My mom is good. Jenniver keeps her busy, but Elsa wouldn't want it any other way. She adores her and wants to spend her free time with her," he tells me. "We'll be wrapping up this series of shows in a few days. I would like us to get together afterward, maybe at your place. Jenniver likes being outside the city, as she can pick flowers in the fields. We need time together."

I have lost so much time with everyone and will not waste any more time. They are my family, and I want to be with them. "I would like that. One thing I learned about being held captive is the importance of loved ones. Thank you for watching out for Mother all these years. It truly means everything to me," I express to them. "I'm sorry

I missed your wedding. I bet you looked amazing, Lindsey. You'll have to tell me about it sometime. I bet he was a nervous wreck." Looking at Rox.

"You're partly right. She did look amazing, but she was the nervous one. At one point, I thought she would pass out during our vows," Rox teases Lindsey.

"We don't have to bring that up again, do we? A wedding is a big day in a girl's life. I was nervous. I still married you, didn't I?" Lindsey punches Rox's arm softly.

Seeing them interact, I am grateful for being with them once again. I missed this. We sit together, talking and asking questions about our time apart, trying to reconnect as best as possible. It feels awkward, and I am sure they feel it, too, but we keep talking until it feels a little more natural, like in the old days. Looking out the window of their home, I can see it's getting close to evening. I should get going, as Mother is most likely checking outside to see if I am coming up the path every few minutes.

"I should be heading back home. I promised Mother I would be back before nightfall, and I can't break that promise to her. Please give Elsa warm wishes for me."

They walk me to the door and are about to follow me out. "I can find my way out. Be with Jenniver. Time goes by faster than you think."

Lindsey kisses my cheek. "I'm glad you're back."

"Me too," I tell her.

"See you soon." Placing my fist out to Rox, who bumps it with his fist.

"Definitely!" he says.

I head down the hallway and the stairs, feeling good.

CHAPTER 29

THE DRAGON TAIL

Leaving the theatre, I take my old routes through the city to see if some places I used to go to are still around. I'm the most curious about the Dragon Tail. I have many fond memories of that place. Walking down the alleys, it doesn't take long before it's in front of me. The dragon mounted to the front of the building is still smoking, and I am getting faint smells of roasting meat. Curious, I walk in to get a quick drink before heading home. The place is busy and looks the same, but it's different; it's a bit brighter and cleaner. I see the bartender behind the bar and head over. I walk through the tavern and notice someone eyeing me from his table. He has small tusks protruding from his lower lip. He sees me looking back at him as I head to the bar.

"How's it going? What can I get for you?" the bartender asks.

"Cider or Ale, whatever you think is better," I answer.

"I recommend the pear cider. It's new and good," he tells me as he wipes the bartop with a rag.

"Pear it is." Dropping a silver coin on the bartop.

As the bartender gets me my cider, I look around. A set of stairs on the back wall goes up to a landing of rooms that weren't there before.

"Are those rooms for rent up there?" I ask.

"Yes, the new owner is making this place a full inn. They bought the whole building last season and have been getting this place turned around. Need a room? We have two free. Fifteen silver per night," he says.

"I'm good."

"Here you go. I hope you like it. By the way, I'm Thomas, but everyone calls me Rooney. If you need anything else, let me know." He places my cider on the bar.

Grabbing the mug, I take a large sip of it. It's sweet with a slight bite, and the pear is coming through. "It's good."

"Glad to hear it. You look familiar. Have you been in here before?"

"I used to come here years ago, but I just got back the other day," I tell him.

Going for my second sip, someone bumps me, and I spill some of my cider onto the bartop. I look at the person who bumped me. It's the individual who was eyeing me before.

"I saw you looking at me. What's your business here?" he asks.

"Just here for a drink and checking out the old place," I tell him.

"Something about you doesn't seem right. You smell funny to me, and my nose never lies to me," he tells me snidely.

Placing my cider down, I grab the bartop with my other hand. "You're about to open a door you don't want to walk through. You better back off," I warn him.

"She's having a drink at the bar. Let her be," the bartender injects himself into our exchange.

I know he isn't going to back off by his confident tone and stance. Why can't people leave me alone? This day was hard enough, and now I have to deal with this asshole.

"Door, what door?" He turns to his tablemates. "Do you see a door I don't want to walk through?"

He leans in and whispers, "I like to see you try—"

Before he finishes his statement, I slam his head into the bartop, which causes it to bounce off, and he stumbles backward. He looks confused at what happened before he falls to the ground, completely out of it.

"I told you not to open the door!" I exclaim, standing over him.

Someone grabs my arm, and I turn quickly, ready to strike. When our eyes meet, I freeze. Maddie is standing in front of me. I can't believe I'm looking at her.

"Calm down. Let's talk over there," she says. "Rooney, can you take care of Burock? Get him back to his table and give him an ale. I think he learned his lesson."

"You know this asshole?" I ask.

"He's a regular. He has a chip on his shoulder and feels everyone dislikes him because he's half-orc. He'll be fine. He has a hard head. You just rattled it," she explains.

She leads us to a table in a corner under the stairs. On it are a bunch of books and other items.

"Welcome to my office. This is where I run this place. We have a lot to talk about," she says, sitting down.

I pull out a seat and sit down to join her. I can't believe she's in front of me.

"Been a long time, hasn't it," she says.

"Long time. What are you doing in Mountain Side? I am trying to get my head around you being here and in front of me."

"I decided to do my own thing and be more. It took me a while, but I finally did it. I know the ins and outs of running a tavern from watching my brother, so I figured, why not? I wasn't sure where I would be going—well, that's not true. I did, with the hopes of possibly running into someone. I guess it's working out," she says.

I lean in and say, "So you left the Trading Post and ventured up to Mountain Side to start a tavern with the hopes of possibly running into me. Your logic seems a little off to me. How were you able to afford this place?" I ask.

Maddie smiles. "My logic seems to be quite good. You're here, aren't you? As for purchasing this place. I saved all my earnings from the start. I only spent a little here and there when I had to. By the time I was ready to leave, I had saved a large sum of money. Two large chests full, to be exact. Enough about me; you seem different. You have an edge to you that wasn't there before," she says, with a softer tone.

The bartender places my cider on the table and has one for Maddie.

"Thought you might like these," he says to us.

"Thanks, Rooney. Make sure we're not disturbed," she tells him.

You got it, boss," he says.

Before returning to the bar, he turns and says, "The painting, that's why you look familiar. You're the girl in the painting."

"Painting?" I say, confused.

I watch Maddie grab her mug and move her eyes to the left. I look at the wall near us with a painting on it. It takes me no time to realize it's a painting of me from when I first met her. I can't believe she has a painting of me on the wall. Feeling very awkward, I place my face in my hands.

"Why do you have a painting of me?"

"I missed you, and painting you was a way to keep you in my thoughts. You don't look all that different from that painting."

"You missed me?" I ask.

"I did. I'm happy you're here. I hope you plan to stay for a while."

"That's the plan; I need to be around family and friends and work through some things. The person you painted isn't here anymore, but I hope to find parts of her again."

"I can help you if you like. I remember that person, and I am pretty sure I can get her out of you," she tells me in Maddie fashion.

Looking at her grinning at me, I also can't help but smile slightly. She is devilish and loves to cause chaos, but in a good way.

"You did drive me crazy back then."

"You loved it, if I remember correctly," she says before taking a large drink of her cider. "Do you have work or anything lined up?"

"I plan on helping at home with the fieldwork and anything else that needs to be done. It's getting hard for Mother to do that type of work. Other than that, no."

"Don't take this the wrong way, but I don't see you as a farmer or field worker. Based on what you did to Burock, you can take care of yourself, even more so than I remember. Hear me out; sometimes, things can get unruly, and having someone here to keep everyone in check would be nice. I will pay you, plus it will allow us to spend time together. What do you think? Any interest?"

Seeing her in this light is odd. She now owns and runs the place I spent countless hours in when I was younger. Thinking of her as my boss is even stranger. I know she will get a kick out of giving me orders, but at the same time, I'm confident I could get away with doing things that others might not. I don't have anything lined up, so having this to keep me busy might be good.

"You know what, I'll take you up on your offer," I say, raising my mug to her.

"Really? That's great. I won't give you special treatment. Everyone is treated the same here," she says, raising her mug to mine.

We both drink down our mugs, slamming them on the table simultaneously.

"I have to be getting back as it will be dark soon, and I promised Mother I would be back before nightfall. I don't want to worry her," I say, standing up.

Maddie walks around the table and grabs my hand. I look down at her hand over mine and then at her. The next thing I realize, we are hugging each other.

"When do you want me to start?"

Continuing to embrace me, "How about next week? We can work out a schedule on your first day."

"Sounds good," I say as we release our embrace.

Making my way out of the tavern, I look at Burock, who is

nursing an ale with his friends. I can't help myself but yell over, "See you next week; she just hired me."

I watch his eyes widen at what I just told him. I'm pretty sure he's not happy at the thought of seeing me regularly.

CHAPTER 30

FOREVER CONNECTED

Walking up the path to home, I notice the sky has shades of yellow, oranges, and pink, with clouds illuminated by the sun that nestles between two mountain peaks. I forgot how pretty the sunsets can be this far north in the valley. Walking to the house, I see the old tree and grave markers under it, and head over to them. Looking down at Jenny's grave, I go to my knees, feeling a wave of emotion come over me. Hoping to feel closer to her, I place my palm on the ground.

"I finally made it home, and I can't help but think you were the guiding force behind getting me home. What were the chances that Forge ended up in that place? It was you who kept me going all this time. When all I saw was darkness, you showed me light. You would pick me up when I needed it the most. I wish I hadn't been so scared to tell you the truth, but I think you knew somehow. After all this time, I finally understand it's not about moving forward without you, but instead moving forward while honoring our memories. You will forever be a part of me, no matter where I go."

As I say my last words, I feel a hand on my shoulder.

"I'll come in a minute," I tell Mother.

"That is all I wanted for you. For you to find a way to be happy again and discover your place in the world."

That voice! I look behind me, and Jenny is standing behind me. I spin around and stand there gazing at her. She looks as she did all those years ago. She's wearing an off-white dress with a decorative leather vest on top. Her hair is perfect and falling just past her shoulders. I embrace her tightly, never wanting to let go of her.

"Are you real?" I ask.

"In a way, but this is the last time I can crossover. I am pretty sure I used all the favors at this point. I know you will be fine, as I have seen things. Please know that I am safe and in a good place. Promise me that you will grab life and be who you are meant to be.

Lean on our family and friends to support you when you need it. They love you and want to help you. You are more than this and will do great things."

"What do you mean?" I ask.

Jenny squints her eyes at me slightly, which tells me there is more to what she is saying.

"I am not allowed to say, but trust me. I have to get going as my time is running out."

"Will I see you again?" I ask, with tears filling my eyes.

"Someday, we will be reunited, but not for a long time. Know that I will be watching always."

I squeeze her tightly so I feel as much of her as possible, and she does the same. Jenny, let's go of me, and I do the same. She steps back and starts to fade away.

"I like Maddie; she keeps you on your toes. I approve," she says, smiling.

"I love you more than you can imagine," I tell her.

She smiles, and just before she fades away, "I love you the same."

Staring at the space where Jenny was, I wipe my eyes. Even though I am crying, I feel at ease. Maybe that's all I needed all this time ... a way to say goodbye to her in my own way. I know now that she is in a good place and wants me to be happy, and I can't let myself or her down.

"Till we meet again."

I turn, walking to my home. Opening the door, I see Mother setting the table for the evening meal. "As promised, home before nightfall."

She looks at me and smiles. I smile back.

ABOUT THE AUTHOR

David has always been passionate about fantasy, science fiction, and anime. His love of these genres and active imagination have intertwined into his art, shaping his creative journey.

Kyra of the North is his first novel and a testament to his belief that anything is possible with hard work and perseverance. During the early years of David's education, it became evident that he struggled with reading and writing and was not progressing with his classmates. After being tested, he was classified with a learning disability, which affected how he comprehended and understood the structure of words when reading or writing. With the help and support of his family and educators, David was enrolled in special programs and classes to help him adapt and develop tools to help him throughout his life.

David obtained a BA in Graphic Arts from Western Connecticut

State University and later an MS in Interactive Communication from Quinnipiac University.

Even with success in his education and career, he still feared and often avoided writing. The worry about making mistakes or being misunderstood held him back until writing *Kyra of the North*. Not only did he find a passion for writing through this experience, but he also learned not to fear trying something new.

To learn more, visit https://www.mountainsidemediallc.com/